PRAISE FOR
FIRST DROP

"Sharp keeps the plot moving at a lightning-fast pace . . . [Charlie Fox's] lethal abilities and winning personality combine to make her a compelling figure."

—*Chicago Sun-Times*

"Charlie Fox [is] a gal with moxie and deadly accuracy with a Sig Sauer. Slick, hard-boiled fare."

—*Kirkus Reviews*

"Action-packed, tightly plotted . . . irresistible."

—*Publishers Weekly* (starred review)

"Charlie Fox is something entirely new in crime fiction, a genuine female action hero—with passport. Fans of Thomas Perry's Jane Whitefield series are sure to relish Charlie Fox, a true Brit with true grit. Zoë Sharp's original voice, breakneck pacing and crisp prose make for one riveting thriller. Charlie Fox is here to stay. Read *First Drop*, and then tell me if I'm wrong!"

—Julia Spencer-Fleming, author of *All Mortal Flesh*

"Zoë Sharp writes with a casual freshness that makes it all seem easy: her fully-fleshed characters, her closely observed settings, her satisfying plot. American readers will be glad for the chance to get to know her."

—S.J. Rozan, author of *Absent Friends*

"Zoë Sharp is one of the brightest of the new generation of British crime writers, and Charlie Fox is a memorable creation—a welcome addition to the ranks of strong female characters who have turned crime fiction on its head."

—Stephen Booth, author of *Dancing with the Virgins*

MORE . . .

FIRST DROP

ZOË SHARP

St. Martin's Paperbacks

First published in Great Britain by Judy Piatkus (Publishers) Ltd.

FIRST DROP

Copyright © 2004 by Zoë Sharp.
Excerpt from *Second Shot* copyright © 2007 by Zoë Sharp.
"Postcards from Another Country" copyright © 2007 by Zoë Sharp.

Cover photo of roller coaster © Alan Schein/Zefa/Corbis
Cover photo of eyes © Jupiter Images

Library of Congress Catalog Card Number: 2005045490

ISBN: 0-312-93704-0
EAN: 978-0-312-93704-1

Printed in the United States of America

St. Martin's Press hardcover edition / September 2005
St. Martin's Paperbacks edition / September 2007

St. Martin's Paperbacks are published by St. Martin's Press, 175 Fifth Avenue, New York, NY 10010.

For Andy,
who's absolutely convinced . . .

ACKNOWLEDGMENTS

Taking Charlie on her first American adventure wouldn't have been so much fun without the assistance of a number of people. First of these has to be Maryellen and Paul Papadeas of Soundcrafters, organizers of the Spring Break Nationals—the World's Most Famous Sound-Off. Maryellen and Paul not only graciously allowed me to use their event as the location for some of the action in this book, but were also absolutely wonderful about digging out obscure bits of information on Daytona Beach. If you haven't been to SBN, then go. Experiences like Charlie's happen in the pages of novels only!

Richard and Beth Smith of Seattle were another pair of friends who patiently provided excellent and detailed advice on the correct use of numerous Americanisms, and I shouldn't forget to mention the contributors to the DorothyL website who had their say on teenage speech patterns. Thanks to all of you.

Also, Dr. Perran Ross of the Florida Museum of Natural History, who told me all about the feeding habits of alligators; Ian Cottam and Lee Watkin, who taught me how to win a dirty fight; and Glynn Jones for making suitable armament suggestions. Any slip-ups are undoubtedly by my own hand.

Various people eviscerated the first draft to try and help me keep the mistakes to a minimum. A big thank you for this to Peter Doleman, Claire Duplock, Sarah Harrison, Iris Rogers and Tim Winfield.

As always, my husband Andy has been my best critic and biggest fan. Thank you, too, to my editor, Gillian Green; my publisher, Judy Piatkus; and to my copy editor, Sarah Abel, who keeps me on my toes.

Also, grateful apologies go to our temporary neighbors, Robert and Caroline Roper, for putting up with much pounding of computer keys in the flat above them late into the night.

And finally, special mention needs to go to Andrew Till, librarian *extraordinaire,* who always wanted to be a character in a book. I hope you approve, Andrew!

ONE

FOR THE THIRD time that morning I shut my eyes tight in the absolute and certain knowledge that I was just about to die. Around me, people were screaming. Lots of people, but the prospect of dying in company did nothing to alleviate the terror.

My stomach lurched as we started to fall. Actually, fall doesn't begin to describe our horrifying descent. Plummet was more like it. An endless roaring plunge. My hair whipped at my forehead, the sheer punch of the wind pulling my cheeks back to bare my teeth in a final death-mask travesty of a smile.

I just prayed that the expression didn't stay with me post-mortem. Otherwise, although I was unquestionably about to die young, it seemed I was destined *not* to leave a beautiful corpse.

Then we bottomed out, the rollercoaster squatting into the compression. Before I'd time to be thankful I'd survived another first drop, we crested a small rise and bowled into a left-hander so severe the wheels of the open car I was riding in seemed to bounce right out of their tracks and shimmy sideways toward the outside of the bend. Beyond the token piece of safety railing, it had to be at least fifty feet to the ground.

The coaster was constructed out of what had looked to my dubious eyes like a hastily nailed-together clutch of old railway sleepers. I tried to tell myself they were checked, religiously, every day, that the theme park owners would be fools to let anything happen to their paying customers. But in the back of my mind I could already hear the sober voice-over of the dramatic reconstruction after the accident.

And surely even wooden coasters weren't supposed to rattle and shudder this much? We were vibrating so hard my eyesight was blurred. The graunching of timbers as we thundered over them was like the crepitus of broken bones grinding against each other. I knew without a doubt that the damned thing was shaking itself to pieces right underneath us. I could picture each popping nail.

Another bruising turn, another sudden downward swoop that left me tightening my grip on the handle on the seat back in front of me. The chicken bar. As we'd climbed the first lift hill I'd mentally sworn that, no matter what, I would not give in and grab hold of it. Right now I didn't care.

"Jesus Christ!" I yelped.

In the seat alongside, Trey Pelzner stopped waving his arms in the air and whooping just long enough to throw me the kind of utterly contemptuous glance that only fifteen-year-old boys can truly master.

Oh man, it said. *You are* so *old.*

I'd spent the last few days trying to be cool in front of the kid. Trying to be on his level. Trying to be his friend. Someone he really didn't mind hanging out with instead of grudging, enforced company.

Wipeout.

Having started to go downhill, things took on a momentum all of their own. Much like a rollercoaster, I suppose. But without the ups.

In this case, the line of cars was grabbed by its final set of brakes and we slowly clattered back into the station. Had we not paid fifty dollars a head for the privilege of getting into the park, torture sessions like this would have been banned by the Geneva Convention.

As soon as the thrills ceased, Trey's animation went with

it. He dropped back into morose silence like someone had just unplugged him. If sullen equated to cool, then he was the coolest kid there by miles.

I'd already sussed out enough ride etiquette to know that you were supposed to look bored to tears on the way in and out. It was only during the minute or so of terror that masqueraded as fun were you allowed to squeal and wave your arms. In fact, it was almost obligatory. Holding on for grim death was the ultimate *faux pas*. In teenage terms, I'd just ordered Pot Noodle at a three-star Michelin restaurant.

The cars stopped, the lap bars unlocked, and we followed the distorted tannoy directions to please exit to the right, being sure to take all our personal belongings with us. I did my best not to snarl at the manically cheery additional instruction that we were to enjoy the rest of our day here at Adventure World, Florida!

We were carefully funneled through the ride-related gift store on the way out. The park's designers had been masters of merchandising as much as the harnessing of kinetic energy. Mostly it seemed that these places were stocked with the same array of hats and shirts as at the other attractions in the park, allowing the wearer to proclaim to the world that they'd ridden and survived.

It wasn't just a kiddy trap, either. I'd noticed people who should have been old enough to know better riding the rides and buying the T-shirts. If age isn't supposed to bring sense it should at least have brought a little dignity.

As for Trey, he seemed determined to flick through every single rack of clothing. Perhaps he'd seen me rubbing the goose bumps on my arms and just wanted to make me stay out of the sun that bit longer. I'd come to Florida told to expect temperatures in the eighties, even in March, but nobody had warned me about the air-conditioning. Every store and restaurant had the dial set so low that if you let your drink stand for long enough, ice formed on the top.

"Hey, I want one of these."

I sighed, moving away from the door with its promise of baking heat just a few feet outside. Trey was near the back of the store by a rack of leather jackets, holding one up by the collar. It was glossy black, with the Adventure World logo beautifully embroidered across the back panel. A lovely piece of work, and no doubt worth every cent of the three hundred and fifty dollar price tag I could see dangling from the cuff. Except for the fact that it was at least four sizes too big.

Before we'd set out from the house that morning, Trey's father, Keith Pelzner, had handed me a folded wedge of cash with the casual instruction that I should buy the boy whatever he wanted.

"Anything?" I'd asked, riffling my thumb across the edges of the bills and realizing just how many of them were hundreds.

He'd shrugged. "Yeah, sure," he'd said, with the air of someone whose current financial status means that large amounts of money can be frittered on an adolescent whim. But even he had paused at the open doubt in my voice, and grinned at me as he'd added, "Within reason."

Now, I eyed Trey for a second to see if he was joking, but there was nothing funny in the mulish scowl. Mind you, the braces he wore to coach his teeth into perfect alignment would probably have been enough to wipe the smile off anyone's face.

"OK," I said, neutral. "Let's see it on."

Trey's glower deepened, but he slipped the jacket off its hanger and climbed into it. Climbed being the operative word. He was a skinny runt of a kid and both of us would have fitted inside the body and still got the zip done up without having to hold our breath first. His fingers never hit the end of the sleeves until he shoved the cuffs right back. Then the leather bunched up round his thin biceps like a Victorian leg-of-mutton costume.

I was careful not to smile, tilting my head on one side as though giving the jacket serious consideration. "Looks a touch on the big side," I offered at last.

Trey sighed, rolling his eyes and shifting his feet like that was the most pathetic excuse he'd ever heard for denying him something so vital. "It's the smallest they've got," he threw back at me, like that settled it.

"Trey, it doesn't fit you," I said, all reasonable. "If you really want a leather jacket, let's look in one of the other—"

The bottom lip came out. The sigh had become a noisy gush. If it wasn't for the rampant teenage acne that peppered his face like woodchip wallpaper, he would have looked about twelve.

"I—*want*—this—one," he said, speaking very slowly and with great scorn. I'd heard him address the Hispanic maids at the house the same way, obviously taking it for granted that their grasp of English wasn't up to any more than basic cleaning instructions. To my immense disappointment, none of them had ever slapped his legs for it.

I glanced round. Even the assistant was taking notice, I saw, edging out from behind the counter to fuss over straightening a display of polo shirts that was strategically between us and the door. One of the other customers, a youngish good-looking guy in designer Oakley sunglasses and a New York Yankees baseball cap, was two racks down doing a poor job of trying to pretend he wasn't listening in. I moved in close to Trey, stuck my face into his.

"It—doesn't—fit—you," I said between my teeth, matching my delivery to his. "You're not having it."

"Dad said you had to buy me anything I wanted."

"He said within reason," I shot back, aware that for years I'd heard adults in supermarkets talking to their offspring in just the same tone of tightly controlled but thin patience. I'd never really understood it until now. I tried again. "It drowns you and it makes you look like a prat. Put it back."

The word "prat" doesn't have any particular meaning to your average American schoolkid, but he caught the gist and knew I hadn't meant it as a compliment. For a moment I thought we were going to have a major showdown right there. Either that or he was going to lie full length on the ground and beat his fists into the carpet. Instead he glared at me for a second longer, his face starting to flush pink round his collar. I knew I'd beaten him at that point, but at what cost?

He scrabbled out of the jacket as though he suddenly hated the thing, flicked me one last, insolent, knowing look, and deliberately dumped it at my feet. Then he stepped over it and sauntered out of the store.

I waited just long enough to get a grip on my temper, picked the jacket up again and put it back on its hanger on the rail. The assistant came hurrying over to check she wouldn't have to make me pay up under the "you break it, you bought it" rule, but fortunately there was no harm done. On my way out even the guy in the designer shades flashed me a commiserative smile.

I found Trey waiting for me outside, sulking, hands jammed deep into the pockets of his baggy knee-length shorts. He could barely bring himself to look at me. I wanted to shake him.

The track of the coaster dipped to within twenty feet directly above our heads and just then a line of cars swooped through another sequence. Their passing was heralded by a howling like wind through canyons. The note rose and fell as they rode the tracks, accompanied by the mock screams and squeals of unreal fear from people who do not know what it is to be truly afraid.

When I looked back at Trey I was relieved to note that most of the pout had left his face. I never thought that having the memory span of a goldfish would turn out to be a virtue in a kid.

"So," I said, "do you want to look for another jacket?" Hell, why not? After all, it wasn't *my* money we were spending.

"Nah," the little brat shrugged. "I kinda, like, changed my mind about that." He smiled at me, all glinting metalwork and colored plastic.

I fell for it long enough to smile back. "OK," I said, trying to get things back onto at least the semi-friendly footing we'd had before. "What now? You fancy something to eat?"

"Nah, not yet," he said, and the smile developed harder overtones. He nodded to the track above us. "I think I'd like to ride this one a few more times first."

Without waiting for a reaction, he turned and made for the entrance to the ride again, leaving me standing there with my own smile fading rapidly.

Oh yeah, smart thinking, Fox. Next time, just keep your mouth shut and buy him the damned jacket.

It took another four runs on the wooden coaster before even a fanatic like Trey had had enough. At least by the time I'd endured that, I wasn't scared of us crashing any more. In fact, I was praying for a serious malfunction of some kind. Anything to make it stop, and I would even have accepted major injury as the tradeoff.

Particularly if it happened to my charge.

Maybe I was just getting better at hiding my panic but, when we climbed out after that fourth turn, Trey didn't immediately head for the repeat rider queue. I knew better than to provoke him by asking if he was done, so I followed him in silence as we wandered away from the timber colossus.

"I'm hungry," he announced, reproachful, like I was the one who'd been keeping him away from nourishment in order to satisfy my own hedonistic urges.

I resisted an urge of a different kind, one that would have involved swift contact between the back of my hand and the side of his head, and shepherded him into the nearest group of restaurants. According to the menu boards they served a whole range of stuff that sounded surprisingly good for that kind of venue, including taco, Caesar, or garden salads, chili beef, and baked potatoes.

I should have guessed that a fifteen-year-old would despise anything not stuffed with E-numbers and MSG.

"Oh gross," he whinged. "I want proper food."

Proper food, it turned out, was burger and fries which we found at one of the smaller concession stands. At least it was warmer sitting out there at the benches provided. You just had to fend off the bold sidlings of the local scavenging bird population. If you chewed with your mouth open they'd practically have your food straight off your tongue. Trey was in constant danger of losing his lunch.

The kid shoveled down his meal doused in ketchup to equal proportions, pushing the lettuce and tomato garnish to the side of his plate like he'd found a slug in it.

Still, it was nice to sit down somewhere that didn't try to

buck you out of your seat. Even in the shade of an awning the day had a bottomless warmth to it that permeated right down to your bones. I'd just spent a cold winter being reminded about all the bones of mine I'd previously broken. Being here was a luxury, I told myself, regardless of having to look after an obnoxious oik like Trey.

The kid finished his burger, slurped the last of his drink up through the straw and got to his feet, dragging the crumpled park map out of his pocket.

"We gotta go ride Demon next," he decided.

Great. Now we have fear and indigestion, too.

I got up and took my time over collecting the debris of our meal and sliding it into one of the nearby bins, trying to give my food some time to go down before I had to stomach another vomit-inducing piece of so-called entertainment. I'd never been on a rollercoaster of any description before today. If, when this assignment in Florida was over, I never got on another as long as I lived, it would still be too soon.

Nevertheless, it went with the territory. When I'd agreed to an alternative career in close protection, to become a bodyguard, I'd agreed to take discomfort along with reward and danger.

Just my luck that I'd got landed with Trey.

The Demon coaster was across the other side of the park. Scarlet-painted bits of its twisted superstructure were visible over the tops of the trees as we drew nearer. It looked immense and tangled, with no obvious sense of direction. Signs we passed informed us that Demon was newer, higher, and faster than anything we'd ridden so far. I was amazed Trey hadn't headed straight for it, and said so.

He shrugged. "It's a steelie," he said, dismissive.

"A what?"

"A steel coaster, not a wooden one. They're OK, I s'pose, but woodies rule. They're, like, awesome."

I tried not to think about the ride quality of something

that didn't live up to the bone-shaker we'd spent half the morning on.

The queue line for Demon was certainly no shorter. We weaved our way in guided by a maze of stainless steel barriers. If you touched them your hands came away sticky with the sweat from a thousand nervous palms. I'm not sure mine were any drier.

As we moved deeper in we came to a split in the path, manned by a young attendant who could only have had a couple of years on Trey.

"Singles to your left," he said as we approached.

Trey started to go left. I caught his arm.

"Hang on a moment, what does that mean?"

He tried to shake me loose. "If you go in the singles line it means you get on the ride faster 'cos they use you to, like, fill up the empty seats."

"No way," I muttered, steering him off to the right. "We'd rather go on together, thanks," I told the attendant, who shrugged and pointed us wordlessly in the other direction, his attention already lost.

As we joined the end of the long, shuffling line Trey was back to sulking again. "Oh man," he complained, "anyone would think you were my *mother*."

I didn't know what had happened to Mrs. Pelzner. She could have been off visiting her folks, spending her divorce settlement, or dead. It was difficult to respond to Trey's jibe without knowing which, so I let it pass.

"Look, Trey," I said, making a valiant stab at tolerance again. "The company your dad works for has hired me to keep you safe. It's hard enough doing that on a bloody rollercoaster to begin with, but there's no way I can do my job if we don't stick together. You don't have to like it," I added, as he opened his mouth to protest, "but that's the way it is, so learn to live with it."

Yeah, right, his expression said, but he didn't speak to me again as we shuffled our way to the front of the queue line.

I had to admit, privately, that the singles route did seem to be moving much faster. I swear I saw one kid go round twice in the time it took us to get there.

I even saw the good-looking guy again who'd been in the wooden coaster gift store. I only spotted him because one of the attendants held the car back while she made him take off his hat and sunglasses. So this one really was going to turn you upside down and shake the change out of your pockets.

The guy was a little sheepish to be singled out for censure. He looked around as though hoping no one else had noticed. And when it was uncovered like that I couldn't help getting the feeling that I knew his face from somewhere.

I only had a moment's glimpse before the car was released and clanked its way up the first lift hill. After what seemed like an eternity, the clanking stopped, there was a pause, and then the usual screaming started.

They were running two sets of cars on this ride, so it wasn't long before the last run was in and emptying. I was worrying too much about what was coming next to bother racking my memory for where I might possibly have known the Oakley guy from. As the attendant checked the overhead harness was down securely over my shoulders and buckled to the seat between my legs, I had other things to occupy my mind.

I was in for a big surprise.

After the woodies that had been my introduction to coasters, the steelie was a revelation. It was blisteringly quick, yes, but it was smooth the way a sports bike ridden hard on an open road is smooth. It inverted us so many times I lost all comprehension of which way was ground and which was sky, but for the first time I began to see what all the fuss was about.

"Now *that*," I said when it was over, "is more like it!"

Trey immediately lost all interest in further turns on Demon. He hurried out along the ride exit, his amusement now blighted by my unexpected pleasure. I realized belatedly that all I would have had to do to curtail my earlier torment would have been to make a show of enjoying it. At that moment I could cheerfully have strangled him.

I went after the kid, determined not to scurry to match his petulant pace. Outside I spotted him over by some shops, perched on a low concrete wall with his arms folded and shoulders hunched. He was too cross even to put on an act in front of the two teenage girls who were sitting next to him. As I walked across the open area between us, I saw the guy from the coaster again out of the corner of my eye, now back in his Oakleys and his Yankees cap.

And something about the predatory way he moved sent the hairs rising on the back of my neck in a way no rollercoaster, however scary, would ever be able to do.

He was already closer to Trey than I was and moving closer still, focused on him, intent. His shirt was hanging loose outside his chinos but his right hand was stealing underneath the hem, going for something that was concealed at his waistband. Something I couldn't see, but could certainly guess at.

I broke into a run, using my arms to pump up instant speed like a sprinter leaving the blocks. At the last moment Trey became aware of my full-pelt charge and looked up, startled out of his surly guise. Oakley man was watching his expression. He started to twist, head turning.

And that's when I hit him.

I ducked my shoulder and caught him with a full body slam without breaking stride. I hit him hard and low, and was lucky to stay on my feet in the process. I was luckier still I didn't snap my damned collarbone. He wasn't carrying muscle bulk but he was solid, all the same.

Oakley man went down in an ungainly sprawl, letting go the .40 caliber Smith & Wesson he'd been unholstering as he went. The pistol clattered onto the concrete and spun out of both our reach under the legs of the nearest group of fleeing passers-by. I didn't stop to wait for him to retrieve it, just hurdled his legs and kept on going.

I grabbed hold of Trey's shirt by the front and the collar and hauled him sideways off the wall, ignoring his wail of protest. But for once, he didn't argue about doing what I suggested, or going where I wanted him to go.

Out of there. Fast.

I pushed the kid ahead of me, trying to keep my body between his back and our unexpected attacker. I knew I should have just kept my head down and kept running, but I couldn't resist a quick glance behind us.

Oakley man was still on the floor. His hat was missing but the sunglasses were still in place, giving his face a terrifyingly blank stare. Worse, he had managed to recover his gun. He was clasping it firmly in both hands and swinging the muzzle in our direction, heedless of the crowd.

Finding the nearest exit suddenly wasn't as important as finding cover. I jerked Trey sideways just as the first two shots rang out, so close together the second report sounded like an echo of the first. After that I didn't need to urge him to greater speed.

Panic ripped through the immediate vicinity. I'd heard people screaming all day but this was different. This was the real thing. A scattering became a stampede as everyone strove to get out of the firing line. In doing so they inadvertently put themselves directly into it.

Oakley man wasn't deterred by having human obstacles in his way. He fired another two-shot salvo toward us just as a terrified woman darted across our path. Both rounds caught her in the body. The second passed straight through in an explosion of blood. She was so close to us that we were both splattered with it as she tumbled.

I didn't even stop to check if she was dead.

In a heartbeat, Trey had shifted from pain in the backside to principal. My sole concern was to get him away from the source of the danger and to keep him alive. Nothing else mattered.

I'd automatically taken in enough of the park layout during the morning to know where to find the exits. The security guards we encountered on the way were too busy heading for the trouble spot to try and detain us, despite our freakish appearance.

We bolted out through the turnstiles and I was suddenly glad Trey had insisted we pay for preferred parking so he didn't have to walk from the far parking area to the front gate. Nevertheless, by the time we reached the Mercury Sable I'd been allocated, the sweat had glued my polo shirt to my back and drenched through where it was tucked in to the waistband of my shorts.

I fumbled with the key in the door, then bundled Trey straight across the front bench seat into the passenger side, jumping in after him. As I jammed the key into the ignition and cranked up the engine, my eyes were frantically searching the nearest rows of cars for the first sign of those wraparound shades.

I yanked the column-mounted gear lever down into drive and released the parking brake, chirruping the tires as we set off. I forced myself not to put my foot down too hard on the way out. If Oakley man didn't know what car we were driving, there was no point in making it obvious. My eyes constantly scanned the rearview mirror.

Trey sat huddled in the corner of the passenger seat furthest away from me, his eyes wide and blank with shock. I knew I should do something to reassure him, but for the life of me I couldn't think what.

"Put your seatbelt on," I said instead, calmly. He threw me a disbelieving glance, but buckled up without demur. *Shit, he really* is *frightened.*

I followed the signs for the freeway doing my best not to exceed the posted speed limit. No cars seemed to be making an effort to get close to us. Still, I didn't start to breathe again until we were on I-95 heading away from Fort Pierce, south toward Fort Lauderdale.

It was only then, as my heartbeat finally began to settle and my brain started to come out of survival mode, that the question returned of where I'd seen Oakley man before. It lurked brooding at the back of my mind, an itch I couldn't scratch.

I pulled the mobile phone they'd given me out of my pocket, noticing for the first time the blood on my bare forearms, and I remembered again the woman who'd been shot in front of us. I glanced down and saw that her blood was all over the front of my pale fawn polo shirt as well, a livid splash of color already turning dark as it dried. Trey had a few flecks, but I'd caught the brunt of it and looked like an extra from a Tarantino flick. No wonder he'd been unnaturally cooperative.

I hit the speed-dial for the house. Whitmarsh was in charge of house security and he was going to go ape-shit. But that was nothing to what my boss, Sean was going to do when he found out my low-risk babysitting job had ended in a full-scale assault. The fact that, technically, Whitmarsh had authority over Sean would make very little difference.

The Pelzners' home number rang without reply, the endless long burr of the US phone system. I let it ring until it clicked off, then tried it again, checking carefully that I'd punched in the right number. I steered with one hand, flicking my eyes from the phone to the road. There was no mistake.

I tried Sean's own personal mobile, but all I got was a recorded message telling me the number I was calling was switched off. I knew that the house was never empty and my boss never had his phone off without leaving it on divert or answering machine.

Right there, in a big car on a big stretch of open road in a big country, I suddenly began to feel very small, and very lonely.

And then, because I'd pushed it to some peripheral part of my brain, my mental retrieval system finally connected and spat out the information I'd been searching for. I remembered exactly where I'd seen Oakley man before and I wished to God that I hadn't.

It was just about this time I realized how much trouble we were *really* in.

TWO

THE FIRST STATE Trooper flashed past in the opposite direction less than ten minutes after we left the park. He was going like hell, lights and sirens at full bore, in a black and tan Chevy Camaro. Even the cops out here had cool cars.

The distance across the grassy central reservation was such that he couldn't have seen us in any detail. Hell, in London they would have built housing on a tract of land that size, but Trey still ducked down further in his seat.

"Are you OK?" I asked him, taking my eyes momentarily off the road, but he just hunched his shoulders in a jerky shrug and turned his face away. If he'd been alone, I realized, he probably would have been crying. If I'd been alone, maybe I would, too.

I sighed, trying not to snap at him for clamming up on me right when I needed him to tell me everything and anything he knew. And I was pretty sure he knew more than I did.

Still, for all his pseudo grown-up posturing he was still a kid. An immature kid, at that, and he'd just been through an experience that would have left most adults little more than a puddle of jelly on the floor mat. At least he'd held it together long enough to keep running.

But from what?

Even though I'd worked out who our assailant had been, that hadn't got me much further forward. I still had no idea why he'd been after Trey. Kill or capture? I wasn't sure about that one either.

A stark, vivid snapshot of the woman who'd run in front of us exploded out of nowhere, action frozen at the moment when the bullets struck and the blood sprayed outward. I hoped with all my heart that she had survived, but I couldn't find it in me to feel more than fleeting concern for an unlucky stranger. A fractional shift of fate and timing and that could have—would have—been us. There but for the grace of God . . .

I gripped the steering wheel tighter in an effort not to lose all self-possession. I focused on my anger instead. It was much safer ground.

I'd been kept out of the information loop ever since I'd arrived in Florida. With the clarity of hindsight I wished I'd pressed for more background, but they'd just kept patting me on the head and fobbing me off. I'd let it go because I was aware of being new in the business and I hadn't wanted to make waves, to come across as too pushy.

What a time to turn over a new leaf.

At the time of the abortive attack on Trey Pelzner I'd been in America for just four days. I'd flown into Miami International airport expecting a laid-back couple of weeks' jaunt in the sun, and no trouble.

Officially, I'd been working for Sean Meyer's exclusive close-protection agency for six weeks by then. Unofficially, my involvement in the world of the professional bodyguard had begun at a dodgy training school in Germany shortly after New Year.

When that particular course had ended in disarray Sean had sent me off to study with various experts on a one-on-one basis. By the beginning of March they'd reckoned I was ready for my first assignment.

The Florida job had come up at short notice. I'd been away up in Lancashire visiting friends when Sean had phoned one morning and told me to get back down to King's Langley fast, and to make sure I'd got my passport with me.

"Where am I going?" I'd asked, almost flustered. "What else do I need to bring?"

"Just pack some clothes for hot weather," he'd replied. "We're supplementing an existing security team and they'll provide any equipment we need once we get out there."

I heard the "we" rather than the singular and couldn't help the relief. "Who's the principal?"

"Nobody you've ever heard of; don't worry—this is not a celebrity job," Sean had said, and I could hear the lazy amusement in his voice. "It's for a small software company based in Miramar in Florida. They've had some threats made against their staff and they're getting jumpy, that's all."

I'd frowned. It didn't exactly sound like cause for a mad dash halfway down country, let alone across the Atlantic. "So why are they bringing us in?"

"I came across the company's director of security when I was teaching a hostage negotiation course in Virginia last year and we hit it off," he'd said. "When they needed extra manpower, she came to me."

She, I'd thought, and tried to suppress the unexpected spike of jealousy. After all, I had been the one who was putting the brakes on the relationship Sean and I had tentatively agreed to resume. I had been the one who was being cautious to the point of timid. Hell, it had been more than two months and we hadn't even made it to the bedroom.

There were times when I'd wondered if he still wanted me the way he once had, with that kind of desperate, all-consuming intensity. Was he just being considerate because of what he now knew I'd gone through, or did the wounds we'd both received at the hands of the army still run deep, even after five years?

Maybe I'd been just too proud, or too scared, to make the first move and find out. If it all went wrong this time, that would be the end of it.

"OK," I'd said, checking my watch. "I'll set off as soon as

I'm sorted. I should be back down there in less than three hours."

He'd restrained himself from reminding me that just shy of two hundred and thirty miles separated us. It may be colder, wetter, and more exposed, but riding a motorbike also means you don't sit in traffic jams on the M6 all the way past Birmingham.

"That's fine," he'd said. "I'm just about to leave now, but Madeleine's booked you on a flight out of Heathrow first thing tomorrow morning. I'll make sure she puts together some background info for you to read on the plane."

But by the time the American Airlines 777 touched down in Miami the following afternoon, I didn't feel much more enlightened than I had done before I'd taken off. The promised dossier was scant, to say the least. Even from my limited association with Sean's company, I knew he never took on a job without being fully aware of the facts. I wondered at his tie with this unknown female director of security, that he would drop everything for her to fly nearly five thousand miles apparently so ill-prepared.

The security director's name was Gerri Raybourn. The file told me that much at least, and included a badly pixellated black and white picture of a slight blonde woman wearing a power suit and a don't-mess-with-me expression.

The company she worked for was only vaguely described. They were a small independent software house, specializing mainly in accounting packages and data manipulation. Their turnover was modest and didn't seem to be matching up to anyone's projections, least of all their own.

In truth, the company's markets were being swallowed up as the big boys stamped conformity across the sector. Taking it at face value, they were not quite sinking yet but the decks were certainly awash.

Ms. Raybourn's department within the company was more diminutive than her impressive title might have suggested. She just had a deputy director and two additional operatives to play with.

The step-up in security concerned one of their key program developers, Keith Pelzner, but no specific threats or incidents were noted.

It was a long flight and I hadn't thought to buy a paperback at the airport, so I read and reread the file several times, trying to squeeze the last few drops of information out of every word and phrase. Despite that, nowhere did the document even begin to suggest why they should feel the need to import close protection personnel from the UK.

It was only much later that the thought occurred to me that maybe they just didn't like the idea of getting their own people killed.

The flight had landed on time but it had taken a while to shuffle through Immigration and then my bag had, of course, been the last one off the carousel. When I finally made it out into the arrivals lounge I was disheveled, tired, thirsty, and surprisingly chilly.

Gerri Raybourn herself was waiting to meet me in a tailored mint-green suit and the kind of four-inch heels I couldn't have successfully negotiated a flight of stairs in. She was holding up a piece of white card with my name written on it in a slightly childish hand. Her impatience showed only in the way her long painted nails drummed against the edge of the card. Her face was a perfectly made-up mask.

"Ms. Raybourn?" I said, halting in front of her. There was a faint lift of one plucked eyebrow. I nodded to the card. "I'm Charlie Fox."

Her confusion was momentary, quickly cloaked, and she held out her hand. I engaged it with care, not only because of those talon-like nails, but also because in the flesh she was a tiny woman, her hands half the size of mine. I needn't have worried. She had a grip that could crack walnuts.

"Well, if you're all set I'll take you right on over to the house," she said, looking dubiously at my rip-stop nylon squashy bag. I couldn't tell from her expression if she thought I'd brought too much luggage, or not nearly enough.

She led me outside at a surprisingly brisk pace considering

those shoes. As the sliding doors opened the wet Florida heat hit me in the face like a sneezing dragon. The surface of my skin went from shiver to sweat almost instantly. Then we were climbing into Gerri's illegally parked Mercedes and she cranked the air-conditioning on full almost before she even started the engine. So that was how she stopped her makeup sliding.

"So, Charlie," she said as she pulled out fast into traffic. "I take it you've worked in the States some before?"

"No," I said, wondering what exactly Sean had told her about me. Less, it would seem, than he'd told me about her. "Actually, this is my first time."

She frowned, then said with the faintest touch of bite, "Well, I guess you'll find we like to do things a little differently over here."

Uh-oh, I thought. *Where did that come from?* But I said nothing, just smiled and nodded as though she'd spoken without the undercurrents. Nevertheless, it made it more difficult to phrase a question that didn't show my ignorance still further. Like what the hell was I supposed to be doing?

In fact, it wasn't until we'd navigated our way out of the airport complex and were onto the highway that I plucked up the courage to do so. But my tentative opening gambit of "Excuse me, but can you tell me wh—" was cut short by the shrill ring of her mobile phone, amplified by the in-car kit it was slotted into.

She peered down at the tiny display, then leaned across and pressed a button to receive the call on hands-free.

"Hi, it's Gerri," she said, slightly singsong, speaking loudly enough to combat the muted background noise. "And how are you today?" She sounded like someone out of every American film I've ever seen. And I've seen a lot.

"I'm good, Gerri," a man's deep voice rumbled. "But you're not gonna like what I have to tell you. Are you alone or do you wanna pick up?"

She shifted her eyes sideways and decided in an instant that I was slightly above invisible servant level. She grabbed

the big pearl clip-on on her right ear and yanked it off before
snatching the phone out of its dash-mounted cradle.

"OK," she said, and the singsong tone had turned to steel.
"Shoot."

There followed a fairly lengthy, mainly one-sided conversation, only punctuated by the occasional "uh-huh" on Gerri's
part. Her voice may have stayed neutral, but after the first couple of minutes her left hand started to flex around the Merc's
leather-rimmed steering wheel. High-carat stone rings glinted
on most of her fingers like ornamental knuckledusters.

I tried not to look like I was eavesdropping, staring out of
the window at the odd mixture of low squat concrete discount
warehouses and tinted glass skyscrapers that we passed. All
the really plush buildings seemed to be banks. I recognized
maybe one in four of the makes of car around us.

Eventually Gerri ended the call, almost slamming the
phone down. For several minutes afterward she drove in simmering silence, then her only words were a muttered, "Son of
a bitch."

I didn't think now was the right time to strike up a friendly
conversation. I kept my lip buttoned until we left the freeway
twenty minutes later and turned east toward the coast.

The closer to the water we got, the more expensive the
housing became. This year's fashion accessory seemed to be a
very large motor yacht parked at the bottom of your lawn, and
when your garden backed onto an inland waterway, all things
were possible. It was only when Gerri finally turned into a
quiet side road that I realized perhaps I should have paid more
attention to the route.

She was still spitting feathers when we drove up to a set of
motorized gates at the end of the road, tapping her fingers impatiently against the steering wheel until they'd swung wide
enough for the Merc to get through.

The house itself, set back in the trees, was so massive that
for a moment I wondered if it was split into apartments. Gerri
left the Merc at a jaunty angle on the front driveway and
rushed up the steps to the double front door almost before I'd

time to grab my bag out of the back of the car. I had to jog to catch her up just as the door was opened by an unsmiling Hispanic maid.

Gerri hurried past the woman without a second glance. I nodded, tried a tentative greeting and was rewarded by a fleeting smile. I've always thought you can tell a lot about somebody by the way they treat other people's staff.

A well-built black man in neatly pressed slacks, a blue Oxford shirt and loafers with tassels on the front met Gerri in the cool, tiled, circular hallway. A double staircase curved around the sides of the walls and the domed glass ceiling was thirty feet above our heads.

"What the hell is going on, Chris?" Gerri snapped at the man before he could open his mouth. "I've just had a phone call telling me it's all over the goddamn press."

"I'm sorry, boss," the man said, eyes widening with surprise at the sudden onslaught. "We only just got the news ourselves." His gaze skimmed toward me a couple of times as he spoke, but Gerri didn't bother to introduce us.

"How's Keith taking it?" she demanded.

"Well, I guess you could say he's kinda upset right now," the man said, picking his words with care.

Gerri sighed noisily. "OK, where is he?"

Chris waved a hand toward a pair of glass doors behind him. "Out back in the lanai, by the pool."

She headed out, the whole exchange having been carried out without her actually breaking stride, so that Chris had to shift into rapid reverse to stay with her. Unsure whether I was supposed to follow or not, I stayed right behind her, lugging my bag with me. It seemed like the safest place to be.

The back of the house was as breathtaking as the front. A paved terrace swept down to an expanse of lawn so big it should have had herds of wildebeest grazing on it. Clusters of palm trees were grouped at the edges of the grass and then you were straight out onto the waterway.

The pool Chris had mentioned was off to the left and the lanai, I surmised, was the giant mosquito net structure over the top of it and joined onto the far wing of the house. The pool itself was fed by a waterfall at one end and lined with pale turquoise tiles. An array of slatted wooden sun loungers was arranged around the sides of it, their teak faded to a soft-sheen silver by the constant blazing sunshine. Even with the breeze coming up off the water, the heat had a mass all of its own.

There were two men by the pool, but neither of them seemed to be enjoying the amenities. One was tall with artistically graying hair and a very good tan. He was dressed in shorts and a knitted shirt with a designer label, and deck shoes with no socks.

The other man was younger, on the scrawny side, with a wispy mustache and beard, and little wire-rimmed spectacles with badly matched clip-on sunglasses over the top. He was wearing a cheap-looking Hawaiian shirt, swimming shorts and plastic flip-flops. He was also carrying a small net on the end of a long pole. Until the three of us got close enough to hear the conversation they were having, I assumed he was just there to clean the pool.

"I'm real sorry, Mr. Pelzner," the gray-haired man was saying, "we don't know how it happened."

"How can you not know how it happened for Chrissake, Lonnie?" the bearded man snapped. "What in hell's name do I pay you for?"

There was a small doorway set into one side of the lanai. As Gerri pushed it open the hinge squeaked and both men looked up sharply. I could almost see Lonnie's muscular shoulders relax when he recognized Gerri and realized he was about to be rescued. Then they tensed again as he caught the thunderous expression on her face.

"Gerri!" the bearded man yelled, throwing the net aside and striding to meet us—as far as it's possible to stride in flip-flops. "Will you tell your guys to get their butts into gear? How can they have let this happen?" He let out a frustrated exclamation of breath, shook both fists in the air and whirled away.

"Now just calm down, Keith," Gerri snapped. "Until we find out exactly who leaked that information to the media I'm not having my guys taking any heat."

"The media?" Keith Pelzner said, his tone rising to an outraged squeak as he spun back to face her. "Who gives a shit about the media? I'm talking about my son, for Chrissake. I'm talking about Trey."

For a moment Gerri was silent. Whatever the phone call in the car had been about, I realized, that wasn't it.

She glanced at Lonnie and Chris, neither of whom would meet her eyes. "OK," she said in the falsely controlled voice of one who is hanging on to her temper by the slenderest of threads. "Now I've just had a call saying one of the top financial weekly magazines has run with an article blowing our supposedly top secret project wide open to the world, and laid the company open to hostile takeover bids that could see us all out of a job, which *I* personally feel is something we ought to 'give a shit about', huh?"

She emphasized the last few words using her fingers to scratch twin quotation marks in the air, casting a ferocious look in Keith's direction, but he was just staring at her with his mouth open. "OK," she went on. "Would anybody like to fill me in here on what *else* has gone wrong today?"

"Er, well Ms. Raybourn," Lonnie said. "Trey's been AWOL outta school again and this time he's been caught shoplifting down at the Galleria."

Even Gerri was momentarily speechless to that one. "And where is he now?" she managed eventually.

"The cops are bringing him home," Keith told her. "Jim and the limey have gone to smooth things over with the store but he shoulda had somebody watching him, for Chrissake. Anything could have happened!"

"Well now we have someone to watch him," Gerri said, gesturing toward me. My heart sank.

Keith seemed to notice me for the first time. "Oh, hi. Keith Pelzner." He wiped his hand on his shirt and held it out for me to shake. "And you are?"

"Charlie Fox," I said, and couldn't resist adding, "Another limey."

He gave a nervous laugh but was saved from having to find a way out of that verbal hole by the appearance of another group of people at the double doors where the lanai joined the house. The same Hispanic maid who'd let us in came out first and pointed wordlessly in our direction. Two policemen strolled out next, with a junior version of Keith between them.

The kid had his head down and was dragging his feet, but insolence rolled off him like sweat. Whatever it was he'd been caught doing, he was totally unrepentant about it. His gaze floated briefly over me, the newcomer, and carried on without interest.

One of the cops came forward and looked straight at Lonnie. "Mr. Pelzner?" he asked. He had sergeant's stripes on his sleeve and a belly big enough to ensure he had to use a mirror to check his fly.

The real Keith Pelzner stepped forward. "I'm Pelzner," he said, sounding resigned. "What's he done this time, officer?"

"Well, sir," the sergeant said, glancing round meaningfully. "Maybe we could talk about this some place more private?"

Keith sighed and started to lead them back toward the house.

"I think I better be in on this one," Gerri said. "Lonnie, get Juanita to show Charlie her room, then contact Jim and find out what the score is."

"Yes, ma'am," Lonnie said smartly, and to me: "If you'd like to come this way?"

"So," I asked as I fell into step alongside him, "does the kid do this kind of thing a lot?"

Lonnie rolled his eyes. "Oh yeah," he said, a slight smirk forming as he recognized somebody further down the pecking order than he was. "But I guess you'll find out soon enough—seeing as how you're gonna be looking out for him."

He wouldn't say much more, handing me over to the Hispanic maid in the hallway. On the way to my room I tried to gently pump Juanita for information about how much trouble Trey Pelzner managed to get himself into, and on what kind of regular basis. Either her English wasn't good enough to understand the question, or she was being loyally tight-lipped. She just led me to the appropriate doorway, waved me inside with another smile and departed.

My room was in the block above the garaging, which

makes it sound less luxurious than it really was. "Suite" would be a better description. The whole place was painted white with blue and pink trimmings which would have looked gaudy anywhere else but the subtropics. It had a tiled floor and the kind of finishing touches that have been added by an interior designer rather than a homeowner.

There was an ensuite just off the bedroom, with a shallow but wide bath that I couldn't have laid down in, but which had a huge shower head over the top of it. Everything had been done in white marble.

Another doorway from the bedroom led to a small sitting room, with a mammoth TV set and a balcony. I opened the wooden shutters and stepped out onto it, discovering that I was at the front of the house, but right over to one side. If I leaned out and craned my neck, I could just see the police cruiser parked next to Gerri Raybourn's Mercedes.

As I watched, the two cops who'd brought Trey home walked down the steps and climbed into their car, their audience with Keith Pelzner over. The sergeant took the passenger seat, while the younger guy, clearly his junior, went round to the driver's side.

Just before he got in, the second policeman unfolded a pair of expensive Oakley sunglasses and slipped them on.

THREE

"OK, TREY," I said, keeping my eyes on the road ahead of us. "I think now would be a really good time for you to tell me who's after you."

I was rewarded by another silent hunch of the boy's shoulders. Still he wouldn't meet my eyes.

I pressed my lips together and let my breath out slowly through my nose, willing the tension to escape with it. The technique didn't work particularly well.

In reality, I didn't need him to tell me who was after him. I already knew that. What I really needed to find out, though, was *why*.

We'd passed the exits for Boca Raton and Deerfield Beach. Maybe, once, they'd been individual places, but now they just seemed to be part of one huge urban sprawl. It started around about West Palm Beach and went all the way down to Miami in the south, swallowing Fort Lauderdale on the way. We were nearly at the junction for the house.

I knew I needed answers before we got there. Trey hadn't spoken at all since we'd got back into the car. I was only too well aware how shock has its own way of shielding the mind, but I didn't have time for gentle psychology.

"Is this a straightforward kidnap?" I wondered, more to myself than to the boy. "Was he planning on holding you to ransom?"

Trey snorted suddenly. "For what?" he demanded. "You

gotta, like, have a lotta dough to be kidnapped, don't you? We're broke."

"Broke?" I echoed blankly, thinking of the mansion and the wedge of cash in my pocket.

"Yeah," he said, scathing at my lack of comprehension. "The people Dad works for rent the house and give him, like, an allowance. Like he was a kid or something."

"Well somebody's after you." I said. "You do know who that guy was, don't you?" It was almost a rhetorical question. After all, the kid had been brought home by Oakley man, sat in a car with him, been torn off a strip in front of him. How could Trey possibly have failed to recognize him?

The kid glanced at me, little more than a sliding skim that settled longest, I noticed, on the blood which had dried on my shirt and on my skin. I resisted the impulse to scratch at it.

But I'd caught something in his eyes. Something knowing. Something that made me suspect he wasn't as horrorstruck by what he'd seen as he was making out.

"Why was a cop trying to kill you, Trey?" I asked now, more brutal, trying to shake it loose. "What have you done?"

"I ain't done nothing!" The words had burst free before he had the chance to stop them. Too fast, perhaps? The way the guiltiest kid in the class will issue an instant denial before he's even been accused of the crime. "I ain't done nothing," he repeated, quieter this time.

"You must have done something for those two cops to have picked you up at the Galleria," I said. "It was only the day before yesterday. What happened?"

Of course, I'd heard the official version of events from Gerri Raybourn's second-in-command, Jim Whitmarsh. He'd filled me in later, on the day I'd first arrived, although it was only after he'd begun speaking that I'd worked out that the Galleria was the name of the local shopping center—a place so mammoth it made Meadowhall in Sheffield look like the corner SPAR.

Trey had been caught near a store that sold computer accessories with a considerable amount of unpaid-for merchandise stashed in his school bag. The store manager had been all for pressing charges until Whitmarsh and Sean had been down there.

It was Sean, I'd gathered, who had politely pointed out the name of the company Trey's father worked for. It might not have been up to Microsoft standards, but it still had enough clout in that field to dampen the guy's enthusiasm for a prosecution. Particularly when Sean had hinted that the company might possibly be needing a rake of new hardware in the near future. By the time they'd left, he'd told me, the manager was falling over himself to be helpful.

Now, I waited for Trey's side of the story. It took him a while to get it straight in his head before he tried it out on me.

"They set me up," he muttered.

I ducked my head to catch the words, unsure for a moment that I'd heard him right. I couldn't believe he'd actually come out with that one as a viable excuse, but I put a lot of effort into keeping my voice neutral. "Who set you up?"

Again, that sideways flick of the eyes from beneath his lashes, to check how this was going down. "That cop and my dad," he said at last. "He didn't want me to go up to Daytona for Spring Break, so he set it up just so's he could ground me."

I actually felt my mouth fall open, had to consciously issue the instructions to my jaw to close it. *Don't jump,* I told myself. *Think it through before you rip his head off.*

It was certainly true that after the shoplifting incident Keith had, in no uncertain terms, forbidden his son to go to Daytona Beach for the annual Spring Break weekend coming up.

This was, I gathered by Trey's reaction at the time, a major catastrophe. He'd sunk past being upset and had moved almost into grief-stricken at the prospect of missing out. In the end I had to brave Lonnie's condescending attitude and check with him what the story was.

"It's the first major school vacation since Christmas," he'd told me. "The kids kinda go a little wild, let their hair down, y'know?"

"So what happens at Daytona Beach that's so special?"

"Lots of partying, lots of drink, maybe a little drugs," he'd said, flashing me the kind of perfect smile Trey would be able to muster in a few years' time if he kept up with those braces. "The kids with the cool cars go down there and hang out, do some cruising on the beach. There's a big car stereo competition they all go to. It's a cool time, y'know?"

"So, missing out on it is a big deal?"

"Oh yeah," he'd said. "It's a big deal all right. Trey is not gonna forgive him easy for this one."

Now, as I took in the thin set line of the boy's mouth, I would have to say I agreed with Lonnie that Trey hadn't forgiven his father. To the point where he was prepared to spin me this ludicrous story to explain what had just happened.

"Don't you think," I said, allowing a trace of acid to leak through my voice, "that there were easier ways of your dad stopping you going to Spring Break if he didn't want you to, other than organizing an elaborate setup with a couple of local cops?"

The sudden thought occurred to me that what if Oakley man wasn't a cop at all? What if his fat sergeant hadn't been a cop either? What if this whole thing had been a setup right from the start? Where did that leave us?

"You don't believe me," Trey said, flushed and defensive. "No one ever does! I'm just a kid, right? I don't know nothing, right? Well how the fuck do you explain what that cop did then, huh?" His voice had risen sharply, the note cracking. "How do you explain *that*?" And he waved his hand toward the bloodstains on my arms and clothing.

I didn't answer straight away because, the truth was, I didn't have one to give him.

I deliberately exited I-95 a junction early, turning left toward the sea. I'd quickly discovered that most of the city layouts were dead easy to navigate. If you made a mistake, there was no need to do a U-turn when everything was laid out on a grid pattern. Two wrongs may not make a right, but in the States three lefts generally do.

I was searching for something specific. Somewhere I could

leave Trey in reasonable safety. It went against all my instincts not to have him with me, where I could protect him, but for what I needed to do now it was just too risky to take him along. I'd just have to pray I'd been good enough for them not to follow me from the park this far. For both our sakes . . .

It wasn't long before I found what I was looking for. A little independent diner with few cars in the parking area. It was only after we'd actually stopped that Trey seemed to notice where we were.

He eyed me with disgust. "You wanna *eat*?"

"No," I said. "Look, Trey, I'll level with you." Which was more than he was doing with me, I reckoned, but one of us had to make the first move. "No one's answering the phones at the house. I need to go back and check what's happened there and I don't want to take you with me while I do that."

"I can handle it," he shot back, touchy. "I'm not a baby."

I shook my head. "I don't doubt it," I lied, "but that's not the reason." I paused while I gathered my thoughts. Treating him like a kid wasn't going to get me anywhere. Besides, I'd already proved how bad I was at handling kids. I was going to have to pick another strategy.

"OK, let's look at what's happened today," I said. "Someone's made an attempt on you. A pretty serious attempt, yes?" Trey's face froze up at that, as though he was trying to keep some emotion from skating across the surface, but he nodded at least.

I tried a reassuring smile, not sure if this was the best approach, but at the moment it was the only one I'd got. "OK, so far we don't know if this attempt extends to Keith or not," I went on, using his father's name to detach the whole thing, make it into an academic exercise, depersonalize it. "If I take you back to the house now, I could be delivering you into a trap, you understand? I need you to sit tight here and if it all looks OK, I'll come back and get you."

For a few moments Trey said nothing, staring at part of the dashboard and biting his lip. I almost thought that the events of the day had finally caught up with him, that they were finally beginning to sink in.

"If you're the main target," I added, aiming to appeal to his ego, "we'd be giving them exactly what they want."

"I don't see why I can't come with you," he said, as stubborn and sulky as he'd ever been. So much for treating him like an adult.

"It might be dangerous." I regretted the words as soon as they were out of my mouth. *Yeah, smart thinking, Fox, that's really going to put off a fifteen-year-old boy who spends his free time riding rollercoasters.*

"So what?" He flashed me a resentful look. "You're going and you're just a girl! You're just somebody's girlfriend who came along for a free ride—" He broke off then, abruptly, as if he'd suddenly realized that he'd said way too much.

"And where exactly did you get that idea?" I said, hearing the soft note of anger in my own voice.

Trey swallowed, hung his head. "I overheard Mr. Whitmarsh talking to Dad this morning," he mumbled.

I was glad he wasn't looking at my face as he spoke. *Well, that explained a lot. And there was I thinking Sean and I had been so careful . . .*

"Well, look on the bright side," I said with a touch of bite, opening my car door and climbing out into instant heat. I ducked back and met his eyes. "I may just be 'somebody's girlfriend' as you put it, but I've managed to keep *you* alive 'til now."

As we walked into the diner one of the waitresses grabbed two wipe-clean menus from the rack and hustled toward us. She was middle-aged and the kind of slim you get from constant hard work rather than fashionable exercise. But even her jaded gaze fluttered slightly at our appearance.

"Hi there, how ya doing?" she greeted us, her mouth on automatic pilot as though bloodstained people walked in off the street all the time. Only her eyes betrayed the hint of nervousness. "Just two? Smoking or non?"

"Non," I said.

She led us to a corner booth. I sat with my back to the window, facing the door. Trey slid in opposite.

"Can I get you guys anything to drink?" the waitress asked, plonking the menus on the scuffed laminate in front of us. Her badge said her name was Joyce and she was happy to help.

Despite his distaste at the idea of food, now we were sitting down Trey ordered a Coke. I shook my head and asked the way to the ladies' room instead. It was right at the back, Joyce told me, next to the kitchen.

On my way there I took a long but casual look at the other occupants of the booths, but nobody set the alarm bells ringing. Inside the washroom I got my first proper look at myself in the half-length mirror, and Joyce's apprehension became all the more understandable. The blood might have lost some of its impact now it had dried to a dullish dark hue, but there seemed to be a hell of a lot of it. Some had even splashed up onto the underside of my chin.

I suppressed a shudder and ran hot water into the sink. There were no plugs so I had to wad toilet paper into the plug hole until I'd got half a basinful, then I scrubbed at my arms and face until the skin was pink, although I couldn't do much about my shirt. I'd just have to wait and change when I got back to the house.

I left the washroom and moved out past the kitchen again. Ahead of me, at the counter, Joyce was talking in low tones with one of the cooks, glancing constantly in the direction of the restrooms. She broke off quickly when she saw me coming.

By the doorway was a staff notice board which seemed to be covered more in personal photographs than official paperwork. My eye landed on one of the snapshots, which was unmistakably of Joyce, kneeling on a lawn with a pair of German shepherd dogs.

Inspiration was born of desperation.

I walked as casually as I was able back through the diner toward our booth, managing to snag the waitress between tables.

"Joyce," I said, earnest, "I need to ask you a really big favor."

She eyed me warily, her jaw working gum as a reflex action. "What is it, honey?"

"Well, I'm supposed to be looking after Trey over there," I said, nodding in the direction of the kid's back. "And well, this afternoon his dog got loose on the road and got himself run over."

"Oh jeez, that's terrible," she said, her face animating for the first time as the relief flooded in. "Oh, the poor kid."

"Yeah," I said, waving a hand toward my shirt. "It wasn't nice. We did everything we could, but . . ." I let my voice trail off, shaking my head, getting into my stride. "The thing is," I went on, "I've got the dog in the back of the car and I really need to go and take him to the nearest vet's where they can, you know, dispose of him, but I don't want Trey to be any more upset today. You see, it happened right in front of him."

I swear I saw a tear start to well up in Joyce's eye and I felt a stir of guilt at playing on the woman's emotions like this.

"No problem, honey, you leave the kid right here and I'll take real good care of him for you."

I dug in my pocket for some of the cash Keith Pelzner had given to me that morning and pulled out a fifty. "Would you get him whatever he wants to eat until I get back?" I asked. "I'll try to be as quick as I can."

She nodded and smiled, relaxed now as she followed me back to the table. I put my hand on Trey's shoulder.

"OK," I said carefully, "I'm going to go and take care of Rex now, so I want you to stay here with Joyce for a while."

Trey opened his mouth to ask what the hell I was talking about. I surreptitiously dug my thumb into the front of his protruding collarbone hard enough to shut him up. He squirmed out from under my hand and glared at me with resentment.

Joyce watched this display of belligerence indulgently. "Don't you worry," she said to me. "He'll be just fine." Some waitressing sixth sense made her aware then that one of the other diners was approaching the counter, clutching his bill. "I'll be right with you," she said and hurried away.

"No arguments!" I warned Trey quietly when she was out

of earshot. "Now, for God's sake try to look upset about this mythical dog who's just been run over, and stay put until I get back."

I straightened up, was about to turn away when he stopped me.

"So what happens," he said in an uncharacteristically small voice, "if you don't come back?"

"Trey," I said, passing him a grim smile, "I don't think you could be that lucky, do you?"

It was only when I was safely in the Mercury and had pulled out onto the road that I allowed the real worry to surface. It welled up and washed over me like a blocked drain, only smelling twice as bad.

I reached for the mobile and re-dialed the numbers for the house, Whitmarsh, and Sean, but with no joy on any of them. I stuffed the phone back into my pocket, frustrated. Instinct told me that going to the house wasn't a good idea, that my actions were being dictated to me, but what else could I do?

I knew this wasn't a straightforward kidnap attempt on the boy, otherwise I would have been able to contact them by now. All the worst possibilities I could come up with flooded in, but whatever had happened, I told myself, it was better to know now.

I considered calling the cops and letting them check it out, but then I remembered Oakley man. I couldn't identify him by name and I hadn't been close enough to him when he'd come to the house to read his badge number. Supposing he was the one they sent to investigate? I could try explaining the whole scenario but I knew just who the police were likely to believe first. And it wasn't me.

OK, Fox, on your own again.

It took less than ten minutes before I was turning into the end of the Pelzners' road and crawling down toward the house. The dead-end layout made it impossible to do a drive-by. I was going to have to go straight in and get it over with.

I drove slowly right to the end and swung the car in a circle, as though I was simply turning round. The house looked quiet, but then, all the houses along this road looked quiet. It was too upmarket an area to stand for untidy rowdiness on the front lawn.

The opener for the electric gate was attached to the Mercury's sun visor, but I didn't want to take it right into the driveway. Instead I pulled up by the curb next door, leaving the car facing the main road. No other vehicles had followed me into the street and none were already parked there. Nevertheless, I'd already started to sweat before I even got out of the car and it had little to do with the heat.

I took the opener with me, walking quickly across the road and through the gap as soon as it was wide enough, then closing the gates behind me. I did a rapid circuit of the exterior of the house, checking for obvious signs of forced entry. There weren't any.

I even peered in through a couple of the ground-floor windows. The furniture was all in its usual carefully coordinated positions. Juanita and the other maids kept the place immaculate, as though in readiness for a magazine photo shoot. If Keith Pelzner had been taken from here, he—and his bodyguards—had gone without a fight.

I went in via the door to the kitchen, which was the only one I had a key for. There was a keypad for the alarm next to it. A glance at the panel on my way in told me the system hadn't been set.

I did a fast sweep of the ground floor rather than a thorough search but even so there was nothing to find. No disturbance. No breakages. No sign of hurry. It was like they'd all simply got up and walked out of the front door. And then someone had sent the cleaners in.

I carefully used the bottom of my shirt to touch the door handles. If the place had been wiped down I didn't want mine to be the only prints they found.

Upstairs I ran through the bedrooms in the main part of the house but they were all empty. Nothing in the drawers or the wardrobes, no personal effects at all. Even Keith's study had been stripped of its usual mess of paper printouts and notes. His computer was gone, too.

With my heart in my mouth, I walked along the corridor to the rooms they'd given to me and to Sean. I looked in my own first. My bag and all my clothes had been taken.

I'd put my passport in the top drawer of the dressing table. I almost didn't have to check to know it wouldn't be there but I couldn't suppress the squirt of panic when I proved myself right, even so. The feeling of being trapped with no back door out of there was suffocating me.

I took a couple of deep breaths, acutely aware of the amount of time I'd been in the house already. The longer I was there, the greater the risk. Still, I couldn't put it off any longer. I moved from my room to Sean's. They were next door to each other, back to back. His was a mirror image of mine.

I knew the layout pretty well, because I'd spent the previous night there.

I'd gone simply to talk to him. At least, that's what I'd told myself to begin with. Not so much talk as argue, really. I was pissed off with the way the job was unfolding and he was the only one I could shout at about it.

Ten minutes after I'd heard him go in I was outside, banging on the door. At first I thought he was avoiding me. He'd seen at dinner how annoyed I was at Whitmarsh's automatic assumption that my sole purpose in life was to look after the kid. It was only Sean's warning glance and his murmured, "Later," that had stopped me shooting my mouth off there and then.

I knocked again, louder this time. I was about to give it a third go when the door opened and there was Sean, wearing nothing but a towel round his hips, water glistening across his naked upper body.

"Sorry," he said, rubbing at the back of his dark hair with another towel. "I was in the shower." He stepped back, opening the door wider. "Come on in."

I swallowed, the action ungluing my tongue from the roof of my mouth. "Look," I said, my anger fleeing, "you're busy. I can come back la—"

"Charlie," he said, cutting me off in mid-waffle, pinning me with that deadly gaze. "Shut up and come in."

I did as I was told almost meekly. He shut the door and turned to face me, a smile playing round his lips. I was trying not to look at the expanse of skin on view, but I couldn't help it.

Even though he'd been out of the army for the best part of four years by that time, Sean was still fighting fit in the true sense of the word. Every lean inch of him was packed with the muscle of an athlete rather than a weight-lifter. He'd always been wide across the shoulders but he'd never used that as an excuse to bulk up.

My eyes strayed to the small scar just below the point of his left shoulder. The memory of how close I'd come to losing him hit me like a blow.

I realized Sean hadn't moved but was just standing there without conceit, watching me watching him. I tore my eyes away, face heating, and sat down on the bed rather abruptly.

"So," he said, "what's on your mind?"

The flush, which had been starting to subside, flared painfully.

He laughed softly, then reached over to a chair and picked up a bundle of clothing. "Tell you what," he said, "I'll take myself out of your sight into the bathroom. You can yell at me from here."

It was only when he was safely in the other room that my brain seemed inclined to resume normal service. "What the hell is going on, Sean?" I demanded, trying to pick up the thread of my earlier indignation. "Did you know I was going to be here as some kind of glorified nanny?"

"No." His voice floated back to me. He'd left the door open just a slit and I could see him moving about behind it in a series of tantalizing snatches. "I can't start kicking up too much of a fuss about the way Whitmarsh is handling you, because as soon as he asks for a list of your previous jobs, we're a bit snookered. It's one of those difficult situations where nobody wants you without experience, but to *get* the experience . . ." I heard rather than saw him shrug. "You've no idea how much bullshitting you have to do to get started in this business."

"So I just have to bite my tongue, is that it?" I said, aware of a weary kind of resentment.

"No," he said again, emerging from the bathroom. This time when he appeared the towel had been replaced by a pair of dark tan chinos. But he had yet to put on a shirt, or buckle the belt. It seemed a wanton invitation.

My eyes suddenly became fixed on the chevron of dark hair that disappeared beneath the waistband of his trousers. I could feel my body reacting, however much my mind told it not to.

"Keep looking at me like that, Charlie," Sean said, his voice husky, "and talking is the last thing we're going to be doing."

He moved in closer, pulling me to my feet, running his fingers lightly down my arms. My skin came up in goose bumps instantly.

"I though you'd lost interest," I managed, suddenly breathless.

He shook his head. "Oh no," he said, rueful. "I've been going cross-eyed trying to let you move at your own pace, but I really think you ought to leave now, because otherwise I'm going to be tempted to push you faster than you want to go."

I had every opportunity to move away from him then, but I didn't. It was time. I was ready. I stepped in closer and lifted my face to his, my voice little more than a whisper. "Who says I don't want that, too?"

It was only later—much later—that we had resumed our conversation.

"To go back to an earlier subject, something's clearly wrong out here, and I think both of us are being kept in the dark about it," Sean said, settling so I could lie with my head resting on his shoulder and listen to his heartbeat recover its steady rhythm. Above us, I could hear the quiet rustle of the ceiling fan as it gently cooled the sweat on our bodies.

"I know," I said. "While you were out today a taxi arrived to take Keith and Trey to the airport."

"The airport?" Sean queried. "Are you sure?"

"Yeah, I spoke to the driver myself, until Keith came out and made out like he hadn't ordered a taxi, it was all some big mistake. He was getting quite irate, though it was hard to tell if that was because the taxi had turned up at all, or because I'd intercepted it."

"What happened?"

"Well, in the end Keith paid the guy off and he went away swearing merrily in that cheery way of disappointed taxi drivers the world over."

I felt rather than saw Sean smile into the darkness. "So," he said, "is Keith planning a great escape, or is somebody just trying to wind him up?"

"You think there might be something serious going on here after all?"

He shrugged slightly. "Could be."

I started to shift round to face him. As I did so my hand brushed against something cold and hard under the pillow. I hardly needed more than that to identify the object for what it was.

"Sean," I said, my voice calm, "why have you got a gun under your pillow?"

"It could just be that I'm pleased to see you," he said. He eased away from me, leaning across to flick on the bedside light.

I blinked for a moment, propping myself up on one elbow while he retrieved the gun. It was the same model of Sig Sauer nine-millimeter pistol that I'd used in Germany, a P226.

"How the hell did you manage to get that onto a plane?"

He grinned at my consternation. "I didn't," he said. "I was working out here a couple of years ago and I left this behind. All I did this time was detour on my way from the airport and pick it up."

"Does Gerri Raybourn know you're carrying?"

He shook his head. "No," he said, "and that's how I aim to keep it. I learned the hard way never to play all your aces at once."

"So," I said, "what happens now?"

"Well give me a minute, Charlie," he said, mocking. "I'm only human."

I shot him what I hoped was a stern glance. "That wasn't what I meant."

"OK, OK," he said, laughing. "I've arranged a meeting with Ms. Raybourn tomorrow while you're babysitting Trey at the theme park. By the time you get back I should have some answers, otherwise we're on the next plane out of here."

"Just do me one favor."

"What?"

I nodded to the Sig. "Take that with you," I said. "I've got a bad feeling about this."

"Don't worry," Sean said. "I wasn't planning on going anywhere without it."

Now, I walked into the room that had been Sean's and looked around me. It was as empty and as lifeless as my own, as though he'd never been there at all. On impulse I picked up one of the pillows, just to see if it still smelt of him. I sat down on the bed and pressed my face into the cotton cover. The faintest trace of his aftershave still lingered somewhere in the fabric.

But as I went to put the pillow down again I noticed something just sticking out from under the sheet. When I pulled the covers back, there it was.

Sean's Sig.

I picked the gun up slowly, slipped the magazine out and saw that it was fully loaded. And suddenly a rush of emotion came rocketing up out of the depths of nowhere and hit me in the face. Tears exploded. I sat there, on my own in a deserted house, clutching a gun and sobbing my guts out.

Sean had said he wouldn't leave the house unarmed, and that could mean one of two things. Either he'd been taken prisoner, against his will.

Or he was already dead.

FOUR

I LEFT THE house the same way I got into it, locking the kitchen door behind me and wiping the handle once I was done. My search had told me everything and nothing. But had it been worth the risk?

At least I'd managed to find a fresh shirt. None of my own clothes were where I'd left them, but I remembered seeing something crumpled up behind the small bar by the pool. I made a small detour through the lanai and found it, a rather tatty man's striped shirt with a white collar and cuffs. Still, it didn't look so bad once I'd put it on and rolled the sleeves back three or four times. It had the added advantage that at least it didn't have blood on it.

The tails were long, almost down to the bottoms of my shorts, but I left them untucked nevertheless. At least that way it covered the fact I'd shoved Sean's Sig into the back of my waistband. The gun was momentarily chill against my skin but it took on body heat fast. I couldn't deny that the weight of it was reassuring.

I'd splashed cold water on my face in the bathroom before I'd ventured out. It had taken down some of the puffiness around my eyes and the redness out of my nose. Still, it didn't take a genius to spot I'd been crying like a spoiled kid. I had eleven years on Trey, but right now I felt little better than his baby sister.

I slipped through the smallest gap in the gates, closing

them behind me. Outside, beneath the dappled shade of the rows of palm trees, the street looked as quiet and deserted as it had done when I'd arrived. I tried to use its very normality to calm my shattered nerves.

I'd almost made it back to the Mercury when a man's voice froze me in my tracks.

"Hey there!"

After the briefest hesitation, I kept walking, picking up the pace. The man called again and this time I heard his footsteps approaching behind me.

Just for a second, I considered the wisdom of drawing the gun but dismissed it just as quickly. The Sig was my safety net. My last resort. I wasn't quite that far gone yet.

I halted, turned, trying to contrive a faintly irritated expression. Behind me a trim upright guy in his early sixties was hurrying down the paved driveway of the house next door.

Livingston Brown III had seemed an unlikely friend for a computer nerd like Keith Pelzner. I'd wondered if their paths would have crossed at all except for the accidental fact that the company Keith was working for had rented the property next to Brown's, but the two of them seemed to hit it off strangely well.

Brown was a tall, slightly gangling figure, tanned to the color of a pecan and just as wrinkled. He was one of those perfect adverts for why you should use sunblock and big floppy hats in this kind of climate. He wasn't wearing either today and the perspiration pasted thin wisps of gray hair to his scalp.

"Hi there," he said, puffing, as he caught me up. "Thought I'd missed ya. Carly, isn't it?"

"Charlie, sir," I said. "Hello, Mr. Brown." I kept my voice polite but noncommittal, as though he was keeping me from some minor task.

Now he'd got me, he seemed a little lost as to what to do with me. "I saw the truck this morning," he said at last. "Couldn't get over the fact that Keith never said he was moving out sooner." He pulled out a voluminous handkerchief and blew his nose loudly, peering at me over the top of it. "So, you forget something?"

"You saw them go?" I said, sharper than I'd intended. "What time was this?"

"Oh, well now, lemme see," he said, so slowly I could have rattled him. "Well, I do believe I'd just had my midmorning swim. Fifty lengths every day, come rain or shine, did I ever tell you that?"

"Yes sir," I said dryly. He'd mentioned his daily constitutional on both of the occasions we'd met over the last couple of days, but I'd already worked out that men as rich as Livingston Brown III did not accurately recall names or conversations with their neighbors' staff unless you gave them undue reason to. It wasn't rudeness particularly, he'd just had money for so long that he couldn't remember what it was like talking to people who dared interrupt his ramblings.

Now, he beamed at me and stuffed the handkerchief back into his pocket. "Well now, yes, I heard the sound of the truck arriving and I came out for a little look-see, 'cos it's pretty quiet round here. Must have been right around eleven."

Eleven. Right about when Trey and I were getting off the wooden coaster. Right about when Oakley man had been casually lingering in the gift shop and observed the kid's temper tantrum. Right about when he'd smiled at me with such apparent sympathy and friendliness.

"Who was with the truck?" I demanded now. "Did you see them?"

Brown frowned, unaccustomed to quick-fire questions. I wondered how he'd managed to accrue the personal fortune through shrewd property dealings that he was rumored to possess. Maybe he just delegated to smart cookies and let them get on with it.

"Well, just a couple of ordinary-looking guys, I guess," he said, in the kind of doubtful tone that discredits eyewitnesses the world over. "Like I said, I came out and there was this U-Haul truck backed right on up to the front steps."

"And you didn't see any sign of Mr. Pelzner?"

"Oh yeah," he said, surprising me. "Keith came on over to the fence when he saw me out front. Seemed in kind of a hurry—not like him. He's always been a laid-back guy, y'know? Anyways, he said as how he was having to move out kinda unexpected."

"Did you see anyone else—Jim Whitmarsh, or Sean?"

Brown rubbed the back of his head, fluffing his hair up from its comb-over style across the top of his scalp. "Sean?" he repeated, puzzled. "Oh, you mean the Brit guy? No, no, I don't think so. Come to think of it, I didn't see any of the usual guys either. Just the ones with the truck, I think."

A nondescript beige Buick saloon turned in to the end of the street then and started to slowly cruise down in our direction. Inside were two suited men wearing sunglasses. Neither had their seatbelt on. They both had big necks and square jaws and could possibly have been double-glazing salesmen who liked to work out a lot, but I wouldn't have bet on it.

"Did Mr. Pelzner say where he was going, or give you a forwarding address?" I asked quickly, starting to edge toward the Mercury. If it hadn't already been telling me it was time to go, my mind was now screaming *"Leave!"* repeatedly in my inner ear.

"No, no he didn't, which I must admit I thought was kinda strange, but he did ask me if I'd pass on a key to the realtor. He seemed kinda nervous, y'know? On edge. Said they'd be stopping by this afternoon to see about leasing the place out for the summer. I guess they might know. I think I maybe have a card some place in the house if you wanna come in for a mo—"

"No!" I said. The Buick had come to a halt about halfway down the street. It was hard to tell if the two men were watching me, because I couldn't see their eyes, but they were sitting very, very still.

"No," I said again, less vehement this time as I took in his offended face. "Look, Mr. Brown, I'm sorry, but I'm afraid I have to go now. I don't want to keep you standing out here."

He was around four or five strides away at that point. Too far for me to be sure of getting him into cover if things went bad now. We were both way too exposed.

"Oh, well OK," he said, still looking a little put out.

Just get back inside, you stupid old git, I wanted to yell at him. *Get off the battleground!* I breathed in, rolled my shoulders. Under my shirt the Sig had already stuck to my back with sweat that wasn't entirely brought on by the heat. It wasn't in a holster and I wondered how long it would take me to bring it out.

Longer, I calculated grimly, than it would take the two men to draw and fire the guns I just knew they were carrying. *If you can't run, then take the passenger down first. He's more likely to get out of the car faster than the driver.*

I took another couple of steps toward the Mercury, keys already out in my hand, when Brown called a final question.

"Say, young lady, weren't you supposed to be looking after Trey today?"

Christ, the old boy had a death wish. "Er yeah," I said, glancing back at him as I wrenched the car door open. "I've left him with a friend." I thought of Joyce. At the moment she was the nearest thing I'd got.

"Oh," Brown said, clearly nonplussed at my cavalier attitude toward proper childcare. "Oh well, that's OK then, I guess. You take care now, Carly."

I didn't bother to correct him again, just jumped in and cranked the Mercury into life. In the rearview mirror I saw Brown shaking his head as he turned back into his own driveway. I waited until he'd got another few steps toward comparative safety and hoped that, if the guys in the Buick were as dodgy as I feared, they wouldn't mistake the old guy as one of my allies and go after him as well.

I needn't have worried on Brown's account. As soon as I put the car into gear I had their full attention. I tried not to make direct eye contact as I passed within a few feet of the other car but it was impossible not to let my eyes slide sideways, just a little.

The two men were craning to see into the Mercury, lifting up in their seats as they did so, making no bones about it. It was immediately obvious that I wasn't the one who interested them. They were checking to see the kid wasn't hiding in the back. When they saw he wasn't they swung the Buick in a tire-squealing circle and hooked it onto my tail.

It wasn't subtle but they knew, just as I did, that I couldn't leave Trey where he was indefinitely. Sooner or later I was going to have to make a move to collect him.

And when I did, the game was going to be over.

It had to go on record as one of the slowest car chases ever. Instinct made me turn left at the top of the street, trying to slow down my pursuers by making them follow me across four lanes of traffic to copy the maneuver. Fat chance. They pulled out smoothly with only two cars between us.

Damn, but driving on the right was taking some getting my head round.

I trundled through the next two sets of lights sticking bang on the speed limit. Bearing in mind Oakley man's profession, I didn't want to risk getting pulled by the cops.

The only experience I had of American traffic stops came through reality TV shows and the movies. If they were anything to go by, even if the officers involved were on the level I was likely to get hauled out of the car and subjected to a patdown search. I'd no idea if the gun I was carrying wedged into the small of my back was officially registered, but even if it was, it certainly wasn't in my name.

Mind you, it always seemed to be the State Troopers of the Highway Patrol who engaged in that kind of gung-ho behavior, rather than the city police or Sheriff's department. I vaguely recalled that Oakley man had been with the city police. Just how interconnected were the various departments? Was he working on his own, or was someone else lurking in the shadows pulling his strings? I didn't have a clue.

I kept driving, the area taking a step down with each passing block. My brain was frantically concocting and dumping solutions to my current situation. The beige Buick had moved up to one car behind me, keeping station. Checking in my mirrors, I could see the guy in the passenger seat talking on a mobile phone. If they were calling in reinforcements I couldn't afford to delay much longer.

I had to do something, but what?

Then something caught my eye up ahead on my left. Every

little roadside shop and store, it seemed, stated their business on a sign about twenty feet up in the air, like all their customers were incredibly tall.

"We service and repair Harleys," this one proclaimed in hand-painted letters that were peeling at the edges. *"Bikes bought for cash."*

It struck a chord. I was a dedicated biker myself and had been so for far longer than I'd held a license to drive a car. If bikers in the US were anything like they were in the UK, then I might have found an ally.

I took a flyer, diving across the road and into the parking area without bothering to indicate as I did so. A driver coming the other way blared his horn and shook a desultory fist, but it was more force of habit than passion. The Buick pulled up a little further along on the other side of the road. The two men twisted in their seats and calmly waited to see what I was up to.

The business I'd picked looked run-down and slightly seedy, which was exactly what I'd been hoping for. There was no showroom as such, just a grubby workshop with a huge roller-shutter door to one side, halfway open. Stacks of rusting exhaust pipes decorated the entrance and all the windows had bars on them.

I jumped out of the Mercury and hurried into the workshop. The floor felt sticky underfoot and a hard rock station was playing on a slightly off-tune radio somewhere in the back. Two of the biggest guys I've ever seen were working on a stripped-down Electra-Glide with severe front-end damage, while three more blokes of equal size stood around and watched and drank beer.

They were discussing something that involved use of the word "fuck" at least twice every time they opened their mouths, and some of them were being monosyllabic. When they spotted me they shut up fast.

"Oh my God, do you have a phone?" I cried, racking an edge of hysteria into my voice as I rushed forward. "I need to call the cops. Oh God!"

"Yeah, we got a phone," one of them said slowly, although

his manner clearly said that fact didn't mean I was going to get to use it. The others exchanged nervous glances at any mention of the law. "What's the trouble?"

"They hit him and just never stopped!" I said, pressing my hands to my face. "I didn't know what to do, and now I think they're following me!"

"Who hit who?" asked the biggest guy of the bunch with mild interest, as though any fight he wasn't personally involved in wasn't high on his list.

"Two guys in a beige Buick," I said. "They ran a red light and took out some poor guy on a Harley, just wiped him clean out. And they never even slowed down! I need to call the cops."

The big guy forgot all about the next mouthful of beer he'd been just about to take from his long-neck bottle of Budweiser. Suddenly I had their utter and complete attention.

"A Harley?" he demanded. "What kinda Harley?"

"I don't know," I said, wringing my hands in a suitably girlie way. "It was just one of those big gorgeous bikes, you know?"

"It wasn't kinda purple, was it?" another of the group asked.

I made a show of deep thought, frowning. "Er, yeah, it might have been."

"Fuck," the same man said, taking a step back and shaking his head like a dog coming out of water. "Must be Brad. He left here no more'n five minutes ago."

"Is that the two sons of bitches over there?" growled the first guy, pointing to the car across the street.

"Oh my God, yes," I said, feigning terror. "That's them! They must know I saw the whole thing and I'm going to report them."

"Don't you worry none about the cops, lady," said the big guy, carefully putting his Bud down and picking up a tire iron. "You just leave 'em to us."

The five of them walked out of the workshop and headed straight for the two men in the Buick, uncaring of the traffic that squealed and swerved to avoid them. My pursuers took one look at the grim intent and the makeshift weaponry that was bearing down on them, and took off.

The gang ran back to the workshop and jumped onto the grubby assortment of bitsa bikes that were parked up outside, leaving me standing alone next to the Mercury. I watched them give chase until the Buick made a frantic right turn at the next signal and the convoy disappeared from view.

"There's one thing you can say about us bikers," I murmured to myself. "When the shit hits the fan we certainly stick together."

Then I got back into my car, pulled out in the opposite direction and headed sedately back to the diner.

I found Trey elevated on a stool at the counter, recounting a frankly ludicrous story about the fantastic exploits of his recently deceased mythical dog. He had Joyce, another of the waitresses, and two of the other customers as his audience. I walked in on the tail end of it and had to suppress a wince at the sheer lack of believability.

Nothing like keeping a low profile, Trey . . .

Joyce's expression when she caught sight of me showed she clearly knew something was amiss with the whole setup, even if her younger workmate was proving more gullible. When he realized I was standing behind him Trey bounced out of his seat and shut up, looking more than a little guilty.

I slipped Joyce a tip out of all proportion to the cost of the food Trey had managed to consume in the time I'd been away. She tucked the folded bill away into the pocket of her apron so fast it was almost sleight of hand, but her face stayed cool.

"So, what's up?" Trey demanded as we walked out of the diner. "You went home, yeah? Is Dad OK?"

I didn't trust myself to answer him until I'd unlocked the car and we were back inside, then my temper flashed.

"For fuck's sake, Trey! Do the words 'acting suspiciously' mean anything to you at all?" I threw at him. "When I left you all you had to do was look miserable and say as little as possible. Why you should find that difficult, God only knows! You've certainly managed it perfectly well all day. But no, you had to go shooting your mouth off."

The shell grew back around him almost instantly. I watched it harden over and cursed myself inwardly. *Oh great, now we have the sulks again.*

I sat back in my seat and let my breath out. "OK," I said, trying to start again, calm, sensible. "Yes, I went back to the house. There was nobody there. Not only that, but the place has been cleared out—no clothes, no personal possessions. There's just the furniture left. It's like you were never there."

"What about Dad?" Trey asked, sounding subdued.

"I'm sorry, there was no sign of him," I said, as gently as I could. "I ran into one of your neighbors—Mr. Brown. He reckoned he saw Keith loading up a U-Haul truck this morning. Even asked him to give a key to an estate agent." I paused, flicked the kid a sideways glance. "Did you know your father was planning on moving out today?"

Trey shook his head mutely and that was the last I could get out of him. I didn't think telling him about the two guys in the Buick was going to gain me anything other than scaring him half to death, so I kept their part in the proceedings to myself. With another sigh I started the Mercury up again and pulled out onto the road.

It was a little after four o'clock. Traffic was starting to heavy up for the evening rush hour and the quality of the light was already changing, softening down from the usual harsh brightness. I'd discovered that night arrives fast in Florida. You get maybe twenty minutes of sunset around six-thirty, then the day's dead.

The idea of driving around all night didn't appeal to me. Not in a car that the bad guys could easily recognize. Particularly not with Trey in the passenger seat. We needed shelter and somewhere to hide, and the sooner the better.

I was already heading toward the coast and the closer to the sea you got, the greater the proportion of motels to other buildings. I picked the first one that looked reasonable. Not too smart, not too shabby. The neon sign out front said they had vacancies and free HBO. Nevertheless, Trey looked horrified when I turned in.

I drove straight through the parking area to the back of the small diner next door where the Mercury couldn't easily be seen from the road, and reversed into a space. The car only had a numberplate on the back and there was no point in making it easy to read for anyone doing a casual drive-by.

I switched off the engine. "Stay here," I said. "Lock the doors when I'm gone and if anyone comes, hit the horn and don't let them in. OK?"

He shrugged and muttered, "OK."

I walked back to the reception via the central courtyard. The motel was made up of ugly two-story blocks of accommodation lining the car park on three sides. Each block had ten rooms per floor. Their doors were all accessed from open walkways at the front with stairwells at either end. It looked more depressing from here than it had done when I'd picked it, but I wasn't going to go back and admit defeat to Trey.

I walked into the reception, which was small and nastily lit by a string of fluoro tubes across the water-stained ceiling tiles. It smelt of coffee that was brewed two days ago and has been on the hot plate ever since. The black girl behind the counter met my arrival with unsmiling lack of enthusiasm. Her name badge told me her name was Lacena. She had hair so elaborately styled and set it looked like a sculpture, and her fingernails were too long for her to have been able to put contact lenses in without the serious danger of losing an eye in the attempt.

She took an imprint of my credit card and a cursory glance at the photograph on my UK driver's license. Apart from my name, I filled in a completely fictitious set of details required on the registration form and took the key, making as little eye contact as I could get away with.

Trey hadn't shifted when I got back to the car. He'd even had the sense to slump down in his seat. I tapped on the window and he followed me silently to the room we'd been given.

We were in the left-hand block, on the top floor in the end

room furthest from reception. The number on the key fob read 219, which was ambitious considering there were only around sixty rooms. Maybe they were just trying to make the place sound bigger than it was.

I opened the door on a pair of twin beds with cigarette-singed floral covers. The low-wattage bulb made the whole place look dingy and depressing.

"Oh man," Trey moaned. "This place is a dump."

He grabbed the remote control for the TV and flopped down on one of the beds. Even channel-hopping didn't appease him, as he soon discovered that the promise of Home Box Office movies was a broken one. The picture on the other channels was so badly adjusted they were just about unwatchable. Still, there were hundreds to go at and he seemed determined to try every one.

I left him to it, pulling the edge of the curtain back slightly and looking down on the car park. It all looked quiet. No one new had arrived since we'd checked in.

In my head I backtracked, replaying the conversation I'd had with Livingston Brown III outside the house. So Keith Pelzner had gone, apparently of his own accord. Sean, on the other hand, had not gone quite so willingly. I would have put money on it.

Then a man who'd come to the house as a policeman—and I could only assume he was a genuine cop—had followed Trey and me to the amusement park and tried to grab the kid. Something about the setup didn't quite hang true. I kicked and pummeled at my lumpy thoughts, trying to break the sense out of them. Then my brain tilted, and in the light of what Brown had told me I began to look at things from a slightly different angle.

Supposing Oakley man hadn't followed us? Supposing he didn't need to, because he already knew where we were going to be? After all, Keith knew exactly where his son was heading. Exactly.

Just after he'd handed me that wedge of cash that morning, he'd turned to the boy and said, "I suppose you're gonna drag Charlie onto your favorite old woodie until one of you is sick, huh?"

Oh yes, Keith had known precisely the area of the park where we could be located, and that's just where Oakley man had picked up our trail. I saw again the gun in his hands, the people scattering. The woman he'd shot fell again before my eyes.

But if the cop was there simply to snatch Trey, why had he fired at us?

I let the curtain fall closed and turned away from the window, moving to sit on the empty bed.

"Trey," I said. "We need to talk."

He sighed and clicked off the TV. I got the feeling his reluctance was more to do with a desire to avoid the subject rather than fascination with a fuzzy game show.

"OK," he said. "Talk."

"Have you any idea where Keith might have gone, or why he's disappeared?"

He shrugged. "Sounds kinda like he's run out on me, doesn't it?"

I might have known this would be all about Trey. "Why would he do that?"

Another hunch of those skinny shoulders.

I waited, and when that seemed to be as much of an answer as I was going to get, I added carefully, "Is there any reason you can think of why your father might want to harm you?"

His head snapped up at that, eyes unnaturally bright. "Oh yeah," he said. "I can think of plenty."

I sighed. *God preserve us from teenage angst.* "He's your father, Trey, why would he want to do that?"

"Why not?" the kid threw back at me, his voice oozing with bitterness. "He already murdered my mother."

FIVE

FOR A MOMENT I sat very still, my face expressionless while my mind reeled. I skimmed back over every chance remark and casual word I'd overheard since I'd arrived in the Pelzner household and came up blank.

No one had mentioned Trey's mother.

From somewhere I'd formed a vague impression that it was a bit of a sticky subject as far as Keith was concerned, but I'd no idea what the official line was on her whereabouts.

I glanced at the boy. He was worrying at one of the burn holes in the bedspread with the end of his finger, staring fixedly at the bed. His other hand was clamped onto his own wrist so tight the knuckles showed up as a row of whitened double indentations. I wavered over believing him or dismissing the whole thing as another of his fantasies.

"What happened to her?" I said quietly.

"When I was a kid we were living up in Daytona and she and my dad used to fight all the time," he said, speaking so low I could hardly hear him. "One night they had this mega row, like total war, screaming at each other and throwing stuff. The next day, when I got home from school, Dad told me she'd gone."

"It happens," I said, disappointed at the lack of concrete evidence—or just of fresh-laid concrete in the back garden. I tried not to put anything into my voice, one way or another. "Marriages break up every day."

He speared me with a single vicious look. "She would never have left me," he said, vehement. "Oh she talked about going, but she swore she'd take me with her. She *swore*. Every time after they'd been fighting she'd come into my room and sit on my bed and cry and tell me how she'd find a place for us real soon, and it would just be the two of us."

He sniffed, letting go to wipe the back of his arm across his nose. He'd been gripping so tight he'd left reddened finger marks on the skin of his wrist. His hand still picked at the burn hole in the bedspread, which was now big enough for him to get his fist into, and growing all the time.

I eyed the oblivious destruction. "How long ago did your mother disappear?"

"Five years," he said. "It was right around the time I turned ten. She'd promised me this real big party. The best ever. Dad was going on at her how we couldn't afford it, 'cos he wasn't doing so good then. But that's how I knew, when she didn't come home, that it was down to him."

I closed my eyes momentarily, trying to get a handle on the logic. OK, supposing just for a moment that there was any grain of truth in all this. Supposing Keith Pelzner *had* murdered his wife five years ago. It seemed far-fetched, but then, so did being pursued and shot at by an imitation or off-duty cop in an amusement park. So did being followed in broad daylight by a couple of hardcases in a Buick.

"So why has he waited until now to do anything about you?" I asked.

He shrugged. "Dunno," he said, looking up at me but unable to hold my gaze for long. "Maybe it's 'cos I wanted to go to Daytona for Spring Break this year. Maybe he thought if I go back up there I might find out what really happened to her."

Now that really *was* stretching it.

I shook my head slowly. "I just don't know, Trey, it sounds a little—"

That was as far as I got. He jumped off the bed like someone had turned up the gas under him. "Oh sure," he cried. "That's right, tell me I'm talking weird, just like Dad does whenever I try to talk to him about Mom. Why don't you tell me I'm delusional, too? Drop a few hints about how maybe I should, like, see a shrink, huh?"

And with that he stormed into the only place he could get away from me—the bathroom—and made sure he slammed the door behind him hard enough to set the wall light fittings jiggling.

I sat there on the bed and put my head in my hands. Of all the training I'd had in the army to prepare me for stress under combat, nothing compared to trying to keep a stroppy teenager under control.

"Jesus, Sean," I murmured under my breath, "where are you now when I need you?"

I reached behind me and pulled the Sig out of the back of my belt. With automatic movements I dropped the magazine clear and thumbed the rounds out into a little pile in front of me, counting them. I had the full eight, but no spare magazine. I hadn't expected Sean to carry a gun that wasn't fully loaded, but if people were going to keep shooting at me, it was nice to be sure, even so.

The sight of the pistol and the copper-nosed bullets brought back all the rush of emotion I'd felt at the house. I had to take a couple of deep breaths and clamp down hard on it, scowling at my reflection in the mirror on the wall behind the TV.

Sean might still be OK, I told myself. After all, he had said he was going to see Gerri Raybourn this morning to find out what the real story was with Keith Pelzner. Maybe it was Keith himself who'd intercepted him. Maybe Sean had never got there. If he had, I tried hard to ignore the fact that he had promised to go armed and had clearly not done so. There could be any number of reasons he'd left his gun behind other than the one that was uppermost in my mind.

And there was one way to find out.

I quickly refilled the magazine and tucked the gun away again out of sight, then dug the mobile phone out of my pocket. I didn't know the direct line number for Gerri Raybourn but, along with the obligatory Gideon Bible, there was a Bell South Yellow Pages in the drawer by the bed. I looked up the number for the software company Keith worked for and dialed.

As I waited for the phone to be picked up I checked my watch. It was well before five, but for a while I feared they'd already left for the afternoon.

Eventually the phone was answered by a girl who spoke so fast I could hardly tell what she said. I gave her my name anyway and asked to be put through to Gerri's office.

She put me on hold and for what seemed like a long time I listened to the quick-fire presentation of the local commercial radio station. Then the lady herself came on the line.

"Charlie!" she yelled, her voice strident enough to make me jerk the mobile away from my ear. "What the fuck are you playing at?"

Well that answered the question of whether she'd been informed about the bloody battle at the park, I suppose. Not quite the face of concern I'd been hoping for, though.

"Well thanks a bundle, Gerri," I bit back, hackles rising defensively. "That kind of attitude's going to get us a long way, isn't it?"

For a moment there was silence and I had visions of her building up to a real explosion. But when she spoke again her voice had that reined-in quality which told me she'd been using the time to get a grip on her temper. "OK, OK, I'm sorry," she ground out, surprising me with the apology. "Just let me talk to Trey."

I glanced at the bathroom door, still firmly shut. "He's not available to come to the phone right now," I said dryly.

I heard Gerri's breath hiss out in annoyance. "Godammit, Charlie, he's just a kid. I need to know he's all right, you understand me? I can't help you unless I know he's OK."

Oh great, so you don't give a shit if I get killed in the process? The thought was fully formed before it dawned on me that was exactly what I was being paid for. I suppose it was the realization of my own expendability that allowed more sarcasm to creep into my voice than it should have done.

"You'll just have to trust me when I tell you that he's unharmed," I replied. "And I am doing my best to keep him that way."

"OK, OK." Another long pause, then the words came out in

a rush. "Look I'm here to help. I really appreciate that you've contacted me, but I need for you to tell me what it is you want me to do."

"Want?" Her question was so banal I had to wrestle a sudden splurge of temper. *Jesus, and I thought these people were supposed to be professionals.* "What I want you to do," I snapped, "is help me find a way out of this mess."

"OK, that's good," she said, sounding distracted now, as though she was also trying to carry on a second conversation at her end of the line and was only managing to give me half her attention. Either she wasn't taking this seriously or she was so far out of her depth she needed a wetsuit. "That's good," she repeated. "We can help you. Are you under threat at this time?"

"Hang on." I moved over to the curtain and peered down onto the parking area. Two cars that had been there when we'd arrived had now gone, but no new vehicles had taken their place. In particular, there were no beige Buicks. "No," I said. "I don't think so."

"OK Charlie, that's good. Now, just tell us where you are and we can sort this whole thing out."

There was something about that slightly agitated tone that was setting all my instincts on edge like the fur down a dog's spine. "What about Sean?"

That got an immediate reaction. "Jesus, Charlie, there's nothing I can do—" She stopped abruptly, obviously realizing what I was asking and that she hadn't picked the most diplomatic manner of breaking the bad news.

"Look, I'm real sorry about Sean, Charlie, but you're gonna have to let him go," she said, making a fresh start and hiding the fact she didn't give a damn behind the quick apology, her voice oozing with insincere concern. "Let's just concentrate on getting you and Trey to safety, OK? We can work out the details later. Just tell us where you are and let us come get you."

It was my turn to go quiet, fighting not to let the tears come. For a moment there was nothing but the occasional click of static on the line, then her patience broke. "Come on,

Charlie, cut me some slack, huh?" she bit out. "I'm putting my neck on the line for you here."

"All right," I said and gave her the name of the motel and a rough idea of its location, trying to ignore the mental klaxon that was blaring in the back of my skull.

But not completely. When Gerri demanded the room number I squinted through the gap in the curtain at the block opposite, but the room numbers themselves were small and I couldn't quite read them clearly at this distance. The room directly across from ours was in darkness, unoccupied. On impulse, I directed her there. "Right-hand block, left-hand end room, first floor," I said.

"We'll find it, don't you worry," she said. "Now sit tight, Charlie and wait for us to come get you. And don't worry. You've done the right thing. Everything's gonna be OK."

So why, as I ended the call, did I get the feeling I'd just made a big mistake?

I knew there were a hundred other questions I should have asked Gerri while I had the chance, but I was still shell-shocked about Sean. I went backward and forward over that part of the conversation, recalling with a stark clarity the way Gerri had blown up at the mention of his name. She'd been evasive, too. Whatever had happened to him, it must have been bad to have provoked that kind of reaction.

I was still sitting there, staring at nothing when the bathroom door opened and Trey shuffled out, looking a bit sheepish. He'd been attempting, I noticed, to clean up his shirt. The front of it was still wet. Not just sulking, then.

I don't know what he saw in my face, but his stride faltered and he came to sit on the side of the bed opposite. When he spoke, his voice was almost tentative. "What's up?"

I glanced up at him, tried to force a smile that took more effort to produce than the end result was worth. "I've just called Gerri Raybourn," I told him. "She's coming to pick us up."

His face spasmed momentarily, like a kid let out with the grown-ups who's just been told it's bedtime. "When?" he demanded.

I shrugged. "Soon, I expect," I said.

It occurred to me then that Gerri might have been just the person to ask what had really happened to Trey's mother. If the company carried out any kind of background checks before they took people on, a suspicious disappearance of a spouse was just the kind of thing that should have jumped out at them. They must have looked into it further. Still, I suppose there would be time enough to find that out later, once the kid was off my hands.

Trey was fidgeting, but he stilled when he caught my inquiring glance. "I kinda don't trust her," he mumbled.

This time I didn't have to push the smile out. "Neither do I—not entirely, which is why I've told her we're in the room across the way," I admitted. "We'll watch from here what she does when she arrives before we go out there."

That got me a quick, unexpected grin. I blinked, and it came to me that Trey must have been a pretty-faced child. Once he'd got over the gawkiness and the tantrums, the acne and the braces, he would no doubt turn into an attractive adult. His mother must have been a looker, I concluded, because he certainly didn't get that side of his genetic makeup from Keith.

"So we wait here, yeah?" he said. And just when I thought he'd been doing some rapid growing up, he added with a hint of his old whingey tone, "I'm hungry."

There was no way I was going to go out to the diner, and I vetoed Trey's idea that we should order in pizza, even though there was a menu from a local takeaway next to the TV. In the end we compromised on raiding the vending machine I'd spotted at the top of the stairs when we came up. There had been a bank of them offering everything from cans of soft drink to snacks, as well as an ice maker.

I used some of the stash of money Keith had given to me that morning. There was still a heap of it left and I was glad I hadn't given in to Trey's whim on the leather jacket. Even with Gerri Raybourn on her way to get us out of here, it was always good to have a contingency fund.

We went to the vending machines together and I let Trey have a free hand with the food. He seemed intent on grabbing one of just about everything in the glass-fronted machine, stabbing at the selection buttons so fast I couldn't follow him. By the time we'd gathered an armload each I was anxious to get back to the safety of the room.

It was past six now, but the temperature was still as balmy as an English summer day. The light was starting to drop fast, though, the sky a vast wash of turquoise and shell pink. Already the cars on the road outside had their headlamps on. I wondered what was keeping Gerri, how long it would take her to get to us from Miramar. I hadn't been to the company itself, had only a vague idea of the distance involved from a glance at the map.

As Trey fiddled with the key to get us in, I scanned the car park, but there was nothing untoward. The room opposite our own was still in darkness.

We sat on one of the beds and inspected our haul. I had no clue what most of it was, and it seemed he'd dropped in one or two surprises.

"My God," I said, suddenly finding myself trying to bite through a piece of spiced conveyor belt webbing. "What the hell is this?"

"Teriyaki beef jerky," he said, tearing a chunk off with his teeth and chewing with his mouth open. "You like it?"

"I'm sure it would come in very useful if I was training a dog, but otherwise—no."

Trey laughed and started to come back with a smart remark, but then I heard the sound of a car engine pulling in slowly off the road and I held my hand up for quiet. For once he shut up straight away.

I hopped off the bed and clicked the light out before easing the curtain aside. A dark-colored Chevy saloon was idling in the middle of the car park. As I watched, the front doors opened and two men climbed out, giving the whole area a thorough but apparently casual scrutiny as they did so.

One was thickset, running downhill from muscular toward just plain fat, but he moved lightly, like he didn't know it yet. He was going bald from the front in a big way, leaving a two-inch band of short-cropped hair around the back of his head from ear to ear. The other guy was younger, black, and in great shape by comparison. I recognized both of them the moment they stepped out of the car.

"Hey, it's Mr. Whitmarsh and Chris." Trey was by my shoulder now, looking down. "Let's go."

Still wary, I grabbed his arm. If Keith and Sean were out of the picture, how had these two escaped unscathed? "Not yet," I said. "Let's see what they do first, hm?"

The two men strolled toward the block opposite, still checking around them, but to my surprise they ignored the stairs. "Now why aren't they going to the right room?" I wondered out loud, more to myself than to Trey. "I *know* I told Gerri the far left-hand room on the first floor."

"That's where they're heading," Trey said, sounding confused. "We're on the second floor."

I stared at him. It hadn't occurred to me that the Americans would refer to the ground floor as the first, and the first floor as the second. I shifted my eyes back to the room below the one I thought I'd indicated. There was a light on and I could see somebody moving around behind the curtains.

"Oh shit," I muttered.

Whitmarsh and Chris were at the door now. I expected to see them knock and wait, but Chris pulled a silenced semi-automatic out from under his jacket and calmly put two rounds through the door around the lock. He did it smoothly, without hesitation. This had been the plan from the start, not some last-minute impulse decision.

Jim Whitmarsh reared back and kicked the door, using his arms for balance. Whoever was inside the room couldn't have put the safety hook across, or maybe it was just weakly mounted. Jim was a big guy and he looked like he'd done this kind of thing before. The door broke open with a crack, bouncing back against the inside wall. By the time the two men dived through the doorway, they both had a gun out.

I froze, drenched in shock. Whatever I'd been expecting, that wasn't it.

"Jesus," I muttered. "What the hell are they—"

Because of the silencers we didn't hear the sound of the

shots, and the muzzle flashes were reduced to little spurts of light, spilling out from the open doorway. I desperately tried to remember who'd been in there, but I hadn't seen anybody, hadn't known the room was occupied.

And even if I had, it wouldn't have made any difference, I realized with a sick taste at the back of my throat. I simply hadn't known that I'd given Gerri Raybourn directions to the wrong room.

"What's that?" Trey asked in a small voice. "What are they doing in there?"

For a moment I couldn't answer. Then Whitmarsh and Chris reappeared, stalking out, moving fast. The set of their shoulders betrayed their anger. Whitmarsh tucked the gun away under his arm, bringing out a mobile phone and hitting speed-dial. Whoever he was ringing must have been waiting for the call.

"They're not here," I heard him say tightly into the phone, his voice loud with anger and tension. "How the hell should I know?" There was a pause while the person at the other end of the line had their say. "OK," he added, glancing back at the room briefly. "You'd better send a clean-up crew out to the motel."

He snapped the phone shut again and they both climbed back into the Chevy before swinging out of the car park. The whole thing had taken less than three minutes.

The door to the room they'd burst into was still standing open and I eyed it with major apprehension. Everything in me was screaming to get out of there, to run and keep running, but I knew I couldn't do it without knowing what devastation I'd caused, however unwittingly.

"Stay here," I said to Trey. "I'm going to have a look."

I could hardly see his face in the gloom, but I took his silence for compliance. I let myself out of the room, shutting the door quickly behind me. Despite the onset of evening it was still pleasantly warm outside, with the cicadas clicking constantly in the background.

I moved to the stairwell and hurried down it. The motel's outside lights had come on and there weren't any shadows to offer a comforting hiding place to linger. I was just going to have to get this over with as quickly as I could.

Nevertheless, once I'd reached the far block I paused at the doorway to the room, feeling Trey watching me from the other side of the car park but unable to walk straight in. *Come on, Fox, where's your courage?*

When I stepped over the threshold, I needed all of it.

A girl lay sprawled over the bed, limbs flung wide. She had clearly just got out of the shower when they'd killed her. There was a bath towel knotted loosely around her body, and another around her head like a turban.

She'd been shot twice in the body, the blood a livid stain against the white cotton of the towel, splashing up the wall behind and across the same floral bedspread as in our own room.

I stood for a moment and stared down at her, this girl whose death I was ultimately responsible for. She was young, maybe in her early twenties, but she could even have been still in her teens.

From the bathroom came the sound of running water. I moved through there and found her boyfriend had never made it out of the shower before they'd shot him, too.

He must have grabbed at the plastic curtain as he'd fallen, snapping it off the rail and pulling it on top of him as he'd gone down. He sat slumped in a corner of the bath with the water still beating down on his head and bubbling across his open staring eyes. It hit the wall behind him, washing the last traces of his blood away down the drain. An expression of horror was forever frozen on his youthful features.

Without the curtain to hold it back, the bathroom floor was already flooded. I didn't venture in. I didn't need to in order to know there was nothing I could do for either of them. I turned and walked out, using the tail of my shirt to pull the splintered door as far closed as I could behind me.

As I walked back across the car park I felt nothing inside me but a cold, brightly burning rage against Whitmarsh, and Chris, and Gerri Raybourn. They would pay for this. At that precise point I had no idea how but, in the end, they would pay.

I would make sure of it.

SIX

I TOOK THE steps back up to the room two at a time and knocked on the door twice in the time it took Trey to get his skinny backside off the bed and let me in. He took one look at my face and backed away from me.

"What was it?" he demanded, but he looked like that was a question he didn't really want an answer to.

I didn't give him one. Instead I grabbed the thin plastic bag out of the unused rubbish bin and swept the remaining snacks off the bed into it.

"Come on," I said, twisting the top of the bag shut. "We're leaving."

Trey didn't say anything further as we walked out of the room. I slipped the key into my pocket on the way out, even though I had no intention of using it again.

As we reached the bottom of the stairs a crowd of people had gathered round the doorway to the ground-floor room on the other side of the car park. A fat woman in the kind of loud check trousers you normally only see on a golf course pushed to the front to have a better look, then started screaming when she got what she was after. Trey faltered. I hooked my hand under his elbow and kept him moving all the way to the Mercury, which was still sitting behind the diner next door.

It was only as we pulled out into traffic that he finally spoke.

"There were people in there, weren't there?" he said, curiously neutral. "Are they, like, dead?"

I took my eyes off the road briefly to glance at his set face in the flashes of reflected light from the shop fronts and restaurants along the sides of the road.

"Yes."

He nodded and swallowed, his Adam's apple bobbing. Then he said, "Why would Chris and Mr. Whitmarsh do that?" and his voice was nearly plaintive, as though it wasn't fair.

There wasn't an easy way to say it. So, better to say it fast and get it over with. "Because they thought it was us."

I'd come to that conclusion almost as soon as I'd walked in on the scene. In the split-second it would have taken Whitmarsh to take a bead and fire, he wouldn't have had time to recognize that the girl who'd just got out of the shower wasn't the me he'd been told to expect. Not with a towel covering her hair and shock distorting her face.

And after that? Well, maybe they were just being tidy. It still didn't tell me if they were trying to take Trey alive, or if they'd wanted him dead from the outset.

"If they're the ones trying to kill us, why did you call them and tell them where to find us?" he asked now, and the sudden anger in his tone made me wary.

"Trey, I didn't know they were going to do that and anyway, I thought I'd directed them to the room above," I said, not liking the defensiveness that was creeping in when it should have been cool command. "I thought I'd sent them to a room that was empty."

"Yeah, you *thought*," he threw back, half twisting in his seat to face me. "Jesus!" He shook his head. "Just how long have you been a bodyguard, Charlie? How many VIPs have you saved, huh?"

I waited a beat before I answered. The temptation to lie was great, but I knew in the long run it wouldn't get me anywhere. "Well, if *you* count," I said, "then you're the first."

He slumped back, letting his arms lift then flop back to his sides as though weighted down with despair.

"Oh man," he muttered, "we are *so* screwed."

◆ ◆ ◆

For no particular reason other than the fact I recognized the road number, I headed north on A1A. We were traveling parallel with the Atlantic and somewhere over to my right, endless rollers crashed and broke in the darkness.

For a time we drove in silence. I kept strictly to the speed limit, indicating religiously whenever I changed lanes and stopping for amber lights as well as reds. I was being so legal it was downright suspicious, but I suddenly couldn't remember how to drive any more casually.

I don't know what thoughts were tumbling around inside Trey's head. I was too occupied with my own to care.

The first couple of times I'd seen dead bodies I'd been physically sick. At least that hadn't happened this time. Perhaps my stomach was hardening with experience, or perhaps it was simply because the murdered couple in the motel room were complete strangers.

Then I thought of Sean, who was so much more than a stranger to me, and felt the familiar twist in my gut, the hollowness up under my ribcage and the slight buzzing in my ears. I dropped the window a couple of inches and gulped at the blast of warm air it allowed into the car.

Trey recognized my moment of weakness mostly for what it was. "You gonna hurl?" he demanded.

"No," I said firmly. I took a final breath and wound the window back up again. The Mercury's air-conditioning immediately returned the interior to its former temperate state. The moment passed.

We were moving further out of the built-up area now. The buildings had thinned out and were punctuated by longer and longer clumps of scrubby trees and palms. I found my fingers had locked into tense claws round the steering wheel and I flexed them a few times, trying to relax a little more with every mile we were putting between us and the motel. I'd almost begun to think we might have made it clear.

And then, just at that moment, I saw the flashing lights come on in the rearview mirror.

The cop didn't switch his sirens on straight away, as though he didn't want to spook us into running. He started out just with the lights. It was only after I'd ignored the first three or four convenient places to pull over that he hit the loud button.

Trey jerked upright as the screeching wail started up and squirmed round in his seat to stare out through the back screen.

"Aw shit," he said. "You gonna stop, or what?"

"What, probably," I murmured. I reached behind me, awkwardly, with my right hand and pulled the Sig out from under my shirt. I wedged the wheel with my knee just long enough to yank back the slide with my left hand, snapping the first round into the breech. Then I stuck the gun just far enough under my thigh so that it was out of sight of anyone leaning in through the window, but within easy reach.

I glanced over at Trey. He was staring transfixed at the little bit of the pistol grip that he could see peeping out from between the seat cushion and my leg. When he lifted widened eyes to mine they were suddenly a whole lot more guarded than they had been.

"Keep quiet and leave it to me. We'll try and talk our way out of this first, hm?" I said tightly. "But be ready to make a run for it."

Then I indicated and pulled over onto the sloping dirt shoulder of the highway.

I let the car roll slowly to a halt, raising dust as we did so. There was a ditch and a post and rail fence to the right-hand side of the car and beyond that I could just make out a sandy piece of waste land, probably an undeveloped building plot.

On the other side of the highway were lock-up industrial units with chain-link fencing round the boundary and orange sodium lighting. A little further on I could see a stuttering neon sign advertising a small bar.

The cop brought his cruiser to a halt about three or four meters behind our rear bumper. He cut out the siren but left his lights on, which made it impossible for me to tell what car he was driving. All I knew was that the red and blue light bar meant he was with the county police.

I palmed the Mercury's column gear lever up into neutral, keeping the engine running and my foot on the brake pedal so our lights cut down his visibility into the rear of the car. Then I released my seatbelt, put both hands on the top of the steering wheel and faced forward. All the time I was covertly watching his approach in the driver's side door mirror.

Any hopes I might have been harboring that this was just a routine traffic stop went out of the window as soon as the cop got out of his car. When you ride a motorbike you're used to being pulled over, but this guy didn't swagger up with all the confident bravado of someone who has the power at his disposal to take your driving license away from you and the temperament to abuse it.

Instead, he came out in a fast nervous crouch, his gun already in his hands, and started to crab toward my door.

"Out of the car! Out of the car!" he was yelling, his voice pitched high and close to breaking point. Even in the poor light he didn't look old enough to shave, let alone drive a car or graduate from a police academy.

Trey had started to fidget in his seat.

"Keep still, for God's sake, and stop giving him a good excuse to shoot you," I snapped under my breath. The kid froze.

I didn't move either. The cop's advance stalled about four or five feet away, reluctant to come any nearer. He was only too aware of the possibilities of my trying to make a break for it by thumping the car door into him. He didn't want to come and get me, and I didn't want to go to him.

Stalemate.

Closer to, I could see he was holding a large-caliber Glock semi-automatic and his hands were shaking. He was still bawling at me, sounding breathless now, as though he hadn't stopped to draw in air.

Because of the lights from the cruiser I didn't immediately see the second car pull up softly behind the pair of us.

When I did notice it, my first reaction, with a sinking feeling in the pit of my stomach, was that the cop had called for back-up. If we were as dangerous as his manner clearly suggested, he'd been taking a huge risk stopping us on his own to

begin with. I reckoned that a keen and youthful brand of inex-
perience had probably come into play there.

In my mirrors I saw the car doors on both sides of the newcomer open. The young cop whirled round but he didn't look
relieved. Not more cops, then. He seemed unable to decide
which of us now presented the greater threat. He ended up
dancing a fretful jig in the middle, the barrel of his gun swinging wildly between the two of us.

"Stay back!" he barked. "Remain in your vehicle!"

I ducked my head a little, trying to see what was going on
behind me without actually turning, but I couldn't make out
anything clearly. The cruiser's lights acted as a shield.

The cop cast another look at me, still sitting immobile behind the wheel and made his decision. He took a couple of
steps back toward the newcomers. That was as far as he got.

Both men from the car behind the police cruiser opened up
at the same moment. Small arms, probably, but I couldn't see
what they were using.

At least four rounds hit the young cop in the head and upper torso. In the rotating swirl of the lights I saw his body jerk
like he'd just been wired to the mains. He dropped to his
knees, giving a soft surprised gasp as his lungs emptied for
the last time. He let the pistol trickle from his lifeless hand,
then he pitched forward very slowly onto his face in the dirt.

I had the gear lever rammed down into drive almost before
the cop realized he was dead. I stamped my foot down hard
onto the accelerator, sending the car scrabbling for grip along
the earth shoulder while I wrestled with the wheel, trying to
steer us back onto the highway.

The two men who'd shot the cop started pouring bullets
into the back of the Mercury. The rear screen shattered and
Trey gave a squeal, balling himself up in the seat.

Either by luck or by judgment, our attackers took out the
passenger side rear tire when we'd barely made fifty meters.
The car reacted immediately to the hit, lurching onto the rim.
I lost my battle with the ditch. We slithered into it nose down
and the passenger side front corner slammed into one of the
upright fence posts, tearing it out.

The charges in both the Mercury's front airbags exploded instantaneously. I'd always assumed those inflatable white sacks were soft and pillow-like, but they're not. It's like being hit in the face with a bag of wet cement. Still, considering I'd taken off my seatbelt, at least mine saved me from heading straight out through the windscreen.

The bag started to deflate at once. I paddled it away, aware that the whole of my face was burning and there was blood coming out of my nose. I shook my head to try and clear the ringing in my ears but it wouldn't go. Even so, I heard the sound of an engine revving up behind us. Shit!

I twisted round in my seat and saw that the two men had jumped back into their car and had swerved out round the cruiser and the fallen cop. They were now bearing down on us with the doors still wide open.

I clutched at the boy's shoulder, shaking him. "Trey, come on, we've got to move now!" I was rewarded with a dull groan. He wasn't going anywhere.

I reached under my thigh and found, in spite of the crash, that the Sig was still wedged there. I hauled it out and tried to open the door. It was jammed and I had to hit it twice with my shoulder before it gave way with a sharp crack. Because of the cockeyed angle we'd come to rest, I had to wedge it open with my feet so I could struggle out on the uphill side.

I dropped straight onto my hands and knees on the sandy bank of the ditch, just as the other car squealed to a halt at a slant on the road above us. It was a light-colored Buick. Either the bikers I'd set on the two men who'd tailed me from the Pelzners' place had failed to catch their prey, or they hadn't inflicted any lasting damage when they had. More's the pity.

I held the Sig in both hands with my elbows resting on the ground, keeping low as I waited for my chance. The guy in the passenger seat was closest. He was big and still wearing the suit that had made him look like a salesman when I'd seen him outside the house. He got out first, so I shot him first. Two rounds high in the chest. He let go of his gun and fell backward into the car with a kind of heavy grunt.

The driver came out with a hell of a lot more caution, using his door for cover and firing through the open window so that only an inch or so of his head was visible. The bullets thunked into the Mercury's bodywork, much too close for comfort. The noise alone was terrifying.

I carefully lowered my aim and planted two rounds through the door panel itself, right in the center. I knew I should have kept firing until I saw the driver go down, but I didn't have the ammunition to spare to go by the book. As it was, hit or not, he stopped shooting at me and that was enough for now.

And then, in the distance to the south of us, came the unmistakable sound of police sirens. Lots of them. I glanced back at the dead cop and knew that staying here was just about to get a lot more dangerous.

The driver of the Buick must have made that decision, too. I saw the nose of his car bounce as he put it into gear and wheelspun for the first thirty meters. The force of the takeoff slammed both doors shut, carrying both him and his fallen colleague away from the scene.

I jumped up, reached back into the Mercury and grabbed hold of Trey by the front of his shirt, yelling at him to move. This time he responded, scrambling out after me.

I ran, dragging Trey behind me with my hand fisted into his collar, uncaring of his cries of protest as we went. I fled like an animal, looking for darkness, looking for somewhere to hide. Across the highway, through a narrow alleyway that formed an access road between the industrial units and into cover on the other side. The sodium lights didn't reach this far back and it was all the darker for being just outside the scope of their glare.

The sirens were growing louder all the time. I just prayed that when the cavalry arrived they didn't have dogs with them, otherwise this was going to be over very quickly. I'd deliberately chosen not to head onto the waste land because our footsteps would be too easy to track across the soft sandy surface. Asphalt would make it just as easy for a dog.

The first of the reinforcements slid to a messy stop alongside the cruiser. I stopped, struggling to make out the sounds of pursuit over the drumming of the blood in my ears. My breath was coming harsh and loud, so I had to hold it in when I was trying to listen. I wasn't a sprinter any more than I was a long distance runner, but I'd given our short flight everything I'd got and it had shattered me.

Gradually, as I stood there in the darkness, I felt my body begin to put aside the shock of the assault I'd just inflicted on it. My heart no longer seemed about to rupture with every beat. The balmy night air dried the sweat on my skin without chilling it and my eyes were sharpening.

We were hidden for the moment but vulnerable to anyone with methodical determination and a powerful torch. I remembered the way the cop had fallen. Whoever came looking for us would bring both, backed by shotguns and anger. It would be best if we weren't here for them to find.

I lifted the tails of my shirt and slipped the Sig back into my belt. Having it in my hand would only encourage the law to shoot me and, anyway, I wasn't planning on killing anyone else tonight if I could help it.

Behind me, Trey was sniveling quietly into his hands but I daren't soften toward him. Survival was all that mattered now. Compassion could come later. Roughly, I urged him on.

We picked our way through the debris that littered the backs of the units until we came to an area where the chain-link fencing was sagging enough to climb over. Beyond it was the car park behind the bar I'd seen earlier.

It was a single-story building with wooden siding and neon signs for Bud Light and Coors beer that flickered intermittently. I spent a moment watching the bar entrance but it wasn't exactly bustling. The kind of place where the regular clientele arrive as the doors open and have to be persuaded to vacate at closing time, usually with each arm across someone else's shoulders.

There was an array of vehicles parked up outside, mainly pickups. I worked my way along them, trying all the handles, but nobody had been in such a hurry to get a drink that they'd overlooked locking the doors when they'd arrived. I could have simply smashed a window, but even if I did, I'd no idea how to hot-wire a car.

And then, just when I'd almost given in to despair, I caught sight of the line of motorbikes against the far fence. Now bikes, on the other hand, I was much more familiar with . . .

I hustled Trey behind the bar itself, keeping him out of sight of the highway. I could still see the flashing lights reflected from the industrial buildings.

"Stay here," I hissed, then made my way over to the bikes. There were a dozen or so of them, parked up neatly, noses toward the fence like cowboys' horses outside the saloon. I ducked down into the shadows as I checked over each one.

"What are you looking for?"

I turned. Trey had followed me out and was standing a few feet behind one of the bikes. In plain view.

"A way out of here," I bit back in a savage whisper. "Either stay out of sight or find me one that isn't chained up. No mechanical locks and no alarm."

He looked at me for a moment as though he was going to ask questions, then he shrugged and moved away with a lack of urgency that almost made me want to scream at him.

As I went through the bikes it seemed that most of them had additional security of some form or another. I couldn't blame them for that. I carried a roller-chain wherever I went with my bike and I always used it to hobble the rear wheel. The end one of the machines here was tied with something very similar, except it was also threaded through the side bull bars of the nearest pickup truck. I hoped the respective owners knew each other, or things were going to get rough at chucking-out time.

When I reached the other end of the line I found Trey hovering, hands shoved into his pockets and shivering like he was cold.

"Will this one do?" he asked. I gritted my teeth but said nothing as I quickly checked it over.

The bike was a Kawasaki GPz 900 Ninja, not in the first flush of youth and much abused if the dirt-engrained scars in the fairing were anything to go by. The counterweight on the end of the clutch lever was missing and one indicator dangled by its wiring. Not exactly somebody's pride and joy, then. Well, that was good.

Better still, there were no extra locks or chains and no warning stickers for an alarm system. Just the steering lock, which held the handlebars cocked hard over to the left.

"Yes, it will," I said at last, trying to force my lips into an encouraging smile toward the boy. "Well done."

I straightened up, put one hand on the pillion seat, reared back and kicked the scuffed bar end with as much force as I could put into it, given the angle. The bike lurched on its side stand like it was shying away from the blow. As soon as I could be sure it wasn't going to go down, I hit it again.

This time the whole of the front end bucked as the steering lock sheared. The bars rebounded off the far side of the fairing as they broke free. I had to grab the body of the bike to stop it diving forward off the stand. My muscles cramped as I took the full weight of it, straining to keep it upright. It was like slapping a particularly nervous racehorse round the muzzle and then having to stop it bolting afterward.

Trey stood mute, looking puzzled, not making any attempt to help as I wheeled the Kawasaki out of the line. I cast him a single vicious glance as I set the bike back onto its stand, then flipped the fuel tap on and fumbled in my pocket for my Swiss Army knife. I folded out the slot-head screwdriver bit and rammed it into the ignition, using the leverage of the handle to break up the inside of the lock and twist it to the run position.

"OK," I said to Trey, "get on the back. If this works we might have to get out of here fast."

He climbed onto the pillion seat without a word. I closed my eyes briefly, then hit the starter.

The Kwak, good reliable old hack that it was, fluttered and caught. The neglected engine was rattling like a bag of old spanners and the exhaust can was in dire need of replacement, but at least it ran.

No one came rushing out of the bar to rescue their trusty steed.

I toed the bike into gear, feeling weird to be riding without a helmet for the first time in my life. Trey wrapped his arms round my waist and clamped himself to my back like a monkey as we trundled across the uneven car park.

When I got to the highway I checked both ways carefully before I pulled out. The cluster of cop cars was about a third of a mile further back down the road. As I turned in the opposite direction I tried not to look too hard, and I made sure I went up through the Kwak's gearbox slowly and smoothly enough not to attract their attention.

As I rode north into the subtropical night, I could see the visual disco of their lights behind me for a couple of miles before they finally disappeared from view.

SEVEN

I MANAGED TO get us forty miles away from the scene of the shoot-out, across two county lines and almost into West Palm Beach, before I had to stop.

There was a wooden shack by the side of the road, with a faded sign by the side of it to tempt passers by with the offer of homegrown citrus fruit for sale. The shack looked as though it hadn't had anything fresh inside it for years. A thick coating of weeds was the only thing holding the rotting timbers upright. I slowed and rode carefully in through the open doorway, paddling the Kawasaki round with both feet down, clumsy.

As I pulled the clutch in and we finally came to a halt, I muttered over my shoulder to Trey, "OK, *now* I'm going to hurl."

He almost tripped in his effort to be off the bike faster than me. I staggered to the doorway and stood bent over with my hands braced on my knees. There was a roaring growing louder in my ears like I was standing in the shallows waiting for the surf to wash over me. I didn't have to wait long.

The teriyaki beef jerky tasted no better on the way up than it had done on the way down.

Trey stood by the bike inside the shack, watching me throw up with irritating intensity. I could feel his distaste, but sensed it wasn't so much at the fact that I was vomiting, as at my need to do so. He despised my weakness without sympathy. I wasn't so keen on it myself.

When I was finally on empty I came upright slowly, buffeted by dizziness and fresh nausea. Considering I was relatively uninjured I felt like hell. My eyes were gritty from squinting unprotected into the hot wind that had blasted up over the bike's fairing. I seemed to have been hit in the face by every living species of insect in Florida. It reminded me why I never even rode with my visor open at home, never mind with no helmet at all.

I put a hand up to wipe the bug splats off my face. I swear my nose was at least twice its normal size. I prodded gently at the bridge with my fingers but I didn't think it was broken.

The moonlight was clear and startling by the doorway and it seeped inside the shack. I noticed for the first time that Trey had acquired a small cut over his eyebrow when the airbag had gone off in his face. A little blood had trickled down past the side of his eye. Apart from that he looked OK. More or less. He was staying further back in the gloom and it was difficult to tell.

"Are you all right?" I asked.

"Yeah, 'course," he said, with a defiant edge to him. Reminding him at this point of his tears and listless shock as we'd run from the cops would not, I thought, be a way to gain his friendship and trust. I let it ride. Besides, I soon found out that he had other things on his mind.

"Was that—" he broke off, took a breath and tried again, his voice detached. "Was that the first time you've like, y'know, killed someone?"

Again, I was tempted to lie. Again I didn't see the point. "No," I said.

Trey gulped. "Did it . . . Did you throw up then, too? Afterward, I mean."

I cocked my head, as though giving the question serious thought. "Probably. I don't remember," I said, trying to be truthful. "I didn't exactly come out of it in the best of health myself and the paramedics were giving me a lot of painkillers. Things were a little hazy."

I didn't explain any further than that, but Trey nodded seriously, as though what I'd just told him made perfect sense. "Can I see it—the gun?"

I eyed him doubtfully. There was a kind of fearful eagerness about him now. He'd got over the shock of watching me shoot the men in the Buick and all the ghoulishness of your average schoolboy had returned. Nevertheless, there was no good reason to refuse him.

I sighed and pulled the Sig out of my belt again. He moved forward, his gaze locked on the gun. I deliberately dropped the magazine out and removed the chambered round before I handed it over to him. His contained excitement outweighed the offense he took at having his judgment so obviously mistrusted.

"Awesome," he said. Even knowing the gun was unloaded, he handled it with exaggerated care, surreptitiously reading the maker's name off the side of the barrel, but not wanting to let me see him do it in order to recognize what it was. "Sig Sauer, huh? Where d'ya get it?"

"From the house," I said. "It's Sean's." I couldn't quite bring myself to talk about him in the past tense. Not yet.

"Where d'you learn to shoot like that?" His stance had altered, I noted. He was holding the Sig in a showy double-handed grip now, posing almost, with both elbows bent sharply in best movie tough-guy tradition. So the camera can pan in good and tight on the hero's face and still get the gun in the same shot.

"In the army," I said, short.

"Yeah? Why'd you leave?"

"I had my reasons," I said. I could have added a whole lot more to that, as well. The Special Forces course I'd been on when I'd been unceremoniously chucked out had taught me an awful lot more about firearms than basic training had ever done, but he didn't need to know that.

I busied my hands feeding the loose round back into the magazine. I had just four left. I tried not to dwell on what I'd done with the other four.

My job?

Or murder?

No, far better to concentrate on what I had left.

"Will you show me how to shoot?" Trey asked, trying out

the feel of the Sig one-handed, with his arm outstretched. It was heavier than he'd expected. His narrow muscles began to shiver with the effort of keeping it up there.

"Yeah, sure," I snapped, my nerves edged into sarcasm. "Let's go and buy you a .357 Magnum and then we'll go out robbing banks together."

Trey stared at me blankly for a moment and I remembered all of a sudden that irony was a concept lost on him.

I sighed. "No," I said, holding my hand out.

He scowled, hesitating for a moment before he surrendered the gun, slapping it down onto my palm. I slipped the magazine back into the pistol grip and tucked the whole thing back into my belt, watching him all the while. My patience was starting to wear so thin that keeping a check on it was giving me a bad head.

"What makes you so damned important, Trey, that four people have died today because of you?" I demanded. It was more like an accusation. I was feeling like shit and he was the nearest person I could take it out on.

The body count could be more than that by now, I realized as I spoke. The woman at the amusement park for one.

"I dunno," he muttered.

I rubbed my eyes, which had the effect of sandpapering my retinas a little flatter. "Why the hell has Keith done a runner? What's he up to?"

"I dunno!" Trey said, more emphatic this time. He let his head droop and was back to mumbling again. "Maybe it's like, y'know, connected somehow with the work he does for the government."

That brought my head up. "What kind of work?"

He shrugged. "It's classified," he said, snotty with it, like he'd always wanted to say that line.

I tried for a sigh, but my breath came out too fast to qualify, so it ended up more as a hiss. "Trey," I said carefully, "it may have escaped your notice, but I've just had to kill a man to protect you and right now I don't feel too good about that. So tell me what you know."

He would only look at me for a half-second at a time. The

rest of the time his eyes swiveled away into all the far corners of the shack. "I don't know what kind of work he was doing," he admitted at last, sulky. "You think he used to tell me stuff like that?"

"No," I said. "I don't."

I fell silent for a moment, trying to assimilate these new disclosures into the incomplete jigsaw of what I already knew. Keith Pelzner working for the government. If anything, it made the presence of the two armed men in the Buick more sinister, not less.

I recalled again the way they'd gunned down the young cop, their casual ruthlessness. It had not, I recognized, been their first time out. And suddenly they'd moved up from simple outlaws into something so much more. Now there was the possibility that they might be backed by limitless authority.

And I'd just shot one of them dead.

My anger slumped into weary resentment, sending a more up-tempo beat surging outward across my temples. "Why didn't you tell me any of this earlier?" I said quietly.

"Why?" he lashed out. "What difference would it have made?"

I opened my mouth, preparing to launch in, then thought better of it. "Probably none," I allowed weakly. "But I'm trying to work out who's out to get you and right now it seems to be just about everybody—the cops, your dad, Gerri Raybourn and Jim Whitmarsh—you name it. And exactly who those two guys in the Buick were, I've no idea." I shrugged, letting my hands fall back against my sides. "Sean's missing. He could be dead," I went on, my voice flat now. "I'm running out of ideas."

Something of Trey's own resentment seemed to leave him at my admission. Maybe it was the first time an adult had consulted him for his opinion. He was silent while he thought about it.

"We could go to Daytona," he said, almost diffident, the way kids are when they're asking for something that's desperately important to them and trying to make it look like they don't really care.

"Why? What makes Daytona safer than here?"

He stuffed his hands into his pockets. "I got friends there," he said. "We can hang with them—hide out if we need to."

"Are you sure we can rely on them? No, think about it," I said when he started to make an automatic response. "After tonight there are going to be a lot of people looking for us."

"Trust me." He smiled, an abrupt cocky grin that showed off all the metalwork behind his lips.

It wasn't reassuring. In fact, the more I thought about it, the more heading up to Daytona Beach seemed like a bad idea, but I was damned if I could come up with a better suggestion.

I swung my leg back over the Kawasaki and jerked my head for him to climb on the back.

"OK," I said heavily. "Daytona it is."

We stayed on A1A, traveling steadily northward and trying to stay inconspicuous. By the time we were passing through Indian River Shores the Kawasaki's fuel gauge was showing we were running on fumes. Not knowing the bike, I wasn't sure how accurately it read and the last thing we could afford to do was run out by the side of the road. I pulled into the first quiet-looking filling station we came across.

There was a sign on the pump that told customers they had to pre-pay after dark. I thought the fuel prices were high until I realized they were per gallon, not per liter. I sent Trey in with a more than adequate twenty-dollar note while I broke the lock on the filler cap with my knife, making as little fuss about it as I could. The tank seemed to take a long time to fill and I stood with my back to the CCTV cameras, trying not to look furtive whenever a car drove past on the highway.

According to the window posters, the filling station also sold coffee and hot dogs. The slightly burned greasy smell of them permeated out into the warm night air. I knew I ought to put something in my empty stomach but the thought of doing so brought on a rising queasiness I struggled to suppress. The snacks we'd brought with us when we came away from the motel, I remembered, had been abandoned in the Mercury.

A sudden thought had me checking my pockets, then cursing. The food wasn't the only thing that had been left behind at the crash site.

The mobile phone had gone, too.

The feeling of having just severed my last lifeline to the outside world was a strong one. It wasn't a mistake I wanted to boast about to the kid.

I hung the nozzle back into the pump and flipped the filler cap closed. I'd already climbed back onto the bike by the time Trey reappeared from paying for the fuel. He didn't offer to hand over any change and it seemed petty to push for it.

He was looking wired. "Hey, there was a TV on in there," he said, jerking a thumb over his shoulder. "We made the news!"

"Jesus! What did it say?" The speed with which the story had got out surprised me, but I suppose the murder of a cop in the line of duty is always going to be an emotive subject. "Did they mention us by name?"

Trey scratched at his armpit, frowning as he was overtaken by a sudden worry. "Nah. It just said there was a double homicide at a motel and that a cop was gunned down by the side of the highway."

As I restarted the Kwak's motor he hopped onto the pillion seat, grabbing on round my waist. He leaned forward. "That means they know it was Mr. Whitmarsh and Chris, yeah?" he said in my ear, and there was a painfully hopeful note in his voice. "That means we're, like, in the clear, right?"

Now would have been a good time to stop being so truthful with the kid, I recognized, but it seemed a shame to break the habit.

"No, sorry," I said, grim. "It means now we're in the shit twice as deep . . ."

It was late in the evening by the time we arrived in Daytona Beach. The whole place was bright and brash and lit up with neon like Blackpool sea front on steroids. Lots of steroids.

We crossed over the inland waterway and came in on South

Atlantic Avenue, past block after block of high-rise luxury flats that were perched on the narrow ribbon of land between the road and the beach. The motels and hotels lined both sides, mostly with signs out welcoming the Spring Breakers. The bars and surf shops all seemed to still be open, bright and brash and loud. They were doing a roaring trade if the number of teenagers thronging the pavements was anything to go by.

I stopped before we got too far into the thick of things. The sight of numerous police cruisers pulling teenage drivers over in the center turning lane for traffic and drink driving offenses was enough to make me want to get us and our stolen motor-bike off the road, and fast.

I turned into the first reasonable-looking motel that had a vacancies sign lit up and tucked the Kawasaki away behind a massive pickup truck.

"I'll stay with the bike," Trey offered as I cut the engine and we climbed off.

I nodded and walked into the reception. There were a crowd already in there, including a family of harassed and sunburned Brits who were complaining about the noise.

"I'm real sorry, sir," the thin youth behind the desk was saying, "but you have to understand that this is Spring Break."

The man kept grumbling until the duty manageress was wheeled out to discount his bill. He accepted the reduction with poor grace and stalked out, his crotchety-looking wife and family trailing after him. His plastic sandals squeaked annoyingly on the tiled floor as he went. As they passed me I noticed that the backs of their collective necks were scorched to the color of a red brick house.

A group of American teens were next in line, all good tans and gum and braces. I busied myself leafing through a rack of local attractions by the main desk, mainly so I could avoid eye contact with people. I didn't want to stick in their memory if I could help it.

I quietly checked out my reflection in the mirrored glass panel behind the reception desk, but to my surprise I didn't show any signs of having just lived through a car crash and a bloody shoot-out. My nose looked a little puffy, sure, but if you didn't know what it looked like normally, you wouldn't notice. And the reddened patches on my face from the airbag would pass for too much exposure to the Florida sun.

It was at this point I noticed the sign on the corner of the desk. The one that said, "IT IS THE POLICY OF THE MANAGEMENT TO REQUEST VALID ID WITH CHECK-IN DURING SPRING BREAK WEEKEND. THANK YOU FOR YOUR COOPERATION."

I thought about that one for a moment, then turned and headed for the door.

"Excuse me, ma'am, can I help you?"

I half-turned, smiled and waved the leaflet for the Daytona Motor Speedway that I was still clutching. "No thanks," I said, smiling. "Just wanted one of these."

Trey was leaning nonchalantly on the Kawasaki when I got back outside. Too nonchalantly. I wondered briefly what he'd been up to while I'd been gone.

"They have a room?"

I shook my head. "I didn't get that far," I said. "They've a sign up asking for ID, and in view of the fact that I showed my driver's license when we checked into the motel in Fort Lauderdale, I didn't think that was a good idea."

Trey didn't have to ask me to explain my reasoning. OK, so we were in a different county and I had it in my head that the US police were a lot more territorial than back at home. Even so, when the murder of one of their own was concerned, I'd bet they wouldn't have much trouble getting assistance from other departments.

Besides, the cop who'd stopped us had known we were the ones he was after. That much was obvious as soon as he'd got out of his car. They must have discovered we'd disappeared from the motel after the shooting and decided that running away from a crime scene made us instant suspects. What had happened afterward would have put us right at the top of the list.

Either that or the young cop was in league with Oakley man and had simply wanted us dead. In which case, whose side were the men in the Buick on?

I shook my head, setting the fading headache off again. I was too tired to think straight tonight.

There were a couple of pay phones on the wall outside the reception door. I looked at Trey and nodded toward them. "Any chance you can get in touch with your mates tonight and see if we can cadge a bed from them?"

"I called already but they weren't home," he said. "I left a message that we'd meet up tomorrow, down at the Ocean Center."

"What's going on there?"

"It's the Spring Break Nationals," he said, as though I should know straight away what he was on about. "It's, like, y'know, the biggest car audio competition in Florida. In the whole of the States, probably. It's just awesome."

A car audio competition. Only in America, I thought. As if to prove the point a car went past us with its stereo system cranked so high the spot welds holding the roof panel together were buzzing loose. All four windows were down but I still couldn't name that tune.

"I can't wait," I muttered. "So, what do we do tonight?"

Trey shrugged. "This is Spring Break," he said. "We do what everyone else does if they can't get a room—we sleep on the beach."

EIGHT

THE AMOUNT OF police cars cruising about in Daytona Beach soon convinced me the Kawasaki was going to have to go. Trey and I rode back down the strip until we came across a big hotel with an underground car park and ducked into there.

I found a quiet corner next to the laundry room and that's where we left it. I retrieved my Swiss Army knife from the ruined ignition and gave the bike a last pat on its battered tank. It had served us well and I was sorry to see the back of it.

As an extra precaution, I unscrewed the rear numberplate and took that away with us, just to slow down the identification a little. I dropped the pressed ali plate down the first storm drain at the side of the road we came to. It must rain like hell in Florida, because they had openings in the gutter that would have been big enough to lose a medium-sized dog.

The prospect of sleeping on a beach, in March, without any camping equipment or a sleeping bag was not one that filled me with excited anticipation.

Still, at least it was Florida. The last time I'd been forced to rough it like that had been doing Escape and Evasion exercises in the army. The Brecon Beacons at the same time of year is a whole different ball game.

On foot now, we crossed over the highway and walked

along the strip until we came to one of the big surf shops that was still open.

"What do we want from here?" Trey asked.

"Beach towels," I said. "They may not be quite up to blanket level, but at least they'll keep the sand out."

I picked up a couple of what felt like the warmest, but Trey balked at the prospect of owning anything with twee cartoon mermaids on the front so I let him choose his own. The one he came back with was a leftover from the previous year's bike week and looked half as thick as my choice. I didn't have the energy to argue with him. There was only a desultory crowd as we went to the check-out, but the cashier was looking jumpy.

When I followed his gaze I noticed a couple of teenagers, probably a year or two older than Trey, hanging around by the surfing gear. One was a skinny kid, wearing a bandanna and an open shirt over a white vest that showed off his concave chest. His jeans were slung fashionably low, just about clinging on round his protruding hip bones and showing off two inches of underpant over the top. He walked like he thought he was hot stuff.

His mate was shorter and fatter, still trying to shake off his adolescent puppy fat and look like a mean dog instead. It came over as clumsy bluster. The thin kid was the dangerous one. Neither of them looked like they were about to splash out on a new Lightwave longboard.

I realized when I dug in my pockets that I'd let Trey have the last twenty to pay for the fuel. I had to break one of the hundred-dollar bills Keith had given me, which I would rather have done without the audience, particularly as the cashier counted my change out loud into my hand. The only good thing was that he was so busy watching what was going on behind me he didn't spend long looking at my face.

When we walked out of the shop and back across the road, I checked behind us regularly but as far as I could see there was nobody following.

Beach ramps were spaced at regular intervals along South Atlantic Avenue. According to the signs, if you paid your fee you were invited to take your car down there and ride up and down the sand all day. It sounded like an invitation to major corrosion problems to me. The ramps were gated off at night but it was only to stop traffic. Trey and I walked past them, carrying our towels, and stepped out onto the soft sand.

It wasn't truly dark out there. There was too sharp a moon, caught and reflected by the white water of every breaker. The navigation lights of a big commercial ship far out to sea shimmered toward us.

Moving heavily through the dry sand, we worked our way further down the beach. Someone had gathered enough odds and ends of driftwood together to light a campfire, in spite of the notices strictly forbidding such an activity.

The night had taken on a chill now and it would have been tempting to stay near the fire, but I didn't want to be around if the cops arrived to tell them to put it out. We skirted round the edge and kept going.

The flames momentarily wiped out my night vision, so I didn't see the skinny kid from the surf shop until he was a few meters in front of us. He was tight and wired. There was a cheap knife in his right hand.

"Gimme the money," he said. No wasted time on banter.

I glanced over my shoulder to check Trey's position and saw that the fat teen was now behind us. His hands were empty. I turned back to the skinny kid. The glint and shadow from the fire shifted satanically over his face.

"We don't have much," I said.

"Don't lie to me, bitch," the skinny kid said, raising the knife. "You got plenty."

Better to buy our way out of trouble if we could. I dropped the towel at my feet and reached into my pocket. I separated a couple of notes from the fold with my fingers and pulled my hand out. I held the money out to the side of me, wanting to make him work for it.

The skinny kid smiled unpleasantly and nodded to his companion, who came forward just far enough to grab the money, then retreated again to check his booty. It was obviously a system they'd used before.

"It's just a coupla twenties," he said, disgusted.

The skinny kid's smile became a sneer.

"What kinda fool d'you take me for?" he spat. He took a couple of steps forward, rolling the knife almost delicately between his fingertips so the blade flashed in the light. "Gimme the rest."

"No," I said.

He stopped. For a moment the only noise was the steady crash of the waves on the shoreline and the crackle of the fire behind me.

Trey had moved up to my right shoulder but I was under no illusions that he was about to act as my wing man if it came down to it. His body was rigid, jaw clenched. When our eyes met he let his slide meaningfully down toward my back where the Sig was lying under my shirt. I gave the briefest shake of my head and turned back to the kid with the knife.

I sighed. "Look," I said. "I've had a very shitty day. I'm tired. You've just made twenty dollars each for ten seconds' work. Be smart and quit while you're ahead."

He bared his teeth. "Wise-ass, huh? Always heard you English chicks didn't put up much of a fight," he said and something else was gleaming in his eyes now. "Always heard it was like fucking a corpse. Looks like we've found ourselves a fighter, huh?"

My heart accelerated, starting to flood my system with oxygenated blood. I could hear the echo of it thundering in my ears. "You have no idea," I murmured.

He came at me fast then, leading with the blade. I went to meet him, taking a couple of quick steps forward to keep him away from Trey. I blocked his knife hand with my left forearm and snaked my arm around his so his wrist was locked up under my armpit.

He jerked at his trapped arm and when he couldn't immediately free it he tried to launch a wild left-hand punch instead. I tightened my grip, jamming my fist up under his elbow to force the joint straight beyond its limit. He gave a surprised grunt, the pain preventing him from turning far enough toward me for the blow to connect. I steadied him for a moment, then turned my body in toward his and jerked my knee up into his groin, quick and hard. The fight was over.

The skinny kid's eyes bulged as his legs gave way and he began to gag. I loosened up enough to let him fall to his knees, putting some twist onto his right hand as he went down to prise the knife out of his fingers.

The fat kid hadn't moved an inch while all this had gone on. He just stood there with his mouth hanging open.

"Beat it," I told him.

For a moment he didn't move. I hefted the knife one-handed, tossed it up and caught it by the blade, then brought my hand back like I was a circus knife thrower going for the big finale. *"Now!"* I said.

The fat kid didn't wait to see how good my aim was. He gave a kind of startled squeak, hurled the twenty dollar notes down onto the sand, and then he turned and ran.

I let go of the skinny kid's arm and stepped away from him, but I needn't have worried he was about to launch a counter attack. He just took it back and, very carefully, tucked both hands between his legs, cradling himself. His breath came quick and shallow, almost a pant, and his eyes were wet with tears.

I leaned down, keeping my tone conversational. "Now, I wouldn't like you to kid yourself that I've just been lucky and caught you off guard, because we both know that isn't true, don't we?"

He managed a weak nod. The action shook loose a couple of tears, which tracked down the sides of his nose and dripped to the ground.

"Good," I said, still calm and pleasant. "So, we're going to leave now and you're going to crawl back to whatever hole you came out of and you're going to stay there, aren't you?"

Another feeble nod.

"Good boy," I said encouragingly. I held the captured knife up in front of his face and watched the fear sharpen into focus as it caught his attention. "Because if you don't, next time we meet I'm not just going to kick you in the bollocks, I'm going to cut them off, is that clear?"

"Y-yeah!" he yelped.

I straightened up, jerking my head to Trey. He picked up the fallen money and the towel I'd dropped, then stood looking down at the skinny kid for a moment, his face expressionless.

"OK, let's go," I said gently. We carried on along the beach, leaving our would-be robber behind us, crying quietly into the sand.

We kept walking, away from the campfire and the brightness of the big hotels and toward what looked like a residential area. Trey was quiet as we trudged along. I left him to work out what it was he wanted to say.

My heart rate was slowing to its normal level, the tension going out of my body now.

After I'd left the army I'd taught self-defense classes to women. Dealing with a situation like the one presented by the skinny kid and his mate was exactly the kind of thing I'd covered, week in and week out, for the best part of four years. There was no way he could have known that, so he'd woefully underestimated me.

Sometimes that was annoying, being mistaken for less than I was, but at others I had to admit that it came in very handy.

"Why didn't you shoot him?" Trey asked suddenly.

"What?"

"You had a gun," Trey said, sounding petulant, as though I'd somehow cheated, "so why didn't you just, like, shoot him?"

"I've already shot my quota of people for today," I said, flippant.

I heard his breath huff out.

"Look, Trey, it's not as simple as that," I said. "What if he'd had a gun, too? Suddenly we're in the middle of another shoot-out. If you pull a gun, you have to be prepared to use it. I wasn't—not against a couple of chancers like those two. Besides anything else, I don't have the ammo to spare. And if I'd just threatened them with the gun I'm sure they would have remembered us. This way, well, I don't think matey-boy's going to be in a hurry to go round telling anyone he's just had his arse kicked by a girl, do you?"

"No, I guess not," Trey said. A slow smile spread across his face as the truth of it dawned on him. "'Sides, man, it wasn't his ass you kicked."

We found a secluded space by the side of a pair of weather-beaten wooden steps that led up into the dunes and that's where we spread out our beach towels for the night. I'd seen the amount of tire tracks all over the place and I didn't want to put us somewhere we were likely to be run down in our sleep.

Trey rolled himself up in his towel and went out like he'd taken a punch, leaving me to lie awake listening to the relentless sea and the noises of the insects clicking incessantly into the night, and to think about the fact that I'd killed a man.

Now the immediate dangers were past, that inescapable fact surfaced again. I replayed it over and over. Saw in minute detail the Buick slewing to a stop, the guy in the passenger seat putting his left hand on the A pillar to pull himself out of the car, the gun leveling in his right, the clenched concentration in his face.

I tried to remember my own emotions, to put my actions down to extreme fear, or anger. Anything but the cold calm deliberation with which I'd shot him. In the end I couldn't do it. I couldn't blame heat for what I'd done because, in truth, beyond a determination not to let them get to us first, I hadn't felt anything at all.

Nothing.

So what did that make me?

Maybe it was partly down to my familiarity with guns. I associated them with sport, with accuracy and skill more than death.

I'd been a first-class shot in the army, selected by my training instructors for the shooting teams in very short order. The first Skill At Arms meeting I'd done they'd brought me out almost as their secret weapon, gleeful as the scores came in for this unknown WRAC private. If I didn't know better I'd almost say that most of the senior NCOs had put a bet on.

But target shooting was different. Targets fell, or developed holes. They didn't bleed. They didn't scream. And they didn't die.

It wasn't until I'd gone for Special Forces training that my temperament had been recognized for what it was. By Sean, of course. He'd been one of my sergeants then and he'd always seen too much. I suddenly remembered a conversation I'd had with him the year before, when we'd met again for the first time since the army.

"You were one of the best shots with a pistol I've ever come across, Charlie. Cool-headed. Deadly."

"There were plenty who were just as good."

He'd shaken his head. "A lot of people had a reasonable ability to aim. That doesn't mean they'd got the stomach to pull the trigger for real. Not like you, Charlie. You had what it took. Still do, at a guess."

I'd refuted it at the time, hadn't wanted to admit he might have been right. Events in Germany had made any arguments I might have come up with redundant. I'd finally accepted that an ability to kill was part of me and I'd better learn to live with it if I didn't want it to destroy me. Becoming a bodyguard had seemed the best way to channel such a talent, if that's what it was.

Maybe "curse" would be a better description.

Trey shifted and mumbled in his sleep. Not surprising that he would have bad dreams after what he'd seen today. I watched him for a moment, but he didn't wake.

I didn't like him, I admitted to myself, dispassionate. When all was said and done he was just a spoiled bratty kid, and I hated spoiled bratty kids. In normal circumstance I wouldn't have crossed the road to spit on him if he'd been on fire.

Odd then, that my chosen new profession meant I was now supposed to lay down my life, if necessary, to protect him.

Next morning—Friday—I woke with the sunrise. My body clock was still partly tuned to UK time, running some five hours ahead.

I sat up with a groan. You think sand is nice and soft until you try spending the night with nothing between you and it except a towel. My hips creaked and grated every time I moved and I realized I should have dug hollows under them. Ah well, maybe next time.

The sun was cranking up slowly from beyond the far horizon, casting the sky with a stunning wash of pinks and pale blues. I sat, wrapped in my towel against the early chill and watched it climb steadily over the teeming bird life.

All along the shore line quick little piebald wading birds darted into the bubbling water as the sea advanced and retreated, nipping at the wet sand. The seagulls seemed like slow bruisers by comparison, lurking with their thumbs in their pockets, looking for trouble. Across the tops of the swells a strung-out flight of pelicans cruised effortlessly, as though they were air surfing just for the fun of it.

Trey was still spark out and I let him sleep, but I wasn't the only one awake early. Lots of people were out for their morning exercise along the beach. In the golden dawn light they looked aggressively healthy as they power-walked briskly past us, elbows pumping. Most were elderly, dressed in shorts, pale shirts and those tinted sunshades that golfers wear. Nearly all were carrying insulated mugs. I smelt their coffee, and was envious.

Not everybody was in a hurry. One young couple wandered at the waterline, hand in hand, soaking up the primitive peace of the sun's ascent. I thought of the couple at the motel, pointlessly slaughtered, and it set up a dull aching pain behind my breastbone.

Strange how I could feel more distress at the deaths of two people where I'd been little more than a bystander, rather than the one where I'd actually pulled the trigger myself.

Now, the couple paused a little way off to my right with the waves lapping gently at their ankles. They turned their faces toward the sea and embraced. I shifted my gaze, unwilling to intrude.

I suppose there'd been a time, once, when I'd wondered if

that would ever be Sean and me—strolling barefoot on a sub-tropical beach at sunrise. Instead we'd spent more time with our backs to the wall, fighting for our lives. Violence, mostly not of our own making, had always seemed to come between us.

We'd come back from Germany after New Year, though, with the air clearer than it had ever been, promising we'd try again from the beginning. No more baggage.

And we had, to a certain extent.

The first time Sean and I had got together we'd rushed into a wild and passionate affair that had "self-destruct" written all over it. Sure enough, it had ended in disaster for both of us.

This time around, he'd taken his time, courted me, and I'd been bemused to discover he had a gentle, thoughtful side I'd never previously suspected. It didn't fit with everything I'd ever known of Sean. It had made me hesitate.

Looking back over the past few months I realized that I'd been holding back, hoping for something that would lend sub-stance to my caution. Failing to find it had only made me more wary, as though I'd been afraid that he was too good to be true.

And then, only the day before yesterday, I'd let my guard down just long enough for Sean to slip through, under my skin again. It had been every bit as magical as I'd recollected. Every bit as magical as I'd feared it couldn't be.

And now it looked as though circumstances had brought our fledgling relationship to an end in the most final way possible.

I glanced over at Trey, the cause of all this. Drool stringed from his slack mouth. He was beginning to stir, rolling over onto his back with a short grunt like a sleeping dog. As I watched, his eyes fluttered open, squinting against the sunlight.

He struggled into a sitting position, scratching at his neck as he yawned and stretched. The hair sprang up around the back of his head in tufts.

"What's up?" he said, rubbing at his face, his voice thick with sleep. "You were looking at me kinda weird."

"Nothing," I said, turning my face away. I indicated the vista with my hand and added with a touch of irony, "Another day in paradise."

A flash of black and white further down the beach caught my eye. Tense, I got quickly to my feet, shaking the sand out of my towel. "Time to go," I said abruptly.

"Aw man, what's the hurry?" He stared up at me, not moving. "It's early. We ain't gonna meet up with the guys 'til around eleven."

"That's as may be," I said, keeping my voice low, "but there's a pair of cops over there, checking IDs of all the kids sleeping on the beach."

I'd tried to keep my body language casual, but Trey immediately spun round, staring at the two cops. They were wheeling mountain bikes through the sand. I'd always thought the cozy image of the local bobby on his bike belonged firmly in the leafy villages of Agatha Christie's England. Looks like I'd been wrong.

These two looked nothing like familiar English coppers. Both men were wearing cycling shorts, gunbelts and trendy sunglasses. The image of Oakley man momentarily overlaid on top of them, sending my pulse soaring.

The pair handed ID back to the group of kids they'd been talking to and started moving toward us. They were barely thirty meters away. I cursed my own lack of attention, that I hadn't spotted them earlier.

"You reckon they're looking for us?" Trey asked, jumping to his feet now, nervous.

"Best not to find out, don't you think?" I murmured.

The only immediate way off the beach was the set of wooden steps we'd slept alongside. Trey snatched up his towel and I led the way up the short flight. I concentrated on breathing evenly, trying not to make it look as though we were in a hurry, or running away. Difficult, when we were doing both.

In the dim light of the night before I'd thought the steps were simply a way up onto the dunes, but once we were at the top in daylight, I could see they actually led to someone's private garden.

In front of us was a scrappy lawn of tough-looking grass punctuated by stubby palms at the borders. The trees had all grown leaning away from the beach and the prevailing wind.

It wasn't a big area, not like the garden of the Pelzners' rented mansion back in Fort Lauderdale, but it had a lived-in feel. A child's plastic slide sat on a paved patio closer to the house, with a brightly-colored football and a mini trampoline.

The house itself was low and squat and painted white, battered by its proximity to the sea and the salt. A trellis of rust trails ran down the walls from every metal fixing. Almost the whole of the wall facing the ocean was made of glass that tilted downward, presumably to fend off the glare from the water. I didn't know much about real estate prices in Daytona Beach, but if the view alone counted for anything, then this was right up there. Until the next hurricane hit, of course.

The two cops had almost reached the foot of the steps. They were studying Trey and me, trying to work out if we belonged in the garden, or if they had a good enough reason to follow us up.

"Keep walking toward the house," I whispered to the kid. I let my gaze scan casually across the cops, nodded and gave them a smile and a cheery wave. Failing to make eye contact doesn't work with people who've been trained to spot someone acting shifty.

I turned back toward the house, then swore softly under my breath as a gray-haired woman in a loose sacky dress appeared at one of the windows. She stilled, narrowing her eyes and sticking her chin out as though she needed glasses to positively identify us as strangers at that distance.

I glanced round, making the pretense of pointing out a diving pelican to Trey. Out of the corner of my eye I saw one of the cops lean his bike against the stair rail and put his foot on the first step. His partner stayed on the beach.

A trickle of sweat ran between my shoulder blades. I hunched them, feeling the Sig dig into the back of my belt. The knife I'd taken from the skinny kid the night before weighed heavy in my shorts pocket.

Oh shit . . .

"Morning, officers," said a man's deep voice at that moment. "Can I help you boys?"

We all turned to find a slim elderly man with a neatly

trimmed white van Dyke beard approaching up the beach, his stride long and rangy. He wore a battered Panama hat and a very faded T-shirt that had once advertised the 1989 Daytona 500. In his right hand he carried a bulging string bag.

"Oh hi, Walt, how you doing today?" said the cop who'd been about to climb up after us. He turned and stepped down onto the beach again.

"I'm doing good, Mikey," the old guy said. "So, you boys smell breakfast cooking, or what?"

"No." The cop laughed and shook his head. "You have folk visiting?" And he nodded in our direction.

Walt looked up then from under the brim of the Panama and a pair of piercing gray eyes under bushy eyebrows locked onto mine, straight and steady. I stared back at him and tried to impart pleading and desperation. I suppose there was a certain amount of fear there, too.

For what I'd have to do if he said no.

For a long moment, Walt didn't move, then he gave me an almost imperceptible nod. "Yeah," he said, his voice slow and rolling, like he was reading a story on the radio. "You guys hungry?" he called to us. "Harriet's making her special blueberry pancakes."

I checked the house again. The old woman had moved to the open doorway now. She was standing just behind the mosquito screen, looking anxious.

Walt climbed the steps and came toward us. He paused a few strides away to turn and wave a small salute to the police. The cop he'd called Mikey waved back and collected his bike. The pair of them began to move off.

Walt watched them go, then turned back to us. Close to, I could see the bag he'd been carrying was filled with seashells.

"So," he said calmly, "can I ask you folks what you're doing in my backyard?"

"I'm sorry, sir," I said, "we made a mistake—took a wrong turn. We were just looking for the way off the beach and—"

I broke off as Walt's wildly sprouting eyebrows did a strange jiggle of surprise. "English, huh?" he said. "I have a daughter went to college over there—Manchester. You know it?" He pronounced the name with all the emphasis on the *Man,* like it was two words.

"Er, yeah, I'm from that part of the country. My mother and father still live near Manchester," I said, grasping at the association. I thought of my parents' substantial Georgian house in the stockbroker belt of Cheshire and reckoned that my mother would faint at the suggestion that they were any-where near the outskirts of the city itself, but they weren't here to contradict me.

Walt beamed. "Well, that's just great," he said. "Why don't you both come inside and you can tell Harriet and me all about Manchester while we have a bite of breakfast?"

"Oh really, sir, we couldn't put you out like that," I said quickly, even though my empty stomach was already grum-bling at the mention of those blueberry pancakes.

"No, no," Walt said. "It's no trouble. Harriet always cooks for a full house. That woman could feed a battleship. There'll be waffles, bacon, eggs, hash browns . . ."

He let his voice trail off artfully, those canny eyes shift-ing between the two of us. The expression on Trey's face was so pained at my continued resistance to food it was al-most comical.

I flicked my eyes past him. The two cops were still in sight, stopping someone else further along the beach. I looked back and found Walt had been watching me carefully.

I smiled back at him. "Well, if you're sure, then that's very kind of you, sir," I said. "We'd love to stay for breakfast."

NINE

WALT LED US into the house through the screen door where his wife had been uneasily observing our approach. She stepped back without speaking as we trooped into her kitchen, confining whatever doubts she may have had about Walt's foolhardy actions to a single hurried look.

"Now, now, Harriet," Walt said, catching it. He hooked the Panama onto a peg by the door and dumped the bag of shells on a worktop. Then he turned to face her, taking both her small hands gently in his, engulfing them completely. He was a good head taller than she was and he had to drop his chin to meet her eyes. "This young lady here's from Manchester, where Grace went to school. How could I hear that and not invite them in for some good home cooking?"

She smiled indulgently at him, but didn't look much reassured.

I moved forward and put my hand out. "I'm Charlie and this is Trey. It's very nice to meet you," I said in my best well-brought-up voice. "I've never been to America before and I'm overwhelmed by your husband's generosity in inviting us into your home like this."

Her shoulders relaxed a little. That was different, I saw. National pride was at stake. She disengaged herself from her husband and took the hand I'd offered. Her grip was firm rather than strong, the skin thin and soft.

"You're very welcome," she said. "I'll get right on it. How d'you take your coffee?"

She poured us both a cup of the real stuff from a pot on the side. I added sugar to mine to try and stop my hands from shaking, aware that I hadn't managed to keep anything down since that midday snack at the park yesterday. Besides, there's only so much adrenaline your body can produce without giving it an outlet and mine was threatening to swamp me.

Trey and I hovered and drank our coffee while Harriet cooked and Walt fussed around, setting the table and generally getting in her way. They kept up a friendly banter between the two of them as they worked together. Trey watched, fascinated.

"OK, we're nearly all set," Walt announced, putting four glasses and a jug of iced water onto the large oval table near the kitchen window. "Either of you two kids need to use the bathroom before we eat?"

I glanced down at the dirty state of my hands and took him up on the offer. He pointed me in the right direction and left me to it, which was rather more trusting than I would have been, given the circumstances.

The back of the house, the one facing the water, was almost entirely open-plan, with just an island unit between the dining kitchen and the large living room, and a study area at the far side. Two ceiling-mounted fans lazily stirred the air in the living room.

Off that room were two hallways, one of which contained the bathroom and what looked like a couple of spare bedrooms. The bathroom was clean but shabby, the short little shallow bath marked by years of hard water.

As I scrubbed my hands I glanced at my reflection in the mirror above the sink. The side of my face still looked a little bright, but you might simply have taken that for overexposure to the sun. In fact, with my reddish-blonde coloring, if I didn't take care when we were outside today it really *would* be sunburn.

I pulled back my perspective a moment and looked at my

whole face, realizing that the eyes staring steadily back at me showed no signs of guilt for what I'd done. I'd been hoping for some mark of inner torment, something to show that I was normal, that I was just like everyone else.

Not just a cold-blooded killer.

I looked away, turning to dry my hands on the towel hanging from the rail, then walked out of the bathroom taking care not to meet my eyes again.

When I got back to the kitchen I found Harriet serving up the promised blueberry pancakes. They looked more like thick Scotch pancakes than the familiar thin-style crêpes. She handed me a small jug of what appeared to be golden syrup, but turned out to be maple instead.

Walt and Trey were chatting about car stereos by the sound of it. The old man had a way of listening with his head on one side, like what you were saying was the most important thing he'd heard in ages.

It worked really well with Trey, who was sitting taller in his seat, puffed up with pride as he enthused to Walt about the big sound-off competition going on at the Ocean Center. Trey had already cut his pancakes into strips and slathered them with maple syrup. Now he abandoned his knife and started shoveling the sodden bits into his mouth with his fork, not bothering to stop talking while he ate. He shut up abruptly when I sat down.

I smiled at Harriet to cover the awkward silence. "You have a lovely house," I said. "Have you been here long?"

"Oh, since we got married," she said, fetching a plate of thin crispy bacon strips and indicating that we should dig in and help ourselves. "Walt and his daddy started building this place in the fall and we moved in in the spring, right after the wedding. Forty-five years ago next month."

"My family's been in construction going back three generations," Walt put in.

"It's been a good family home," his wife said, contented.

"It still is, by the looks of it," I said, finding that bacon went amazingly well with maple syrup. Even if it hadn't I still would have eaten it. I hadn't realized just how hungry I really was and it took some effort not to let my table manners slip to Trey's level. "Do you have a lot of grandchildren?"

Harriet frowned. "No," she said, "we've never been blessed."

Surprised, I nodded to the toys in the garden and Walt smiled.

"We foster. Y'know—kids from problem homes," he explained. "Try and set 'em back on the right path."

I thought about Sean's sister and his younger brother, who'd taken his parents' broken marriage much harder than Sean had done. His kid brother, in particular, had gone off the rails in fairly spectacular fashion the winter before. We'd since managed to retrieve him, more or less, but how either of them were going to react when they found out that the big brother they idolized was dead, I couldn't begin to guess.

"So," Walt said now, mopping his mouth with a paper napkin and sitting back in his chair, "Charlie here's from Manchester, that much I know, but that doesn't sound like an English accent you got there, Trey. Where you from, buddy?"

It was casually slipped in. If it hadn't been for the shrewd look in the old man's eyes, I wouldn't have read anything more into the question.

"Oh, well, we've lived in a bunch of different places," Trey said airily. "My dad kept us, like, moving around a lot."

I glared at him. If he was trying to make it sound like Keith was a petty criminal, he was going about it the right way. "Trey's from down near Miami," I put in quickly. "I'm just looking after him."

Now it was Trey's turn to scowl. He didn't like the idea that I was his nursemaid any better than he liked the idea that I was his bodyguard.

"Uh-huh," Walt said slowly. He poured himself a glass of water, offering the jug to the rest of us before setting it down again on the tabletop. His movements had a slow precision to them, as though he weighed the merits of each one before he did it. "So how come you were sleeping on the beach last night?" he asked.

It was a reasonable question, I couldn't argue about that. What to tell him was the problem.

"We got robbed yesterday," Trey said. And just when I thought that maybe he was starting to think on his feet at last he had to go and embroider it unnecessarily. "Four guys jumped us—with guns. Took all our money."

Harriet immediately made sympathetic noises, but I was watching Walt. His only reaction was to let his eyes flick up briefly from under those disordered eyebrows. He let his wife run on a little, then said, "Gee, that's bad luck, Charlie. So what did the cops say?"

I took another sip of coffee while I thought furiously about my answer. Damn Trey's smart comment. I hadn't a clue what the American police would be likely to have told us in such a situation. I put my cup down again. "We didn't go to them," I said at last. "The guys who mugged us threatened to come back for us if we did and anyway—" I shrugged "—we didn't have much money to give them."

"Musta had your credit cards, though—if you couldn't get yourselves a motel room last night," Walt said, apparently busying himself forking a slice of watermelon from the central platter onto his plate. "I know it's Spring Break an' all, but there's still plenty of places further out with vacancies."

For a moment I didn't answer. This was getting sticky. I glanced at Trey's worried face. "We'll sort something better out for tonight," I said. That, at least, was true.

Walt nodded at that, his eyes hooded and his face serious. "So," he went on, his voice still slow and pleasant, "was that before or after you crashed your car?"

I went utterly still, eyes fixed on Walt's face. How could I have ever thought he was just a nice friendly old man? He was ruthless. Relentless.

"Oh Walt," Harriet protested with a shaky laugh, "I'm sure you're mistaken about that."

"You were driving, young lady," he went on mildly, ignoring her. The sheer certainty in his tone sent the blood thumping in my ears.

"Whatever gives you that idea?" I asked, hearing the

slightly steely note that had crept into my voice, however hard I tried to maintain my neutrality.

He had been trimming the skin off his watermelon with one of the table knives, and now he used the rounded blade as a pointer, waving it toward my bare forearms where they rested on the table top.

"When the airbag went off it burned along the inside of your arms as it deployed," he said conversationally. "I've seen it happen plenty before. It's one of the sure signs if the driver and passenger have tried to swap places after the event."

"I see," I said, unable to stop myself shifting my hands into my lap. If I'd remembered my upbringing and kept my elbows off the table to start with, I reflected, I might not have been rumbled. "You seem very well-informed about the mechanics of road traffic accidents for a third-generation construction worker."

"Walt never followed his daddy into the construction business," Harriet said. She was sitting very straight and very still, I saw. Her voice was unnaturally calm and clear. "After the navy he spent twenty-five years with the Bureau."

The Bureau. Even a non-American like me knew that meant the Federal Bureau of Investigation. Shit. We'd escaped from the cops and walked straight into the arms of the silver FBI.

I pushed my chair back and stood up. Trey followed suit, almost scrambling to his feet. Walt and his wife didn't move to rise with us and they both kept their hands still. Harriet's jaw was tight. I hated being the cause of her sudden fear.

"We're really very grateful to you for feeding us," I said, giving her a small smile, "but unfortunately we really must be leaving now."

I backed toward the door we'd come in by, pushing the kid ahead of me. Trey shuffled, as though he could hardly move under his own steam.

As I reached it, Walt asked sadly, "What do you think you're gonna achieve by running, Charlie?"

"Right now? Staying alive," I said, flat.

"Maybe I can help."

I shook my head. "The people we're dealing with have no compunction about killing bystanders," I said. "This is not your fight, Walt. You'd be better off staying out of it."

"If you change your mind, call me. I mean it. Any time— day or night," he said and reeled off a ten-digit number. "You want me to write that down?"

"I can remember it," Trey said. I glanced at him and he shrugged. "I got a head for figures."

I pushed open the screen door and thrust him out into the garden. As I stepped through it myself Walt threw me a final question.

"This trouble you're in—it's that bad, huh?"

I gave him a grim smile. "Keep watching the news," I said.

We spent most of the rest of the morning lurking on the beach around the busy Boardwalk area, which was like an old-fashioned seaside promenade, complete with a pier. We tried to stay out of the way of anyone who looked vaguely official and I gave all the wrinklies a wide berth, too. However harmless they might first appear.

Closer to the center of Daytona, where South Atlantic crossed over and became North Atlantic Avenue, there was a funfair with one of these contraptions that turns people into human bungee balls. They winch a circular cage down to ground level, strap you in, then release it. The cage goes catapulting up into the sky, suspended by elastic from two support towers. Trey was desperate to give it a try.

I had no desire to become reacquainted with my breakfast so soon after eating it, but I talked him out of having a go on the grounds of poor security.

"If the police spot us when we're up there, we're sitting ducks," I told him. Thankfully, he seemed to believe me.

By ten-thirty, in any case, he was itching to get to the sound-off at the Ocean Center to meet his friends. We crossed back to the west side of the main drag, braving five lanes of traffic that didn't seem to pay any attention to the WALK/ DON'T WALK pedestrian signals at the crossings.

The police were everywhere. I kept my head down and hoped that some quirk of fate didn't make the Sig slip out of its place behind my belt and clatter to the floor in front of one of them.

The banners strung across the front of the Ocean Center announced, "SPRING BREAK NATIONALS—THE WORLD'S MOST FAMOUS SOUND-OFF." If I'd never heard of it before, I couldn't help but hear it now.

There were half a dozen wild-looking cars spread across the expanse of concrete in front of the building. They had amazing paint and graphics, the kind of thing I'd only seen at custom bike shows in the UK. We walked past a Cadillac Escalade with chrome wheels that, according to the tire size, were a mind-boggling twenty-four inches in diameter. The truck was riding so low that I couldn't have got four fingers between the side rail and the ground. How on earth did they drive them?

I'd never been particularly interested in cars. To me they were a means to an end. A preferable way to travel, but only if it was snowing, or the rain was being driven down horizontally. If it wasn't, I would far rather have used my bike.

But nobody seemed to be looking at the vehicles themselves. They were too interested in the outlandish stereos inside them. Each competed for the crowd's attention with the system wound up louder than the last. They made the whole of my chest cavity vibrate just walking past.

The kids weren't content with that, though. They wanted to actually cram their heads into the interior, which struck me as an occupation only slightly less risky than trying to train a bunch of sharks to take morsels of food out of your mouth.

Either way you were likely to lose your head.

In spite of my misgivings, we paid our entrance fee on the door and moved into the building itself. I stuck my nose in one of the programs they were handing out so I had a viable excuse not to be looking at any of the security guards in the lobby area.

Back when I was in the army I spent plenty of time out on the ranges during live-firing exercises. Since then, I'd worked nightclub doors, found myself in the thick of an urban riot and involved in a full-blown firefight, but nothing prepared me for the sheer barrage of noise inside the Ocean Center.

It had started out life as music but when a hundred different sound systems are all playing a hundred different tunes, it gets hard to tell. All you could feel was the pound of the bass.

There were customized vehicles of every type, from monster civilian versions of US military Hummers to new-shape Mini Coopers, even a Ferrari and a couple of full-dress Harleys, though I couldn't quite see the reason for the bikes at a car stereo show.

Inside, the main conference hall was a huge open space, now filled with stands from equipment and accessory manufacturers. They varied from little more than a cloth-covered table laid out with boxes of product, to elaborate modular structures with space for two or three vehicles. One stand even seemed to be strung with inflatable small green aliens. I didn't quite get the significance but no one else was acting like it was out of the ordinary.

The place was heaving with people, mainly teenagers perhaps a few years older than Trey. They didn't seem at all bothered by the din, although when I looked closer I saw that quite a few of them were wearing little yellow ear defenders like the ones I'd used for shooting in the past. I still had a load of them at home but it wasn't something I'd ever thought to pack for this trip.

I reached forward and tapped Trey on the shoulder as we wended our way through the crowd, putting my mouth close to his ear. "Where are we supposed to meet your friends?" I bellowed.

He pointed over into a corner of the huge conference center hall. "By the main stage," he yelled back. "Yeah—there they are!"

There seemed to be any number of people clustered round the raised stage area, sitting on the floor and sipping cola or eating junk food from the nearby concession stand, so I didn't immediately spot Trey's mates. It was only when one of them noticed him and waved that I got the idea.

There were three of them, two boys and a girl. The girl jumped to her feet and came bouncing over to greet Trey, wrapping herself onto his arm like bindweed and eyeing me up suspiciously.

"So, who's this?" she asked, arching her eyebrows. She had a mass of ringleted dark hair and smooth caramel-colored skin and, purely in my subjective opinion, way too much makeup for someone her age.

She was wearing shorts and a microscopic little crop top. The latter showed off a flat tanned midriff at the front and a painful-looking tattoo of a rising sun at the bottom of her spine. I could hear her chewing her gum even over the background noise.

"Oh, this is Charlie," Trey said, trying to be cool and casual, like he was introducing me to his posse. "Charlie, meet the guys—Scott, Xander, and this is Aimee."

Scott was taller than Trey but just as gawky, with short spiky hair dyed an aggressive white blond and studs through the left-hand side of his nose, his eyebrow and the middle of his chin. His shorts came down to below his knees, showing only a small section of tanned calf between the hem of the legs and the tops of his absurdly large basketball boots.

Xander was a little shorter, his skin a deep Caribbean black and badly pockmarked by teenage acne. His hair was shorn to within five mil of his scalp and had intricate designs and swirls razor-cut down to his skin.

He was wearing a *No Fear* T-shirt that advised anyone who read it to "drive it like you stole it." When he grinned in welcome he revealed a gold tooth in his upper set. None of them looked older than about seventeen.

I kept only part of my attention on the group as Xander and Scott went through some mystic teenage ritual of slapping palms with Trey rather than shaking hands. I was painfully aware that the two cops on the beach had come within a hair's breadth of catching us this morning and I didn't want to get caught napping like that again.

"What's happening, man?" Xander asked. "Your message was kinda cryptic."

"We're in big trouble," Trey said impressively. He was going for nonchalant but his pride took the edge off it. "Got the cops on our tail and we need a place to hide out for a coupla days, 'til the heat's off, y'know?"

The boys were nodding sagely, pretending that this kind of situation arose for them all the time. I didn't like to break the mood by telling them that with four people dead it was likely to take longer than a few days for the manhunt to subside.

I hadn't seen any news reports to know if they'd connected the couple at the motel with the dead cop. When they did, things were going to get thoroughly nasty. Always supposing that Walt and his wife hadn't already brought in the cops. Or his former colleagues in the FBI.

"Cool," Scott said. "My mom and dad are in the Carolinas. You can crash at my place."

"So, what have you done, Trey?" Aimee asked with a giggle.

Trey glanced at me for guidance but I kept my face expressionless. They were his friends and I was interested to see what story he'd come up with.

"Dad's gone AWOL," he said at last, "and there's these guys after us. They shot a cop down in Lauderdale but we, like, got away." He saw the shock register on their faces and swallowed. "It's kinda hard to explain here."

I let my eyes slide away from him and roam over the sea of faces around us, looking for anyone who was staring too hard. Anyone who seemed to be trying to remember if that Identikit picture they'd seen on the TV this morning might really be one of us.

And then, over near one of the exits, I saw the pair of cops, led by a security guard in a uniform blue blazer. They were pointing their arms like they were designating a search area and talking into hand-held radios.

I moved forward and nudged Trey's arm. "Time to go," I said, loud enough to be heard.

This time he didn't question my reasons, just looked round for the cops.

"You got your truck, man?" he asked Scott.

Scott shrugged and jerked his thumb. "In the back lot," he said. "We leaving already?"

"Unless you want to watch us being arrested," I told him, "I think that would be a very good idea."

But as we started to move toward the closest exit the doors opened and another couple of cops walked in. If it hadn't been for the press of people, Trey's sudden about-turn would have been more than enough to flag our whereabouts.

They could have been responding to some other emergency in the hall, but I very much doubted it. Someone—most likely some sharp-eyed security guard—had spotted us on the way in. Getting out might prove somewhat more problematic.

We pushed and hurried our way through to where the crowd was thickest. A whole swathe of it seemed to be gravitating toward one of the big industrial doors that led out of the main hall and into a corralled outdoor arena.

We allowed them to sweep us along and carry us out into the blazing sunlight, hoping it would be enough to cover our escape. Then, just when I was beginning to get my hopes up, the advance of people slowed and stopped.

They seemed to be gathering round a big electronic scoreboard and PA system that was set up in a corner of one of the parking areas. I glanced behind us and spotted a couple of peaked caps in among the baseball hats, heading in our direction, but without the urgency to suggest they'd actually spotted us. I kept pushing Trey toward the forward edge of the crowd, trying to put as many bodies between us and authority as I could.

Eventually we came up against a steel barrier fence, about waist high. On the other side a fat little Chevy van was pulled up in front of the scoreboard, surrounded by what looked like a ground crew. One of them was holding a control box, with a thick bundle of wires leading to a socket behind a fuel filler cap on the van's rear panel.

Then the guy who was manning the PA said, "Hit it!" and every panel on the van began to buzz. Somewhere in the depths of the vehicle, muffled like it was buried under rock, there came an incredible deep bass rumble. The ground seemed to be jumping under my feet. I stuck my fingers in my ears but it didn't seem to do much good.

The electronic scoreboard shot up to 165.3 and stuck there. The guy with the control box shrugged and shook his head and shut the system down. Everybody clapped and whistled.

Xander was standing next to me, cheering.

"What the hell is this?" I demanded.

"IdBL," he said. When he saw my totally blank look, he sighed and added, "It's a competition for measuring who has the loudest, most kick-ass system, you understand what I'm saying? Whose system kicks the hardest."

"And how hard does this one kick?" I asked, risking a quick scan for the police, then turning back to the van. The crew were unclamping the doors and taking the measuring microphone and its stand out of the interior.

Xander nodded to the scoreboard. "Says it right there— 165.3dB."

"Is that dB as in decibels?" I said. He nodded again. "Christ, that's more than enough to kill you if you sat in there."

Xander smiled serenely. "Yeah," he crowed. "How cool is that?"

Further to my right, another cop appeared. Or it could have been one of the same cops. I wasn't paying attention to their faces. I turned away from him, and saw another away to my left. At least they were still searching, I saw. They didn't know how close they were.

In front of us, the crew with the van had finished uncoupling it and were now positioning themselves around the body, starting to wheel it slowly out of the arena and toward the parking area beyond. Clearly all that stereo equipment hadn't left any room for an engine.

"Come on," I said, and squeezed through a gap between the barriers.

The five of us gathered round the back bumper of the van, heads down as we helped push. There were a couple of event officials sitting under sunshades on folding chairs between the arena and the car park but they were paying more attention to stopping unauthorized people getting in than they were to stopping unauthorized people going out.

We kept pushing until the van's crew steered it into their pit space in the parking area and nosed it to a halt.

"Hey, thanks, guys," said the kid who'd been operating the controls.

"No problem," Xander said. "Good score, man."

Scott fished into one of the front pockets of his shorts for his car keys. The pocket was so long he had to bend down to reach the bottom of it. We threaded our way between the cars and trailers and trucks in the competitor car park until we reached the far end. He pressed his alarm remote and the lights flashed on a lowered Dodge pickup with blacked out windows and a mountain of colored beads hanging from the door mirrors.

I wondered how five of us were going to fit into the pickup cab, but Xander and Aimee climbed straight into the rear load bed. Trey and I piled onto the front bench seat, with Scott behind the wheel. He cranked the engine up and roared out of the car park, raising a cloud of white sandy dust.

"I think it might be a good idea if you tried *not* to get pulled over for driving like a prat, don't you?" I said mildly.

"She means a dork," Trey supplied when he looked puzzled. "She's from England," he added.

"Oh, er, yeah," Scott said, but at least he drove more sedately out onto the road behind the Ocean Center. As we joined the jam of stationary traffic waiting for the next lights, a couple of police cars came screaming into the car park we'd just left. The cops jumped out and went running into the exhibition hall.

I was suddenly glad of the tinted windows. Trey slunk down in his seat and put his elbow on the door frame so he could partly cover his face with his hand. The lights took forever to change in our favor. We all held our breath.

Finally, they flipped onto green. Scott gunned the motor and as we turned out onto the main road he gave a whoop of relief.

"Man, that was a close one," he said, grinning as he reached for his sunglasses which were hanging from the rearview mirror.

He flicked the stereo on to a local hard rock station and started slapping the top of the steering wheel in time to the music. "Tell you one thing," he added, "if you're gonna be around here a few days, we are gonna *have* to do something about a disguise for you two."

It was the first sensible thing I'd heard him say.

TEN

"PINK?" I SAID, allowing the disgust to win out clear in my voice. "Of all the colors you could have chosen, and you went for *pink*?"

"Aw, c'mon, Charlie!" Aimee said and I could tell from the suppressed laughter in her voice that she'd been the one behind it. "I think you'll look kinda cool."

"We're supposed to be keeping a low profile, not making prats of ourselves," I said sourly. "Who the hell has pink hair?"

Aimee started to giggle, hiding her mouth behind her hand like she was still in junior school, setting Trey off as well. I wanted to knock both their heads together.

We were in the upstairs den of Scott's parents' place in Ormond Beach. Having said that, the house was actually a bungalow, like so many in Florida, with dark glass windows and a huge arched porch over the front door. The exterior stucco was painted salmon pink, so I suppose that should have been a warning of things to come.

The house was on a quiet residential side street of properties similar in size, if not in style. Scott had driven his pickup right up to the doors of the built-in triple garage at the left-hand side of the main entrance. He'd waited impatiently while the automatic mechanism ploddingly cranked the door up out of the way, then drove straight in, braking hard enough to make the tires squeak on the painted concrete floor. The garage door slowly closed again behind us.

However Scott's parents made their living, they clearly
weren't doing too badly out of it, I reflected, as he led us
through a utility room and into the house itself. It was another
mainly white interior, enlivened by a sprawling collection of
Native American art and sculptures.

The hallway opened out into an open-plan lounge, dining
room and kitchen. A massive picture window ran floor to
vaulted ceiling on the opposite wall, giving a view into the
greenery of the garden outside. To one side was an open-tread
staircase leading to a loft that looked down onto the lounge
below.

I don't know how long his folks had been away, but the
house showed obvious signs of lone teenage occupation. Dirty
clothes littered the cream leather corner sofa and a mess of
old takeaway food containers was strewn across the glass-
topped dining table, along with empty cans of high-energy
soft drink. Like kids in the States really *need* that extra hit of
sugar and caffeine.

Scott made straight for the stairs and we followed him up to
what turned out to be the den, complete with computer and
games console. Scott had yet more sugar-loaded pop in a
mini-fridge up there, too. So the poor lamb didn't have to
traipse all that way down to the kitchen when he got thirsty.
He chucked everybody a can without asking if they had a
preference, and slumped down into a chair.

"So, Trey, you wanna tell us what the fuck is going on,
man?" he asked.

I let the kid tell the story in his own way without interruption, mainly because I was curious to hear his take on it. And
from the way he described the last twenty-four hours I almost
managed to recognize them as the same ones I'd also been
through.

What was interesting was how much he emphasized my
role in the proceedings. Mind you, he built his own part up
some, too. No mention was made of the fact I'd had to practically carry him away from Oakley man at the theme park, or
drag him out of the crashed Mercury. On the other hand, I
hadn't realized he'd witnessed quite so much detail of the

shoot-out with the men in the Buick. It had clearly made a lasting impression.

"You should have seen it, man," he enthused, coming half out of his chair and gesturing with his arms as he recounted the tale. "She just jumps out of the car and caps this guy, like, blam, blam! And he goes down and we take off and, like, just steal a bike and head up to Daytona."

He paused, nodding, to slurp from his can of drink. The other three were sitting tense and still, hanging on his every word. Trey looked at their absorbed faces and I saw his ego start to climb at the respect he was getting.

"So you're a bodyguard, right, Charlie?" Xander said, eyeing me up and down. "Like, for real?"

I took a sip of my drink, trying not to wince as my teeth instantly began to melt, and nodded in reply.

He looked at me for a moment longer, a smile beginning to form. It was as if he just *knew* he was having his leg pulled and didn't want to come across as too gullible, but there was this edge of doubt there, too. Eventually he sat back and looked at Trey and laughed. "No shit, man?"

"You shoulda seen her last night on the beach," Trey said, a trace of defensive anger in his tone now. "These guys came after our dough, like, with a knife. And Charlie, she just tore them apart. Go on," he added to me, "show 'em how you did it."

I raised one eyebrow, not making any moves to comply. "I am not," I said mildly, "a performing seal."

Trey colored at that, but pushed on regardless. "She was in the military, right? She rocks, man, I'm telling you."

This last seemed to convince them a little. At least enough not to express their skepticism out loud. Maybe women played a more active role in the US forces so there wasn't quite the same resistance I'd always encountered.

But I could feel their excitement more than their apprehension and it scared me. In spite of Trey's lurid reconstruction, they hadn't the faintest idea how serious this all was. They were just a bunch of middle-class kids pretending to be gangsters, playing at rebellion.

Maybe they would never have agreed so readily to help us

if they'd stopped to think. I offered a silent cynical prayer of thanks that none of them were great thinkers.

One thing that everyone agreed on was that we needed to do something about our appearance. Xander offered to take Scott's truck down to the nearest superstore and bring back enough stuff to change our hair and clothing, and to try to make me blend in with the rest of the Spring Break crowd.

As soon as shopping was mentioned, Aimee jumped at the chance to go with him. She looked critically at my tired secondhand shirt and grubby shorts and said, "Trust me, girl, you *need* some help."

After they'd gone Scott unearthed the remote, switching on the giant projector TV in the lounge and channel-hopping until he found a news report. We soon discovered we'd made the headlines in a big way.

"Broward County police are today mourning the loss of one of their fellow officers, gunned down in the line of duty last night," said the serious-voiced but plastic-faced news anchor. "The officer, who had been with the department just six months, was the victim of a brutal slaying during a routine traffic stop on the county's roads yesterday evening . . ."

The report ran on, showing a lingering hand-held night shot of the Mercury crashed in the ditch with the punched-out rear screen and the obvious bullet holes in the back end. I watched it with detached interest, as though it hadn't happened to me at all.

The logical half of my brain told me that, when they'd had a chance to properly analyze the scene, the police would know the men in the Buick had been there. The young cop hadn't got a shot off, his gun would be fully loaded and unfired. Surely they had to ask where all the rounds in the Mercury had come from?

I remembered, also, that I hadn't even thought to stop and pick up the brass shell casings the Sig's eject mechanism had scattered into the ditch. I'd been too busy running for our lives. At least if they linked those to me they should work it out that I wasn't the one who killed the cop.

Apparently not.

The sound of my own name brought me up short. In a corner of the screen, just by the newscaster's head, they'd put together a half-reasonable likeness to go with it. Having said that, the description they read out would have fitted half the female population.

The only worrying thing was they knew about the scar on my neck.

That shook me. I'd acquired the injury that had caused it nearly a year and a half before. It was a permanent and sobering reminder of how easy it would be to get myself killed.

Since I'd started working for Sean, the glamorous Madeleine had taken me under her wing as far as the use of makeup was concerned. Given enough opportunity and a shelf full of wickedly expensive cosmetics I could now make a tolerable job of concealing the scar unless you were right up close. But I was still self-conscious about it.

Since I'd arrived in Florida I'd been very careful to avoid awkward questions from Gerri Raybourn's men by keeping it covered up beneath polo and standard shirt collars.

I'd even done my swimming in the house pool early enough in the mornings not to have the rest of the household around staring at me. It was only quite by chance that Keith Pelzner had unexpectedly come out into the lanai on the second morning and caught me in the act.

I could tell he'd spotted the scar straight away but he hadn't made any comment. Question was, had he mentioned it to anyone else? And if not, how had they found out?

". . . Broward police have also announced that Fox is wanted in connection with an earlier double homicide at a motel in the Lauderdale area that left a young couple tragically slain. They advise anyone who identifies Fox to approach only with extreme caution . . ."

"You really have a scar like that?" Scott asked, taking his eyes off the screen for a moment. Trey was looking at me, too.

Without speaking, I peeled back the collar of my shirt and showed it to them. A pale and ragged five-inch line around the base of my throat. If my neck had been a clock face, it would have run roughly from six until nine.

"How d'ya get it?" Scott said. He swallowed. "I mean, was it, like, saving someone's life?"

I had a brief mental snapshot of the moment the knife had gone in and the sheer hate on the face of the man who'd been wielding it. I'd believed completely that I was on borrowed time from then on. That nothing I did after that point mattered any more because I was already dead. I wondered if it had colored all my actions since.

"Yes," I said.

"Wow, that is intense," Scott said, shaking his head. "So you have a gun, right?"

"Yes," I said again. I wasn't trying to unnerve him by the monosyllabic answers, there just didn't seem to be any more to say.

"That's cool," Scott said. "My dad has a coupla hunting rifles but he won't let me touch them. When he and Mom went on this trip he locked them away and, like, took the key with him so—"

The shrill buzz of a mobile phone cut through the tail end of his sentence. He instinctively started looking round for his phone but to my utter amazement it was Trey who reached calmly into a pocket and pulled out a mobile.

" 'S'up?" he said into it, then handed it over to Scott. "It's Xander for you, man."

"No shit? Why didn't he call me on my own cellphone?"

"Because you left it in the truck, stupid," Trey said. "What d'you think he's using to call me on?"

Scott grabbed the phone. "Hey, Xander, get off my cellphone, asshole!" he said, laughing. " 'S'up, dude?"

As he went over by the window to have his conversation I grabbed Trey's arm and steered him to one side, out of Scott's immediate earshot. "Why the hell didn't you tell me you had your own mobile?" I demanded.

He shrugged out of my grip. "You never asked," he said, both truculent and shifty.

I rolled my eyes. "For fuck's sake, Trey," I ground out, "I lost mine in the car. There are people I could call in the UK who might be able to help us get out of this mess and I haven't been able to do it. And all this time you've had a damned mobile phone and not thought to tell me?"

"I thought you knew," he said, but he wouldn't meet my eyes. "You were the one who told me to call the guys last night. Why do that if you didn't know I had a cellular?"

"I thought you used the payphone outside the motel," I said. *Why hadn't he really told me about his mobile? What was he trying to hide?*

"Anyway," Trey said, sulky now, "I can't use my phone to call long-distance. There's, like, a block built in to it."

I sighed. "Trey, if I'm going to protect you in all of this you're really going to have to start communicating with me."

"Protect me?" he said, his voice low but scornful. "How? First you send Mr. Whitmarsh into the wrong room at the motel so they, like, kill those people who didn't have nothing to do with this. Then you crash our getaway car. You've never even done this before."

"Hang on a minute!" I stared at him in surprise. "You're the one who's been making me out to be some kind of Wonder Woman in front of your mates."

"Yeah," he said, churlish. "What did you expect me to tell them—that you're just, like, the nanny who's in way over her head? No way!"

Scott ended his call and ambled back across the lounge to hand the mobile back to Trey. "What's up?"

"I really need to call someone in the UK," I said. "Can I use the phone here?"

He looked sheepish. For a moment my temper sparked. He was prepared to help us outrun the police, but the prospect of a transatlantic phone call was too much to ask.

"I'm quite happy to pay for the call," I said through gritted teeth.

"It's not that," Scott said quickly. "It's just that, well, when my folks were up in New England skiing last winter I kinda used the phone a lot when they were away. I mean *a lot*." He glanced from one of us to the other, clearly not keen to reveal his misdemeanors in front of his friend. "Dad went ape when he got back and found out. He, like, totally lost it. So now, when they go away, they have the phone company put a block on the line. All I can do is make local phone calls 'cos, like, they're free, y'know?"

"Great," I muttered, turning away in frustration. "That's just great."

Scott stuck his hands in his back pockets, making his shoulders round. "These guys you need to get in touch with," he said, diffident. "Can't you just e-mail them?"

I turned back, slowly. I'd been a latecomer to the information super highway. I still didn't own a computer and I'd only occasionally used the ones at Sean's office to surf the Internet.

Then, I regret to say, it was usually looking for cheaper quotes for motorbike insurance, rather than sending e-mail. It just hadn't occurred to me that it was the perfect way to get in touch with Madeleine, regardless of the time difference.

"Scott," I said, smiling at him, "you're a genius."

He grinned back at me.

Trey didn't like that much, either.

The message I sent to Madeleine was short and to the point, more like a telegram than an e-mail. "Job blown up. Locals hostile. KP disappeared. TP with me. SM missing. Instructions?"

I put Scott's phone number on there as well and sent it with a certain feeling of relief, like I'd got an SOS out from a sinking ship. I hoped the whole thing wasn't too cryptic, but I was reluctant to say much more without knowing who might be monitoring e-mail traffic.

All I could do now was wait for a reply.

Then I checked my watch and realized with a sense of dejection that it was 12:37 PM, Eastern Standard Time. Add five onto that and it was just outside office hours in the UK. And on a Friday afternoon, as well. There was always a chance that Madeleine wouldn't even pick up my cry for help for another two days.

By that time, we could both be dead.

Downstairs, a door slammed and we heard chattering voices. Scott leaned over the rail and called for Xander and

Aimee to come up. Trey was still hunched over the computer keyboard, logging on to his own e-mail account.

It was at that point I discovered Aimee had bought a packet of pink hair dye that she was fully expecting to use on me.

"It's not, like, permanent," she pointed out, pouting. "It'll wash out in about a month."

I thought about the picture on the news report.

"OK," I said, resigned. "Let's get this over with."

I had to wash my hair first anyway, so they let me shower in peace in one of the guest bathrooms. I stood under a shower head the size of a dinner plate and let the hot water pummel my face and body for a long time. After twenty-four hours on the run, it felt indescribably wonderful to be clean again. I could have stayed in there for days.

Eventually, I reluctantly shut off the water and stepped out. I toweled myself roughly dry and opened one of the brown paper bags that Aimee had handed over. Inside was one of the smallest bikinis I've ever seen and a pair of flip-flops with plastic flowers on the straps—also in pink.

I glanced at the limp pile of clothes I'd discarded on the bathroom floor, but I couldn't face the prospect of putting them back on again. I wrapped myself firmly in a bath towel, draped another round my neck, then grabbed the bag and ventured back out into the lounge.

The kids were all clustered in the kitchen. Someone had switched channels so MTV was playing loudly enough in the background for you to have to raise your voice to talk over it.

Trey was on a chair in the center of the tiled floor, his hair covered in gunk. He didn't seem to have changed out of his old clothes and he certainly hadn't showered.

They all stopped talking when they saw me.

"Is this all you've bought for me to wear?" I asked, holding up the bag.

Aimee giggled. "If I'd left it to Xander—yeah," she said. Her hands were still encased in the throwaway plastic gloves she'd used to spoon the dye onto Trey's hair. She nodded to the nearest worktop, where a rake of other brown paper bags were scattered. "There should be some, like, y'know, green silk pants in there someplace."

Fearing the worst, I searched through the bags for the article described, but discovered she actually meant a pair of loose-fitting trousers in a rather restrained color that was close to olive drab. The only problem was that the waistband was held up by a drawstring that was nowhere near strong enough to contain the Sig.

I turned back and realized all four of them were watching me with a certain amount of anxiety.

"We got you a bag and a shirt, too," Aimee said hesitantly.

I kept looking. The bag was a tiny thing with straps for you to wear it on your back like a rucksack. It was just about big enough for the gun. At least the shirt had a collar, even if its shortened tails were designed to be knotted to show off your midriff, so that left no room for the Sig either.

I tried not to show impatience with them. I'm sure that concealing an illegal firearm wasn't something Aimee normally had to think about when she went clothes shopping with her pals. Considering what she *could* have picked out for me, she'd done a good job.

"That's great," I said, relieved. "Thanks."

I took my haul back into the bathroom and got dressed. The bikini top seemed at least a size too small. If I made any sudden moves, even someone of my relatively limited attributes was likely to fall out over the top of it.

I gave up on the flip-flops. The thought of trying to run anywhere in them didn't bear thinking about. Instead, I washed out my socks in the sink and hung them to dry on the towel rail. That way I could put my boots back on. The trousers sat quite low on my hips and would be plenty long enough to cover the boots when the time came.

I slipped the Sig into the backpack, together with the blade I'd taken away from the skinny kid on the beach. Just those two items filled it enough for me to have trouble closing the zip and I had to slip my Swiss Army knife into my trouser pocket. What were people actually expected to carry in these things?

By the time I was dressed and went back out again Aimee had Trey's head bent into the kitchen sink, rinsing the dye off. She glanced up and grinned at my appearance.

"You'll have to lose the shirt," she said. "I don't wanna, like, get dye all over it."

Reluctantly, I complied, shifting uneasily as Scott and Xander did a double-take at the sight of me in a bikini top. Aimee grinned again at their reaction. "I thought so," she said airily, sounding a little smug. "I got just the right size."

She suddenly seemed businesslike, less silly, as she set to on Trey with a pair of scissors and enough gusto to make me nervous. But by the time she'd finished snipping and blow-drying and gelling his hair, Trey had a short white blond spiky cut, very like Scott's. It was quite a change.

"Now why couldn't I have gone blonde as well?" I wanted to know as I sat down and prepared for my turn.

"Too close to your natural color," Aimee dismissed. She picked up a strand of my still-damp hair. "You have great hair. This *is* natural, yeah?"

"Well, it was," I murmured. She grinned and began spooning the gloop onto my head.

I had to sit still while the dye did its thing. I spent the time ignoring the chatter that was going on above my head and trying not to watch the clock and wonder if Madeleine had picked up her e-mail.

Eventually, Aimee peered closely at a bit of hair and said. "OK, you're done."

She washed it off in the sink again but I backed off when she got her scissors out.

"Aw, c'mon, Charlie, don't sweat it," she said. "I'm not gonna do yours real short like Trey. And you need it cut anyways."

So I let her do what she wanted. Whenever I've had my hair cut in the past I've always had a mirror in front of me, so I can see what they're up to, and that's when I'm dealing with professionals. This was something of a leap of faith.

It seemed to take her a long time, trimming a bit here and there. She blow-dried it and finished off by plaiting two small sections of my hair into thin braids, just above the outside corner of my right eye, with colored beads threaded onto the ends. If I turned round suddenly the beads clunked irritatingly against my cheekbone.

"I've got some more beads you can wear round your neck that will, like, cover up your scar," she told me, her voice chatty.

I made a noncommittal reply, uncomfortable having something I'd always viewed as so private discussed so publicly.

Aimee didn't stop with my hair. She fished out boxes of makeup and started smoothing it onto my face with her fingertips. I would have objected but I'd seen the length of her fingernails and didn't want to do anything that might make her jump when she was so close to my eyes.

Finally, she stood back, hands on hips as she studied me. "OK, Charlie," she said, "you're all set. Go have a look."

I stood up, brushing the bits of loose hair from my knees. Nothing seemed to stick to the silk trousers for long. I went back through to the bathroom and stared at my reflection in the mirror.

Only it wasn't me.

Aimee had done something to my face that brought my cheekbones out and made my eyes look huge. The pink hair was in more of a bob than my usual rather straggly style and, I had to admit, it really quite worked. So did the braids and the outfit.

I struck a pose, giving it some attitude and putting my hands on my hips like I'd seen Aimee do. If I worked my jaw like I was chewing gum with my mouth open, the transformation was complete. Sure, I still looked older than Trey, but not by much.

I went back out into the lounge. Aimee looked up, expectant.

I shrugged awkwardly. "It's amazing," I said. "Thank you."

She flushed and smiled, her cheeks dimpling prettily. "You're very welcome," she said.

We stayed in the house for most of what was left of the afternoon. Trey seemed to spend most of it up in the loft, either playing computer games or surfing the Internet. It was the only time I'd seen him look really at home anywhere. He seemed to lose his gawkiness when his right hand was clawed round a mouse and his eyes were locked on the screen. Mind you, then he just looked nerdy instead.

I even had a bit of a go at surfing myself, although I won't say I was anywhere near being at his level. I tried putting in a search for the name of the software company Keith Pelzner worked for. That gave me their official website, which failed to tell me much more than I'd found out from Madeleine's original report.

But it also found any references to the company, including one that I guessed must be an online edition of the financial paper article that had so annoyed Gerri on the day of my arrival.

I scanned quickly down the page. All it said was that the company was on the brink of launching a new program that would mean big things for anyone intra-day trading on the futures markets, whatever that meant. It was not only couched in wildly technical terms, but also written in a style so leaden my eyes started to glaze over by the time I was halfway down the first page.

There was still no word from Madeleine.

Later, we ordered takeaway pizza delivered to the door. You couldn't get to the surface of the dining table, so we ate with the huge boxes open on our knees, watching the news reports.

They'd expanded since the first ones we'd seen that afternoon. Now they'd linked me to the shooting at the theme park as well. *Jesus,* I thought, *how many different guns do these people think I've got?*

"Wow, this is getting wild," Xander said. He shook his head and looked speculatively at Trey. "Who'da thought it, huh?"

"Shush!"

A new face had appeared on an outside broadcast camera but I'd missed the opening introduction. Not that I needed it to recognize who she was.

"Aw crap," Trey burst out, "it's Ms. Raybourn!"

"Will you shut up," I snapped, "and let me listen!"

". . . more about the missing teenager?" the reporter was asking.

Gerri nodded, her face doing a perfect impression of serious solicitude.

"Sure," she said. "Naturally, we are extremely concerned at this time for the safety of both the Pelzners—father and son—but particularly so for Trey, who is just fifteen years old. We are appealing to the kidnappers to release the family."

"I believe you have already had some contact with the kidnappers. Can you tell us anything about their demands?"

Gerri shook her head. "Not at this time," she said. "Though clearly we are dealing with some very dangerous people and we are really looking forward to writing the bottom line on this without further loss of life."

"Like hell you are," I muttered, still reeling.

The outside broadcast cut back to the studio and the beginning of the next story. For a moment none of us reacted.

"Kidnappers?" Scott asked, looking from one of us to the other. "What the fuck do they mean, man—kidnappers?"

"I don't know," I said slowly. "I don't know what on earth Raybourn hopes to gain by trying to make out that I've kidnapped Trey—or Keith for that matter."

"*She* was the one who sent Mr. Whitmarsh after us at the motel," Trey said blankly.

I nodded. "Yeah, and they didn't manage to get us that time, or afterward, and now with that cop getting killed, it's all got well out of hand." I looked around at their faces, still and a little pale now. "If I had to guess, I'd say good old Gerri's trying to make sure she's got a suitable scapegoat ready to take the blame for whatever it is that she and your Dad are up to," I said. My lips twisted into a mocking smile. "Looks like I'm it."

ELEVEN

"SO, THE QUESTION is," I went on, "what exactly *are* they up to?"

Trey shrugged. "Dunno," he muttered, but I'd seen the way his eyes had nervously scanned across his friends, as though checking they weren't about to tell me anything he didn't want me to know.

Time to press him, then.

"Is it something to do with your mother's disappearance, do you think?" I asked carefully.

"Could be, I s'pose." He shot me a dark look, but there were no great reactions from the other kids. They clearly knew all about his theories in that direction.

The more I thought about that one, though, the less likely it seemed. If Keith was trying to cover up the murder of his wife, which had apparently passed unnoticed by the authorities for five years, why would he now try to keep it hidden by sending a hitman to kill his son in such a public place?

Surely, if he had the kind of connections Trey had hinted at, it would have been far easier to have arranged a teenage suicide or accidental drowning in the pool at the house. Why the urgency, all of a sudden?

Unless Keith had needed witnesses to the snatch of his son in order to prove its authenticity. Hell, at the time it had seemed pretty authentic to me. But if that was the case, why hadn't Keith handled his own "disappearance" better? Why let a neighbor see the van he was using to move out, and then give that same neighbor a key for the letting agent?

It didn't make sense and, worse than that, it was amateurish. And this was the man who had supposedly arranged the murder and disposal of his wife so professionally that nobody had suspected a thing for half a decade.

Or had they?

I glanced at Scott, who was frowning in concentration and clicking the back of the stud that passed through his bottom lip against his teeth. "Can we use the Internet to look up old news stories?" I said.

He looked at me with a touch of scorn, like I'd just asked if we could use a refrigerator to keep milk cold. " 'Course."

He led the way back up to the computer in the loft, with the others in pursuit. Only Trey was showing any signs of reluctance.

"OK," I said when we were there, crowded round his chair, "let's see if you can find any reference to Trey's mum. Exactly when was it, Trey?"

For a moment he scowled at me, his expression mulish, then he muttered, "Five years last January."

He gave out information with all the joy of a kid forced to share his last packet of sweets. Scott went onto one of the local newspaper sites and tapped in the full name of Trey's mother and the area of Daytona where they'd been living at the time.

Nothing came up.

He tried again with other news sources, but each time we drew a blank. It was like the woman had never existed. And the more he tried, the more twitchy Trey became.

"*See?*" he said at last, a little snappy. "Like I told you— she's dead, OK? *He* made her disappear. What did you think you were gonna find?"

"This doesn't prove she's dead," I said gently. "There's still a chance that she might have just left of her own accord."

I'd meant it to appease him but it had the opposite effect. Trey's face shut down, turning white, then as pink as my hair. He swung round, body rigid like he was ready for a fight.

"Take it back!" he yelled, in my face, shaking now. "She would never have left me! You take it back!"

I didn't react, didn't say anything at all, but I didn't back off, either. After a few moments, some small manifestation of sanity seemed to tap Trey on the shoulder and whisper in his ear that maybe taking me on wasn't such a good idea. The anger faded into nervousness and his eyes flickered away. He turned and slouched down the stairs into the living room, throwing himself onto the sofa. Aimee pulled a face and went after him.

Xander let his breath out through his teeth. "Phew, you sure know how to go stirring up trouble, Charlie," he said quietly, shaking his head. "Trey's real touchy about his mom."

Scott gave up on his searches and sat back, staring moodily at the computer screen. "If his dad *is* tied in with some government agency then you wouldn't expect to, like, find any trace of her," he said slowly, almost to himself. "They can just wipe anybody off the face of the earth."

"Yes, OK," I allowed, "but what's Keith doing that's so vital to the US government that they would go to those lengths to protect him?" I looked from one of the boys to the other, but they just shrugged. "He's just a computer programmer who writes financial software, not anything for the military."

For a moment the only noise in the loft was Scott clicking that stud against his teeth again. Downstairs, over the drift of MTV I could hear the earnest murmur of Aimee's voice, giving Trey a pep talk.

I sighed. Keith Pelzner worked in an industry where talent made you rich and the bottom line was that he wasn't a wealthy man. The house in Lauderdale had been rented by the company who employed him. He'd flashed his cash around but even that had all been provided by them. So what made him important enough for this?

It just didn't fit together. I couldn't reconcile a geek like Keith, however talented a programmer he might be, playing any role vital to national security. Nothing that would explain armed men being sent out to try and kill his son, at any rate. I saw again the man in the Buick falling. I pushed it away.

"Try another search for me, would you?"

"OK," Scott said, sitting forward again, "but we've been through just about everything I can think of."

"This one's just for any reports on a man's body turning up in the last twenty-four hours. He'll have been shot."

Scott glanced at me and his eyes gleamed as the realization hit of exactly who I was looking for. He bent over his keyboard with fresh vigor, his fingers rippling across the keys. He went back and checked most of the same places where he'd just been looking for any sign of Trey's mother. We came up with the same result. Nothing.

"He's probably gator food by now, man," Xander said with a certain amount of relish. "Plenty of places in Florida to get rid of a body, if you know where to go." He glanced at me sideways. "That's if you're *sure* you really wasted him, huh?"

"I'm sure," I said. I'd known instinctively as soon as I'd shot the man in the Buick that he was dead. There was something about the way he'd dropped, the sound he'd made. I couldn't quite put my finger on it, but I'd known, nevertheless. Now it seemed that whoever he'd been working for was big enough, or powerful enough, to dispose of the body without leaving a trace.

Did that just make them organized?

Or did it make them federal?

I looked at the boys, found them watching me expectantly. "Maybe," I said slowly, "we can't discount some kind of government involvement after all."

"All right!" Scott whooped, punching the air and grinning. "I just *knew* this was a big conspiracy."

Aimee reappeared at the top of the stairs at that point, with Trey trailing behind her. He wasn't quite dragging the toes of his scuffed trainers along the carpet as he came, but it was a pretty close-run thing.

"Hey, man," Xander said, clapping him on the shoulder, "looks like this is all part of some major cover-up. You know what that means, huh?"

The four of them looked at each other with the air of cartoon characters who are just about to rip off their shirts to reveal they're all wearing different colored superhero costumes underneath.

"We need Henry," Trey said. He even managed to raise a smile.

"Who the hell is Henry?" I demanded.

For a moment none of them spoke, just stood and grinned inanely at each other. The way kids do when there's an in-joke on the go and you're firmly on the outside of it.

Finally, it was Scott who took pity on me. Maybe he was just a better judge than the others of how far I could be pushed without exploding.

"Henry's this really cool guy who moderates a site about conspiracy theories—y'know, who shot JFK, is the government covering up the existence of aliens, all that kinda stuff."

"Henry will know what's going on," Xander put in firmly. "He's the man."

I shrugged. I didn't like it, but *still* there was no word from Madeleine. What other choices did I have?

Scott sent a cryptic e-mail to the mysterious Henry asking only if he could shed any light on events currently in the news. Whatever my personal doubts about contacting a stranger, at least he was paying more attention to his e-mail than Madeleine.

A reply came winging straight back. It was misspelt and curiously constructed, but at least it was prompt.

scott, if told u evrything i know about wots going on behind evry news story, wed be hear forevr, it said. *specifics?!*

"Hang on a moment," I said as Scott reached for the keyboard again. "What exactly do you know about this guy?"

"Oh he's, like, ex-CIA," Scott said airily, trying to be ultra casual. "He worked in Iraq and the Middle East and he was in Kuwait during Desert Storm."

"So says he," I muttered under my breath. I had a nagging feeling in the back of my mind about this. I didn't know much about the CIA, but I'm sure they at least require their personnel to be able to pass a basic literacy test.

Scott was waiting, expectant, his hands hovering over the keys. "Well?" he said. "Do I tell him, or what?"

Trey flashed me a defiant glance. "Yeah," he said. "What have we got to lose?"

So Scott typed in, *Trey and Keith Pelzner.*

Almost as soon as he'd sent it, Henry was back again. *both been kidnapped,* he'd put, *keiths work v intresting. i no lot of hi up folk love to see him fail. software co in big truble without him!*

"See?" Trey said as soon as he'd read the message. "He's plugged right in, I'm telling you."

"Not quite," I said. To Scott I added, "Try telling him that Trey hasn't been kidnapped. Tell him that he's right here."

I glanced at Trey while Scott tapped in the words. The kid was looking even more morose than usual, head down, hands stuffed into his pockets. Mind you, the way Aimee was clinging on to his arm and murmuring in his ear, maybe he didn't have a reason to drop the troubled teen act.

It took Henry longer to reply this time and when he did, his e-mail seemed to have more attention to it.

u r in big truble. i can help. i can negotiate on yr behalf. MUST meet with u! trust nobody!

He didn't say if this last was himself included, but I was way ahead of him on that one.

"He's never suggested a meet before—like, *never,*" Scott said, sounding slightly awed. "What you wanna do?"

Trey sighed and rolled his eyes, as you would if someone's just asked a stupid question to which the answer is obvious. "Like, *yeah,*" he said. He didn't even glance at me for confirmation.

Where and when? Scott sent.

Henry must have been poised over the keys waiting for an answer. He came back right away, naming a small bar near the Port Orange Marina, on the Atlantic side of the Intracoastal Waterway that separated the Beach Shores from the rest of Daytona. *be in parkng lot in 27 mins,* he'd added. *i in red vette. come alone.*

"No way," I said. For the start, specifying such an exact

time smacked of pretension. Like someone who's watched too many spy movies, rather than someone who's ever been involved in the real thing. Secondly, if you're involved in the undercover world you don't drive round in a red Corvette. You have some sludge-colored invisible saloon. And as for the "come alone" bit, he must think Trey was even more stupid than he . . .

"I gotta go!" Trey said, his voice whiny. "Your people never even got back to you, so how can—"

"Trey, I'm not trying to stop you going," I said, cutting him off in mid-whinge, "but no way are you going on your own. I'm coming with you."

"He told me to come *alone*," Trey muttered, sulky.

I moved across to him and linked my arm through his on the side that wasn't already attached to Aimee. "You'll just have to tell him you'd got a hot date then," I said, "won't you?"

Aimee pointedly disengaged herself. "That might work," she told him, smiling sweetly. "If he believes you go for *much* older women . . ."

Scott dropped us off just outside the marina twenty minutes later. Xander wanted to lurk nearby to catch a glimpse of their mysterious hero but Trey was against the idea.

"He'll spot you right off," he complained, "and then he won't show."

The others reluctantly agreed that someone with Henry's eclectic espionage background was bound to check out the area thoroughly before he made contact. They withdrew to the safety of a diner two blocks away and said they'd wait for Trey to call.

Trey and I waited in silence in the shadows, listening to the rumble of traffic over the bridge behind us. I'd noticed a sign on the way across that told me it was the Congressman William V. Chapell Jr. Memorial Bridge. Some memorial.

Everywhere was the buzz and click of exotic insects. There was a slight breeze coming up from the water that stirred around my bare midriff. Underfoot, the dark asphalt was still warm from soaking up the sun all day. It was now slowly giving out heat like it was exhaling.

My body was tense but a part of my mind was on standby. It began pondering on the completely different outlook that was required when you lived in a consistently hot climate like Florida, knowing you can rely on the weather most of the time. It might be constantly sunny, but it was also harsh and somehow unforgiving.

I thought of my bikes sitting at home, the new Honda not yet seriously ridden because I didn't want the final dregs of the winter road salt to pit its pristine aluminum frame. The last time I'd seen it seemed a long time ago.

A sudden image of Sean rose up out of nowhere. A brief snapshot of a country house restaurant he'd taken me to the month before, near Henley-on-Thames. Perhaps it was the very Englishness of it, against such a setting, that had sparked off the memory.

I'd dressed up for the occasion, probably the first time Sean had seen my legs in public. We'd eaten in an elegant high-ceilinged dining room, our table lit by a pair of tall silver candlesticks. The cool ivory linen was so starched the napkin had barely drooped when the waiter had laid it across my lap.

And afterward, when they'd cleared the debris of our meal, I'd glanced up and found Sean watching me intently and frowning.

"What is it?" I'd asked.

"You do realize," he'd said carefully, twirling the stem of his wine glass between those long and clever fingers, "that what you're proposing to do for a living is not exactly the safest profession in the world, don't you, Charlie?"

It was the first time he'd voiced it out loud and that had made me pause a moment before I'd replied.

"Yes," I'd said, my voice calm, "but I also know what I am." I shrugged, a little helplessly. "What else would you suggest I do with it?"

He'd smiled. One of those slow-burning smiles that made the blood thump in my ears so hard I could hardly hear other people speaking because of it.

Nobody observing us then—just another absorbed couple out for another quiet supper—would have guessed the violence that laced our history. Sean slid into the cultured skin very well. It hadn't come naturally to him, but he'd persevered until it fitted and perhaps because of that there was always an air of contained force, of submerged danger about him. He had taught himself how to walk the thin line between civilization and savagery and was just as at home on either side.

And he was just too good at what he did to have been taken out so easily. I had to cling to that thought.

Or what else was there for me to live for?

The vision snapped shut again, its passing riffling the air like the closing pages of a heavy book. I blinked and the hazy reflections of the flames against hallmarked silverware and gilt-edged bone china re-formed into the glitter of streetlights on the darkened water.

Trey nudged my arm. "He's here," he said.

A red Corvette swung a touch too fast into the parking area, its tires letting out a protesting squeak as it made the turn.

I haven't come across a lot of Corvettes, but even I could tell this wasn't a collector's item. It was just at that age where it's too old to be a new car, but not old enough to be a true classic. At that moment it was probably languishing right at the bottom of its depreciation curve.

The body was mostly red, as though its owner had got halfway through rubbing it down and then got bored with the idea. When he pulled up and cut the engine, one of the pop-up headlights didn't close all the way. The car looked like an outclassed boxer at the end of a tough fight.

Trey took a step forward but I grabbed his arm and kept him in the shadows. I had the bag Aimee had given me slung over my shoulder and I'd already partly unzipped it. Now I put my hand inside and curled my fingers around the Sig's pistol grip.

"Let's just see what he does," I murmured.

The driver climbed out and peered around him, like his night vision wasn't too good. Henry was both younger and fatter than I'd pictured him. Even in the light air he was sweating noticeably.

"Hey, Trey!" he yelled, turning a slow circle. "You out there, man?"

I pulled Trey further into cover behind a parked minivan. "The guy's a total waster," I whispered, trying to keep my disgust mostly hidden. "The nearest he's ever got to the CIA is watching a Tom Clancy movie. Let's get out of here."

Trey yanked his arm out of my grip and glared at me, shifting to the corner of the van so he could take another look at Henry.

"Hey, c'mon, Trey," Henry called, his voice still louder than I was happy about. He wiped the back of his hand across his mouth. What did he have to be so nervous about?

"Hey, either you want to know about your old man or you don't, but don't fuck me around, huh?"

That did it. Trey lunged round the corner of the van before I could stop him and trotted out toward the Corvette. Cursing under my breath, I followed.

It took Henry a while after he'd spotted Trey to notice me. His eyes narrowed.

"I thought I told you to come alone," he said.

Trey half glanced over his shoulder and mumbled something that included the word "girlfriend" but I didn't catch the rest of it.

"Oh, OK then." Henry smiled wolfishly at me, looking everywhere but at my face. It was the kind of smile that makes you want to go and scrub yourself down with an abrasive cleaner afterward. I tried not to let that show.

He turned back to the car. "You'll have to cozy up some, then," he said. "This baby's only a two seater."

"Like, where are we going?" I asked, copying the rising inflection the American kids used when they spoke. Trey looked at me sharply but didn't comment. Henry didn't seem to notice anything amiss.

"My hide-out," he said. "I keep a little place a few blocks from here."

I hesitated, but Trey was already opening the Corvette's passenger door and climbing in. It was either drag him out of there by force or go along with it, even if allowing yourself to be taken from a relatively public place to a private one of someone else's choosing was madness in these circumstances. It went against everything I'd ever taught or learned, but I reminded myself that I was the kid's bodyguard. If he went, I went. It was as simple as that.

With a sigh I climbed in with Trey, uncomfortably aware of his bony body pressing against me and the fact that I probably weighed more than he did.

Henry eased his bulk behind the wheel and grinned at the way we were tangled together alongside him. I'd tried to keep the bag reachable but, even so, I doubted I could actually get to the gun to use it if I had to.

That jolted me. In the course of a few days I'd gone from never carrying a gun to being unhappy to be parted from it.

We set off, the poor old Corvette's engine occasionally firing on all the cylinders it was supposed to. The inside of the car smelt of old cigarettes and damp. Henry drove sitting upright, hunched over the steering wheel. He glanced sideways at us a couple of times once we were out on the road, still smiling.

"You've done a real good job on those disguises," he said casually, his tongue flicking out to wet his lips. "I wouldn't have recognized either of you from the pictures on the TV."

Either of you. My heart started to belt against my ribs. Maybe Henry wasn't quite as dumb as he first appeared.

When neither of us responded, Henry said, "You sure don't look like a kidnapper—Charlie, isn't it?" I gave him the briefest nod. "So what's your angle?"

"I'm just supposed to be looking out for him," I said. It was a compromise statement. I knew Trey would object to my saying I was looking *after* him.

Henry nodded sagely. "You wanna tell me your side of the story?" he asked.

I gave him the edited highlights in the sketchiest form possible, little more than the fact that someone was seriously out to get Trey and there was the possibility that the authorities were involved.

"Well, they're sure putting out a different story to yours,"

Henry commented when I was done. He turned off the road into a dimly-lit residential street. "Ah, here we are. Home, sweet home."

The street was in a run-down district. I didn't have to know much about the demographic of Daytona to guess it wasn't exactly an up-and-coming area. Most people seemed to have a dead pickup truck on their front lawn and there weren't enough wheels to go round.

Henry swung left off the road and brought the Corvette to a halt in the dirt driveway of an ugly single-story building with a covered porch along the front. The whole structure was raised a couple of feet off the ground, like a mobile home that's had its wheels removed. A patchwork of trellis covered the gap between the base and the earth.

The house itself looked like some of the worst council-owned dives I've seen in the UK. Trey and I struggled out of the passenger seat and followed him up the uneven steps onto the porch.

"C'mon in," he said when he finally managed to wrestle his own front door open. He went ahead, flicking on lights to illuminate a dingy little one-bedroomed house. There was no air-conditioning inside and the wet heat clenched itself around me as soon as I stepped through the door. I swear I saw something that was the size and color of a stoned date with legs skitter across the cracked floor tiles.

Henry led the way through into what might once have been the living room, but was now packed with computer equipment. It looked like a complicated setup and, judging by the way the cases gleamed, most of it was fairly new. I couldn't see anything staying spotless for long in that environment. Henry had set up a couple of fans that were stirring the turgid air around rather than actually cooling it.

The lone battered-looking typist's chair, its cushion repaired with silver duct tape, was the only place to sit down in the entire room if you discounted the floor, which I already had. Henry eased himself into it with a sigh of relief to be off his feet again and picked up part of a cold hamburger that was sitting congealing in its wrapper next to his keyboard.

"So, any ideas who's holding Keith Pelzner?" he asked, biting off a chunk and beginning to chew.

Trey didn't answer, so I said, "As far as we can tell, no one's holding him."

Henry's jaws stopped working for a moment. He swallowed, then said, "You mean he's gotten loose?"

"No," I said, "I mean it doesn't appear he was ever kidnapped in the first place."

Henry put the remains of his hamburger down again, very slowly, and distractedly wiped his hands on the front of his shirt. It clearly wasn't the first time he'd used his clothing as a napkin. And all the time his eyes skated from side to side as though he was scanning a document only he could see. One that brought him very bad news. His lips were moving but for a while no sound came out, then he muttered, "Crap in a hat," very softly, under his breath.

"Why do I get the feeling the fact that Keith Pelzner has apparently disappeared of his own accord is not exactly what you wanted to hear?"

Henry jerked to his feet, hands to his face now. I thought of the residual hamburger grease on his fingers and tried not to squirm.

"Why?" he echoed, faintly at first, then with growing vehemence. "Why? Because the only goddamn reason for him to run is if it doesn't work, that's why!"

"If what doesn't work?" I asked blankly. Henry spun to face me, checking out Trey's reaction to all this on the way. I glanced at the kid myself but he'd hung his head like he'd retreated into himself. No clues there, then.

"You mean you have no idea what Pelzner was working on?" Henry demanded, surprise making his voice rise and spraying me with flecks of half-chewed burger.

I backed off a step and shook my head.

Henry turned away and groped for the arm of his chair, lowering his bulk into it again. He took a moment to gather his thoughts.

"OK," he said. "Keith Pelzner's a computer programmer, yeah?"

"You can skip the part about the earth cooling and the fish learning to walk," I said. "I know he's a programmer and I know he was working on something to do with the financial markets. Take it from there."

He reached for the hamburger again, a reflex action, but when he got it to his mouth he suddenly seemed to realize what he'd done and plonked it back on the desktop. "This new program he's been working on is dynamite." He looked at me then, a little haughty. "I don't s'pose you know the details, right?"

I would have loved to have been able to tell him he was wrong but he wasn't, so I had to take it on the chin and simply shake my head.

"OK, there are a lot of financial programs out there that track the stock markets," he said. "They've gotten to the stage now where they're pretty sophisticated, yeah? They're based on mathematical algorithms. They follow the trends and use stuff like Fibonacci fan lines and moving averages to try and indicate whether the stock price is going to rise or fall, so you know whether to buy or sell, yeah?"

He glanced at me, checking I was with him so far. I nodded encouragingly to show him I was just about keeping up.

"OK," he went on, "but all these programs do is track. What Keith Pelzner was working on was a system that could take into account stuff like current affairs, financial reports from around the world, news, and could actually predict what was going to happen to the stock prices. Not guess—predict. We're talking software that's capable of learning from its mistakes, here. We're talking artificial intelligence. I'm dumbing down, you understand?"

"I understand," I said, a little tartly. I paused. "So, this program—do you reckon it's worth killing people over?"

Henry sat back in his chair and looked at me with his mouth open. "I don't think you've grasped the concept here, huh?" he said. "If you got a hold of this program you could trade the futures markets with absolute certainty, yeah?" He stopped, searching for the right way to penetrate my tiny little brain.

"Look, say you were going to day-trade contracts on the

futures market, like the S&P 500, yeah? You think the market's gonna go up, you go into a long trade. You think it's gonna go down, you go into a short trade, yeah?"

"Yeah," I said slowly. He was losing me but I didn't want to interrupt the flow.

"OK, so if you're ahead of the game and you know when to go long and when to go short, then every time the market rises or falls in your favor, you make two hundred and fifty bucks a point, right? It don't matter if it rises or falls, just so long as you're in a trade heading in the right direction, you're making dough."

"And how far is it likely to rise or fall in a day?" I said.

"Hey, good question. You're a bright cookie, Charlie, you know that?" he said, wagging a knowing finger at me. "The S&P will only maybe move five or ten points, but if you can jump on the back of every one of them you could be making fifty points a week, easy."

I did some fast mental arithmetic. "That's twelve and a half grand a week," I murmured. Even converting back out of dollars into sterling, that wasn't a bad whack.

"Sure it is," Henry said. "And that's on one contract, yeah? Supposing you were trading ten contracts, or a hundred? It's a license to print money and it's perfectly legit. They can't touch you for it."

He grinned slyly as he watched my face go blank with the realization of just what was at stake here. "You asked if this program was worth killing someone for, yeah? Well, if it hada worked, I tell you, I woulda killed my own grandmother to get a hold of it. In a heartbeat!"

For a second there was silence. I stood in Henry's rank little living room and let the consequences of what he'd told me seep slowly into my brain like blood into the dirt.

More than a million dollars a week.

Every week.

Legally.

Holy shit.

I looked up. "But the fact that Keith's done a runner . . ." I murmured.

"Yeah, you're on it," Henry said bitterly. "Why would he run unless he can't get the bugs out of the system and he knows that he's never gonna be able to make it work? Hell, the company he's working for has banked every last cent on it. They're practically bust. I been following this pretty close, y'know? When I heard he'd been kidnapped I thought he musta finally cracked it. But now—" he broke off, shaking his head. He sounded close to tears.

And then, behind me, Trey cleared his throat.

"It works," he said. It was the first time he'd spoken. "I know it works," he repeated, more firmly this time. We both turned to stare at him and he muttered, "I know 'cos I've, like, tried it out myself."

TWELVE

FOR A FULL five seconds after Trey made his announcement, nobody spoke, then Henry said faintly, "What do you mean, you've *tried* it?"

Trey shrugged again, kicking at the curling edge of the mat with studied casualness. "Dad wanted to integrate a neural network into the program, which is, like, artificial intelligence," he added to me, with that airily precocious tone I disliked so much. "He did all the setup on it, but he couldn't get results that were, like, consistent enough and he gave up on it. So I've been kinda playing around with it some."

"And you've gotten it to work," Henry said. It was a statement, not a question, with a touch of something in his tone that could have been wonder.

"Not yet," Trey admitted, coloring, "but I'm real close. I reckon Dad just expected it to learn real quick. He just kinda underestimated how long you gotta spend hitting the neural net with data before it learns the patterns, breaks it down into numbers. It just needed more time, that's all."

"Your dad must be real proud of you," Henry said. I glanced at him sharply but his face was as guarded as his voice.

Trey flushed. "He doesn't know," he said. "Not how far I've gotten with it, anyhow. I've been kinda working on it someplace else—where he wouldn't hang over my shoulder all the time, y'know?"

"Bet that took some processor power," Henry said, and Trey nodded.

"So that's why you were nicking stuff from that computer shop at the Galleria," I put in and he flushed again.

"Dad's never believed I can do anything," he threw back at me, and the old whiny note was back well in evidence. "Even when I was a kid, he'd buy me model aircraft and stuff, then he'd kinda take them off me and put them together himself. It was like he never trusted me to do it right."

"So nobody knows you've been working on this alongside your dad?" Henry said. There was something calculating about him now. "You've done this all by yourself?"

"Yeah," Trey said, defiant.

Henry shook his head, smiling. "That is outstanding," he said at last. "Absolutely outstanding. I would sure love to see some of what you've done."

Trey stared at him for a moment as the realization of actual adult approval settled on him. "No problem," he said, his enthusiasm bubbling over. "It's all with—"

"Hold it right there," I cut in. I turned to Henry who quickly hid his flash of annoyance at my interruption. "You're the one who told us to trust no one. What makes you an exception to that rule?" I demanded. "Half the people we thought we could trust have been trying to kill us over the last twenty-four hours and now—finally—I think I know why." I glared briefly at Trey. He dropped my gaze like a hot brick. "You said you could help us, Henry. Well before Trey goes handing over anything, I think you should show us how exactly you intend to do that."

Henry pulled a rueful face. "OK, OK, I can appreciate your caution. And you're right, why should you trust me?" He leaned back in his chair. The frame creaked under the strain. For a moment he just smiled at us, spreading his palms wide. I could almost hear his brain turning over furiously while he tried to think up a good reason. At last, he said, "Let me just ask you this, Charlie—what other choices do you have, huh?"

I didn't answer. Silence is always the best course of action if you don't have anything worthwhile to say.

"Face it, you *need* help," he said. "I been watching the

news. I know the kinda crap you're in. You need to negotiate some kinda deal with the people who are after you, otherwise you're gonna be running for the rest of your lives." He sat forward again, intent. The sweat prickled across his upper lip, forming a pale mustache of perspiration. "I can do that. I can negotiate that deal for you."

"How?"

Henry indicated the array of computer equipment surrounding him. "Check it out," he said with pride. "I can reach anyone with this setup, anywhere in the world."

"How are you going to find them? We don't even know for sure who they are," I said, ignoring Trey's quick wriggle of dissent.

Henry gave me a crafty look. "I got a few ideas where to start. I been following the story kinda closely and besides—" he tapped the side of his nose with a forefinger "—I've kinda done this sorta work before."

"Yeah, so I've been told," I said, cynical. "Desert Storm, wasn't it? You must have been about twelve at the time."

He had the grace to color, glancing at Trey. "Yeah, well," he said, shrugging, "the kids go for that kinda thing. Sometimes you gotta embellish a little, y'know? Adds to the rep."

I regarded him for a moment with my head on one side. "So what's your angle, Henry? Why are you offering to help us?"

"Easy—I want a copy of that program," he said, and his voice had hardened now. "Maybe a little startup capital, too—though I can round up enough to get me started," he added hastily when he saw the warning glint in my eye.

I raised an eyebrow at Trey. After all, he had more say over what happened to this program than I did.

The kid shrugged. "OK," he mumbled. "I guess."

"OK," I said to Henry. "You've got a deal." I gave him the number of Trey's phone. "Call us when you have something to tell us, OK?"

"No problemo," he said, struggling to his feet. He was almost bouncing now, his glee almost uncontained. "You won't regret this."

"I hope not," I said, keeping my gaze flat and my voice cool. "I sincerely hope not."

I declined Henry's offer of a return trip to the car park by the bridge in the ailing Corvette. Instead, we left on foot. Trey phoned Scott as soon as we were off the front porch and we walked to intercept him.

Apart from that brief call, Trey trudged along in silence with his head bowed and his hands deep into his pockets. I left him to ferment his thoughts for half a block or so before I butted in.

"Why didn't you tell me about the program?" I said quietly. "Why all that bullshit about your dad working for the government, hm?"

He didn't answer right away. In fact, he took so long I nearly repeated the question. Finally, he looked over and regarded me gravely.

"I guess I was scared to, like, tell you the truth," he said at last and his voice sounded raw, teetering on the edge of tears.

"Scared?" I echoed, nonplussed. "Scared I'd do what?"

He hunched his shoulders. "Want it for yourself, I guess," he said.

I thought of Henry's greedy face and nodded slowly. It was a reasonable fear, I supposed.

"Trey," I said. "My first duty is to protect you. Everything else comes after that."

"Yeah," he muttered. "Whatever."

Stung, I grabbed his arm and yanked him to face me. "No, I'm serious," I snapped. "Don't just dismiss me like that. This is what I do. It's what I am."

Trey met my eyes for a moment, his face stubborn with his disbelief. "Yeah," he said. "Just like Ms. Raybourn and Mr. Whitmarsh and Chris, huh?"

For a moment I didn't reply. What could I say to him?

He pulled out of my grasp and spun away so I wouldn't see him crying. I let him weep. I suppose, in the circumstances, I would have felt pretty gutted, too.

• • •

Scott picked us up two blocks away from Henry's place. His shiny Dodge looked too cool and too new in the shabby neighborhood where all the cars had a two-tone thing going between the paint and the rust.

Scott clearly wasn't prepared to wait until we got back to the house before hearing all about the meet. He jumped straight in with a hundred questions. Aimee and Xander had shifted to the back to let Trey and me have the seats in the cab, but it didn't stop them chiming in through the small sliding window behind us. They were too full of themselves to notice that Trey wasn't contributing much to the general conversation.

I took my lead from the boy, giving brief answers that were as vague and noncommittal as I could get away with.

Eventually, Scott shook his head in exasperation.

"I swear to God, man, that Henry must be some piece of work," he said, and I could still hear the excitement running through his voice, just under the surface. "One meeting and you're even giving us the whole Big Secret thing, huh?"

"There's nothing to tell," I said. "He promised to help." But I was watching Trey as I said it and I couldn't help wondering—if Henry was the answer to all our prayers—why the kid suddenly looked set to cut his own throat.

It was late by the time we got back to Scott's place. The opportunity to sleep somewhere clean and comfortable, and relatively safe, was too tempting to pass up on. I left the kids sprawled in front of the TV and turned in.

I wasn't sure if I was supposed to unravel the beaded bits in my ridiculous pink hair, but felt stupid asking so I left them as they were, but I dropped the necklace Aimee had provided in a heap on the bedside table. I took the Sig out of the little backpack and shoved it under the pillow, just in case.

I undressed slowly, weary beyond words. The guest room had mirrors on the wall behind the double bed headboard. The sight of my strange reflection kept catching me out, like someone else was in the room with me.

I climbed into bed and was just reaching for the light switch when there was a hurried tap on the door. Before I could speak it opened and Aimee stuck her head round.

"Oh hi," she said. "I was kinda hoping I'd catch you. Can we talk?"

I sat up, trying not to hug the bedclothes around me too prudishly.

"Help yourself," I said, waving a hand toward the end of the bed.

She came in, closing the door behind her. Instead of sitting down she came and stood by the bed with her hands in her back pockets. It made her shoulders hunch forward awkwardly. Her eyes kept dropping down past my chin, then popping back up again, nervous.

I sighed. "What's on your mind, Aimee?"

"I was just wondering what—" she broke off, thought some and tried again. "How did you get that scar?"

I was silent for a moment, mentally arguing over whether to tell her the truth, a convenient lie, or simply to tell her to mind her own bloody business.

"Someone jumped me," I said at last, watching her face. "They tried to cut my throat."

She nodded without showing surprise. There was little more than curiosity in her voice as she asked, "What happened to them?"

Now that question I wasn't sure I was prepared to answer. "Why?" I hedged.

"Well, aren't you scared that one day they'll, like, come back?"

Now there was one thing I could be sure of . . .

"No," I said.

"Oh." She eyed me for a few moments, then nodded and started to turn away.

"Why the quiz?" I asked as she reached the door.

She shrugged. "I just wanted to know that Trey's gonna be OK. I've known him since we were six—like, forever," she added. "His birthday and mine are a week apart, so when he lived up here we used to have, like, joint parties and stuff. He's the brother I never had."

The mention of birthdays sparked a memory. "So you were around when his mother disappeared?" I asked. She nodded. "You remember anything about it?"

Another shrug. "Not really," she said. "I know what Trey thinks might've happened, but I heard my mom and dad talking about it, a while after. They said she was always gonna go sometime—Trey's mom, I mean. She just never liked giving up her job to bring up a kid. I think she resented him, or something. He just can't see it, that's all."

"Yeah well, parents can give you the impression they think you're a waste of space sometimes," I said tiredly, thinking of the ups and downs I'd been through with my own. "I think it's part of their job description."

She smiled, with that slightly worried look behind her eyes, like she didn't really get the joke.

"So, you feel any more reassured?" I asked.

She frowned for a moment, hesitating.

"Aimee," I said, straight and steady. "I won't let anything happen to him—or any of the rest of you, for that matter. Not if I can help it."

She carried on frowning for a moment, her eyes flicking over my face. "Yeah," she said, then, slowly, "I guess you won't."

I watched the door close behind her and debated in passing on turning the key but quickly dismissed the idea. If anything happened in the night, I didn't want to have to waste time fumbling with the lock.

I reached up and killed the light but sleep eluded me. I lay awake in the gloom, my eyes just about able to make out the twirl of the ceiling fan above me, and let my restless mind roam. A good many questions had been answered tonight, but at the same time just as many new queries had been thrown up.

I struggled to stop my mind turning things over, so that when I eventually drifted into sleep, it was edgy, fitful and disturbed by savage dreams. I woke distressed, reaching for Sean, only to find the bed beside me cold and empty.

Saturday morning dawned with that hazy brightness of English midsummer, which seemed to indicate it was going to grow up into another hot and sunny day. Did it ever do anything else round here?

I was up and showered and dressed by seven, so I sat out on the small screened rear deck, drinking coffee and watching the nimble little geckoes flit across the concrete path just beyond the mesh.

From where I was sitting I could hear but not see the neighbors. Over to my right the kids had been bribed into washing the family speedboat. They were using a hose with a spray nozzle on the end of it and the exercise soon degenerated into a shrieking water fight. Then it all went suddenly quiet and I heard the murmur of adult voices. Just when I thought the kids were getting a ticking off for the noise and the mess, hostilities resumed. By the sounds of the squealing laughter, the parents had now joined in.

I tried to picture my father, a consultant surgeon, or my mother, a Justice of the Peace, indulging in such juvenile behavior but my imagination wasn't up to it.

I wondered what their reaction would be when they heard it on the news that their daughter was wanted for murder and armed kidnapping. It would have been reassuring to have known, without the shadow of doubt, that they'd support and defend me regardless. Past experience, however, told me they would probably want overwhelming proof before they'd believe my side of the story about what had really happened.

I sat and wallowed in a little bitter remembering, the way you'd kick your heels in a muddy puddle, just for badness. It took a while before I'd got it out of my system and stopped feeling sorry for myself. It might be dirty water but it was all under the bridge now. My relationship with my parents had certainly improved lately, even if it hadn't quite recovered completely.

Unlike Trey's.

Trey had claimed that his father must have set him up at the Galleria—that he'd arranged in some way for Oakley man and his partner to catch him shoplifting. I wasn't actually convinced that the boy *hadn't* been stealing. By all accounts it wasn't the first time he'd been brought home in disgrace for petty theft. The chances were, if he hadn't been doing anything wrong on that particular day, then he was caught for something he'd got away with in the past.

But if Keith had paid Oakley man to snatch his son, why not do it then, when the boy was alone? Why wait until he had his own bodyguard, however inept they believed me to be?

It simply didn't make sense.

I made a mental note to grill Trey for the details on his arrest when he surfaced, then I went into the kitchen and poured myself another coffee.

I had to wait another hour before Scott appeared, by which time I was back out on the deck, soaking up the shaded heat. He poked his head round the open sliding-glass door with his hair sticking up more haphazardly than it did normally. How *do* teenagers do that?

"Hi," he said, groggy and sounding slightly gurgling, like his throat was full of phlegm. "You wanna Coke?"

I indicated my coffee cup and shook my head. He withdrew back into the house. That was the last I saw of anyone until after nine, when Xander and Aimee rang the front door bell.

Scott let them in. He was wearing the same clothes he had on yesterday. So was I, come to that, but he had a choice.

"So," Xander said, rubbing his hands together. "What's the plan for today, man?"

I shrugged. "We wait for either Henry to call, or Madeleine to e-mail," I said. "Then we act on whatever happens first."

Xander looked deflated. "You're not gonna spend all day hanging around the house?" he said, making it a question. "It's Spring Break, man!"

Scott shuffled, looking uncomfortable. "I guess she's right—we oughta stay put," he said miserably.

Xander and Aimee both cast reproachful eyes in my direction. When I couldn't stand the guilt they were putting onto me any longer, I retreated back out onto the deck with yet another coffee. At the rate I was consuming caffeine, I wasn't going to sleep for a week.

I hadn't time to finish my cup when Trey slid the door open and came out. I could tell by the set of his face, and the fact that he shut the door behind him, that he was there for an argument.

"I wanna go out," he announced, scowling. It was as much of a shock to see him with his startling white hair as it was to see myself. "I don't see why we have to sit around on our butts all day. When Henry knows anything, he'll call."

I sat back in my chair and looked at him for a moment. He hadn't mentioned the possibility of missing contact from Madeleine, and neither did I. "So, the fact that between us we're wanted for murder by half the police in the state has no bearing on this?" I said mildly.

He glowered some more, his bottom lip starting to edge out.

I sighed. "Where do you want to go?"

"Excellent!" He flashed me a fast grin, his expression changing in a second, like he'd flicked a switch.

"Don't get all excited," I said, scowling myself now. "It was only a question." Then I noticed the other three standing up close to the inside of the sliding door, flattening their noses against the glass and crossing their eyes.

Trey saw them and his grin widened. "Looks like you're kinda outnumbered," he said.

I sighed again, heavier this time and got to my feet. "Story of my life," I said.

In the end, we compromised. We spent the morning at the house, which included Aimee reapplying my makeup disguise, then climbed into Scott's Dodge and headed for the main strip, and the action.

Scott checked his e-mail just before we left the house, but

there was still nothing from England. I think I was halfway resigned to the fact that we weren't going to hear anything until
Monday morning. I just hoped that Henry hadn't managed to
get us into even more trouble by then.

We had brunch at a little diner on the corner where Earl
Street met North Atlantic Avenue. The five of us sat at a table
outside, shaded from the sun by a giant umbrella. All the kids
with the flash cars were cruising past along North Atlantic,
playing their music loud and fighting over who looked the
coolest in the heat.

Some of the cars were fitted with hydraulic suspension. If
they thought they had an audience, the drivers made them hop
and bounce along the road, occasionally lifting one wheel off
the ground completely like a giant mechanical dog in search
of a very large tree. I marveled at the ingenuity and wondered
at the point.

There were bikes, too, big custom-painted Japanese stuff,
mostly ridden by suntanned kids wearing little more than
swimming costumes. I was wincing too hard at the prospect
of gravel rash if they came off to be impressed by the rolling
burn-outs they indulged in. When they stopped I could see
they'd worn their back tires almost completely flat in the center, which would have made the bikes go round corners like a
drunken tea trolley. I started to feel old and sensible.

The cops were a heavy presence but their eyes seemed to
glide over the group of us as we sat there, drinking malted
milk shakes like we hadn't a care in the world. The white
spiked hair made Scott and Trey look enough like brothers to
avert suspicion and Aimee's work on me was holding up under the strain. Besides, weird-colored hair seemed to be the
order of the day round here. I almost began to relax.

And then Trey's phone rang.

"Yeah?" he said and mouthed, "It's Henry," at me. I
hutched closer, putting my head next to his so I could listen
in on the call.

"I've had a response from the people we were talking
about," I heard Henry say, "but they want proof I've got, er,
access to you. They wanna e-mail you a coupla questions and

you gotta be here to answer right off. You gotta get down here in half an hour, or the deal's off. You understand?" He was talking fast, his voice breathless.

Trey glanced at me. I shrugged, then nodded.

"OK," Trey said. "No problem."

"Outstanding," Henry squawked. "Remember—don't be late or the deal is off. These people are kinda serious."

"We're on our way," Trey said and ended the call.

Yeah, a voice in my head piped up, *but to what?*

Scott was already on his feet, dropping a few dollars onto the table. "All right," he said, "let's roll."

As the others pushed back their chairs I held my hands up. "Hang on a moment," I said and everybody stilled. "Henry asked just for Trey. Now Trey doesn't go anywhere without me, but that doesn't mean all of us are going."

Xander pulled a face. "Aw, c'mon, man," he moaned. "You can't shut us out now."

I caught Aimee's glance, looked away. "I can't look after all of you," I said.

"We're not asking you to," Scott said quickly. "It's just—" He broke off, slumping back down into his chair and grimacing as he searched for the right words.

"Don't cut us out of this—not now," Xander said with a note of quiet pleading in his voice. "You can't let us get close to the action when it suits you, man, and then kinda dump us when it don't, y'know."

I looked at Aimee again, hoping she would be the voice of reason. She just smiled and picked the keys to Scott's pickup off the table. "You *don't* take us with you," she said sweetly, swinging the keys tantalizingly from one finger, "and how you gonna get there in time?"

Getting to Henry's place in time was the thing that proved the most difficult. After my reluctant capitulation Scott retrieved his Dodge from the car park behind the Ocean Center where he'd left it and edged out into the slow-moving traffic on North Atlantic. It had snarled to a crawl, not helped by the police cruisers which seemed to be pulling over an unending stream of cars into the center lane and booking them on the spot.

After fifteen minutes we'd barely made three blocks and I had to make a conscious effort not to look at my watch every thirty seconds. Besides, Scott was looking nervous enough for all of us, fingers beating a relentless tattoo on the top of the steering wheel.

"Aw, come *on*, will ya?" he kept muttering through clenched teeth as he forced his way into a gap that didn't really exist in the next lane on the grounds it had moved six inches further forward than the one we were in. The driver he'd just cut up blew his horn and gave him the finger.

"Same to you, asshole!" Scott shouted into the rearview mirror.

Four cars ahead of us a traffic cop was writing a ticket for some other poor unlucky driver at the next intersection.

"Hey, calm down," I said, eyeing the cop. "The last thing we need right now is for you to get involved in a road rage punch-up."

Unfortunately, the cop's attention had been grabbed by the horn and the raised voices. I saw a pair of sunglasses swing in our direction as his head came up. *Christ, why did they all wear dark glasses?* I started to pray silently that he'd let it ride, ignore us.

I should have known we wouldn't be that lucky.

As the lights changed and Scott began to move forward, the cop pointed firmly at the Dodge and then to the center lane with a contemptuous flick of his wrist. His manner had an overwhelming authority about it. I could feel Scott start to cringe in his seat.

"What do I do?" he asked, his voice tight with either excitement or fear. "You want me to make a break for it?"

I looked at the sea of creeping vehicles that surrounded us. The cop's partner had joined him now and he was staring in our direction, hand drifting toward his hip in a reflex gesture. There was another police car waiting in a motel forecourt less than two hundred meters further on.

Alongside me, both Scott and Trey had turned as pale as

their hair. Aimee and Xander were kneeling behind the cab, their faces pressed in through the sliding window. They looked scared.

I glanced down. The Sig was in the open bag on my lap. I had four rounds left.

I couldn't risk it. I couldn't risk them.

I sighed. "No," I said, aware of a sickly taste in my mouth. "I think we'd better see if we can talk our way out of this one. Just do what he wants, Scott. Pull over."

THIRTEEN

IN THE END, the cops neither recognized nor arrested any of us.

They read Scott the riot act about lane discipline and proper signaling, and they made a big deal out of checking the truck over but in some ways it was all routine. We were just the latest in a long line of kids they'd booked that weekend for some minor violation or another. Not the first and definitely not last by any means. They didn't even bother to search the rest of us and they didn't ask for ID.

As soon as I realized there was nothing sinister about the stop, I felt the muscles across my shoulders begin to unlock, one by one. I took my hand off the pistol grip of the gun in the bag and propped my elbow on the edge of the door instead, resting my chin on my palm. Then I sat in my side of the cab and chewed gum with my mouth open and tried to look teenage and bored.

Scott stood in front of the Dodge, between the two cops. His whole body language was submissive, head bowed, hands clasped behind him. Every now and again he stole a glance back into the cab. If the cops had been a little more on the ball they should have taken that as a cue to rip the inside apart looking for a stash of soft drugs at the very least. I suppose the kid must just have had an honest face.

And all the while, the seconds ticked on into minutes. By the time ten had passed, Trey had started to fidget.

"I'm gonna call him," he whispered to me, talking out of the side of his mouth. "I gotta tell him we're gonna be late."

He eased the phone out of his pocket and started flicking through the buttons, but soon discovered that Henry's number had been withheld. I realized that an e-mail address was the only contact we had for the man. OK, we could find his house again, but being able to give directions doesn't generally mean much to Directory Inquiries, unless the US version was much more accommodating than it was at home.

Trey held the phone in front of him, so tense that it almost vibrated in his hands, hoping for another call. But as Henry's deadline approached he didn't make contact again.

With the engine, and therefore the air-conditioning switched off, the heat expanded inside the pickup cab until it was crushing us into our seats. It didn't seem to make any difference that the windows were all open. In fact, that probably made it worse.

By the time the first cop finally handed Scott his ticket and told him to beat it and to be more careful in future, we were already twenty minutes beyond our half-hour maximum time limit.

Scott climbed back into the cab, looking very pink around the ears as he twisted the ignition key.

"For God's sake don't spin the wheels setting off," I said quietly, "or we'll be here all day."

He threw me a miserable glance but drove away with commendable sedateness, still clutching the crumpled ticket in his right hand.

"Jeez," he said, close to tears, once we were on the move again. "I'm real sorry, guys. I let you down."

"It was just luck," I said, pinching Trey's arm when he opened his mouth to disagree. "Just be thankful they didn't do a full search." I threw him a quick reassuring smile. "And don't worry about it. It could have been worse."

Me and my mouth.

* * *

Once we were away from the main crush Scott put his foot down, but it still took another six minutes to reach Henry's street.

Scott turned in so hard the truck gave a little wriggle as the suspension overloaded. In the back Aimee and Xander were clinging on to the side panels and laughing to each other like it was an amusement park ride.

As we sped along the street I was checking out parked cars and empty driveways, comparing the layout against the mental image I'd snapped the last time we were there. It all seemed quiet, normal, with no new cars too smart for the area, no suspicious vans. I was aware of a slight disorientation, even so, in trying to overlay my nighttime memory onto daylight.

Following Trey's directions, Scott pulled up hard enough in front of Henry's run-down house to have the neighbors twitching. If this had been the kind of estate where the neighbors bothered taking notice of what people got up to.

The place looked worse in the harsh sunlight. The wooden siding of the house itself had once been done pale blue, as though with paint left over from a swimming pool. The broken trellis that skirted the bottom pretended to be white, as did the window trims and the wooden supports for the porch, which leaned very slightly over at an angle. This gave the effect that the whole structure was collapsing slowly sideways off the front of the house. For all I knew, that might have been the case.

My bag was still unzipped, ready. I swung it onto my shoulder as I opened the passenger door. "I suppose it's pointless to tell you to stay in the car?" I said but I wasn't really expecting an answer. Besides, the four of them had already hopped out onto the dusty dirt driveway. The sight of their ready grins made me scowl.

I led the way past the battered Corvette and up the rickety steps. I leaned on the bell, hearing it ring through the house but no one came to answer. We stood like that for a few moments, waiting. The kids' grins had become a little more forced now and they began to squabble in a lighthearted undertone among themselves.

I tuned out the bickering, wishing they were anywhere but behind me on this. All the time I let my eyes drift across the scene over the road from Henry's place but there was nobody in sight. It jarred.

Saturday afternoon and nobody in sight. Not a single person. Not even a dog. As soon as we'd hit the end of the street something had spooked me and now I knew what it was.

Henry had been very specific about time. Why? Anyone needing proof of his connection to Trey couldn't reasonably have expected him to have the kid on tap, instantly available, so why the tight deadline? Why the urgency? Unless . . .

My heart had begun to pump again, setting that tingle along my forearms, that shiver between my shoulders. I dropped my right hand nonchalantly into the open bag hanging from my shoulder as I pulled open the outer screen door with my left.

The inner door was old, the paint faded although with two tough-looking shiny locks at different heights along the leading edge. When I tried the handle, it turned without resistance and the door opened.

I heard Xander suck in a breath. "Man, are you sure we should—"

"Shut up," I murmured, and nudged the door all the way wide. It swung slowly back against the wall of the hallway, revealing the same grotty little living space. The door at the end of the corridor was the only one closed. I took one step across the threshold but that was all I needed before I knew the smell.

When I brought my hand out of the bag the Sig was in it. I shrugged the bag onto the floor. Without looking over my shoulder I said tightly, "Get back in the truck. Turn it round and have the engine running."

They didn't argue with me. Maybe they'd caught the odor too, even if they couldn't identify it. Living in a climate like Florida's, how can you fail to recognize the smell of death for what it is?

"Is it—is it him?" Trey's hushed voice by my shoulder sounded a little wavery.

I glanced back at him, took in the pale but determined face and didn't repeat my last order.

"Yes, I think so," I said. "You up to this?"

He nodded once and I wasn't going to ask him again. Together we took the few short steps along the hallway and opened the door to Henry's lair.

The man of the house was sitting in the chair where we'd last seen him, amid a sea of wreckage and destruction.

And blood.

Henry's massive torso had been tied into position with nylon rope and his wrists had been handcuffed to the metal arms of the chair, then double-secured with silver duct tape around his forearms. They must have needed the two methods of holding him down while they methodically broke every one of his fingers.

They'd gagged him while they'd done it, wrapping more duct tape around his face, half covering one ear. It was tight enough to distort Henry's bulging cheeks and make his jaw sag, like his whole head was being squeezed in the middle. The dirty dishcloth they'd forced into his mouth was just visible beneath the lower corner of the tape, poking out like a lizard tongue.

His head was slumped forward so his chins rested on his chest. His eyes were closed, but I didn't bother to check for a pulse. After the men who'd tortured him had finished extracting whatever he had to give them, they'd put a single bullet through the center of his forehead. They'd held the barrel close enough for the explosive discharge to tattoo an imprint into his flesh around the small neat hole. Henry would, without a doubt, have known exactly what was coming to him.

It hadn't been a small caliber gun they'd used, either. The impact had lifted off the back of his skull, radically redecorating the window and far wall of the room in the process. The round had kept going, scattering the slats of the venetian blind and taking out the small center pane of glass, then traveling on to God knows where in the trees beyond.

Behind me I heard a slithering bump and I turned to find Trey had concertina'd slowly down the door jamb. He was still clutching desperately at the woodwork even after his skinny rump had hit the floor.

I opened my mouth to say something but realized there wasn't much I could say that was going to help in a situation like this. I stepped carefully further into the room, trying to keep my feet out of the blood. The flinty taste of it was sharp on the back of my tongue as I breathed.

So that was why Henry had sounded breathless on the phone.

Not excitement. Not greed.

Pain.

Poor bastard.

But who had done this to him? And were they still waiting around to do the same to us?

With an acute awareness of time passing, I eyed what was left of Henry's prized computer array. Every piece of it had been trashed and I didn't know nearly enough about them to work out if anything could be salvaged from the ruins. But I was damned if I was going to come this far and leave with nothing. I turned back to Trey. He hadn't moved a muscle.

"Trey," I said, loudly. "Would any of this gear still work?"

He shook his head a little as if to clear it, like a boxer who's just taken a good strong combination to the jaw and is doing his best, against all expectation, to stay in the fight.

"Wha-what?"

"Henry's computers," I said, slow and clear. "Would any of them still work enough for us to find out who he was in contact with?"

"I dunno," Trey said, unable to take his eyes off the corpse. It was the hands, I noticed, more than the head that bothered him. It seemed such a deliberately sadistic act to take the hands of a man who lived by the dexterity of his fingers.

I moved in front of the boy, blocking the vision. "Trey," I said again, bending over him. "We don't have much time. Think about it."

It took him a moment to refocus on me, like an old camera struggling to follow the action. "We might get something off of the hard drive, I guess," he said at last.

"Great," I said, giving him an encouraging smile. "Where do I find it and what does it look like?"

"Them," he said. He cleared his throat. "He was using three separate systems. They'll each have a hard drive, and he could have a back-up unit somewhere as well."

"Three plus a back-up?" I repeated. I glanced at my watch. This was all taking much too long. "OK, where are they likely to be?"

Trey shook his head again but just when I was about to snap at him he dragged himself to his feet and wiped his nose across the back of his hand. "Last time we were here I kinda noticed that he only had one machine connected to the Net," he said.

I shrugged. "Meaning?"

"Less chance of picking up a virus and if you do, you don't, like, lose your whole setup, like you would if they were all networked together." He nodded toward one of the tower units on the far side of the room, carefully avoiding what lay between him and it. "That's the only one plugged into a phone jack."

"How difficult is it to take the hard drive out of it?"

"A coupla minutes if I had a screwdriver."

"Here." I pulled my Swiss Army knife out of my pocket and threw it across to him. "Get on with it."

Trey didn't want to come any further into the room than he had done already and he certainly didn't want to touch the computer he'd indicated. It had been behind Henry at the moment he'd been killed and its outer casing had taken on a color and texture not usually available in office equipment catalogues.

He took a quick peek at what was left of the back of Henry's head just once while he worked. That was enough, even for a fifteen-year-old kid who lives on a diet of thrill rides and horror flicks. After that he kept his back slightly turned and his chin tucked down.

As soon as the stained outer casing was removed, his hands seemed to steady and he fumbled less. The hard drive he'd mentioned was about the same size as a double-album CD case. It wasn't long before he stood up with it in his hand.

I grabbed a towel from the kitchen and quickly wiped over the surfaces I thought we'd touched. Better for the police not to find our prints at another murder scene, if we could help it. I smiled bracingly again. "OK?" I said. "Then let's go."

We hurried back down the hallway as far as the outer screen door. I picked my bag off the floor and Trey shoved the hard drive into it.

Scott had swung the Dodge round and was sitting with the motor turning over, as requested. He saw us appear and started to wave, just as a man in a dark suit stepped out from behind the shrubbery of the house opposite.

I elbowed Trey back into the hallway and brought the Sig up in front of me, almost as one move. In the truck, Scott, Aimee and Xander hadn't noticed what was going on behind them and when they saw the gun come out their expressions froze.

"Get down!" I shouted.

The man in the suit reacted to the warning much faster than the kids. I didn't see him pull a gun but one had suddenly appeared in his hand. He kept low, crabbing sideways so that he had the cover of a rusting Chevrolet. I put one round into the front end of it, shattering a headlight, just to keep his head down.

As I did so, another two figures appeared round the corners of the houses on either side of Henry's, closing in fast. This was getting silly.

"Get back into the house!" I yelled to the kids.

Xander and Aimee jumped straight out of the pickup bed onto the scrubby front lawn, hitting the ground already running. Scott should have just hutched across the front seat of the Dodge and left via the passenger door, the one nearest to the house, but panic stole from his logic and left it weak.

He opened the driver's door and got straight out onto the road instead. As he sprinted round the front of the truck the man behind the Chevrolet rose into a crouch. He was holding a silvered revolver with a stubby barrel but he had the advantage of short range.

He fired three shots, the second of which hit Scott in the

back. I'll never forget the look of sheer surprise on the kid's face. He stumbled over his own feet and began to stagger.

"Shit," I muttered.

Aimee, who'd just reached the safety of the hallway, turned as I spoke. When she caught sight of Scott she started screaming.

I moved out fast onto the porch, aware that almost anything was better than staying close to that noise. Scott had made it halfway to us but he was losing momentum and direction. The man behind the Chevrolet had risen into plain sight and was steadying his aim for another shot.

I ran across the grass until I was up against the solid front end of the Dodge and shot the man on the other side of the Chevy, just once, about half an inch below his right eye. He fell back behind the car and didn't come up again. I hadn't expected him to.

His mates took that as their cue to open fire but I'd lost interest in this uneven game. I turned back for the house, ducking my shoulder under Scott's arm as I ran past him, just as his legs gave out and he started to sag. I swept him forward, using all my strength to keep him on his feet. Xander ventured out as far as the porch steps to help take the load. The bullets seemed to be raining down all around us. How the hell could they keep missing?

We all burst through the narrow doorway into the hall and fell onto the tiles. Aimee slammed the door shut behind us, turning the locks firmly like that was going to keep them out.

"Shit, man, who *are* these people?" Xander muttered softly under his breath. "Like, *shit*!"

Aimee had bent and was clutching Scott's hand as he thrashed and twisted. Her eyes were shimmering with tears. "*Do* something!" she pleaded. "He's bleeding."

I knelt in front of Scott who was sprawled where he'd landed, half on his side, propped against the wall to the kitchen. He was still conscious and crying with the pain.

I eased his hands away from his body. The bullet had left a small but messy entry hole just behind his left hip. There was no exit wound, but that didn't make it any better. He was los-

ing blood at a rate that meant most of the loose rug in the hallway was already greasy with it.

"We need to get him away from the door," I said. Xander
and Aimee's faces were gray with shock. Suddenly this adventure game had cracked back and bitten them, big style. It
wasn't fair. "Scott, you're going to have to move now."

"No-o," he wept, writhing when we tried to get him up. In
the end we just grabbed the edges of the rug and dragged it,
with him on top, through the door into the tiny bathroom. He
mewled at every jolt.

I gathered all the towels I could find from the rail and used
them to pack onto the wound. They were pale colors that
turned almost instantly scarlet. "Here," I said to Aimee and
Xander. "Lean on the towel, keep it pressed hard onto his hip.
Like this."

My demonstration was met with a squeal of protest from
Scott. His legs threshed weakly.

"You're hurting him!" Xander objected.

"It'll do more than hurt him if we don't stop the bleeding,"
I shot back. "Keep it pressed on—as hard as you can. And call
the cops."

Xander glanced at me sharply, but he nodded and flicked
his mobile phone out of his pocket. I heard him already speaking to the dispatcher as I got up and moved past Trey, who was
still in the hallway, staring at his injured friend.

"For God's sake stay down and keep out of sight of any of
the windows," I told him.

I tiptoed round the house, skirting Henry's corpse to peer
carefully out of the broken window in that room. Outside it
had all gone quiet again. The kitchen looked out onto the front
porch but from that angle I couldn't see if the man I'd hit was
still lying behind the Chevrolet.

I cursed myself then for shooting him dead. At the time my
only thought had been to save Scott's life, but wounding the
man would have been a far better strategy. That way his com-
rades would have had to tie up manpower and resources to either get him away from the scene, or treat him there, as we

were doing with Scott. Killing the gunman outright meant
they could forget about him until the fight was over.

Which, by the looks of things, wasn't going to take long.

"The cops are on their way," Xander said, the strain clear
in his voice. "They said to just sit tight and wait for them to
get here."

I nodded. I was waiting for our opponents to make the first
move in any case and it wasn't a lengthy wait. Just as I started
to move back out of the kitchen again the first of the shots
came, half a dozen of them in a random pattern straight through
the front door. I dived across the hallway and landed half on top
of Trey, keeping him flattened down hard onto the floor.

After the pandemonium came an eerie silence, broken only
by Scott's quiet moaning.

Then a voice I didn't recognize shouted, "Hey, Fox, we
want you and the kid. Come on out and the others get off."

I lifted my head. "And if we don't?" I yelled back.

I could almost hear the man shrug. "Makes no difference
to us."

I shuffled round until I could look at the bullet holes in the
door again. Sunlight shafted through them, highlighting the
dust motes that drifted and spun inside the hallway. The holes
ranged from a couple of feet off the ground to head height. If
we'd been standing they would have hit us. Not exactly warning shots, then.

I hutched back into the bathroom. Xander and Aimee both
had their eyes fixed on me. They were still keeping the balled-
up towels hard against Scott's hip, their hands bloody with
their efforts. Scott protested less, now. His face had turned almost as pale as his hair and pearls of sweat had formed on his
forehead, sliding sideways to the floor.

"The cops are on their way," I called to the men outside,
hoping that their need not to be apprehended was greater than
their need to kill us.

The man on the other side of the door just laughed. "I
know," he said, almost lazy with it. "Actually, Charlie, we're
already here."

For a moment I was stilled by my own surprise, then I scrambled across the hallway into the kitchen and risked a peek through the window. Outside, behind Scott's pickup, stood a good-looking man I recognized instantly. Even without his trademark Oakley eyejackets.

He wasn't in uniform, like the first time I'd seen him at the house in Fort Lauderdale. Neither was he in casual dress, as at the theme park. Today was different. Today Oakley man was wearing a dark suit and white shirt like the other two men alongside him. Brought a whole new meaning to the phrase "dressed to kill."

I looked at the others while I had the chance, but I knew I hadn't seen either of them before. One was short and stocky, with pale gingery-blond hair. The other guy was dark skinned, slightly Hispanic, with a pencil-thin mustache across his upper lip and a single gold hoop in his left ear. I wondered if all three of them were cops and just how they were planning on explaining the dead man behind the Chevrolet.

I dropped back below the level of the kitchen cabinets. Through the doorway I could see Scott had started to twitch, going almost into convulsions. I could hear Aimee's voice taking on an edge of panic as she whispered to Xander.

I crawled back through to the bathroom.

"It's the same guy," I said to Trey. He didn't need to ask who I meant. The fear froze his face into a tight mask across his bones. "We're going to have to give ourselves up."

He hesitated, just fractionally, then nodded once, not arguing about it.

"OK," I shouted. "I'll bring Trey out, but only if you let us get the kid who's injured out of here first."

"You're in no position to bargain," Oakley man shouted back.

"That's true, but if you have to shoot us out of here you're likely to lose more men. This way's easier."

There was a pause, as though he was weighing up the merit of what I'd had to say. His voice matched his appearance, I realized. I didn't know enough about American accents to pinpoint his origins, but it sounded educated. The kind of voice I would have expected from that attractive collection of features.

"OK, Charlie," he said at last. "Come on out and we won't stop the others leaving."

"No way," I said. "Xander and Aimee will bring Scott out first and put him into the pickup. As soon as they drive away, you get us. Not before."

And if you double-cross us, I didn't add out loud, *then I will do my best to put a bullet in your brain, you bastard.*

"OK," Oakley man said again. "You got yourself a deal."

"Right," I said, more quietly, to Xander and Aimee. "Grab the biggest bath towel and get that under Scott. You'll have to use that to carry him like he's in a sling. Get him to the nearest hospital," I added, trying to smile reassuringly. "He should be fine. He'll make it."

We maneuvered ourselves with difficulty in the cramped bathroom, getting the towel in position. Scott's cries had subsided into a low groaning now and his skin was chilled and clammy to the touch.

Xander was physically strong, so I put him at Scott's head, leaving Aimee to carry the end of the towel at his feet. As they staggered into the hallway with their burden I slipped the hard drive we'd taken from Henry's computer into Xander's pocket.

"If we don't get out of this," I murmured, "that might tell you who's behind it all."

He nodded briefly, face tight with tension. "Good luck, man," he said.

"Right," I called through the door. "They're coming out. Pull your men back to the other side of the street."

I waited a moment or two, opened the door just far enough for the two of them to hustle through it, then slammed it shut again and moved back to my kitchen window vantage point.

Oakley man may have been many things, but at least he kept to his promise as far as Scott was concerned. The three of them watched from the far side of the Chevy as Xander and Aimee struggled to get Scott into the back of the pickup. Aimee hopped into the load bed with him, as Xander got behind the wheel. He set off fast, as though scared they'd change their mind and try to prevent him. I watched the Dodge all the way to the end of the street, until it turned out into traffic and disappeared from view.

And all the time I was furiously searching for a way out of this that didn't involve our surrender. That didn't involve our defeat and capture.

"OK, Charlie," Oakley man said. The three of them had moved forward again, taking up position just to the rear of Henry's old Corvette which was parked to the side of the house. "I've kept my side of the bargain. Now it's your turn."

"How do I know you've let them get clear?" I hedged. "Not exactly one for leaving witnesses, are you? Let's give them a little longer."

He laughed again, but there wasn't much amusement in his voice. "If you're waiting for rescue, Charlie, you're gonna have a long wait," he said. "No one's gonna save you this time."

I didn't answer right away. I knew I didn't have many options left. Not ones that were survivable, at any rate.

For Trey or for me.

I looked down. The hands that were tightly gripping the Sig were covered in Scott's blood. I knew I had just two rounds left in the gun and there were three bad guys left outside. Not good odds, whichever way you looked at it.

"Come on, Charlie," Oakley man said gently. "You make us come in there and get you and you'll regret it."

"Why?" I tossed back, reckless now. "You're probably going to kill us anyway."

I expected some kind of reassurance but it didn't come. Instead there was a pause and then that bloody annoying laugh again. "True, but some ways of dying are harder than others," he said, and the very lightness of his tone made his words all the more brutal, all the more chilling. "Just ask your pal Henry in there."

FOURTEEN

"THERE'S SOMEONE UNDER the house."

"What?"

For a moment I didn't compute what Trey had said to me. His voice was little more than a whisper. I stuck my head round the kitchen door and stared at him across the narrow hallway.

He was sitting with his back ramrod straight against the open bathroom door, hardly daring to move more than his eyes.

"There's someone under the house," he insisted. "I can hear them."

And when I listened, I could hear them, too. Nothing overt, just the faintest cautious scuff and slither of someone trying to ease their way into a position. I felt my mouth dry so that my tongue stuck to the roof of it. *So, Oakley man was trying to keep me talking while his men outflanked us.*

I looked at the floor, as if I was going to be able to spot some sign of this invasion like a lump under a carpet. I'd known when I'd first seen Henry's house that it was constructed off the ground, hence the rotting trellis round the bottom of the outside, but it hadn't occurred to me that the gap might be big enough for a person to squeeze into. If I had I might have considered it as an escape route for Trey.

And now, it seemed, it was too late for that.

Somebody had beaten me to it.

"Get into the bath and keep your head down," I said. The

bath tub was old-fashioned enameled steel and a heavy enough grade to offer some measure of protection—either from the side or from below.

I waited until Trey was safely in, then edged back across the hallway, trying to move very quietly. When I checked out of the kitchen window again, only the Hispanic man was visible, covering the front. There was no sign of Oakley man or Ginger.

Maybe now would be a good time to make a break for it . . .

I thought of Oakley man's last words. So we were doomed anyway. The defeat tasted dirty, like spoiled food. Better to go out fighting, even with a pitiful supply of ammunition.

"Trey?"

He lifted just the top of his head over the rim of the bath and gave me a *What now?* look.

"Change of plan," I said, urgent. I jerked my head toward the front door. "Let's go."

I waited until he'd climbed out and moved up close behind me. "If anything happens," I said carefully, glancing at him, "you run like hell and you keep running, do you hear me? You don't stop and you don't come back, no matter what, understand?"

He stared at me, then nodded, reluctant, even a little sullen.

"Try and stay away from the police if you can," I said and on impulse added, "Go to Walt and Harriet's place on the beach. They'll take care of you." And I realized as I said it that it was true. I trusted the canny old man without quite knowing why.

I also realized, in a detached kind of way, that I wasn't expecting to get out of this alive. So, I'd fooled Oakley man once but that was when he wasn't expecting me to be up to the job. I'd fooled the two men in the Buick, too—I could only assume they were his accomplices—when they hadn't been expecting me to be armed. But now he had the measure of me, for what it was worth.

I stood in that dingy hallway and felt the full reality of it settle on me, like a sense of calm. I was twenty-six years old.

I always thought I'd feel more emotion at the prospect of my own death, when I'd thought about it at all. I wondered if I would have been approaching it with such equanimity if I'd known Sean was out there somewhere, moving heaven and earth to get to me.

I tried to reach out, get a feel for him. I'd hoped for some kind of connection, some suspicion that he was alive or dead, but there was nothing. A big empty void where once he'd engaged some space in my mind. Perhaps there would be a time to grieve for him later.

If I made it.

I eased the locks clear and opened the newly ventilated door just enough to peer through the gap. Still the only person I could see in front of the house was the Hispanic man with the earring. His attention was focused off to my left, toward the corner of the house.

The blood had dried on my hands but new sweat made it tacky again. I took a moment to wipe both palms down the sides of my trousers, then yanked the door wide.

I kicked the screen door open and came out at a kind of sideways run across the porch, leading with one shoulder and the Sig straight out in front of me. I sighted on the center of the Hispanic man's body mass, and felt the muscles in my forearms tense as I began to take up the pressure on the trigger.

I knew I'd come out fast, but my opponent seemed to be faster, swinging his gun up with the kind of easy movement that suggested long hours of practice and a professional familiarity with firearms.

Minute pieces of detail from that moment stuck in my mind. The fact that the man's pencil mustache had been trimmed slightly longer on one side than the other, making his face appear lopsided. The fact that he wore a wedding ring on his left hand, with an ornate turquoise signet ring on the finger next to it. The fact that his gun was a nine-millimeter semi-automatic, a nice piece gleaming with care and pride.

The shot sent me reeling. It seemed far too loud for a handgun, an almost deafening report that I knew I hadn't fired. I'd always been told you never hear the shot that gets you, but if this was it, they were wrong. You heard it twice as loud.

And then it hit me that I wasn't.

Hit, I mean.

I couldn't say the same for the Hispanic man. He staggered a couple of steps backward, tottering in much the same way Scott had done. The front of his shirt was red where only a blink before it had been white. The lower tail of his tie was ripped away and missing but I hadn't seen it go. He looked down at the gaping mess that had been his own abdomen with an expression of puzzled surprise on his face.

The man made a last laborious, heavy attempt to bring his gun up again but the weight of it defeated him. It was all too difficult, too tiring. His feet tangled, twisting him as he fell so he described an almost graceful pirouette and dropped from sight behind Henry's old Corvette.

And directly below my own feet, under the porch, came the unmistakable sound of a fresh cartridge being jacked into the chamber of a pump-action shotgun.

I stared. The porch was only wooden planking. A shotgun blast would come up through it like it was paper. I wheeled, grabbing Trey and shoving him back into the house. The screen door hadn't even had time to slam behind us.

I hit the locks on the front door and hustled the boy back into the bathroom. This time, I climbed into the bathtub with him and we both squatted there, tense and breathless.

Who the hell was under the porch with a shotgun? Not one of Oakley man's team, that was for certain. Not unless he was having severe communication problems with his staff. So who?

For a second I remembered the claims that Henry had CIA connections. Supposing he hadn't been entirely bullshitting about that? Supposing his murder had rung alarm bells somewhere and sparked a reaction that included such a retaliatory attack?

Almost as soon as the thought had formed, I dismissed it. If that was the case they would have taken the Hispanic man out of play before Trey and I ever set foot outside the house.

And they would have brought something a little quieter to do it with. Shotguns were not the kind of gun you were likely to take with you on a covert operation of this type. House clearance and intimidation, yes, but for a surgical strike after a hit? I didn't think so. Too messy.

Outside, I heard voices, raised but not far enough to hear the words, only the tone. Anger, mainly, and not a little measure of surprise. I realized there were two men speaking, voices raised. It sounded like Oakley man and another who could only have been Ginger. He hadn't anyone else left to argue with.

I waited for another blast from the hidden shotgunner, but the man chose to lay quiet, biding his time now. If he was so ready to kill one of the men attacking us, I wondered fiercely, why not finish the rest while he had the chance?

An engine started up, something fairly hefty that throbbed through the building as it stopped outside. It sat there ticking over for a minute or so, while doors were opened and thumped shut again. Then it set off fast, the engine note rising and falling as the auto box ran up through the gears. I listened to the sound of it disappearing toward the end of the street until it receded into the background altogether.

"Have they gone?" Trey whispered.

"That depends," I said, "on who you mean."

"Charlie?" called a new voice, close enough to the front door to make both of us jump. I hadn't heard any footsteps on the porch. "You can come out now. Show's over."

I recognized the man who'd spoken as soon as the drawling words were out of his mouth. So did Trey. I felt him flinch beside me. He was hunched down with his knees bent up in front of him and his arms wrapped round his shins. He was holding on so tight his knuckles had gone white with the force of it.

"Tell me, Whitmarsh," I called back, "why the fuck I should trust *you*."

Jim Whitmarsh gave a kind of a snort that might have signified amusement. But then again, it might not.

"Well, I can think of a coupla good reasons," he said. There was a pause, then the sound of that shotgun again, the oiled mechanism being snatched back and ramming another cartridge home. There was no need for it. It was just a gesture. Just for show. "How's that for a start?"

For a second I sat huddled in the bath and tried to work out what was wrong here. Besides the obvious, that is. Oakley man had wanted us dead and only the arrival of Whitmarsh and his men had prevented that.

But I doubted that Oakley man knew who'd killed the Hispanic man. He could even have thought it was me. Going up against someone you believe to be armed with a half-empty handgun is one thing. Suddenly finding there are people lying in wait with shotguns is something else altogether. Either Oakley man had run, or he'd gone for reinforcements.

So that just left us facing Jim Whitmarsh. The man I'd seen burst into that motel bedroom with one of his men and coldly murder two unlucky innocents because he thought they were us.

He was right, though, about his argument being a persuasive one. Choosing to stay and face a shotgun in a confined space—especially one as flimsily constructed as Henry's house—was suicide.

If they started clearing the place room by room they wouldn't even have to aim. The bathroom was so small that all they'd have to do was put one shot round the open door, or even straight through one of the dividing walls. Not even a cast-iron bathtub would save us then. Open ground was our best chance by far.

I glanced at Trey. He looked so terrified I wasn't even sure I'd get him on his feet unaided.

"We've got to go out there," I told him, almost gently. He shook his head, lip starting to tremble. I moved to brush his cheek, then noticed the blood on my hands again and ended up just touching his shoulder instead. I smiled, tentative. "Trust me," I said with a confidence I didn't feel. "I'll get you out of this."

His bruised eyes called me a liar, but at least he didn't say the words out loud.

I raised my voice. "OK, Whitmarsh, we're coming out."

We got out of the bath and moved through to the front door again.

"Here," I said quietly, and stuck the Sig into the back of the waistband of Trey's baggy shorts. His face paled even further. "For God's sake don't touch it," I warned him. "They're less likely to search you, that's all."

I unlocked the door and pushed the screen open, then moved out onto the porch, keeping Trey slightly behind me and my empty hands where everyone could see them.

Jim Whitmarsh was standing on the scrubby drive, not far from where the Hispanic man had fallen. My gaze swept across the space behind the Corvette but the body seemed to have gone. There was no sign of the man I'd shot on the other side of the road, either. So that's what Oakley man had stopped for.

Whitmarsh was wearing an Oxford shirt and chinos and loafers with no socks. He was carrying a Beretta out of the neat leather holster attached to his belt and he was sweating in the heat. When he saw me his eyebrows went up as he took in the cheesy teenage outfit and the beaded pink locks, not to mention Trey's shock of white hair.

Lonnie was the one with the shotgun, a Remington twelve-bore. He stood a little further forward but well to the side of Whitmarsh, giving him a decent line on us. The fronts of his combat trousers were coated with dirt and dust where he'd lain under the house and shot the Hispanic man through the trellis, unseen and unsuspected. Now, his eyes were constantly ranging across the surrounding houses and along the street, checking for trouble. He barely gave Trey and me a second glance.

I didn't see Chris right away, not until the car arrived. A maroon Ford Taurus braked to a fast halt right outside the house and the big colored guy jumped out of the driver's seat, leaving the doors open and the engine running. He moved round the back of the car and opened the boot.

"C'mon," he said to Whitmarsh, "we don't have much time."

"OK." Whitmarsh nodded. "Check her over, first." To me

he said, "You exceeded my expectations, Charlie. Takes a lot to impress me, but I'm impressed."

"Excuse me if I don't take that as a compliment," I said with a touch of acid.

He smiled. "Yep," he went on as though I hadn't spoken, holding my gaze as he added with a certain cruel deliberation, "you put up more of a fight than Meyer, that's for sure."

I felt my face harden but I wouldn't give him the satisfaction of rising to that one. We continued our stare-out competition as Chris approached and gave me a quick pat-down search. He kept out of Lonnie's field of fire and stepped back when he was done, shaking his head to Whitmarsh. As I'd hoped, he didn't bother with the boy.

"OK," Whitmarsh said, "get them both into the trunk."

"Oh come on," I snapped, edging closer to Trey and stamping on my fear. "If you're going to kill us, just get on with it. You don't have to go through the classic 'taking you for a ride' crap."

Chris flicked his eyes to his boss and in that instant I read just a hint of nervousness there. The sudden realization it triggered was like someone had flicked a switch inside my head and turned on all the floodlights at a Premier League football game.

They didn't want us dead.

In fact, having Trey dead was the very last thing they wanted. To the point where they'd actually stepped in to prevent us being shot by Oakley man and his crew.

It all made a twisted kind of sense now. I'd thought Whitmarsh and Oakley man were all in this together but, when I thought about it, I'd never seen them working as a team. Even though they'd always appeared to have a common aim.

"Maybe we aren't of a mind to kill you," Whitmarsh said, narrow eyed. "You thought of that?"

Lonnie paused just long enough in his constant surveillance to flick his boss a brief, pained glance, as though he considered Whitmarsh was wasting time they didn't have on idle chitchat. Chris was tense, too. For a few moments the only sound was that of the Taurus's quietly running engine.

"Well it certainly looked that way when we watched you slaughter that pair at the motel," I threw back.

Surprise rocked him, then he smiled. "Maybe we've had a change of heart since then," he said and jerked his head to Chris to get on with it.

Trey was right next to me and, as Chris closed on us again, I took a step back, leaving the boy to the fore. Chris's face flickered at my apparent display of cowardice but as I moved I reached behind Trey with my right hand, as though to put my arm around his shoulders. Instead I went under his shirt and grabbed hold of the pistol grip of the Sig, snatching it free.

My left arm snaked round Trey's neck, fisting my hand into his shirt to pin him hard against the front of my body, unashamedly using him as a shield. I brought the Sig up into view, planting the muzzle under his jawline. His head came back as his spine went stiff both with outrage and with fright. All the time I made sure I presented as small a target as possible to Whitmarsh.

He was the one who worried me. If they were as desperate to capture Trey alive as I suspected, Lonnie couldn't risk firing the shotgun when we were so close together. Chris had nothing in his hands. That left Whitmarsh and his Beretta.

But they all froze, which gave me hope to think there might be an escape route still open to us. It was a gamble. All I had to do now was play it.

"You must think I'm amazingly stupid," I spat. "OK, so you've decided you need the kid. So where does that leave me?"

I contrived a suitably whiny note of low cunning into my voice. I was dealing with men without honor. They wouldn't have any difficulty in believing I might have my eye solely on my own interests. A rat who'd suddenly found a life jacket and decided now was the time to leave this ship.

I nudged the barrel of the Sig further into Trey's neck, angled upward where a single shot would scatter his brains all over the lawn, and watched the alarm in their faces.

"You want him alive?" I sneered. "Well in that case you better be prepared to let me walk him out of here, because otherwise he'll be yet another dead body you've got to clean up. And trust me," I added, voice positively dripping with venom, "after two days solid in this little brat's company, it would almost be a pleasure."

For a moment nobody spoke and I feared I'd overdone it, but then Whitmarsh lowered his gun and nodded to the other two. They let me shuffle Trey toward the Taurus, making sure I kept him turning so they never had a clear shot at me while we got there. Not that any of them tried for one. I began to realize that whatever value they now placed on Trey must be a high one.

Getting into the driving seat without exposing myself wasn't easy and I managed it with less style than I would have liked, but we got there. Trey was taut and ungainly, barely seeming able to fold himself into the car.

As soon as we were in I stuck the car into gear and floored it, not caring how much rubber I left stuck to the road. The boot lid bounced up and down a couple of times as we hit a few bumps, then finally latched shut. I kept hunched down in my seat, waiting at any moment for the shots to come through the back window, but they never came.

Either Whitmarsh knew when to admit defeat, or he really was terrified of injuring the boy.

As we reached the end of the street I risked sitting up far enough to glance in the rearview mirror. It was set for a taller driver and I had to tilt it down slightly to use it, but when I did so I found that everyone had disappeared from the front of Henry's house.

I turned and looked over my shoulder, just to be certain, but there was nobody there. Whitmarsh and his men had gone just like they'd never existed.

FIFTEEN

I DROVE WITHOUT direction, heading down the main strip for a couple of blocks then making a series of random turns, just to keep us and our stolen Taurus away from prying police eyes. Not that I thought Jim Whitmarsh would be in any hurry to report the car as taken.

Mind you, we wouldn't have lasted the first ten seconds in a traffic stop. The Taurus had a beige interior and my nervous hands had left bloody prints all over the rim of the steering wheel. It looked like I'd gutted a live rabbit in there at the very least.

And then there was my unlicensed Sig, which I'd stuffed back under my thigh. A gun, bullets from which could now be found in two dead bodies. The thought sent a shiver across my shoulders.

Shit. How had it come to this?

For a time I drove without speaking, barely giving Trey a second glance. The boy was burrowed into the far corner of the passenger seat, his face turned away to the glass. I could tell by the angle of his head that he was sulking and I didn't have the energy to start a fight with him about it. Not right now.

I was too busy trying to make some sense of what had happened at Henry's place. It all seemed such a tangle. Oakley man was genuinely with the police, of that I was now quite certain. Otherwise, how could he have known about—and diverted—Xander's call for help?

It was also Oakley man who had tortured and then killed Henry. He'd admitted as much to us—when he'd been confident we weren't going to live long enough to report the fact. The question was, how had he found Henry in the first place?

The only answer had to be that Henry himself had contacted Oakley man, offering to negotiate for Trey. But if that was the case, where did Whitmarsh and his mob fit in? At the motel I'd assumed they all had a common aim, but now it seemed like they were on opposite sides.

Oakley man had simply wanted us dead, so at least he was consistent in that. Whitmarsh, though, seemed to have changed his stance. A change of heart, he'd called it but I hadn't believed him. I didn't think he had one to change. But he now wanted to take us alive desperately enough that he'd let us go when I'd threatened Trey. And he'd been prepared to use deadly force to protect us when necessary.

But why the secrecy? Why hide in the shadows and wait until we made a break for it to take potshots at the Hispanic man? And why allow Oakley man and Ginger to pick up their dead and run? If Whitmarsh's men were prepared to kill one, what did it achieve to let the others escape alive?

I remembered the young cop who'd stopped us and the men in the Buick who'd intervened. It wasn't just a black and white case of dead or alive, I realized. Neither side wanted us to fall into the wrong official hands, either. So who were the right ones?

I flicked my eyes across to Trey. He was still staring pointedly out of the window.

"Maybe it's time we went back to see Walt," I suggested, a little tentative.

No response.

"Trey," I said, snappier this time. "Did you hear me? I said maybe—"

"I heard you!" The words burst out of him, too loud inside the confines of the car, startling. He twisted round and now I could see the tears running down his face. He pressed his lips together until they were white and without definition, his whole face pinched.

"What's the matter?"

My question only made things worse.

"What's the *matter*?" he shrieked, uncaring that his voice rose and wavered, shrill as a reed. "How the fuck can you go 'What's the matter?' like that, after what you just did?" He broke off, shaking his head for a moment as his temper boiled up under the surface, then he slammed his fist sideways into the door panel. "How *can* you?" he repeated.

"Trey," I said carefully, trying to keep one eye on the traffic through his outburst. "I did what I had to do to get us out of there alive. Surely you realize that?"

He was silent and it dawned on me that he'd taken every word I'd spoken on Henry's porch at face value. My mouth dried. No wonder the kid was so touchy.

"Trey," I said, trying again. "I didn't mean it—any of it. Christ, you can't have thought I did, not after what we've been through these last couple of days?"

"How was I s'posed to know?" he threw back, sullen. "You sure sounded like you meant it."

"If I hadn't been convincing, Whitmarsh would have called my bluff." I broke off for a moment while I looked for another way to make him see it. "I'm here to protect you," I said at last. "It's my job. I *have* protected you. Christ, I've even killed to protect you. Actions are supposed to speak louder than words. Doesn't that tell you anything about me?"

There was a long pause. "I never *asked* you to kill anyone," he muttered.

"Shit, I really can't win with you, can I?" I let my breath out fast, but my annoyance didn't go with it. "I do everything I can to keep you alive and suddenly I'm a cold-blooded killer. But if I hadn't done what I've done, we'd both be dead by now."

"Didn't do much for Scott, though, did it?"

He seemed determined to chuck any argument he could at me. I set my jaw and tried to hang on to my temper. "I did my best," I ground out. "He made a poor call. If he hadn't got out of the wrong side of the truck, he probably would never have been hit."

Trey huffed and threw his hands in the air. "Oh great! He's my friend and he's probably dead and all you're doing is saying as how it's, like, not *your* fault!"

"Trey, don't jump to conclusions," I said, starting to lose it myself now. "We don't know *how* Scott is."

"So let's go to the hospital and find out."

"We can't," I shot straight back. "Don't be a prat. That's the first place everybody will look for us." I waved a hand toward my hair. "And they know exactly what we look like now. We've got dead bodies piling up all around us and Whitmarsh and good old Gerri Raybourn seem determined to make sure I'm the one lined up to take the blame for the lot of them. There's no other way to explain what happened back there."

Trey didn't want to ask me to expand on that, but curiosity got the better of him. "What d'you mean?"

"Why else would Lonnie blow that Hispanic guy away without showing himself? Why let the other two get away when they had plenty of opportunity to shoot them, too? I think they wanted Oakley man—the guy from the theme park—to assume I'd done it, though Christ knows where I was supposed to have suddenly acquired a shotgun from."

Trey was still frowning. "So?"

"I don't know," I said, more quietly now. The traffic slowed and stopped as the next light turned red ahead of us. "The only thing that's changed since yesterday is that Henry found out about your part in this program of your dad's. We need to find out who he was in touch with. And for that we need to find out what was on the hard drive we took out of Henry's computer."

"Which you gave to Xander," Trey put in, and there was a slight accusing note in his tone.

"Which I gave to Xander," I agreed, adding pointedly, "when I didn't think we were going to live long enough to do it ourselves."

"So we gotta go to the hospital now anyways," Trey said, his jaw coming out, stubborn. "We gotta find Xander."

"No." I shook my head. "We'll wait until later and catch

him somewhere else—at home, maybe. It's way too dangerous to try now."

"I *want* to go to the hospital. If you're too scared to go with
me," he said, loud and scathing, "let me out of the goddamned
car and I'll go on my own!"

"You can't go on your own, Trey. Use some sense for
once."

"I'm not running out on my friends!" He was almost
yelling at me now. "You can't hold me against my will. That's,
like, kidnapping. You can't—"

The people in the car alongside us had begun to stare.
"OK, OK," I said, cutting him off. "For heaven's sake! We'll
go to the bloody hospital. Just calm down, will you?"

He subsided into his seat, sniffing loudly and mopping his
nose on the back of his hand. He looked too close to smug in
victory for my liking. I couldn't help wiping that off his face
with a quiet reminder. "But if I have to shoot anyone to get us
out of there, just remember whose idea it was, OK?"

The Halifax Medical Center on Clyde Morris Boulevard was
more like a sprawling office complex than a hospital. I left the
stolen Taurus reverse parked against the wall in a corner of
their cavernous multi-story car park and we followed the signs
for the Trauma Center.

We'd already stopped off briefly at a shopping mall, just
long enough to find a quiet restroom where I could scrub the
blood off my hands and wipe the worst of it from my silk
trousers. It had turned black against the green, which didn't
look so bad, but I still thought it wasn't a good idea to walk
into a place where, in theory, they should be able to identify it
for what it was.

I sent Trey into the store with some money to buy me a
cheap bag, something I could use to conceal the Sig. He'd
come back with a lurid Barbie-pink plastic over-the-shoulder
job, decorated with bright violet and yellow flowers. He tried
to look innocently disdainful but I was sure he'd picked that
one out deliberately.

Now we hurried into the main hospital building itself. I slipped on my best worried teen expression along with my best American accent as I asked after Scott at the desk.

The jaded-looking big black woman on the other side eyed me with suspicion. "You a relative?" she asked.

"No, but this is Scott's brother," I lied, nodding to Trey. "He's only fifteen. I brought him in as soon as we heard."

She looked at Trey and for some reason his petulant demeanor caused her to soften. She didn't quite say, "Ah," but it was a close-run thing.

We followed the directions she gave us until eventually we turned a corner and found Xander and Aimee waiting nervously in a corridor and we knew we were in the right place.

Trey broke into a jog as soon as he caught sight of them. "Xander, hey man! How is he?"

Xander turned at the sound of his voice but looked away quickly, like he could hardly bear to have us in sight. Aimee jumped to her feet and came to meet us, looking pale and frightened.

"They won't tell us much, 'cept he's still in surgery," she said. She had her hands wrapped round her upper arms, unconsciously rubbing at her skin. "He lost a lot of blood and there's, like, other complications."

Trey stared from one to the other. "Like what?"

"They took X-rays and they reckon the bullet's pretty close to his spine, man," Xander said, voice compressed. "There's a chance he might not walk again." Just for a moment, his eyes landed on me as he spoke and I knew without it being said that he blamed me—us—for what had happened.

I could have pointed out that no one had forced them to come to Henry's with us. In fact, I'd specifically asked them not to, but there was enough guilt floating around without me adding my contribution.

"They called Scott's folks," Aimee put in. "They dropped everything and got on a plane. They should be here any time. I just don't know what we're gonna, like, tell them."

"Have you said anything to the hospital?"

Aimee shook her head, glancing to Xander.

"We've had the cops hassling us already," he said, "but we didn't tell them nothing."

"Good," I said. "For God's sake don't mention me or Trey to them."

"What?" Xander yelped. He muscled in close, putting his face into mine. He was slightly taller and when he was pumped up on anger and grief he seemed bigger still. Aimee made a protesting noise and put her hand on his arm. With an effort he got a grip on his temper, lowering his voice to a growl. "Our friend could be in a wheelchair for the rest of his life because of you, and all you wanna do is stay out of trouble?"

"Trouble isn't the beginning of it," I said, flat. "At least one of the guys who murdered Henry and then came after us is a cop. Two of them are now dead. If you want to tell the cops—who might or might not be in on this—all about what really happened, then on your own heads be it. Far better to invent a drive-by shooting incident and leave it at that. Everybody keeps telling me it's Spring Break. Wild things happen all the time."

I watched my words penetrate, saw Xander take on board the truth of them and mentally step back. Even if he couldn't bring himself to back down physically. Eventually, Aimee wedged herself between us.

She walked Xander back until his calves hit one of the waiting chairs, then she gently pressed on his shoulders until he sat. He complied without resistance, keeping his eyes on me all the while.

Aimee came back to us, managing a rueful smile. "Look, you guys better go," she said. "Soon as we know anything, we'll call you." Her smile expanded when she turned it on a dejected Trey. "I'm real glad you're OK."

As she made to go back to Xander I caught her arm. "There's one more thing," I said quietly. "You remember I gave Xander the hard drive from Henry's computer?"

She nodded. "You want it back?"

I shook my head. "It's no good to us without access to a computer to put it into," I said. "But we still need to know—now more than ever—who he contacted."

She shrugged, her disinterested look clearly suggesting I was being insensitive to ask after something so trivial at a time like this. "Why?"

I paused, trying not to show my impatience, while I hunted for a way to persuade her. "Because otherwise we're not going to find out who the guys who shot Scott are really working for," I said.

I watched that hit home. She nodded again. "OK, I'll, like, see what we can do."

We left quickly, trying not to attract any attention. Suddenly the hospital seemed to be full of people in uniform but none of them appeared to be looking for two kids. And if they were, we didn't appear to be the kids they were looking for.

Although I was reluctant to abandon our transport, keeping hold of the Taurus would have caused more problems than it would have solved. Nevertheless, I couldn't resist checking it over before we left it for the last time, just in case there was anything tucked away in there that we could use.

It wasn't until I opened the boot that I realized just how carefully Jim Whitmarsh and his men had planned our abduction from Henry's place. The whole of the inside of the boot area was lined in heavy plastic, the kind that builders use. It had been taped down around the edges and, when I cut an experimental slit in it with my Swiss Army knife, I found it was two layers deep.

"What's that for?" Trey asked, still subdued.

"For a man who claimed to have had a change of heart about killing us immediately," I said, voice grim, "Whitmarsh was certainly taking precautions not to leave any forensic evidence that we'd been in his car." I glanced across at him and suddenly felt the need to reinforce my earlier actions. "If I hadn't got us away from him, he *was* planning to kill the pair of us, sooner or later. You do realize that, don't you?"

After a moment's pause Trey nodded, although without making any comment on whether he'd come to terms with what I'd had to do or not. He stood and watched while I wiped the inside of the Taurus down as best I could and locked the doors. Then we walked out of the car park into the blazing heat on International Speedway Boulevard. The massive spectator stands of the Daytona Speedway loomed away to the west of us, on the other side of the eight-lane highway.

I stopped by the first storm drain we came across and dug the keys out of my pocket. But as I dangled them over the slats of the grid Trey's obvious surprise made me pause. "What?"

"You can't just, like, dump the keys down a drain," he said, actually sounding shocked.

I looked at him for a moment, head on one side until he realized how that sounded and colored up. *So, it was OK to shoot at people and steal their car, but . . .*

I shook my head and let go of the keys. They bounced once and disappeared into the gloom. Kids today. I'd been one myself but I swore then I'd never understand them.

We walked as far as the next diner, where we found a bunch of kids who were heading to the strip and were easygoing enough to offer us a lift. Then Trey and I spent most of what was left of the afternoon hanging out around the Boardwalk area, looking at the crazy cars on display, being deafened by the bands that were playing. I hadn't heard of any of them but they were pretty good on the whole. Even if they didn't know where to find the volume control on most of their amplification.

Trey was moody and quiet, which suited me because it left me largely alone with my thoughts. I was still trying to work out what on earth was going on and failing to put together anything that would hold water.

I tried all the permutations I could think of, however unlikely they seemed, starting with the facts as I knew them. Keith had vanished. Oakley man was trying to kill us. Whitmarsh, originally hired to protect the family, had been at first trying to kill Trey, but was now trying to capture him alive—for the short term, at least. Gerri Raybourn was trying to frame me for kidnapping the boy—and possibly the father, too.

It all boiled down, as far as I could see it, to who had possession of the program Keith had been working on at the time of his disappearance. There was too much potential money at stake for it to be a coincidence.

Keith had part of it, although the fact that he'd run when he was apparently so close to completion had suggested to Henry that Keith had realized he was unable to finish the job. But if people thought the program didn't work, why had they put all this effort into going after Trey? Revenge?

But whose revenge?

If it was the company Keith worked for—and therefore Gerri Raybourn and Whitmarsh—that would make a certain amount of sense. Maybe they'd started out for revenge, but then Henry must have let it slip that Trey might just have the missing pieces. Their agenda had abruptly changed from trying to eliminate the boy to needing him alive if they were going to have any chance of their promised millions.

And just when I thought I might have put it together, it all started to unravel again. As I understood it, Trey only had a small part of the program. With Keith missing and possibly in hiding, how were they planning on getting hold of the rest?

Unless Keith was involved, too. But in that case, if he was trying to get rid of Trey because he might stir up trouble over his mother, why stop now? And where did Oakley man fit in? After all, he claimed he was the one who'd tortured and executed poor Henry. Had he been bluffing just to scare us?

The one thing I was trying *not* to think about was what had happened to Sean, but I couldn't help it. Especially not after Whitmarsh's throwaway line. *"You put up more of a fight than Meyer,"* he'd said, *"that's for sure."*

Even so, I wouldn't allow myself to give up all hope. I couldn't allow it.

As the light started to drop we grabbed some food in one of the crowded barbecue places on the main strip, squeezing into a booth to share a table with a group of kids who'd driven down from Georgia just for the weekend.

Trey livened up enough to chat to them over a meal of

burger and fries but I could see the effort it was costing him to act normal. When he thought nobody was looking his eyes had begun to carry a haunted, hunted edge. He'd picked at a hangnail on the side of his thumb until he'd peeled strip after strip of skin away, making it bleed. He was worrying at it now, I noticed, as unconscious an action as a nervous twitch.

He couldn't, I realized, go on like this much longer. He may be an irritating brat with the usual modern teenager's blasé attitude to danger, but faced with its constant reality he was starting to suffer. What had begun as a live-action version of one of his computer games had turned into a nightmare he couldn't just pull the plug on when things got tough.

Whatever I was going to do about the situation, I needed to do it fast. Before he came apart at the seams.

SIXTEEN

IT WAS JUST as we were leaving the barbecue joint that Trey's mobile rang. He dragged the phone out of his pocket and looked at the display almost fearfully.

"It's Xander," he said, not making any moves to pick up the call.

I let it go two more rings, then sighed, lifting the phone out of his hands and hitting the receive button.

"Hi Xander," I said, careful to keep my tone neutral.

"Oh, hi Charlie," he said, sounding just as cautious, just as low-key.

"How's Scott?"

He hesitated and for a second I feared the worst, but when he spoke I realized he'd just wanted to make me sweat. "He's outta surgery. His mom and dad are with him," he said grudgingly. "The doctors still aren't sure if he'll, like, be able to walk real good, but at least he's gonna make it."

Trey, not having wanted to take the call, was hovering at my shoulder, trying to listen in but the passing traffic made it hard for him to hear. Instead, he plucked at the sleeve of my shirt and mouthed, "How is he?" at me.

I gave him a tentative thumbs up and pushed him away. "That's good news," I said to Xander, stalling. There was a tightness in my chest as I worked myself up to asking him about Henry's hard drive, knowing how crass it would make me sound. In the end, I didn't have to.

"Anyways, Aimee said you needed to know what was on that hard drive so's you could nail the bastards who shot him," Xander went on.

"That's right," I said, surprised enough to push my luck. "When do you think you might have the chance to have a look at it?"

"Already done, man. I looked at it soon as I got home from the hospital. Soon as my mom and dad were done chewing me out, anyways. You want the whole thing or just the highlights?"

"Whichever," I said faintly. "Can you tell who he contacted?"

"He sent the first one just to the security department at the company Trey's dad works for. It was kinda mysterious, y'know? Henry just kinda asked them if they'd lost something and what kinda reward was on offer for the person who, like, found it."

Some "negotiation on our behalf," Henry, I thought bitterly. "Did you manage to find the replies?"

"'Course," he said, a little disdainful. "It wasn't encrypted or nothing. I just had to hook the drive up and go look in the In and Out boxes. You don't even need a password. It was a real cinch."

"So what did they say back to him?"

"Well, there was some messing about backward and forward while they go, 'What have you found?' And Henry goes, 'What have you lost?' In the end it was Henry who goes, like, 'You wanna do a deal or not?' and that's when they cut the crap."

"I'll bet they did," I muttered. "I don't suppose they did anything stupid like signed a name, did they?"

"Didn't have to," he said. "Henry's original mail mighta gone just to security@, but the reply came from jwhitmarsh@."

I nodded. No surprises there, then. "So what did Whitmarsh say?"

"He wanted some kinda proof that Henry had gotten hold of Trey for real, so Henry spills it about you and Trey changing your hair color and stuff."

Bastard. I remembered the lack of any real surprise on

Whitmarsh's face when we'd come out of the house and he'd seen our changed appearance. Now I understood why.

"What then?" I asked, keeping my teeth together with the effort of not breaking into a fit of cursing at Henry's obvious duplicity. He'd died terrified and I pitied him for that, but the fact that he'd never had any intention of helping us took the edge off my sympathy.

"Whitmarsh, he goes, 'OK, I'll go check with my superiors about what we can offer you.' And then, like a coupla hours later he comes back online and goes, 'I'm authorized to go to five grand.'"

"Five thousand dollars?" I echoed. *Not even thirty pieces of silver plus inflation?* It seemed such a measly bounty to pay on somebody's life. Two people's lives, when I thought about it. In fact, it was actually quite insulting to have so low a value placed on me. Two for the price of one. It made me feel like a supermarket special offer. "How did Henry react to that?"

"He went kinda nuts, man," Xander said, "really lost it. He accuses Whitmarsh of taking him for some kinda fool who don't know what's at stake. How he knows that without Trey they got zip and how they should be talking about five *hundred* grand."

"I bet that went down well," I said, unable to keep the irony out of my tone.

"You're kidding me!" Xander said, missing it entirely. "So Whitmarsh comes back with, 'You're bluffing. You don't know what you're talking about.' And Henry goes, 'Oh yeah?' and he launches into a load of bullshit about how Trey's been teaching some intelligent software all about how to figure out Wall Street. Is that right, man?" he finished uncertainly.

I glanced at Trey, who'd given up unsuccessfully trying to eavesdrop. He was now sitting on the railing near the door into the diner and blowing bubbles with his gum. He got too adventurous with the last one and it burst all over his face. He tried to peel the exploded goo off his nose and cheek but only ended up sticking his fingers together and increasing the mess. As computer geniuses went he seemed pretty unlikely, I had to admit.

"Yeah," I said. "That's right."

"No shit," Xander said in wonder, and I could almost hear him shaking his head.

"Did they ask Henry for his address?"

"No, but it wouldn't have been hard to find out. He was mailing out from his own website—y'know, the conspiracy theory one we told you about? It was kinda dumb of him if Whitmarsh's got pals in the cops. They'd be able to trace him easy."

"Was there anything else?"

"No, that was it. D'you reckon this guy Whitmarsh is the one killed Henry?"

"Could be," I said, even though I knew it wasn't quite as straightforward as that. "I'm still trying to work it out."

There was a pause, then Xander said, "Look, man, tell Trey I'm kinda sorry I blew up at you guys at the hospital. I was just kinda worried about Scott, y'know?"

"We all were."

"Yeah, well, I know that," he muttered. "Anyway, I gotta go. I'm not really supposed to be on the phone. My folks have gone kinda ape-shit at what's happened. It's really freaked them out. I am *so* grounded."

"Thank you for doing this, Xander," I said, meaning it. "It helps a lot."

"Yeah, well, you're welcome," he said, embarrassed. "Oh, one more thing, you guys. Don't go back to Scott's place. It's not just that his folks are back, but the cops are all over it."

"OK," I said. "Thanks for the warning."

"No sweat," he said. "You could come stay here but, like I say, I think I'm grounded 'til I'm, like, *twenty*."

He made twenty sound both a long way off and an extremely advanced age. I was around twice as many years past twenty as Xander still had to go to get there in the first place. It made me feel suddenly very old.

As I ended the call Trey hopped down from his railing. "So what did he say?" he demanded.

"Well, Gerri seems to be letting Whitmarsh do the talking for her but—"

"Not that!" he interrupted, scathing at my mistake. "About Scott! What did he say about Scott?"

"He's out of surgery," I said. Trey heard the "but" in my voice and made an impatient, get-on-with-it movement with his hands. "There might be some doubt about how much mobility he's going to regain."

Trey stared at me for a moment with his mouth open. The misery spread across his face like a window cracking in slow motion. He slipped his hands into his pockets, hunching his shoulders forward, and turned away from me.

I let him get halfway across the car park before I gave in and hurried after him. He didn't want to look at me, wrenching away when I tried to catch hold of his arm. I tired of this game faster than he did. Eventually my temper frayed far enough for me to catch a flailing wrist and twist a lock onto it. The action brought him up short with a startled cry.

He turned a reproachful, tear-riven face in my direction, staining me with guilt. I pushed it aside.

"Stop it, Trey," I said, snappy as he struggled ineffectually against the lock. "We don't have time for self-pity. It's a luxury we can't afford. So Scott's badly hurt. That's terrible, but there's nothing you can do to help him right now other than doing your best to get to the bottom of this. Giving in and throwing a wobbly makes a mockery of what he's going through. It makes it all for nothing."

He stilled and was quiet for several seconds. I could see his chest rising and falling as he took a couple of deep breaths to steady himself. Then he said, with a surprising dignity, "Would you let go of my arm, please?"

I complied instantly, ready to catch him again if he ran, but he didn't move.

We stood like that for a time. Above us, the sky had taken on that dramatic pinky blue tinge as day fled into evening, leaving a masterpiece of shape and color spread across the heavens. Below it, oblivious to the beauty unfolding overhead, traffic sped by along Atlantic Avenue.

It was only when a bright yellow drophead Mustang full of noisy kids turned in a touch too fast off the road and swung in our direction that we moved. Trey was docile now, allowing me to lead him across the road, jogging obediently alongside me through the gaps between the cars. The light was dropping more quickly and they all had their lights on. We walked down the nearest beach ramp and out onto the sand.

It was only then that the boy cleared his throat. "So," he said, "what did it say?"

I didn't need to ask what he was talking about, but I searched his face as if to check that he really wanted to know this time. There was no trace of sarcasm there.

I gave him the full report of what Xander had told me. When I was done he was quiet again, frowning. Henry's duplicity, I considered, must have been hard for him to take. Trey was learning some tough lessons about trust lately.

"So if it was Mr. Whitmarsh he was in contact with, how did that cop, like, get to hear about Henry?"

I shrugged. "I don't know," I admitted. "The only explanation that occurred to me was that perhaps they were working together."

He stared. "But Lonnie killed that guy . . ."

I nodded. "I did say '*were* working together', but maybe that all went out of the window when Henry let it out of the bag that you could make the program work. Maybe they've somehow got hold of a part-finished version when your dad left and now Whitmarsh realizes he's got the opportunity to make some serious money out of it—*if* they can get hold of you alive. It would explain the abrupt about face."

Trey was still frowning. "How did Mr. Whitmarsh know right off that Henry was talking about me when he wanted proof he'd got a hold of me?" he said slowly. He looked up. "That was what he said, right? But if Dad's disappeared too, how did they know Henry wasn't talking about him?"

"My God, I think you're right," I murmured and found it was my turn to stare. I'd completely missed the significance of that, but the more I thought about it, the more significant it became. Trey was quite right. Whitmarsh had assumed—no, more than that, he'd *known*—Henry was referring to Trey.

So how could he have known?

He couldn't. Not unless Keith was controlling this whole thing from behind the scenes. I did some mental shifting to see if that fitted and it did, after a fashion. But for what purpose?

"Did Xander say anything else?" Trey asked.

"Only that he's grounded until he's an old man, and that we can't go back to Scott's place."

As the full consequences of that piece of news hit him Trey's face grew mournful. "So that means . . ."

"Yeah." I raised a tired smile and waved an arm to indicate the sands all around us. "Looks like we're back to sleeping on the beach again."

It was dark before we knew it, the inky blackness above us spangled with stars. It gave the sky an illusion of a boundary it didn't have, dropping straight down into the sea at the far horizon.

We weren't far away from the area where we'd slept out on that first night, near Walt and Harriet's place. I suppose I needed time to get my head round the idea of asking for help, but first thing in the morning, I promised myself, we'd go and take Walt up on his offer. With any luck, another of Harriet's breakfasts would be part of the deal.

We weren't the only people who'd decided to spend a night out in the open air. The beach itself, as it had been last time, was crowded with kids, half of whom seemed to be courting couples. They grappled with each other in the shadows, tucked up under the walls of the apartment blocks and hotels that edged the seafront, intent on ingraining sand into the most uncomfortable places.

Every now and again we'd get a silvery moonlit flash of naked flesh as we moved past. It was hard to get an adolescent like Trey to concentrate on putting his feet one in front of the other and keep walking. As it was he was so busy ogling that he nearly tripped up twice.

"What d'you want to do?" I muttered eventually, "Give 'em marks for style?"

"It's all right for you," he groused when we reached a quieter stretch. "I bet you've, like, done it loads of times."

" 'Done it'?" I queried. He should have taken the stinging tone as a warning but he had a thicker skin than that.

"Yeah," he plowed on, discomfited but persistent. "Y'know—fucked."

"I don't 'fuck', as you so elegantly put it," I bit back.

"No way!" Trey said. "Mr. Whitmarsh said you were fucking Mr. Meyer. He said—"

"Sean and I have slept together, yes, but that's not the same thing," I cut in, not wanting to hear Whitmarsh's cruder description of what Sean and I had shared. Especially not now. I didn't want to hear Trey talk about it, either. He didn't even begin to have the right to bring up something so private.

"Why isn't it?" Trey wanted to know and I suddenly realized why you heard so many parents answer awkward questions from their kids with the waspish phrase, "Because *I* say so, all right?" through firmly gritted teeth.

Instead, I strapped down my irritation and made an attempt to explain. "Because just fucking somebody is very different from making love with them, where you have a bond, a connection. "Fucking" implies little more than an all-out, selfish, I'm-using-you-for-my-own-gratification kind of act."

Trey was at an age where his squirm at the mention of the word "love" was almost a reflex action. Then he just shrugged. "Yeah—and your point is?"

The strap broke and my temper let fly. I rounded on him, almost unable to see his face for the starbursts going off inside my head. "You asked me once why I left the army. Well, shall I tell you why?" I threw at him, not waiting for an answer. "I left because four of the men I was training alongside, four of the men I was supposed to know and trust, got drunk one night and decided they were going to fuck me, regardless of what I thought about it."

Trey tried to flinch away but I grabbed his arm and spun

him back to face me, not letting him escape my bitter words. Some part of me knew he didn't deserve this but now I'd started I couldn't stop, it just spilled out and kept coming. "And because there were more of them than me, and they were bigger and stronger than I was, that's exactly what they did. They had to beat the shit out of me to do it, but they did it, just the same. And when they were done, they stood around and actually had a discussion about how it might be best to kill me, just in case I decided to kick up a fuss. It was like to them I wasn't even human any more."

I stopped and realized that my chest was so tight it was making me breathless. I made a conscious effort to relax, to speak normally. "Fucking is something you do *to* someone. Making love is something you do *with* them," I finished, calmer now. "That's the difference, Trey. Might not sound a lot, but trust me, it is. It really is."

I let go and this time it was my turn to stamp off, not really caring if he followed or not. After half a dozen strides he caught me up. I could feel him wanting to speak but I wouldn't look at him, wouldn't give him an opening.

Donalson, Hackett, Morton and Clay.

The litany of names went round and round inside my head in time to the fall of my feet in the sand. The names of the men who'd raped me, who'd finished my army career. The names of the men who'd set me on the path that eventually had led me here.

After another few minutes of silent walking I stopped abruptly. "This will do," I said, indicating a relatively sheltered spot in the soft sand at the top of the beach. "Make yourself at home."

I lay down with my back studiously toward him, resting my head on the ridiculous bag containing the bony shape of the Sig. Because of the rumbling hiss of the surf I nearly missed Trey's quietly spoken words behind me.

"I'm—I'm real sorry, Charlie."

In the whole of this sorry mess it was the first time he'd apologized or shown any remorse, the first time he'd made any sign of dropping the act and reaching out to me. Too bad that I couldn't bring myself to meet him halfway.

"You weren't to know," I said shortly, not turning round. "Now get some sleep. We're going to need it."

Despite my words, sleep didn't come easy for me. I lay awake, staring into the semi-darkness. I could tell by his breathing rate that Trey was awake, too, but we didn't speak. It seemed to take a long time before he began to snore.

What on earth had possessed me to come out with all those shameful details? Trey was a comparative stranger. I hardly knew him and certainly didn't like him, and yet I'd told him things I hadn't even shared with my real friends, people I'd known for five years or more. The realization of what I'd done sent a shiver across my skin in spite of the warm sand I was lying molded into.

I hadn't even told Sean the truth, not right away. At first I thought he'd been a part of the whitewash the army arranged to cover what those four men had done, including the ludicrous events of their court martial. What should have been an open-and-shut case degenerated into a farce that had ruined my reputation along with everything else.

It had been years until I'd found out that they'd manipulated Sean as much as they had done me. But once the Powers That Be had accidentally learned of our illicit relationship they'd subtly forced him out of his own career by a war of attrition. The worst thing was that, until we'd met again after five years and discovered what had really happened, he hadn't really known what he was supposed to have done wrong.

And now I'd blurted it all out to a fifteen-year-old boy who undoubtedly didn't have enough sense to keep his mouth shut. *Oh, wonderful move, Fox.* For a while I silently berated myself for my own stupidity, but gradually I recognized what had compelled me to dump that clutch of vitriol onto Trey.

If ever he found himself the aggressor in that kind of situation and it made him pause, just for a moment, then it was worth it. *Yeah, a one-woman crusade, that's me,* scoffed the voice in my head.

Maybe I was starting to lose it. After all we'd gone through, maybe this desire to open up to unsuitable people was one of the first signs. The thought was terrifying. I shut my eyes and willed sleep onto my unquiet mind.

Surprisingly perhaps, the nightmares I'd been half expecting didn't come. I slept sound and quiet and didn't wake until after sunrise the next morning.

And as soon as I did, I knew there was something wrong.

My body woke from the inside out, individual senses coming online first and hitting the mental alarm buttons. I couldn't quite put my finger on how it happened, but somehow I was alert to the danger before I ever opened my eyes and found out exactly what it was.

The brightness outside my closed eyelids told me the sun was well on the way up. The slightly receded lull of the surf told me the tide was on the way out. The mingled odors of sour sweat and last night's joints reaching my nostrils told me we weren't alone any more. It rippled over the top of the fresh morning smell of the salt water, tainting it.

From somewhere above me I heard the snigger of young male voices. *Not Whitmarsh, then. Not Oakley man.* There wasn't time for relief. I kept my eyes shut, regulated my breathing, but my system had started to rev, building up speed like pressure. The Sig was a reassuring lump in the bag under my cheekbone. A last resort.

Eventually, tiring of waiting for us to wake of our own volition, a foot nudged me in the stomach. None too gently. I opened my eyes and saw a sideways picture made up of pairs of tanned legs and baggy jeans. Someone leaned down into my field of vision and smiled nastily.

"Hi, remember me?" he said. It was the skinny kid with the bandanna round his head who'd unsuccessfully tried to rob us that first night on the beach. The one whose knife I'd taken away from him and which I'd left, now I belatedly remembered about it, in the backpack I'd abandoned at Henry's house. Too bad if he'd come to ask for it back.

I'd never even considered that the skinny kid might have gathered reinforcements and be lying in wait for us on the beach. His half-hearted attack had seemed so insignificant compared to the other dangers we'd had to face. Well, not any more.

I sat up fast enough to make him take an instinctive step back. No doubt his reflexes would be sharper this time, in view of the pain and humiliation I'd inflicted on him before. Mind you, he'd partially negated the need for extra vigilance by bringing half a dozen of his mates with him as back-up. Of the fat boy who'd served as sidekick during his last jaunt, there was no sign.

Trey was already awake, I saw, sitting up with his arms wrapped round his shins like he had in Henry's bath. He looked scared and defensive, as though he was expecting this to hurt. He threw me a single reproachful glance, as though I should have seen this coming and somehow deflected it.

"What do you want?" I said, shading my eyes with my hand so I could look up at the skinny kid against the low sun.

He gave a short, disbelieving laugh. "She wants to know what I want, huh?" He looked round at the others who joined in dutifully with his amusement. Then he looked back at me and the smile blinked out. "You know exactly what I want," he said, quiet and deadly. He was doing a pretty good impression of total meanness until the flicker of his eyes telegraphed his intentions.

He swung a vicious kick at my body. I caught his foot before it connected and twisted it sideways. It could have wrenched his knee or ankle out if he hadn't allowed himself to roll with it. He landed hard, sending up a plume of dry sand that was instantly scattered by the breeze.

I bounced to my feet while I had the chance, Trey scrambling up, also. The bag with the flowers on it was in my hand, keeping the Sig only inches from use, but I couldn't bring myself to get it out, even then.

They were just kids. Offensive and repugnant kids, maybe, but kids nonetheless. Perhaps if I drew the line somewhere, I could come back to myself. Perhaps there might still be hope for me.

The skinny kid was back on his feet in a flash, his momentary lapse firing his anger. I turned so Trey was directly at my back and watched the eyes and hands in front of me for the first move.

"Can I ask what the hell you boys think you're doing?" said a sudden familiar voice from a little way off to one side.

We all spun to face it. Walt stood a couple of meters away, staring at the bunch of us from under the brim of his Panama hat. My heart lurched. Before I'd only had Trey to worry about in this uneven fight. Now I had another civilian to protect. The gun was so close. It would end things quickly and I might not even have to use it.

I checked Walt. He didn't have his bag of seashells with him this morning but instead he carried a stainless-steel insulated coffee mug. As we watched he raised the mug to his lips and drank some of the contents. When he was done he looked inquiringly at the group that surrounded Trey and me.

"Well?" he said, with a fine touch of belligerence. "Cat got your tongues?"

For God's sake, Walt. Don't provoke them. You'll only make it worse for yourself.

But he turned to the skinny kid with the bandanna, who had been making out like this was the baddest part of South Central LA and he was the baddest dude in it. "Nathan, isn't it?" Walt said, his voice slow and easy. "What are you doing out when your mother's sick? Shouldn't you be at home helping out with the chores?"

"No sir, er, I mean yes sir," Nathan muttered, hanging his head. "She's much better." He all but scuffed his toes in the sand.

"Well, if you've finished fooling around with these young friends of mine," Walt said, his gaze steady, "we'll let you be on your way."

It struck me then that he was like an old-time Wild West sheriff, facing down the gunslinging brat pack by the slow weight of his reputation alone. One day they might have the courage to take him on, but today was clearly not that day.

Abruptly, Nathan turned and trudged away and his gang

went with him. I studied their retreat but he didn't even dare to go for a resentful backward glance. I gradually allowed my fists to unclench, my shoulders to unlock. It was only now that I became aware of the stiff ache of my body and the dull thumping pain behind my eyes.

I turned back to Walt, who was calmly drinking more of his coffee as though completely oblivious to what might have been.

"Nathan's not a bad kid," he said conversationally. "Gets a little wild now and again but basically he's OK. Harriet and I go to the same church as his mother."

He swung his cool gaze onto me then and I struggled not to quail under it just as the skinny kid and his mates had done.

"Not sure about the new hair style, Charlie," he remarked. "And if you don't mind me saying so, ma'am, you look like hell."

SEVENTEEN

WALT AND HARRIET'S kitchen looked exactly the same as it had the last time Trey and I had been there. More importantly, it smelled the same—of food.

The lady of the house was working furiously at the hob when Walt opened the door and ushered us inside. The smell of bacon frying on the grill hit me straight in the stomach, which immediately let out a clearly audible grumble.

"Well, somebody's hungry," Walt said with a smile. "Can I get you guys some coffee?"

Harriet turned then and it was relief I saw in her face. "Oh, you found them," she said, putting down her spatula. She came forward then, all smiles, wiping her hands on the apron she was wearing over her loose pinafore dress. She pulled out chairs from the table and hastily brought out extra cutlery for us. It was only as I sat down that I noticed there were already three settings.

I looked up at Walt, tense, and saw from his face that he knew right away I'd spotted the extra place.

"My nephew, Andrew," he said calmly, by way of explanation. "He's staying with us for a few days."

At that moment I heard footsteps approaching across the tiled floor of the living room. A young man in a casual jacket and tie appeared round the corner of the kitchen cabinets. He was shorter than Walt, slightly more thickset than the old man but he had a sharp upright stance that usually denotes time in the military—or the police.

Even without that suspicion, his instinctive reaction confirmed my fears. He'd been holding a mobile phone up to his ear with his left hand, making "uh-huh" noises. As soon as he caught sight of the pair of us, he jolted to a standstill and dropped the phone. His right hand snaked for the gun on his hip.

"Now hold it right there!" Walt thundered and his nephew froze automatically. I could just see the Glock 23 service pistol halfway out of its belt holster under the pushed-back hem of his jacket. If he'd ever got to finish it, it would have been one hell of a fast draw.

I had been holding my bag on my lap under the level of the table, which had a wipe-down vinyl cloth hanging over the edges that masked my hands. As soon as I'd made the guy for what he was, I'd stuck my hand inside the bag, trying to sit still and not to let the movement translate into my shoulders. I had my fingers curled round the Sig's pistol grip and already had it clear of the bag when Walt rapped out his command. I froze, too.

"Sit down, Andrew," Walt ordered, quieter now but carrying no less weight because of it. "I will not have gunplay in this house. You keep that piece on your hip, boy." He turned those ferocious eyebrows in my direction. "And you, Charlie, I've put a whole heap of trust in you—enough to bring you into my home like this. Don't let me down now."

I left the Sig lying across my lap and slowly brought my hands above the level of the table, empty. Andrew let his gun drop back into its holster with obvious reluctance and picked up his phone from where it had fallen on the kitchen tiles. The leather cover the phone had on seemed to have saved it from destruction.

"Sweet Jesus, Uncle Walt," he said then, in a slightly strangled voice. "Do you know who this is? Do you have any idea how many people we've got out hunting for these two?" He never took his eyes off me while he spoke.

Walt didn't answer, just raised an eyebrow at him. "Well, let's call a truce while we eat, shall we?" he said mildly. "There'll be time enough to talk about this afterward."

It was a bizarre meal. Trey sat alongside me and ate in complete silence, his gaze fixed on his plate. Andrew took the chair opposite me, with his aunt and uncle at each end. Every time I reached for my water glass Andrew tensed slightly.

I kept my expression bland and my knees up and together so the Sig didn't slide off onto the kitchen tiles, which I felt might have confirmed his worst suspicions. The last thing I wanted to do was give him any reasons to go against his uncle's wishes. As it was, the fingers of his right hand gave the occasional twitch, as though they were anxious enough to be considering independent action.

Nobody did much talking while we ate, although Walt was taking it all with a blithe lack of concern. He played the perfect congenial host, periodically offering juice, fresh fruit, or a plate of pancakes round the table. We accepted with a muted politeness. I knew from our past meeting just how quickly the old man could slip back into the professional skin of his former life. It made me constantly wary, expecting the worst.

In spite of the uncomfortable atmosphere, we were certainly hungry. The food had seemed plentiful in supply but was quickly consumed. It was then that Harriet pushed back her chair and stood, leaning forward with her hands on the table.

"Walt, why don't you take Andrew and Charlie through to the living room? I'm sure you have a lot to talk about and you'll be more comfortable in there," she said, her voice easy even if her body gave her away a little. "Trey, honey, how about you give me a hand to clear the table?"

I half expected Trey to kick up a stink about being excluded from the grown-ups' discussion but to my surprise he jumped up and started stacking dirty plates together like he couldn't wait to be out of there.

Walt and Andrew stood also. I was the last on my feet, mainly because I still had the gun resting across my thighs.

The bag had slipped to the floor and as I reached down for it I managed to stuff the Sig back inside. When I straightened up I found Andrew had loosened his jacket again, just in case, and was watching me with narrowed eyes.

He had dark eyes, a little like Sean's. At this distance it was hard to differentiate the changeover line between iris and pupil. Sean could have that vigilant and impenetrable air about him, too. It was clear that, whatever his uncle's feelings on the subject, Andrew trusted me about as far as he could throw a small car. I suppose I couldn't really blame him for that.

After all, so far I hadn't had particularly good press.

Walt led the pair of us through to the living area and gestured us into the two sofas that faced each other across a shaggy rug and a glass-topped wicker coffee table. We followed him with neither quite wanting to offer our unprotected back to the other.

As we sat there Andrew regarded me for a few moments with a stony face, then he gave a snort of bitter amusement.

"I've come across some fugitives from justice in my time, Fox," he bit out, shaking his head, "but I gotta hand it to you. You have to be one of the coolest."

"Maybe that's because I haven't done anything I didn't have to," I returned. I waited a beat, then added, "Andrew," to the end of it.

"That's Special Agent in Charge Till to you, missy," he shot back.

Special Agent in Charge no less. So he was FBI too, and not just a foot soldier. Nice to keep it in the family, Walt.

The old man held his hand up for peace. "Now, now, Andrew," he said gently. "You've been busting to speak your mind all through breakfast, so let's hear the worst of it."

"This—person," his nephew said delicately, not taking his eyes off me for a second, "is wanted for just about everything from kidnapping to homicide, including in connection with the shooting of a police officer down in Broward County. We've got half the cops in the state working on locating her and the Pelzner boy. And what you're doing now by giving her shelter, Uncle Walt, constitutes a serious felony, as you are well aware."

"You going to bring me in, son?" Walt asked, his voice mild. Andrew flicked him a single barbed glance.

"What happened to innocent until proven guilty?" I asked with just a smear of taunt to the question, "Or doesn't that apply here in the Land of the Free?"

Andrew's face darkened but he didn't rise to it.

Walt, meanwhile, had turned his attention over toward the kitchen, where Trey was dutifully wiping plates dry and being very careful not to drop any.

"I may be a little rusty these days," Walt murmured, "but the boy sure doesn't look like he's being held against his will."

Andrew allowed his eyes to slide in that direction for a couple of seconds. When he looked back, he was frowning.

"If your theory is right," I said, neutral. "I've had him for less than four days. If you're going to play the Stockholm syndrome card and try to say that I've brainwashed him, or that he's formed an unusual attachment to his captor in such a short time, you're going to struggle like hell to make that one stick."

Walt's face didn't show his sudden amusement outright, but I thought I detected a certain twinkle. "You have to admit, she's got a point," he allowed.

Andrew studied his uncle's expression and sat back with a frustrated gesture.

"Perhaps if you'd seen this lady's record you wouldn't be so ready to give her the benefit of the doubt," he said sharply, then started rapping out the facts. He didn't falter and he didn't need to refer to any notes. Nice to see I'd made such an impression since I'd arrived in the US.

"British Army background. Expert marksman—well *that* didn't take much working out. Selected for Special Forces. Then it all goes wrong and she ends up with a dishonorable discharge. Even changes her name. How am I doing so far, Fox?"

"That's Miss Fox to you, laddie," I drawled, mainly to hide the growing unease. I liked my privacy as much as the next person. In fact, considering what my past contained, probably more.

He brushed aside my calculated insolence and kept going. "So after that she's scratching a living teaching unarmed combat. Gets herself involved in a drugs racket. Year before last she ends up killing a guy—with her bare hands, for Christ's sake!"

"It was self defense," I gritted. "I was cleared of any blame."

"Yeah well, looks like the courts over in good old England get it wrong sometimes too, huh?" he batted straight back, keeping his gaze on Walt now, working to convince him. His body was very still as he talked, as though he was putting all his effort into his voice. "Then there's the part she played in a major civil disturbance last fall. There was a shooting there too, wasn't there, Fox?"

I opened my mouth but he didn't give me the chance to speak. "We did a search with Interpol and, surprise surprise, her name pops up again. Trouble in Germany. More shootings. Either you're one unlucky lady, Fox, or you're a magnet for trouble."

"I was cleared," I said again, more quietly this time. "You want to know what really happened with half that lot? Get in touch with Lancashire Constabulary back in the UK and speak to Detective Superintendent John MacMillan. I'm sure he'll be willing to tell you all about the people I *didn't* kill. The ones whose lives I actually helped save."

MacMillan's name was a surprise, I saw, but whether it was because it was familiar or whether the rank impressed him, I couldn't tell. He regarded me gravely.

"I suppose you reckon you have a believable explanation of the events of the past few days, do you?" he asked quietly. "Just like that?"

"I'll give it a go," I said, calmer now. "It may not be believable to you, *Special Agent in Charge,* but it's the truth so it's the best I've got. Tell me, how much do you know about the workings of the stock market?"

* * *

It took a while to tell the full story. The FBI agent made rapid notes in a pocket book and only interrupted me twice. The first time was when I went through the attack on the young cop by the two men in the Buick. As soon as I mentioned shooting the guy who'd been in the passenger seat, Andrew looked up and said, "Shot him with what?"

"A Sig Sauer nine-mil," I said, not making any moves to show it to him. "You'll have found four empty casings at the scene, by the driver's door of the Mercury. They'd already put us off the road by then and the cop was already dead," I added pointedly. "The men in the Buick were using something fairly hefty. I didn't get a clear look, but I would guess at possibly .357s. Large caliber handguns have their own distinctive sound. Oakley man—the guy at the theme park—had a .40, like the one you carry yourself. Whitmarsh and Chris were both using nines at the motel."

He paused a second, looked as though he might throw in another query, then nodded and went back to his notes.

Walt brought fresh coffee but it went cold on the table in front of us. At one point I glanced over and found that Harriet and Trey were standing by the kitchen cabinets, the crockery all put away now. They were listening to every word. The boy was white-faced, as though hearing about it again made it all that bit more real. Harriet had her arm around his shoulders.

Andrew's second interruption came when I got to the part about the shoot-out at Henry's place. As soon as I was done he demanded the details, then relayed the information to his colleagues in a short phone call. He didn't, I noted with relief, explain to them where the information had come from.

I gathered from his reaction that nobody had connected the incident at Henry's with my much-reported killing spree. I wondered how Oakley man had explained away his involvement. If he'd known about Xander's call to the emergency services, did that mean he'd been on duty at the time? But if so, why hadn't he been in uniform? Was he really a cop?

Well, I suppose now was my chance to find out.

". . . uh-huh. Get back to me as soon as you have it," Andrew rapped out now and finished the call without saying goodbye. One of the benefits of being in charge, it seemed, was an ability to dispense with normal politeness.

"Oakley man is the only one I can't work out in all this," I said. "He was one of the two cops who brought Trey home from the Galleria, but that was down in Fort Lauderdale. I assume he really *is* a cop, but if so, what's he doing responding to emergency calls in Daytona Beach? Somebody must be able to identify him."

"I don't think you're in a position to tell me how to do my job, Fox," Andrew said. "You let me worry about the peripheral players in this scenario, huh?"

"Peripheral players?" I echoed smartly. "He's one of the *major* players. Either he's working for Keith or he's working on his own, but he's got plenty of manpower and he's not afraid to kill anyone who gets in the way."

"I'll have people working on tracing him," he said, frowning again. "We're gonna have to check out your story some first. So far, you're claiming a body count of—" he checked the previous page of his notes "—what? Six or seven dead and a couple of wounded? But we've only found the two kids at the motel and the cop. And now this guy Henry." There was doubt in his voice.

"Why would I lay claim to more if it wasn't the case?" I said tiredly. "This looks bad enough as it is. Why do I need to dress it up any further?"

He didn't respond to that question, posing one of his own instead. "And this guy you call Oakley man, you say he stopped for long enough to pick up his dead before he took off from Henry's house, right?"

"Right."

"You have to admit that's kinda convenient. Not leaving behind any bodies, that is."

"Of course he didn't leave them behind—he's a cop," I said, the tension making me snappy now. "There'll still be blood. There'll still be evidence. *If* you care to look for it. Maybe he was trying to leave you pointing at me because he knows from first-hand experience that you'll take the route of least resistance when it comes to pinning this whole thing on somebody."

Andrew's face flushed a little at the jibe and Walt, realizing things were about to deteriorate, spoke up for the first time since I'd begun recounting my tale.

"Why don't you have a look-see if any bodies have turned up over the last coupla days with gunshot wounds?" he suggested. "Might go a little way toward clearing this up, son," he added gently when his nephew still hesitated.

Suppressing a grumpy sigh, Andrew got back on the phone. I leaned forward, resting my forearms on my knees and trying to roll the rigid ache out of my neck. I had the Barbie-pink bag clenched tight on my lap like a talisman.

Walt patted me on the back of my hand and, when I looked up, he smiled, the corners of his eyes crinkling as he did so. Whatever Andrew's qualms, the old man believed me. I was surprised how much that realization gave me hope.

But hope of what? I was stuck in Walt and Harriet's house with an armed and twitchy FBI agent who was fairly convinced I was lying through my teeth in everything I'd said to him. I tried to tell myself that I'd always known it was going to end sometime—we couldn't stay on the run forever. But not like this, I admitted privately. Not like this.

They weren't going to let us just walk out of here again, not without violence that I wasn't prepared to use, but the thought of sitting in a prison cell while Gerri Raybourn and Whitmarsh and Oakley man were still out there, manufacturing more damning evidence against me, made my skin go cold.

Special Agent in Charge Till was getting shirty with someone at the other end of the line. "Well why in the name of hell didn't you tell me about this last night?" he demanded. "Not relevant? You developed sixth sense now, that you can tell me what might be relevant to this case and what isn't? Fax the report through to me right now, y'hear? No, I'm still at my uncle's place." His eyes flickered across me. "No, I think I'll be here a little while longer. Something's come up. OK."

He punched the end call button and let his breath out fast down his nose.

"What is it?" Walt asked.

"Report came in late yesterday. They found a body down near Lake Hell 'n' Blazes in Brevard County. Coupla tourists hired an airboat and happened upon a little more of the wildlife than they bargained for. According to the local boys the guy had been in the water a day or so and he'd been pretty badly chewed up. You throw meat in the swamp and there's plenty out there will take a bite out of it."

"Pretty badly chewed up?" I murmured, not liking the mental image conjured up by his words. "So you won't be able to tell who it is?" In my mind I'd already started running through the list of possibles.

Andrew broke through my thoughts. "He'd been gut-shot—handgun most likely. Not a good way to go. But they found ID on the body. Turns out he was a Brit too. Name of Sean Meyer." He met my eyes level and without apparent guile. "Sound like anybody you know?"

EIGHTEEN

ALL AT ONCE the world stopped. And my heart and lungs stopped with it.

I tried to tell myself that I'd known, right from the moment I'd found the Sig in Sean's empty room, that he was dead. It didn't seem to make any difference to the shockwave that hit me now. Didn't lessen the impact. A part of me fiercely didn't want to believe it, but at the same time another part of me had always known that it was true.

The explosion inside my head was monstrous, but made no external sound. At the edge of my vision, debris started to rain down all around me, but nobody else saw it fall. Fire raged, and froze me to the bone.

I shut my eyes, just briefly, aware of the sting of suppressed tears under my lids. I didn't let them loose.

Then I felt the mechanical jolt as the world started turning again. It had all taken just a split second. All the time out of reality I was allowed.

I opened my eyes and found that the sea hadn't boiled and the sky hadn't turned blood red while I'd been gone. I blinked a couple of times. The FBI agent was watching me closely.

"How sure are you that it's Sean?" I asked, amazed at the calm, level tone of my voice.

"Pretty sure. 'Course we'll need a formal ID, but there was a wallet in the guy's back pocket with credit cards and a Brit driver's license. He was also wearing a real nice Swiss wristwatch—a Breitling. That should be easy enough to trace. Expensive piece and still ticking, so they tell me, which is quite something given the state the body was in. Those Swiss really know their stuff, huh?"

"Shut up!" It was Trey who spoke, his voice harsh and on the edge of cracking. He broke away from Harriet and stumbled forward, glaring at Andrew. "Just shut the fuck up, man! Don't you know she was, like, in love with him? Just leave her alone!"

"Leave it, Trey," I said quietly, too numb even to feel embarrassment at his outburst. The boy glared between us, his mouth tight and an ugly mottled pink splashed across his cheekbones. After a moment he sighed gustily and turned away, letting his arms flop. Harriet gently put her arm across his narrow shoulders and steered him back toward the kitchen.

Andrew Till wasn't being deliberately cruel, I knew. He wasn't trying to hurt or provoke me. Dealing with death on a regular basis gives you a tinge of black humor that it's sometimes difficult to shake. You grow a thicker skin and laugh it off, or you let the weight of old bones bury you alive in ghosts and nightmares.

I got to my feet, still clutching the flowered bag. Till rose, also. His face, which had started to show a hint of pity, sympathy even, turned wary and his eyes went professionally cool and flat again.

"You and I both know who's responsible, don't we?" I said.

"No, but I sure know who you *think* is responsible."

It wasn't much, but at least it showed that he recognized someone else had played a part in all this. It wasn't solely down to me. A tiny blade of hope began to form, to take an edge from dullness.

"So what are you planning on doing about it?" I demanded.

"We are pursuing a number of leads at this time," he said, suddenly coming over all official-speak. "We aren't discounting any theories. It will be thoroughly investigated, Charlie. You have my word on that."

It was something in his voice that tipped me off.

"Tell me," I said, conversational, "how long have I got before your SWAT team arrives?"

Walt looked resigned, I saw, almost a little disappointed. Harriet just stood and gaped disbelievingly. Till almost smiled. His eyes shifted slightly to the face of the clock on the far wall of the living room. " 'Bout ten minutes," he said easily. "Maybe a little less."

"In that case I'm afraid you're going to have to shoot me to keep me here," I said. "I'm not staying to be arrested while you let Sean's killers walk. If you won't find them, *I* will."

I turned my back and took a step toward the door out onto the back lawn, the one we'd come in by.

"Hold it right there, missy!" the FBI agent's voice rapped out. "Don't make me do this."

I turned back and found he'd finally completed that fast draw and brought his pistol out and up and level in a textbook double-handed Weaver stance. From where I was standing the sizeable opening in the end of the barrel looked like the deck gun of a frigate.

"Andrew, don't you dare!"

Outrage deepened Harriet's voice so that, to begin with, I thought it was Walt who'd made the protest, but it wasn't.

"Aunt Harriet, please, get out of the way," Till said, the anguish clear in his voice as the old woman stepped, stubborn and determined, into his line of fire. "You know I have to take her in."

"I know you do, dear," Harriet said, facing him steadily, "but just not today."

Trey edged round her carefully and joined me by the door.

"Stay here," I told him quickly, pleading, one eye still on the FBI agent's gun. He'd lowered it now, but was still ready if he got his chance. "You'll be safe here. Special Agent Till will protect you." *Better than I can. Better than I will for what I have to do now.*

Trey cocked me a sideways glance. "No way, man," he said. "That's your job."

I looked up, taking in Walt and Harriet and Andrew Till in a fast sweep. I shrugged helplessly. "I'm sorry," I said to nobody in particular and pushed open the outside door.

◆ ◆ ◆

We moved up the beach at a hurried jog, trying to put some distance between ourselves and the house. I stumbled along, forcing my limbs into an uneven rhythm. Ahead of me I could see the pier near the Boardwalk and the stepped sides of the Adam's Mark hotel opposite the Ocean Center where the car show was taking place. It seemed a long way away, partly shrouded by the morning heat haze, but it became my target. If we could reach there, the bustle and the crowds, we would have sanctuary.

I didn't look back, didn't want to see if yet another group of men with guns was chasing us. I didn't know if Harriet would hold sway over her nephew, would persuade him to let us run, but somehow I doubted it. Not for long, at any rate.

Trey ran alongside me with an easy stride I hadn't expected for such a gawky kid. I'd thought him too much of a computer nerd to have any flair for athletics. Somehow the two were mutually exclusive.

He kept cocking sideways glances in my direction as we went but I didn't look at him. I just kept running, my eyes on the soft sand in front of my next stride. It was the only way I could see past the wailing that was going on inside my head.

The heat crushed down onto me, weighting my limbs, making me punch-drunk. Eventually, when we'd covered the best part of a mile, Trey dropped back to a jog, gasping. I vaguely registered him falling away but momentarily couldn't work out what it meant. There was a pause, then he caught me up again, staggering now.

"Hey Charlie," he protested, breathless and pained. "Hey c'mon, Charlie, slow down."

Still I ignored him, my only focus on putting one foot in front of the other. It didn't immediately register that he'd grabbed hold of my arm until I swung, half off balance. I looked round, almost surprised to see him clinging on there.

For a moment I failed to recognize his face. He was a stranger to me. His mouth was moving but I couldn't hear the words. Then the noises of the beach suddenly rushed in and regained their natural volume.

"Charlie, c'mon, man, snap out of it!" Trey shouted. There was something in his voice that it took me a moment to place. Then it clicked—panic.

The identification of Trey's fear acted as a catalyst. I shook myself, tried to break free of the all-consuming grief that was paralyzing my mind. As I surfaced, my stride faltered, as though I was diverting energy from my limbs to control my emotions.

I stumbled, going down on my knees in the hot sand. Trey dropped next to me, his skinny fingers still clamped round my upper arm. In the warm gust of breeze from the sea I realized there was a wetness on my cheeks, that the tears were circling my mouth to drip unheeded from my chin.

For a moment Trey seemed utterly lost. He let go of my arm, put a tentative hand on my shoulder instead and gave me a little shake.

"C'mon, don't go all girlie on me, Charlie," he said, and that scornful teenage note was back with a vengeance. Before I could respond, he hit me again, caustic. "They said you were just somebody's girlfriend. Looks like they were right, huh?"

It was the tone rather than the words that cut through and began to bite. I looked up, dazed, expecting to see bitterness and contempt on his face. Instead all I saw was a scared kid who was doing the only thing he could think of to shock me out of my stupor.

It worked.

Slowly, my head began to clear, like feeling your ears pop as the plane makes its final approach. My hands steadied and my legs seemed to come back under my own control. I got to my feet, brushing away the sand that still clung to the sweat-soaked knees of my silk trousers. Trey stepped back, hands hanging by his sides now, watching me.

We were nearly as far down the beach as the Boardwalk but I couldn't quite remember how we'd got there. All I could feel was my own raging thirst and the fact that any exposed areas of skin had started to burn. I needed to get out of the sun. Find a bolt-hole. Somewhere I could regroup and take stock.

Somewhere I could try and come up with a plan to get us out of this mess.

"So, like, what do we do now?" Trey asked. He was panting a little, too. Not just me who was feeling the burden of the heat, then.

I smiled at him. Not a full-blown, reassuring, this-will-all-be-OK kind of a smile but not a bad fake, given the circumstances.

"We need some cover," I said firmly, gesturing to my reddened arms when we both knew I was really referring to the FBI. "Do your ears feel up to another tour of the show?"

I saw his shoulders come down a fraction with a relief he tried not to let show too much. He shrugged, going for nonchalant, going for cool. "Whatever," he said airily.

I guessed that was the nearest to enthusiasm I was going to get from him.

Inside the Spring Break Nationals it wasn't any quieter than it had been the last time we were there on Friday. In fact, I realized that it had probably just been warming up and now, late morning on Sunday, it was building toward its climax.

Most of the exhibitors' booths had acquired a new attraction today, it seemed. Pretty girls wearing not much more than their underwear were signing posters of themselves for queues of adoring, if slightly hungover, teens. The girls all wore exactly the same shade of tan, like they'd been sprayed out of a bottle.

I had to link my arm through Trey's to stop him tripping over his tongue. When he realized he'd been caught ogling he dropped his gaze to the carpeting and kept it there unwaveringly. Until the next scantily-clad lovely, at any rate.

When my eyes and ears had had enough punishment we ventured back out into the heat. I let Trey lead me in apparently aimless fashion up and down the rows of cars on display, with no real clue what I was supposed to be looking for.

To be honest, half my brain was taken up with scanning the people around us, checking not so much for uniforms this time, but for the ones with the watchful eyes and ready hands. Looking for the ones who were looking for us.

It was with a jolt, then, that my eye ran across two faces I recognized but had never expected to see here.

Aimee and Xander.

For a moment I made no moves, did nothing to alert either them or Trey. My first thoughts were suspicious ones. Xander had claimed he was grounded for years. I'd assumed the same went for Aimee. So what were they doing out at all? Were they here as bait for us? If so, who was pulling their strings?

Every nasty scenario I could think of flashed through my head, including that the two were somehow connected to Whitmarsh or Oakley man. No, it was much more likely that they'd been drafted in by the Feds to betray us.

Almost as soon as my doubts arrived I dismissed them, but still I couldn't bring myself to make contact. Xander and Aimee and Scott had thought of Trey as their friend. They'd trusted him—trusted me, more to the point—and had paid a high price for that friendship. Too high a price? Scott was still in hospital. He might not walk again. Even if they were completely on the level I doubted that they'd really want to see either of us right now. Besides, coming hard on top of the morning I'd had already I didn't think I could face another showdown.

Then Aimee turned and caught sight of us, and it was out of my hands.

She gave a whoop and ran across the short distance that separated us, scooping Trey up into a bear hug so fierce I thought his skinny ribs would crack.

I realized then that Xander was watching me and something about the tension in him told me he knew I'd spotted them first. Spotted them and done nothing about it. As he moved across to join us, the nod of greeting he gave me was cautious, to say the least.

"So how did you get out?" I tried but couldn't keep the touch of cynicism in my voice. "Dig a tunnel?"

Xander didn't react to the faint jibe. "Once Mom and Dad got over being angry and being scared they kinda realized it wasn't our fault Scott was caught up in a, like, random drive-by," he said, with little apparent irony in his tone.

"Mine even thought we'd acted kinda brave and responsible, y'know, under the circumstances," Aimee put in, releasing Trey so he could catch his breath.

"So here you are," I said, cool.

"Yeah, here we are," Xander said, matching me, his eyes a little narrowed.

Aimee flicked her eyes over the three of us. "How you doin', girl?" she asked, studying me with her head on one side. "You hanging in there OK?"

"Just about," I said, breaking my gaze away from Xander's to glance at her.

"Anybody thirsty?" Trey asked suddenly, his voice a touch high. "Let's go 'cross the street and grab a bunch of sodas, yeah?"

For a moment none of us gave any sign of having heard him, then Xander blinked a couple of times. "Sure," he said, raising a smile. "Good idea. Why not?"

We walked out of the show area and crossed over the road, dodging the backed-up traffic that was already snarling the main drag. As we went I noticed Trey casting anxious looks at each of us and realized that he'd just been trying to keep the peace. We were the only things so far he'd been able to rely on. He couldn't afford us to be at one another's throats. Not when I'd cracked up on him once this morning already.

We went to the same little diner where we'd been eating when Henry's fateful phone call had arrived. It was only after we'd sat down at one of the round outside tables that the significance of that seemed to occur to him. He shuffled for a moment, looking awkward, but the waitress arrived to take our order and the moment passed.

I hutched my chair sideways until I was mostly in the shade of the umbrella over our table. Even so I could feel the heat radiating from my burned arms like I was sitting next to a furnace.

"You should, like, put something on that, y'know," Aimee said, nodding to them. "It's real bad to let yourself burn like that."

I'd been doing a lot of things lately that were real bad for me.

"I know," I said. She shut up.

The drinks arrived, full to the brim with ice, and I settled for leaning my arms against the sides of the tall red plastic glass instead. It wasn't scientific, but it was certainly soothing.

To begin with the kids were stiff and uncomfortable with each other but gradually they began to loosen up a little and to chat. I didn't join in, just let the conversation flow over and around me. I kept my gaze sweeping over the surrounding area, looking for trouble.

It took about ten minutes before I found it.

One moment my eye had skimmed across the far pavement outside the front of the Ocean Center and it was empty of any threat. On the return pass, however, there was a man standing there.

He stood easily, relaxed, with his thumbs hooked into his pockets, waiting. Waiting for me to spot him and make my move.

I came to my feet automatically, clutching my bag.

"Wait here," I said to Trey, clipped, without shifting my eyes from my target. He followed my gaze and let out a gasp, half rising in his seat. I put a hand on his shoulder and eased him back down again.

"Don't worry," I said, trying a small smile. "If he was out to get us we wouldn't have seen him coming." And I hoped that it was true.

I walked down the couple of steps from the diner and threaded my way through the cars waiting for the next green light at the junction. Not that there would be any gaps for them to pull out into, even when they got the signal.

The man stood still and watched me come to him.

When I reached the pavement I stopped and made a show of glancing around.

"So where's the heavy mob, Walt?"

"No heavy mob," Walt said simply. "No SWAT team. Just me."

He was wearing the same battered Panama hat I'd first seen him in, and now he regarded me gravely from under its brim. I stuck my own hands in my pockets, aware of the tensely frozen audience on the other side of the street.

"Oh really?" I said, not trying to keep the doubt out of my voice.

Walt smiled a little, the action crinkling his eyes until all I could see were pinpoints of a gunmetal gray beneath his washed-out brows. "Let's just say that Harriet and I kinda persuaded young Andrew to call off his dogs until he'd had time to check out your story some."

"And?"

He nodded slowly. "And so far, it checks out."

"So, why are you here?"

I didn't bother to ask how he'd found us. I didn't really need to. That first morning Trey and I had eaten breakfast with the old couple, the kid had been full of the Spring Break Nationals, shooting his mouth off about the event. I remembered thinking at the time that Walt had paid unusual attention to him. Now I realized it was probably from habit of half a lifetime spent in criminal investigation. Never overlook the smallest fact. You never know when it's going to come in useful.

Like now, for instance.

Walt didn't answer straight away, his eye apparently caught by a huge drophead Chevy Impala with Metalflake paint and gold wire wheels that was being driven by a kid who didn't look old enough to buy cigarettes. Walt shook his head and turned back to me.

"I called that young feller you mentioned—John MacMillan," he said. Only someone of Walt's years could get away with referring to a policeman as senior as Detective Superintendent MacMillan as "that young feller."

I started to nod, then paused as a thought struck me. "On a Sunday?"

"Oh, you mention multiple homicide and kidnapping and it

tends to kinda get folks' attention," Walt said softly. "Even on a Sunday."

"Yes, when you put it like that, I suppose it does," I said, my own voice wry. "So, what did he say?"

Walt took his time about replying, giving me a thorough scrutiny. It took effort to stand calm and casual in the face of it.

"He said you'd damned near gotten yourself killed on a coupla occasions since he'd first met you," Walt said, still watching me minutely. "Said you'd just about put your life down to protect the people who were important to you."

His eyes flicked away from me briefly then, shifting to the little group at the diner across the street and to one face in particular. I didn't have to follow his gaze to know which of them he was looking at.

I felt my chin come up and tried not to make it a challenge. "MacMillan say anything else?" I asked, neutral.

"Yeah," Walt returned lazily, swinging his attention back to me. "He said you had good instincts and as how I should probably trust them."

"And is that what you're going to do?"

Again, Walt was silent for a moment, frowning while his mind turned over. I didn't push him. Whatever he was reaching a decision on, it was clearly heavy enough to require such thought. Rushing him would not, I reckoned, be in my best interests.

"I guess so," he said at last, quietly, and he nodded almost to himself. "The guy you called Oakley man?" His tone made it a question.

"Yeah."

"His name is Haines," he said, flat, "and you were right— he's a cop but that's not all he is." His gaze searched my face for reaction but I didn't have one to show him. "When he's off duty he moonlights as a security consultant. Early last year he did a little private work down in Miami for a company manufacturing auto parts."

I shrugged. I didn't see the significance. "So?"

"At that time the head of security at the company was a lady called Gerri Raybourn."

I couldn't keep that one from making its mark. It hit me like a fast unexpected blow to the stomach, stealing the air from my lungs in a rapid hiss. I'd known Gerri was behind Whitmarsh, but confirming her connection to Oakley man made her solely responsible for everything that had happened.

A whole host of chaotic thoughts tumbled out of the back of my mind, jostling against each other, striking sparks. And following them was a slowly spreading black rinse of anger.

Gerri Raybourn had murdered Sean. It might not have been her personally who pulled the trigger, but she'd done it, nonetheless.

I looked back at Walt, aware that my face had locked down and my body had stiffened with the shock.

"Has Special Agent Till picked her up yet?"

"On what grounds?" Walt asked, his voice reasonable. "The only person who's accusing her of anything is you and, you have to kinda admit, Charlie, right now that don't account for a whole heck of a lot."

"So what are you saying, Walt?" I asked bitterly. "If I don't turn myself in, she gets away scot free?"

"No," he said, voice careful. "But it would sure help if you could provide some evidence."

I went still. "What kind of evidence?"

"Well, you're maybe the only person she's likely to make any kind of a confession to," he said. "Just supposing you were to get to talk to her, and just supposing you was to be wearing a wire of some description."

"So, your nephew's looking for someone else to do his dirty work for him," I said.

That earned me a raised eyebrow and a calm stare that made me regret my hasty jibe. It was only stubbornness that kept my face defiant.

"Andrew's a fine agent and he's a fine young man. Fair-minded and thorough," Walt said. "But he has to work within the law, not outside it. If we—you—can bring him something solid, he won't ignore it, that I can safely promise you."

I tilted my head and gave him a cynical smile. "You reckon you can talk your nephew—not to mention the FBI—into planting a wire on me and sending me all the way down to Fort Lauderdale to try and prise a confession out of Gerri?" I asked.

"Gerri's not in Fort Lauderdale," Walt said. "She has a time-share apartment a little ways down the coast from here and ever since there were reports of you and Trey being in this area, she's been staying there."

"And the wire?"

"Well, I don't have the access to that kinda equipment that I used to," he admitted, "but I got one of those little voice-activated memo recorders that works pretty good." He nodded toward my bag. "It would fit in there OK and she's not likely to search you."

I glanced back across the street. Trey was on his feet now, looking poised to flee. I gave him a small wave to try and re-assure him. He sank back into his chair again but didn't ap-pear any less tense, even so.

I thought of Sean, dead and mutilated in a Florida swamp. Of all the ways I'd feared our relationship might end, that hadn't been on the list.

I turned back to Walt, who was standing with his hat brim tilted so the sun was out of his eyes.

"OK," I said. "Where do I find this time-share?"

Walt studied me for a moment, his face grave. "If you're sure you really want to do this, Charlie," he said. "I'll take you there myself."

NINETEEN

WALT DROVE ME south in an eight-year-old Lincoln Town Car with cracked cream leather trim. We didn't speak much once we were on the road and I was happy enough with that. The mood I was in, I wasn't looking for polite conversation.

Walt drove down through Daytona Beach and crossed back over the Intracoastal on the same William V. Chappell Jr. bridge we'd used when Trey and I had gone to meet Henry. There'd been a lot of water under it since then, both physically and metaphorically.

In daylight the buildings looked faded and even a little shabby, the colors washed out without the reinforcement of their nighttime neon. It matched my mood—down-at-heel, subdued.

I'd entrusted Trey to Xander and Aimee's care, much against his will. He'd thrown a controlled tantrum at the prospect of being left behind but I didn't have the time nor the temper myself to stand that kind of bratty behavior from him. After a few futile attempts at whiny persuasion, he seemed to realize as much and gave up trying. He settled for quiet and sulky instead, barely able to bring himself to say goodbye or good luck to me. *Well sod you, then.*

"Look after him," I'd said to Xander and he'd nodded, face serious.

"Don't sweat it," he'd said. "He'll be fine."

Aimee had grinned at me. "Go kick some ass, girl."

I'd promised them I'd call Trey on his mobile as soon as I was done. Then I watched them walk away from the little diner together. They stopped by the curb a little way further down the street and were about to cross when Trey suddenly glanced back at me, frowning.

He knows, I thought. *He's worked it out.* I turned my back on it and jogged through the slow-moving traffic to rejoin Walt, who was waiting for me on the other side of the road.

Whatever doubts I may have had about trusting Trey's safety to anyone else, I dismissed them. The only alternative to Xander and Aimee was leaving him with Walt, which could be the same as handing the kid over to the authorities. I had a sneaking suspicion that the old couple could only hold out against their nephew and the all-consuming government body he represented for so long. Better not to put temptation in Special Agent Till's way by having the boy dangled under his nose. Much better that he simply didn't know where either of us were.

The only other alternative to that was to take Trey with me. That idea was out of the question from the start. If I could get Gerri Raybourn to admit the part she'd played in Sean's death, I was planning on doing more than tape-recording her, and the kid had already seen too much death in my company. Not quite the kind of thing Keith had been hoping for when he'd made some throwaway comment last week about the fact I was British being good for broadening Trey's horizons.

Now, as I sat in the faded luxury of Walt's car listening to something in the rear suspension creaking every time we hit a lump in the road, I found myself wondering coldly where Trey's father fitted in to all this? How much of the responsibility did he share for Sean's death?

The answer to that one didn't so much hit me as rise slowly and uncomfortably into my mind, like sitting in the bath while it fills from a slow-running cold tap. Livingston Brown had told me that he'd seen Keith leaving the house in Fort Lauderdale apparently of his own volition. But he also said the man had seemed nervous and in a hurry.

Supposing that wasn't because Keith had been running

away. Supposing Brown had misinterpreted the reason for Keith's unease and instead it was because his every move was being watched by people who'd told him they had already kidnapped his son.

As the thought formed, I was half-tempted to let it go but it stuck to my fingers like static cling and I couldn't shake it loose. Little things kept popping into my mind. Like the fact that Whitmarsh had known instantly from Henry's e-mails that the one they were missing was Trey, not Keith.

So Keith hadn't done a runner. He'd been taken.

And Gerri Raybourn was the one pulling all the strings.

My resolve hardened along with my certainty. I turned away from the window and glanced across at Walt in the driving seat.

"How much do you know about Ms. Raybourn?" I asked.

"Oh this and that," Walt said, voice easy and casual as ever. "She's well respected in her field. Did ten years with the Bureau, as a matter of fact."

"Ah," I said dryly, "so that's why Special Agent Till doesn't want to move against her without overwhelming evidence—she's part of the old boy network."

"Former agents are treated just the same as everyone else," Walt said firmly but without showing irritation. "I checked her records and she left more'n three years ago. Went through a messy divorce and her ex got custody of the kids. He got laid off from his job so she's having to pay him off and put her eldest through college. I guess she found she could make a little more money on the outside than she could working for the government."

"So she's short on cash," I murmured, "and long on motive."

I remembered our drive from the airport when she'd got the call that told her news of the program had leaked out to the press. Her display of anger then had certainly seemed genuine but I suppose if she was planning on stealing the program along with its inventor, the fewer people who knew about it the better. She'd had me fooled into thinking I could trust her the night I'd called her for help from the motel. And look how *that* had ended.

Walt glanced wryly at me. "Motive for what?"

"For wanting the program for herself," I said. "I think she engineered the trouble at the company recently so she could call in Sean and me as back-up. That way, when she took Keith and Trey—"

"Which she's claiming *you're* responsible for," Walt cut in.

I ducked my head in agreement. "True, she is, but bear with me on this. As I said, that way she already has us in place as fall-guys. She has her boys grab Sean along with Keith and hopes to get Trey and me at the park on the same day. That way she's got the option of either claiming Keith's done a runner, or that we've taken him."

Good as his word, Walt didn't immediately dismiss my suggestion. Instead he nodded slowly, frowning. Ahead of us the lights changed and he braked smoothly to a halt.

"But her man fumbles the ball," he said then.

"Yeah, he did," I agreed. "So, next best thing, she puts it out that *I've* got Trey. But, the last thing she can afford to have happen is for the cops to get hold of us. That might blow the whole thing. So when they nearly do, she has her boys step in and kill the cop. By then she's past caring about getting hold of Trey alive. He was only to secure Keith's good behavior anyway. She just wants us dead."

The lights changed and Walt set the car moving forward again. His measured driving style reminded me of police drivers in the UK. He negotiated a parked truck in the right-hand lane before he spoke again.

"So it's not until that guy you mentioned—Henry—offers you to them on a plate that she realizes that without Trey the program kinda won't work."

"Exactly," I said. "Because after that Whitmarsh was desperate to take us alive, but the message obviously hadn't got through to Haines. I have no idea why not. It could simply have been a cock-up in communications. But Whitmarsh was even prepared to shoot Haines's men to protect us. And to let me go when I threatened Trey myself."

Walt looked surprised. "You didn't mention that part."

"You try living with that kid twenty-four hours a day and you'd want to shoot him, too," I said, only half joking.

Walt frowned again, but whether it was deep thought, or whether he disapproved of my flippancy in the circumstances, it was difficult to tell.

"So you reckon Gerri Raybourn's holding Keith somewhere, hoping she can still get the pair of them."

I nodded. "That's how it seems to me. One's not worth much without the other."

He let his breath out tiredly, almost a sigh. "Makes it kinda all the more important she's stopped, Charlie," he said.

"I know," I said. And inside my head another voice added, *Oh I'll stop her all right, Walt. Don't you worry about that.*

Less than an hour after we'd left Daytona Beach and headed down the coast, Walt slowed the Lincoln to a halt on the dusty shoulder of the highway and nodded toward the other side of the road. The other traffic continued past us at speed, close enough to rock our car each time they did so.

"That's the place," he said.

All I saw was a neatly rendered low white wall bordering suspiciously man-made–looking grounds of part grass and part tropical forest. It looked sculpted for effect rather than natural. The grass was artificially green and bright, and the wall itself seemed to go on for miles in both directions. I tried to remember when it had first started but I hadn't been paying enough attention.

A little way from where we'd stopped was an impressive wrought-iron gateway, next to which was a lavish sign. It showed an artist's impression of a range of Mediterranean-style villas, all white stucco and terracotta tiles, surrounding a lake in the center. Around the edges of the sign were depictions of Prozac-happy couples playing golf, or water skiing, or sharing an intimate after-dinner drink at sunset.

The sign announced a new and exclusive opportunity in vacation resort ownership. It sounded like the copywriters were trying desperately to squirm out of using the word "time-share," with all the sharp-practice baggage that entailed.

"So what are you suggesting—that I go over the wall?"

"You can if you really want to," Walt said, cocking me a wry glance, "but this place is only two-thirds built and half sold. It'd sure be easier for you to just walk up to the front gate and tell 'em you're interested in buying."

I spread my hands to indicate my current garb. "And you really think, me dressed like this, they're going to fall for that?" I demanded.

"Well, OK," he allowed. "Maybe you should tell 'em as how your folks are interested and you're meeting them here. You seem a resourceful kinda girl, Charlie."

I considered. "OK," I said.

But as I reached for the door handle, Walt stopped me.

"Aren't you forgetting something?"

When I didn't respond he leaned across and opened the glove compartment. Inside was a small memo recorder, the kind that takes micro cassettes for business meetings. He lifted it out, checked the tape inside was at its beginning, and handed it over, showing me the voice activation button.

"Just press that and leave it," he said. "It'll start up automatically when someone starts speaking. That way you don't have to worry none about running out of tape."

"OK," I said again. "Just one thing, though, Walt. How much of a confession do you need me to get out of Gerri when I get in there?"

"I reckon you'll know that when you hear it. Just get us something we can use as a lever and we'll do the rest."

We, I noted. *Us.* I wondered if Walt would ever consider himself completely retired from the job.

"I see," I said. I unzipped the bag and crammed the recorder inside. It was a tight fit with the Sig as well but I just managed to get both articles in there and close the bag up again. When I was done I found Walt watching me gravely.

"Don't do anything in haste you might regret at leisure, Charlie," he said softly, but he didn't mention the gun.

I reached for the door handle to get out, then paused. "She's behind the men who murdered Sean."

Walt glanced at me, then let out a long sigh. "Aw hell,

Charlie, I know that," he said. "I guess I'm just hoping MacMillan was kinda right about you."

"Right about what?" I said. I remembered our earlier conversation. "About my instinct?"

"No," Walt said now. "He told me you'd killed, but that he didn't believe you were a killer." He turned his head and gave me a long level stare. "I don't believe that either and I'm kinda praying to the good Lord we're both right, or I just made myself an accessory to the crime."

I got out of the car without answering that one, just shut the door behind me.

"Don't wait for me," I said through the open window. "I'll make my own way back."

I walked quickly to the gateway without looking back, not giving Walt the chance to realize that both he and MacMillan were about to be proved wrong.

Dead wrong.

The iron gates were intended more for decoration than security and looked as though they'd never been shut. I was still aware of a shiver of apprehension as I passed between them. A short distance beyond, there was a guardhouse in the middle of the drive. Next to that was a barrier to block off the road but it was in the up position and it stayed there as I walked toward it.

It was close to midday and the sun was at the highest point of its arc so that I cast a very short shadow on the block paving under my feet. My shirt had stuck to my back and I could feel the back of my neck burning. The little flowered bag containing the tape recorder and the Sig with its almost-empty magazine bumped against my hip as I walked.

As I approached I saw a head appear in the window of the guardhouse, then the figure moved to the doorway and came out to watch me. For a moment I tensed but as I drew nearer I saw the uniformed guard could only have been a year or two younger than Walt.

"Afternoon, young lady," he said cheerfully. "What can I do for you today?"

I manufactured a gormless teenage expression. "I'm

s'posed to be, like meeting my mom. She's got a place here, y'know?" I said, looking about me vaguely, as though expecting her to materialize out of the shrubbery.

The old guard didn't look either fazed or suspicious of my story.

"No problem," he said, picking up his clipboard. "What's her name?"

"Gerri Raybourn," I said, trying not to hold my breath after I'd said it. "She and my dad are, like, divorced and I'm s'posed to be staying with her 'til I go back to college next week. It's a real drag."

Too much information, my mind yelled in my inner ear. *Shut up!*

"No problem," the guard said again. He found the name and made a note against it. "You know where to find her villa?"

I shook my head, hoping the clueless guise would be a good enough excuse.

"Tell you what, then, you step inside out of the heat and I'll have someone come down and give you a ride. Save you the walk. Then if your mom's stepped out you can have a tour or sit by the pool at the clubhouse and have a soda while you wait for her to come get you, OK?"

My God, I thought. *How young exactly do I look?* "Cool," I said out loud, and did as I was invited.

Inside the guardhouse wasn't air-conditioned but the old guy had an oscillating fan set up on the desk right in front of his chair, and it was going full belt. A rake of high-quality security monitors were laid out across the back wall, showing constantly updating views right across the property.

The coverage was impressive and it looked like Walt had been right. If I'd tried to creep in I would have been caught before I'd got halfway across the grounds. This way I didn't even need to worry about directions.

Five minutes later an electric golf cart zipped up outside and a young man bounced out. He was dressed in designer tan chinos and a dark green polo shirt with the resort logo on the front and he was far too slick a professional to look dismayed by the obvious lack of money suggested by my appearance.

"Hi there!" he said. He stuck out his hand. He had great teeth, a great tan, and a manicure. "I'm Randy."

I kept my face as straight as I could manage and didn't inquire if that was an introduction or a declaration of intent.

"Cool," I said again. "Let's go."

As I climbed into the golf cart alongside Randy I realized I could almost see myself as he saw me, a kid with pink hair and an attitude. It was like I had stepped outside my own body, my own mind. Like I was slowly detaching myself in advance from my actions. Hiding from them.

Randy made chatty one-sided conversation all the way along the immaculately tailored drive, going into sales pitch mode as he pointed out the championship golf course, the driving range and the tennis courts, all complete with their own pro instructors. I tuned him out until I realized I'd nearly missed a name I recognized.

"Who?" I said.

"Livingston Brown III," Randy gushed. "He's the property developer. Been doing this kinda thing most of his life. Nearly got wiped out a few years ago when we had the last big hurricane—that one nearly wiped out most of the east coast—but he bounced right back. He shoulda retired by now but I guess the guy just loves his work. He built this whole place. Puts us twenty-somethings to shame, let me tell you. Quite a guy."

"Wow," I murmured, as though I couldn't imagine anyone still being able to walk unaided at such an advanced age, but my nerves tightened at this piece of news. If I was likely to bump into him, would Brown recognize me in this get-up? "Is he here?"

"Oh he's usually around someplace," Randy said and flashed me a slightly condescending smile. One that said no way was the boss man ever going to come into contact with someone as far down the food chain as me, not if he could help it.

On the way to the villa belonging to my "mother" he took a detour to show me the campfire area near one of the pools. "We organize barbecue nights and sing-alongs round the fire in the evenings that you and your mom can join in on," he said. "It's a lotta fun."

"Oh boy, I can hardly wait," I said between my teeth. He looked at me a little oddly but I managed to dredge up a saccharine smile that seemed to convince him I'd been expressing genuine enthusiasm.

If it didn't sound the kind of place I'd want to come and spend my holidays, there were plenty who were willing to be swayed. An army of green polo-shirted staff were leading prospective customers round the lushly planted pathways, or driving them about the place in golf carts similar to Randy's.

The staff were all young and good-looking but that only added to the vaguely sinister feel of the place, like they were the identical minions at the chief baddie's secret lair in a James Bond film.

When I reached the villa Randy indicated I let him knock on the door for me, keeping as far to one side of him as I could, out of sight of the Judas glass set into the center panel. I had one hand dipped into the bag, but not to reach for the voice activation button on the recorder. That remained switched off. Instead, my fingers curled round the pistol grip of the Sig. I became aware of an ever-expanding bubble of tension somewhere deep in my chest.

"Well, doesn't look like she's home," Randy said cheerfully when his loud knocks produced no movement from inside the villa. "We'll try over at the clubhouse."

The clubhouse seemed to be the center of activity. Raucously carnival-type music belted out of speakers on the outside of the building to whip you into the buying frame of mind. As he led the way inside I caught snatches of other conversations.

"If you'da known five years ago what was going to happen to the price of real estate in this area, would you have bought then?" asked another slick salesman.

"In a heartbeat," said the fat man following him.

Randy stopped by the main reception desk and explained he was trying to locate my mother. He waited with a touch of impatience while the receptionist tapped something into her computer. "Just checking to see if your mom's booked in to the health spa, or on any of the courts," Randy explained.

"If you find her, please don't, like, tell her I'm here, will you?" I said quickly. "Just, I kinda wanted to surprise her."

"Sure," he said, easily enough. Either I was getting very good at telling lies, or these people were abnormally trusting.

"OK, I've located Ms. Raybourn," the receptionist said, smiling at me. "She's with Mr. Brown at the moment, then she's due for a massage and a facial after lunch."

Randy glanced at me with something akin to respect. If my mother was important enough to have meetings with the main man, his look clearly said, I'd gone up in his estimation.

"Where's Mr. Brown's office?" I asked. "I'll just go and kinda wait until she's done there."

"He's upstairs and I have instructions not to disturb him," the receptionist said, still smiling but with a touch more steel than before. "If you'd like to wait out by the pool, I'm sure someone will let you know when she's done."

I plastered on a cheery smile and cursed inwardly as Randy led me through the clubhouse itself and out to a paved terrace overlooking a curvy pool with a waterfall and a bar in the center.

Kids were running round the water's edge, shrieking the way only small children can to signify enjoyment. Their parents were sitting in the water drinking lurid-colored cocktails made with half a fruit salad and half a dozen little paper umbrellas. If drowning their sorrows in drink didn't do the trick, there was always the real thing to fall back on. Or into.

But this didn't get me any closer to Gerri Raybourn. And it was much too public for what I had in mind.

Something was folded tight inside now, clamoring to be allowed out. For the first time I was afraid of what might happen if I let it loose. I pushed away that fear.

Randy was making moves to disentangle himself. I could see his greedy eyes flickering over the likely looking purchasers who were being assigned to other salesmen. I could see him calculating his lost commission with every second he wasted on me. My best hope was slipping away.

As he started to turn I reached out and clasped his arm. He tensed under my fingers instantly, trying to make the most of his biceps. Pride was always a useful vanity to exploit.

I gave him my most wheedling smile.

"You're not leaving me already, are you?" I said, a little breathless. "Only, it's kinda hot and crowded out here." I tugged at the collar of my shirt to demonstrate the effect of the heat and the crowds. I loosened a couple of buttons in the process. His eyes followed for a moment, lingered. Encouraged, I even tried a quick flutter of the eyelashes, ladling on the innuendo. "Isn't there anywhere, like, *quieter* we could go?"

Inwardly, I was flinching. Surely nobody would ever fall for such a blatantly awful pickup as this.

For a moment Randy studied me with a slightly narrowed expression. I could almost hear the wheels turning as he made up his mind whether a quick fumble he could boast about in the changing rooms at his local sports club tomorrow was worth missing out on a possible lucrative deal. It only took him a couple of seconds before he decided that it was.

"Well, OK, honey," he murmured, and he'd lowered the pitch of his voice as well as the volume. "I guess I could give you the—" his eyes dipped to my cleavage again "—*personal* guided tour."

I simpered and followed as he led the way back inside. He was hurrying now, his mind totally controlled by some other part of his anatomy.

He hustled me down a short corridor and tried two offices before he found one that was unoccupied, the lights switched off. As soon as the door was locked behind us he had me backed up against a filing cabinet, his hands everywhere. Jesus, here was a boy who didn't need to be asked twice. He had the bad breath of a smoker, despite those gleaming white teeth.

I locked down my revulsion somewhere round my back teeth, hardly feeling it. Under the surface I was crackling like a high-tension power line in the rain. The further into this course of action I got, the less chance there was of turning back. I had to go through with it.

What was more, I wanted to.

I wrenched my mouth free, turning my head away enough to mutter, "Wait. I got something in my bag for you."

I managed to get my arms inside his and lever him away. Looked like he really did live up to his name. He let go of me with reluctance and watched as I reached into the bag.

"You sure came prepared, huh?" he said thickly, giving me a knowing leer.

"Yep, I sure did," I muttered.

When my hand came out of the bag again, the Sig was in it. I had to wedge the end of the barrel against Randy's breastbone and prod him back with it before I finally got his full attention. I wiped his slobber from my mouth with the back of my other hand.

"Hey! What's going on?" he blustered, too annoyed yet by the sudden interruption to be as frightened as he should have been. "What's your game, honey?"

"I am not your 'honey'," I bit out, dropping all pretense at the American accent. I shoved him backward and circled so I was between him and the door. For the first time he began to show alarm.

"I want to know where Brown and Gerri Raybourn are," I said, cold. I made a big show of racking back the Sig's slide to chamber the first round. The noise alone made him recoil. "If you can't tell me, I will shoot you and find somebody else who can."

"I don't know where they are!" he protested. "Jesus, lady, I'm just a freakin' time-share salesman, y'know?"

I didn't speak, just adjusted my grip on the Sig so the business end was centered about on the logo on the front of Randy's shirt.

His face collapsed and he started to cry. "I just work here," he sobbed. He reached out toward me with both hands, pleading, then thought better of it. "Hey, I got a wife and a baby."

I recalled the ease with which he'd been persuaded into the office, and the disgust rose.

"Stop giving me even more reasons to shoot you," I snapped. I stepped back to one of the desks and picked up the phone receiver. "Just call your switchboard and find out where Brown is."

"That's it?" he said, pathetically hopeful now. "That's all I have to do and then you let me go, right? You don't hurt me?"

Letting him go was going to be a tricky one. He was the type who would swear on his mother's grave that he would stay quiet, then scream for security the moment he was out of range.

"Just make the call, Randy," I said.

I stayed close up behind him while he dialed the switchboard operator. Mr. Brown, she told him, was on his usual extension, but he was on a call. Would he hold?

I pressed my finger down firmly on top of the phone, cutting him off, then peeled the receiver out of his hand and dropped it back on its cradle.

"Hey, you promised I could go," he said. His tears had vanished now, his bravado starting to come back with a touch of belligerence, too.

"Take me to him," I said.

When he made to argue, I brought the gun up a little more firmly into view. This time when his eyes followed it they had a hint of cunning to them, as though he was waiting for his chance. What better way to serve his grasping ambition than to save the boss from some gun-wielding nutcase.

It seemed a shame to disillusion him.

"You watch the news much, Randy?" I asked.

He shook his head, nerves making him babble. "A little, y'know. Mostly I'm a sports kinda guy. I just catch the headlines."

"Uh-huh. And have you seen any reports about an English girl who's been shooting people left, right and center over the last couple of days?"

As soon as I said it, it clicked. I saw it in his suddenly bone-white face. He nodded. I never thought all that bad publicity would come in so useful.

"Just bear that in mind," I murmured as I pushed my whole hand, still gripping the gun, back into my bag to keep it out of sight, "if you should think about doing anything stupid or heroic on the way to Brown's office, hm?"

A lamb now rather than a lion, the salesman led me out of the office, back down the corridor and into a lift across the hallway. We only went up one floor but Randy obviously didn't like to walk.

All the time I kept the bag close to him, so he wouldn't be in any doubt. He glanced at it a couple of times while we were in the lift, and I thought I saw him swallow, but he stayed docile. He was lucky that he did.

The energy and the anger inside me was winding tighter and burning brighter with every step. My pulse had started to thunder, beating a harsh tattoo at my temple.

I didn't have a qualm that I'd lied to Walt and that I was about to disappoint all Superintendent MacMillan's hopes for me. I'd known it for a while now that I had the ability to take a life. I'd justified it to myself by saying it was only under the most extreme of circumstances. Only when it was a case of them or me.

Well, not this time.

It was almost a relief not to have to hide behind the pretense of civilization any more.

The lift doors opened and I pushed Randy out ahead of me. In front were more offices, larger this time, their doors more widely spaced. Expensive-looking potted plants livened up the spacious corridor.

At the end was a door with an engraved stainless steel plaque on it which read, "LIVINGSTON BROWN III—PRESIDENT AND CEO." I turned the handle and pushed open the door without knocking.

The man inside was indeed on the phone as the switchboard had claimed. He was sitting behind a huge limed-oak desk, leaning back in his executive chair so he could admire the subtly tinted view of his empire out of the floor-to-ceiling picture window that made up one entire wall.

As we came in he sat up abruptly, his expression first one of irritation, then surprise, as he took in his terrified minion. And me.

Sitting in a chair on the side of the desk closest to me was a tiny blonde woman, dressed today in a lavender power suit and lethal-looking white slingbacks. When she caught sight of me the recognition was instant, despite my disguise. Her mouth rounded into a silent O.

Our eyes locked. My target's and mine. The object of this journey of execution.

"I'm sorry, sir, she made me do it!" Randy gabbled, taking advantage of my distraction to duck out of my grasp and bolt for the door. I didn't bother to stop him going. He'd served his purpose.

"Hello, Gerri," I said, bringing the gun up straight and level so I had a sight picture that put her scarlet-painted upper lip dead center stage. "Remember me?"

TWENTY

LIVINGSTON BROWN III was the first one to move. The old boy had some nerve, I'll give him that. Without taking his eyes off me he said into the receiver, "Something's come up. I'll call you back," and put the phone down slowly and carefully. Then he straightened up and sat forward, linking his long bony fingers together on the desktop. He kept his movements deliberate so as not to alarm me.

I wasn't alarmed but I couldn't say the same for Gerri Raybourn. She tried to scramble further back in her chair, the effort knocking loose one of those white shoes. It dropped to the floor and lay on its side next to a lavender handbag that was a perfect match to the suit.

"Charlie! What are you doing?" she said, her voice harsh with fright. "Have you lost your mind?"

Brown frowned at her, as though he considered making such an accusation to someone with their finger on the trigger was not a sensible move. He wasn't to know it wasn't going to make any difference.

I was planning on shooting her anyway.

"You must have known I'd come for you," I said and the rusty voice that came out of my mouth didn't seem to belong to me. It didn't even seem to be in the same room. "As soon as you had your men kill Sean, you must have known I'd come."

"Kill Sean? What the hell are you talking about?" Gerri demanded blankly, still doing her best to look like she hadn't the first idea what was going on here. "Meyer's with you."

"If Sean was with me, I wouldn't be here," I said with a softness that did little to reassure her. The buzzing inside my head had reached a roar now, enormous and unstoppable like a flight of rapids after the rains. I moved closer, still keeping the Sig out in front of me. The end of the barrel never wavered.

"What was it you said to me back at the motel? That I was just going to have to let him go?" I laughed, a travesty of the sound. "Well you were right about that, weren't you, Gerri? They pulled what was left of him out of a swamp yesterday." The ravening alligators I couldn't reproduce, but I could certainly make sure I shot her somewhere so that she'd die slowly and painfully. I motioned with the Sig. "Stand up."

Gerri clutched at the arms of her chair with those jewel-encrusted taloned claws like I couldn't kill her if I couldn't get her to her feet.

"For God's sake," she said, pale and very shaken now. "You have to listen to me! I didn't kill Sean." Her eyes skittered sideways imploringly to Brown, who was still sitting motionless behind the desk, looking shocked and gray as he listened to the exchange.

"Of course you didn't," I said, almost soothing. "You wouldn't sully your own hands with something like that. You got Whitmarsh to do it for you. Or Haines."

She reacted at the mention of the names of her accomplices. She couldn't help herself. "Haines?" she said and she'd started to sweat now. I could see beads of it pearling along her hairline. "What the hell's he got to do with this?"

"You know," I said. With a bitter irony I added, "He should have killed me at the theme park, when he had his chance."

"I don't know what you're talking about!" she said, louder, like that was going to convince me. She glanced at Brown again. "She's delusional. On something."

I didn't respond to that. I just stared at her coldly, watching as her bewilderment turned to anger, stoked by fear into iridescence. Her temper finally snapped.

"What the hell is it you want?" she shouted.

Even if I'd had an answer to that, I didn't get the chance to utter it. At that moment the door was rammed open hard enough to embed the handle into the plasterboard wall alongside it.

I started to turn as soon as I caught the first sound but it was traveling slower than they were and I was already too late.

Two bulky figures came through the doorway in quick succession, moving hard. One bounced into a crouch, sweeping the room for additional threats with a big silvered Colt semi-automatic clasped in both hands, up and ready.

At the same time the other man simply kept running and hit me with all the ease of a truck taking down a deer that's foolish enough to stand in the middle of the road. I was smacked straight off my feet and bowled over, crashing on top of the chair opposite Gerri's and through the glass-topped occasional table alongside. The table, and the lamp that was sitting on it, both shattered as they hit the floor.

My bag went flying and I lost my grip on the Sig but didn't see where either of them landed. The man was brutal and proficient in his efforts to subdue me without a prolonged fight, and surprise as well as weight was on his side. I never stood a chance.

It was over sooner than he was happy with and I caught a couple of unnecessary extra blows to compensate for his disappointment in that respect. It took a moment after he'd quit hitting me for my head to stop swimming.

When it did I found both the two men who'd burst into the room were standing over me. The one who'd knocked me down had picked up the Sig and was handling it with approval. The other had his own gun firmly trained on me.

They were big men with thick necks and biceps that strained the elasticity of their company polo shirtsleeves. The one with the Colt had rich dark skin and slightly flattened-down features—part genetic, part boxer. The other was blond and had a pencil mustache nesting on his upper lip. They looked like thugs who'd scrubbed up well and weren't entirely comfortable with smart casual attire. I didn't recognize either of them.

I heard a chair go back and looked sideways to see Brown's feet appear from round the other side of the desk. He was wearing suit trousers with turn-ups and shiny black shoes, and he walked like his feet hurt in them. He stopped a short distance away and looked at the two men.

"You boys took your goddamn time," he growled.

"Sorry, sir," one of them rapped smartly, although sounding unrepentant. They'd arrived soon enough, his attitude clearly said, so what was the problem? "What do you want us to do with her?"

My scalp prickled at the prospect of a bullet in the stomach and a ride out to the swamp. More than that I tasted the sour tang of defeat, of failure. Gerri had been stalling me and I'd let her do it. I should have pulled the trigger the moment I'd walked into the office and I berated myself for the weakness of my hesitation. Even without Walt's tape recorder running I realized I'd needed to hear her admit her guilt before I'd done it.

"Get her up," Brown said now and I was hauled roughly to my feet. One of the men produced a set of plasticuffs from his back pocket and used it to yank my wrists together behind my back. I was a good six inches shorter than either of them but they kept a firm hold on my arms, just in case. I don't know quite what they expected I was going to try and do, restrained and groggy. They started to push me toward the door.

"Now wait just a minute," Gerri Raybourn said sharply, smoothing down her suit and retrieving her fallen shoe along with her dignity. "That little bitch was going to kill me. She's not going anywhere until I've gotten some answers out of her."

The men exchanged a brief glance that hinted they thought the only talking that anyone should be doing with me ought to involve a pair of steel-toecap boots. But they did as they were ordered, swiveling me back toward the desk and bracing me in front of it. It was like being forcibly stood to attention and I'd been through too much of that before.

Brown had moved back to his own side of the desk by this

time. He sat down, letting out a slight grunt as his knees bent so far and then dropped him the rest of the way into his seat. For a moment he regarded me, his expression one of bemused perplexity. I tried to keep my own thoughts guarded, even though all I wanted to do was fall to my knees and weep.

"There's nothing to be said," I said, weary when I was trying for defiant. "Just get on with it."

Gerri was on her feet and prowling. "Oh no, you don't get away that easy," she said, her voice tight and vicious now the threat was over. "You can't just come barging in here and accuse *me* of murder when you're the one who's a goddamn murdering bitch."

When I still didn't speak she took a couple of quick steps forward and backhanded me across the face. I wasn't ready for it and my vision momentarily disintegrated into jagged cracks of dark and light.

For someone so slight she packed quite a punch. The force of the blow sent me staggering sideways into the man who'd originally knocked me down. He shoved me upright again with as much care as if I was an unstable piece of cheap furniture. I noticed he was smiling.

"Cut that out!" Brown barked, half rising to lean on the desk. "Goddamn it, Gerri, I won't have that kinda behavior in my office. Get a grip on yourself, y'hear me?"

Gerri had been watching the effect of her strike with narrowed, glittering eyes. Now she turned away and sat down again, tucking her feet underneath her chair almost daintily. She even checked to see that she hadn't broken a nail.

I shook my head to clear it. I had been right in my first assessment of Gerri's rings, I realized. The stones in them had gouged a lump out of the flesh across my cheekbone that felt an inch wide. I could feel a small trickle of blood already running down the line of my jaw.

"Thank you," Brown said, more quietly. He waved a hand toward the plasticuffs. "Now get those damned things off of her and leave her be. She's not much more than a kid herself. Let's try and be civilized about this, huh?"

The mustached man did as he was ordered while the one with the Colt kept me covered, then they both stepped back. I rubbed reflectively at my wrists and looked at Brown.

"Where was your panic button, by the way?" I asked idly. "I was watching your hands and never saw them move. Or did good old Randy raise the alarm?"

Brown scowled a little at the mention of his employee's name. "No, looks like he don't even have the wit for that," he said readily enough, regaining his own seat. His eyes were bright and filled with a deep intelligence that the rest of his easygoing, slightly crumpled features had a tendency to disguise. "I have a switch down here on the floor. All I had to do was put my foot on it."

"Nice touch," I said.

Gerri let out a gusty sigh. "If you've *quite* finished exchanging pleasantries," she said, voice dripping with sarcasm, "I'd like some answers out of her before we hand her over to the cops."

Brown nodded and looked over my shoulder to where his security men were skulking. "Mason, get the lady a chair and then go see if you can rustle up some coffee," he said.

The one who'd knocked me down brought forward another chair like the one we'd broken in the struggle. His feet crackled over the shards of broken glass and pottery as he moved across the carpet. He plonked the chair down facing Gerri's, keeping his attitude just a sliver this side of resentful at being asked to play the waiter. Then he went out, disengaging the handle of the door from the wall panel with a stiff jerk and closing it behind him.

The other man stayed in the background but he kept the Colt out and his attention firmly fixed on me. As I sat down I could almost feel his eyes boring into the back of my skull.

"So, Charlie, you wanna tell us what's going on?" Brown asked then. His tone was calm and reasonable and almost kindly, and maybe because of that I felt much more inclined to answer him than Gerri.

"Keith Pelzner's been kidnapped by Gerri and her boys because they want to get their hands on the finance program he was working on," I said. "They tried to get Trey, too, but—"

"What?" Gerri cut in, strident now. "You and Meyer must be mad if you think anyone's going to go for that fucking crap!"

Brown held up a placatory hand, old-fashioned enough to look faintly embarrassed at the profanity. "Now, now, Gerri, let's hear her out," he said.

"Sean's dead," I said coldly. *And I wish you were, too.* I turned back to Brown. "You remember you told me you'd seen Keith Pelzner packing up and leaving of his own accord on Thursday morning?" I said. "Well I now know he's been kidnapped."

Gerri's brows came together. She, too, turned to the old man. "You saw Keith the morning he vanished?" she said to him, the rising inflection making it a question. She sounded annoyed and puzzled at the same time. "You sure never mentioned that to me."

"Didn't I?" the old man said, his smile fading. "I coulda swore I told you all about it. Maybe it was that Whitmarsh feller." He thought a moment longer, then brightened. "Yes, I do believe it was."

Before Gerri could respond to that the door opened again and the security man, Mason, returned with three cups of coffee, and a little bowl containing three straws and packets of powdered creamer and sugar, on a brown plastic canteen-type tray. He put the tray down on the desk to one side of his boss.

He'd put my Sig into his right-hand trouser pocket in order to carry the tray. I could see the end of the pistol grip sticking out by his hip as he unloaded the contents and just for a second I considered making a grab for it.

Then I flicked my eyes up to Mason's face and found he was watching me out of the corner of his eye with a sneaky little half smile lifting the edge of his mouth, making the mustache wrinkle upward. I didn't want to make his day any more than I had done already so I sat still and kept my hands in my lap. As he moved back to join his mate I contented myself instead with the rudeness of not saying thank you.

Gerri was still apparently frowning over Brown's last remark, making a big performance out of it. The action produced two deep grooves between her carefully plucked eyebrows.

"She and Meyer took them both," she said now, talking firmly to Brown, as though I wasn't there. "I admit I kinda got the feeling Meyer was the ringleader and she was having second thoughts, or she wouldn't have called me from the motel. But maybe he found out what she'd done. By the time my people got down there, they'd already killed a couple who'd gotten in their way and lit out."

I flashed her a dirty look but followed suit, speaking to Brown like he was judge and jury. "I told her we were in a different room," I said. "Partly deliberately, partly by accident. But when Whitmarsh and Chris turned up, they burst straight in there and shot the people inside without giving them a chance." I glanced at Gerri but she was keeping her face devoid of emotion, a smooth, cosmetic facade. "That's when Trey and I did a runner."

She turned to me. "You really *are* delusional, aren't you?" she said with something approaching a sneer. "Why the hell would Jim Whitmarsh kill those people?"

"You tell me," I said softly. "Why would he and Haines be all fired-up for killing the pair of us—until they found out how vital Trey was to your precious program?"

"Now, now, ladies," Brown interrupted, pushing a cup of coffee toward each of us, as though a hit of caffeine might calm us down. He rummaged through the little bowl, picking out four packets of Sweet'N Low which he emptied into his cup along with two packets of creamer. Then he stirred the resultant muddy-colored gloop with one of the straws. Maybe it was a ploy to induce unity. Both Gerri and I eyed the concoction with measures of distaste.

I took my coffee black. It was out of a machine and it hit my stomach thin and sharp and greasy. It was also hotter than hell. I pushed it away.

"So, Charlie, what's all this about them trying to kill the boy?" Brown asked then.

"Between them they've made three attempts so far," I said, ignoring Gerri's impatient gesture which I just caught out of the corner of my eye. "Four, if you count the initial attack by Haines in the amusement park."

"Who's this Haines character?"

"He's a cop down in Fort Lauderdale but he freelances as a security consultant. Last year he did some work for Ms. Raybourn here when she was with a company in Miami that made car parts. Looks like he's working for her again now."

Gerri was frowning again. "A cop?" she said, sounding artfully distracted. "Wait a minute. I remember—he was one of the guys who brought Trey back to the house after he was caught at the Galleria. I *knew* I knew him from somewhere."

I tried not to grind my teeth at her refusal to admit defeat. "Nice to see the myth of the dumb blonde lives on," I said conversationally. "What do you hope to gain by keeping up this act?"

"I'm not the one who needs a new act, Charlie," she shot back, lip curling. "Maybe you'll have time to think on that while you're rotting in a penitentiary somewhere serving your life sentence."

"If anyone's going to prison, Gerri," I said, giving it a little more bite this time, "that will be you."

"Ladies, please," Brown said, starting to look nervous. "Quiet down, huh? I don't want no cat-fight in here."

"Quite," I drawled, pointedly dabbing my fingertips against my cheek. It had stopped bleeding and was starting to scab over.

Gerri's gaze ran over me briefly, lingering on the wound she'd inflicted as if next time she'd like to rip my throat out and spit down the hole.

Not if I get to you first . . .

Brown took a slurp of his coffee and swallowed before he turned to me. "So what was it you said about Trey being part of some program?"

"Keith was writing a program that would accurately predict the stock market," I explained. "He was having problems getting part of it to work but Trey has apparently solved the problem. Something to do with the neural network, I believe. I don't understand the technicalities."

Brown's eyebrows went up, matching the wispy scraps of

hair on his high-domed head. "Young Trey?" he said, sounding doubtful. "I mean, I know he's a bright kid an' all, but you really reckon he's done something his dad couldn't?"

"No, of course he couldn't," Gerri snapped. "It's ridiculous to think for a moment that he could. Keith's a highly talented programmer, otherwise the company we work for wouldn't be basing just about their entire future on his work."

"So why was Whitmarsh trying to kill Trey right up to the point where he found out that the kid might be involved with the program? Then, all of a sudden, Whitmarsh has a chance to shoot the pair of us but he lets us get away because he's afraid of damaging him."

"How did he find out that Trey was involved?" Brown asked.

"Trey went to a guy he knew called Henry for help," I said, not adding my own feelings on the subject. "But Henry contacted Whitmarsh to sell us to the highest bidder. After he'd tried to up the price by telling Whitmarsh what the boy was really worth, Henry attempted to lure us into a trap and when it didn't quite go according to plan he got a bullet in the brain from Haines for his trouble."

Brown went silent, his placid face troubled. "So where's the boy now?"

"He's safe," I said, thinking of Xander and Aimee who were standing guard over him. And Walt, ready to take over if anything went wrong. Not to mention Special Agent in Charge Till, and all that he represented.

"Oh I get it," Gerri said with contempt. "You don't make a phone call by a certain time and he and Keith both get it. Am I right?"

"Something like that," I agreed, wondering why I hadn't thought of telling them something along those lines in the first place.

"Well," she said, smiling nastily at me as she blew that one out of the water, "I'm sure the cops will sweat it out of you in plenty of time to retrieve them both."

She finished her coffee and got to her feet, like this conversation was over. I studied her but couldn't find the faintest sign of panic.

Why on earth had her men killed to prevent Trey and me falling into police hands if she was so eager to see me put there now? It didn't make sense. Unless she was just trying to get me out of here, to get me somewhere quieter and with fewer witnesses.

"Don't you think it might be an idea to check out what she says, even just a little?" Brown asked and I could have cheered at the cool note that had crept into his voice when he spoke to her.

Gerri gave a short laugh. "Why?" The laugh died when she caught the solemn expression on his face. "Oh come on, Livingston! How long have we known each other? You surely can't believe a word this lying little bitch tells you?"

Brown made a "maybe, maybe not" gesture with his hand. "Don't do no harm to check it out, even so," he said easily.

"And how do you propose to do that?"

"Let her call your feller Whitmarsh and offer to make a deal with him for the boy," Brown said. "If he's as crooked as she reckons, he'll go for it." He smiled at me and those bright, clever eyes stared out from beneath their droopy lids like he was a young man inside a geriatric costume mask. "And if he does, well I guess we'll just take things from there."

Gerri didn't like it. In fact, if she'd liked it any less she would have been wailing, but clearly she wasn't in charge here. Brown pushed the heavy cream telephone he'd been using when I'd first burst into his office across the desk toward me. Then he opened one of the drawers and began pawing through the contents.

"My late wife, God rest her, used to love those gadget catalogues," he said while he searched. "You know the ones? A thousand answers to questions you never needed to ask? She was always buying me stuff I never had the heart to send back. Ah, here we are."

He pulled out a small tape recorder, similar to the one that Walt had given me. It jogged my memory and I slid my eyes sideways and spotted the strap of my bag, just poking out from underneath the broken chair.

Brown, meanwhile, was untangling the wires that came with his recorder, which had knotted themselves together the way wire or string has a tendency to do when it's left to its own devices and gets bored. When he'd unravelled these they separated out to reveal a set of headphones at the end of one, and a small sucker at the end of the other.

"You kinda stick that to the receiver, then you can tape your phone conversations," Brown said, checking the batteries were still working in the recorder. "I used it once or twice, just for fun. Can't remember the last time."

He attached the sucker to the side of the handset and pressed the record buttons, then Gerri stabbed in the number of Whitmarsh's mobile phone. Her movements were impatient, her lips compressed. Would her man betray her, I wondered, or was he too canny for that?

She and Brown shared the headphones, putting their heads together awkwardly so they could have one earpiece each. The phone rang out four or five times before Jim Whitmarsh picked up. I don't know what number appeared on the display at his end, but his voice was wary.

"Yeah?"

"Whitmarsh," I said. "It's Charlie Fox."

Gerri Raybourn and I silently locked gazes while I spoke. She sat with her body rigid, as though she was being made to listen to an obscene phone call.

There was a pause at the other end of the line, then I heard Whitmarsh let his breath out in a long rush, close to a sigh with a soft laugh at the end of it.

"Well now, Charlie," he said, voice rich with satisfaction like he'd always known I wouldn't be able to resist him for long. "To what do I owe the pleasure?"

"Cut the crap," I said. "Do you still want the kid?"

"Trey?" Whether it was the abrupt tone or the offer, I felt his surprise. His interest quickened. "You bet."

"Dead? Or alive?"

He laughed again. He had a slightly wheezy laugh, as though he was a heavy smoker. "If I'd wanted him dead, neither one of you would have walked away from us yesterday," he said, coldly matter-of-fact.

"Well, I'm offering him to you now," I said. "What's it worth to you?"

"I don't think you're in any position to start dictating terms, lady," Whitmarsh said but he spoke just a little too fast, his voice just a little too tense. It gave the lie to his confident words.

"Oh really?" I said. "OK, let me phrase that slightly differently for you, Jim. What's it worth to you to get hold of him when he's still alive and kicking, rather than shot in the stomach and dropped into a swamp?"

Another long pause. "News travels fast, huh?" Whitmarsh said then. He laughed again, dustier this time, with more strain showing through it. "Thought it might make you lose your nerve and wanna throw in the towel."

I thought of how close I'd come to doing just that, on the beach after we'd left Walt's place this morning. The memory of my own misery and helplessness hardened something inside me. I would see this through and I would bring them down, whatever it took.

"Well you thought wrong, didn't you?" I said.

"So what do you want?"

"What do I want?" I repeated, letting my voice slip, introducing the rough note of someone pushed close to the edge. It didn't take much faking. "I want to get out of this fucking country and go home," I said, flat. "But I can't do that unless I have something to bargain with. Give me Keith. You don't need him any more."

"Who says we have Keith?"

"Oh come on, Whitmarsh," I snapped. "You took him from the house Thursday morning and you've had him ever since. You must have had plenty of time to copy all his files and notes. Long enough to realize the program isn't complete. And I know Henry told you about Trey's work on the neural net. You need the kid and you don't need Keith. Let me have him."

Whitmarsh didn't say anything immediately. Gerri started to react but I waved her to silence with a curt gesture and added,

"Come on, this is a one-time-only deal. Make a decision."

"OK, Charlie," he said and I could tell by his voice that I wouldn't be able to trust him. "I guess we can do that. When and where you wanna make the exchange?"

For a second my mind went blank, then I remembered the Ocean Center complex. Above the main hall where the show itself was taking place were rows of deserted seating, all fed by corridors and walkways.

"Meet me upstairs at the Ocean Center on Atlantic Avenue," I said. I checked my watch. "You've got an hour." And with that I cut the connection, not giving him a chance to argue.

As I put the phone down both Brown and Gerri Raybourn peeled their earpieces out and put them down on the desktop. I raised an eyebrow at the pair of them. *Well?*

Gerri dipped into the lavender handbag and produced a pack of Kools. She picked one out and lit it with hands that didn't look quite as steady as they had done before I'd made my phone call. She inhaled deeply with all the fervor of a lapsed quitter, closing her eyes briefly.

Brown looked pained but too polite to ask her not to smoke in his office. Instead he shifted his empty coffee cup back onto the tray and put the saucer in front of her. She distract-edly flicked her first build-up of ash onto his carpet anyway. Then she looked up, her eyes skating from one to the other of us in turn, hunted.

"Jim was just leading her on, trying to recover the boy," she said but even she didn't sound like she entirely believed it. The references to Sean were conveniently overlooked alto-gether. She took another drag on the cigarette and the nicotine seemed to build her tattered confidence. I could see it swelling like a reinflating doll until her skin seemed tight with it. "Of course he doesn't have Keith to trade. It's ridiculous."

Brown cleared his throat. "Well," he said slowly. "I guess there's one way to find out." He looked over the top of us to where the two heavies who'd come to his rescue were still loi-tering. "Tool up, Mason, and grab another couple of the boys," he said to them. "We've got less than fifty-five minutes to get up to Daytona Beach."

TWENTY-ONE

I SAT IN the rear of a huge Chevy Suburban with blacked-out glass as it barrelled north up A1A toward Daytona Beach. Alongside me, hunched as far away as she could manage so as to avoid contamination from contact, was Gerri Raybourn. She sat with her knees pressed tight together and her face stiff with outrage.

In the front passenger seat was Livingston Brown, acting like a kid on a big adventure. Mason, the security thug with the pencil mustache, was behind the wheel. Following, at a distance that made it look like they were attached by a short tow rope, was a Transit-sized Chevy van with another three heavies inside. The big black man with the Colt was driving but nobody had told me his name.

Half the reason for Gerri's indignation was that we were making this journey at all. She had done everything possible to talk Brown out of it, even resorting to pointing out that he was too old for such a foolish and possibly dangerous es-capade. That kind of comment had done little to bring him round to her way of thinking.

The other half of the reason was lying across my knees, squeezed with Walt's clandestine tape recorder into the little flowered bag.

As soon as it had become clear that Brown was starting to come down on my side of the fence, I'd asked for the return of my gun. He'd given me a long hard stare. Eventually he'd quietly signaled Mason to hand over the Sig, ignoring the other woman's strident objections.

The security man did so with obvious reluctance, as though he agreed with Gerri's opinion of me. Nevertheless, he was well trained enough not to voice such doubts. They all watched silently as I pointedly dropped the magazine out and checked he hadn't palmed the remaining rounds while he was out fetching coffee. He hadn't.

So I still had a whole two bullets to play with.

It wasn't much, particularly when—if Whitmarsh turned up with both Chris and Lonnie—I potentially had four people to shoot at. My gaze skimmed over Gerri again. I hadn't seen a gun on her and she'd made no moves to reach for one when I'd ram-raided the office.

If it came to it, I decided coldly, I'd leave her for last and take my chances hand-to-hand. I probably owed her a good smack in the face.

Besides, I now had half an army for back-up. Brown had seen our surprise when his professional-looking bunch met us at the front door to the clubhouse and he'd grinned. "I had a whole heap of trouble with people stealing machinery and materials during construction on this place," he said over his shoulder as we rolled out. "They're smart and they're organized and it was costing me a small fortune. Since I took on Mason and the boys I haven't lost a cent. It don't do no harm to be prepared for the worst."

And prepared for the worst they were. Although nothing was visible I could tell each man was carrying a sidearm of some description. Two of them had a shoulder holster leaving a telltale bulge under the armpit of their lightweight zip-up jackets. The black guy with the Colt appeared with a long gym bag that clanked metallically when he placed it in the back of the van.

We didn't talk much on the drive up. Brown switched the radio on and tuned it to a station playing country and western music. He hummed along tunelessly to every song, his hands tapping out cheerfully bad time on his thighs.

I shut my ears to the sound, gazed sightlessly out of the window, and thought about Sean.

It was only then that it began to fully sink in that I faced a whole future without him. It was the prospect of this barren emptiness stretching out in front of me, of being permanently alone, that caused the most internal devastation. I felt something break inside me and begin to crumble.

There had been men before Sean. In spite of what had happened to me in the army, there had even been the occasional one since. The time we'd actually been together had been fleeting, little more than an instant. But nobody understood or accepted what I was, what I might be, the way Sean had.

He was a once-in-a-lifetime deal. I'd thought I'd missed my chance years ago and then, miraculously, a second had been presented to me. And now I'd missed that, too. There would not be another like him. He remained a bright hard diamond amid colorless glass and dull imitations.

The pain of the loss was intense, a deep and endless wound I couldn't begin to imagine time healing.

Before I'd realized it, we were heading into Daytona. Without needing directions, Mason drove straight to the big open car park behind the Ocean Center that said Permit Holders Only next to it. An elderly guard was sitting on a camping chair under a sunshade next to the gate and he got to his feet as we drove up. Mason showed him some kind of ID. I don't know what it was but after a moment's consideration the guard waved both vehicles through without argument.

Mason pulled up at the front edge of the car park and the van slotted in alongside. I slipped the strap of the bag over my head as I climbed out, so it lay diagonally across my body. All Brown's men, I noticed, had their jackets unfastened. One of them had retrieved the gym bag with its sinister contents.

By contrast, they were all dressed in light-colored clothing and trainers or deck shoes. If it wasn't for their combined muscle bulk, they could have been heading for a regatta.

There were more security guards on the way in to the Ocean Center itself, insisting on looking into all the larger bags. Mine escaped notice, but they were curious about the gym bag. Mason flashed his ID again and they, too, let him pass unhindered.

The noise hit us as soon as we were inside the entrance hall area, bleeding out from the main exhibition floor. The entrance way was where they were selling popcorn and giant pretzels and commemorative T-shirts and the crush was immense. For a second I was separated from Brown's men and at that moment I felt a tug on my sleeve.

I turned and found Aimee smiling at me. Of Xander and Trey, thankfully, there was no sign.

"Meet me in the restroom, now," I whispered urgently out of the corner of my mouth, and pushed past her.

The next hand on my shoulder was Mason's, which was a damned sight heavier and rougher than Aimee's had been. He glared at me, suspicious and I tried to look blandly innocent. I'm not entirely sure he was convinced.

"We need to stick together," he said, loudly enough to be heard over the background roar.

"That might be difficult," I said. "I need to go to the ladies' room."

"You'll have to wait."

"I can't wait," I said, stubborn. "Either you let me go to the ladies' or I piss here, but it's going to stink."

He never flickered at my deliberate crudeness. Instead his gaze settled on me for a moment, as though working through the permutations of what I might be trying to pull. Eventually he nodded slowly and jerked his head to one of his men. "Go with her and wait outside," he ordered.

I threaded my way through the press toward the nearest ladies' without waiting to see if the man Mason had tasked was behind me or not.

Inside there were two girls wearing minuscule bikinis and excruciating clear plastic high heels who were applying copious amounts of lipstick and mascara. One was blonde and one was dark haired but they both had identical tans. They looked up as I ambled in, gave me a fast inspection and a little smirk, and went back to their primping.

I washed my hands and took my time over drying them while I waited for them to totter out. Then I went along the line of cubicles, giving each door a gentle nudge. Aimee was lurking in the end one with her hands in her pockets.

"Wassup, girl?" she demanded. "You look, like, way too stressed."

I held my finger up to my lips and shushed her. There was no outer door and even with the general noise level I didn't want to risk being overheard. I pushed her back into the cubicle and shut the door behind us.

"Look, I need you to tell Trey I'm here with Gerri Raybourn and Livingston Brown and his security men," I said, keeping my voice low. "We've arranged a meet with Whitmarsh and he's supposed to be bringing out Trey's dad. If he does, Brown's guys will grab him."

"Cool," she said. "What do we have to do?"

"Just keep Trey out of sight," I said. "I'll call you and let you know when it's over."

She nodded and started to go but as she reached for the door handle I had one last thought to add. "If it's safe for him to come to me I'll say something about his father, his dad," I said. "But if anything goes wrong, when I call you I'll mention Keith by name. In that case get him out of here as fast as you can and tell him to go to Walt's place on the beach. You got that?"

"What about you?"

I brushed the question aside. "Have you got that?"

She hesitated a moment, then nodded. "Father is good. Keith is bad," she said, like she was revising for an exam. "Go to Walt's place. I gotcha."

"OK," I said. "Now give me a minute or so head start before you come out." And I started to head for the exit.

"Oh—and Charlie?"

I turned.

"Good luck, girl," she said.

I managed to raise a poor smile. "Thanks," I said. "I'm going to need it."

◆ ◆ ◆

When we'd been at the Ocean Center before I'd automatically noticed the security guards covering all the staircases leading to the upper floors. Now I wondered if Mason's magic ID card was going to work to get us to the upper level as well—but in the event, he didn't need to show it.

The main stage was close to this entrance and it turned out that our arrival coincided with the build-up to the final of the weekend's bikini contest. So that explained the two girls in the ladies' room.

The guard on this particular set of stairs was about twenty-two and he'd deserted his post to leer round the corner at the half-naked leggy beauties who were gathering in the back-stage area. The eight of us were able to slip past him, under the tape barrier and up the first flight before he'd got his eye-balls back into their sockets again.

The upper floor of the Ocean Center was painted neutral colors and buffed to an institutional shine. It consisted of a network of wide corridors with offices and meeting rooms round the outside of the building and doors leading to the terraces of seating on the inside.

There was another guard sitting reading a magazine between one of the offices and the glass exit doors that led down to the street. She was a fat middle-aged woman with ornate glasses on a chain round her neck and aggressively-dyed orange hair. She got to her feet as we approached, reaching for the walkie-talkie on her belt. I expected Mason to go through his ID rigmarole again but maybe he was getting bored with that approach. Instead he took a gun out from under his jacket and pointed it at her.

"In the office," he said, twitching the end of the barrel in the direction of the nearest doorway. "Now."

The guard jumped to her feet, scared, dropping the magazine to the floor. Mason picked the walkie-talkie out of her nerveless fingers and hustled her through the office door. When he returned a few minutes later he was alone. None of us asked him what he'd done with the woman.

"So, Charlie," Brown said when his boys had checked the

surrounding area and found it devoid of other life. "Where d'you reckon Whitmarsh will put in an appearance?"

"*If* he shows up," Gerri put in sharply. "He could well have just called the cops."

Brown regarded her with one eyebrow raised. "Well, let's see if you're right," was all he said.

Mason came up by his shoulder. "We'd best get ourselves outta sight, sir," he said. "Don't want to scare this guy off." His eyes flicked to Gerri and something happened to his mouth that might almost have been a sign of amusement. "*If* he shows up."

Brown nodded and flashed me a quick smile. "Now don't you worry none, Charlie," he said, patting my shoulder. "Me and the boys'll be close by."

Most of the office doors were locked but that didn't seem to be much of a problem. Mason produced a set of picks from his inside jacket pocket and within moments the doors were open and they were inside.

I was left standing in the center of the polished floor, alone. Beyond the doorways to my left I could hear the thunder of the show coming up from the lower floor. The bikini contest was under way now, by the sound of it, the commentator trying to whip the crowd into an ever-greater fever of excitement as each girl took the stage.

"You gotta cheer for the girl you wanna win," he yelled. "The louder you cheer, the better she'll do. Let's hear it now for Chastity, from Orlando. Come on out, Chastity!"

I don't know how good looking Chastity was. Or, more to the point, how little of her chest was covered by her bikini top, but the crowd went wild.

The noise was suddenly amplified as one of the doors from the balcony looking out over the auditorium further along the corridor was pushed open. I tensed, automatically reaching for the gun in my bag.

There was a pause, then Keith Pelzner stepped out into view.

He was shuffling, looking back nervously over his shoulder. His gaudy Hawaiian shirt was stained and crumpled and his hair was matted down onto his head. Wherever Whitmarsh had been keeping him for the last few days, it wasn't anywhere with a bath and full room service, that was for sure. Keith looked round vaguely, like he'd no idea where he was and didn't remember me either.

I called to him and started forward but I hadn't taken more than a couple of steps before Jim Whitmarsh moved out from behind the open door Keith had just come through. It swung closed behind him.

Whitmarsh pulled his lips back to show me a set of white, even teeth. The gesture came across as friendly as the greeting from a scrapyard dog. He was holding the same Beretta he'd had at Henry's house and looked like he couldn't wait to use it.

"If that hand comes out anything but empty," he said pleasantly, "I'll shoot you."

I carefully let go of the Sig but as I withdrew my hand from the bag I brushed my thumb against the voice activation button on Walt's tape recorder.

Whitmarsh nodded at my compliance. "Lose the bag," he said.

I lifted the strap, ducking out from underneath it, and held the bag out at arm's length beside me. I let it drop gently to the ground so as not to damage or spill the contents. It landed close to the wall and lay on its side.

Whitmarsh was looking in better nick than Keith. He was wearing a striped shirt with buttons that strained slightly over the expanse of his stomach. His weight was causing him to feel the heat and two circles of sweat stained the shirt's armpits. Maybe he was just nervous.

From somewhere below us I heard the commentator shouting to the rabid mob, "And now, from right here in Daytona Beach, it's Tameka. Let's hear it for the lovely Tameka!" The screams and cheers and whistles grew louder.

"OK, Charlie," Whitmarsh said. "Where's the kid?"

"Close."

He shook his head. Not good enough. "Call him."

I shrugged. "I don't have my phone," I said.

Whitmarsh eyed me for a moment, thinking through the

moves like a chess player, trying to see if I was setting him up for checkmate further down the line. When he'd worked out that I had nowhere to go he reached into his trouser pocket and pulled out his own mobile.

"Here." He put the phone on the floor and sent it skidding toward me. I stopped it with my foot, then bent to pick it up without dropping my gaze.

Keith, meanwhile, hadn't moved, apart from a gentle rocking motion backward and forward. He kept his head tilted away from both of us, his gaze averted. I wondered what, if anything, they'd given him to keep him so docile.

I began to key in Trey's number but stopped before I'd got much further than the start of the code. I looked up. "How do I know you won't just kill me and take off with both Keith and Trey?"

Whitmarsh grinned again. "You don't."

"So why exactly should I trust you?" I asked but I knew I was just stalling. *Come on, Mason, what the hell are you waiting for?*

Whitmarsh wiped the sweat from his forehead and studied me seriously. "Well, I could threaten to shoot Keith here if you don't make that call," he said, "but I don't really think you give a damn about that one way or the other."

For a moment he regarded his captive with the contempt for weakness that often befalls despotic jailers, drunk on their own power and total control. Then he was back concentrating on me.

"I could threaten to shoot you. In fact I could make things pretty damn intolerable without actually killing you," he said reflectively and I forced myself not to react other than to remain politely interested, as though in someone important who's telling you a long and pointless anecdote.

In the main hall, the commentator had reached the final bikini contestant. "Last up, all the way from Iowa, it's Jephanie. Whaddya think, huh? Way to go, Jephanie!" The crowd couldn't have shown more savage approval if they'd been watching a public execution.

"But somehow," Whitmarsh went on, oblivious, "something tells me you don't give much of a damn about that either."

Still keeping the gun aimed at the center of my body mass, he stepped back and glanced sideways toward the door he'd just come through, which was standing a little ajar.

"So as a last resort," he said, "I could threaten to shoot somebody I know you *do* give a damn about." He raised his voice slightly and called, "OK. Bring him out."

Just for a second I feared that Whitmarsh's men had somehow got hold of Trey. If they had, I was abruptly surplus to requirements. But if that had been the case, I realized, Whitmarsh would never have showed for this meeting.

And then the door opened again as Lonnie and Chris pushed through it. Lonnie was closest to me and I saw at once that in his right hand he was holding the Remington pump-action shotgun he'd used to such devastating effect in Henry's garden. The length of the gun meant he held it awkwardly, angled upward so that the end of the barrel was resting under the jaw of the figure he and Chris held pinioned between them.

As they turned him toward me and my eyes zeroed in on his face the sound of the roaring crowd below us shrank and vanished like a pinprick of light in space. All I heard was the sharp astounded intake of my own breath.

It was Sean.

TWENTY-TWO

SEAN!

If I thought I'd reacted badly to news of his death, that was nothing compared to the emotional impact of finding him suddenly alive.

The trauma of it went up my body in a fast ripple. Up my shins and the sides of my ribcage, scuttered across my chest and then passed quivering over my scalp like a sine wave. A physical effect that left me shaken and gasping. I was peripherally aware that I'd had to shift my feet to keep my balance.

Sean—and it was definitely Sean—looked like shit. There was no other way to put it. Like Keith, his clothes were filthy and soaked with sweat and from the knees down his trousers were coated in what could have been old mud.

They'd beaten him, too. They'd probably had to in order to begin to subdue a man like Sean. Blood had run and dried from a dozen cuts on his face and body. The bruises had spread like fear. My sense of dread at what had been done to him, at what he'd suffered, ran very cold and very deep.

And at first I thought they'd broken him. I looked and saw nothing in his face. No fright, no pain, not even rage or madness. It was like his emotions had been ripped out, eviscerated.

And then I looked again and, maybe because I knew him so well, I caught a glimpse of what lay past the shield he'd been using to protect himself from damage. Something glittered like ice in the depths of his eyes. A brooding intelligence that still lurked, intact and aware. Waiting . . .

And, recognizing it, my legs spontaneously took me forward.

Lonnie jerked the end of the shotgun up into where the carotid artery pulsed under Sean's jaw, bringing both of us up short. The only difference was that it was me who flinched. Sean didn't react at all. Lonnie had to physically lift his head back, arm muscles straining with the effort. It was only when I was still again that he allowed the gun to relax slightly away from Sean's head.

"Hey, Charlie," Sean said lightly, his voice soft when I'd been half expecting a tight weariness. "Love the hair."

"Yeah," I said, forcing my vocal cords to unclench. "It's growing on me. I may even decide to keep it this way."

He smiled at me then, recognizing my response for what it was. The smile was slow and sexy and it made my heart ache and my throat constrict until it hurt to swallow.

"I see rumors of your death were greatly exaggerated," I managed with surprising equanimity.

"Mm," he said, calm and level but for the first time there was just a trace of the underlying anger. "I expect they hoped you might fold easier if you thought you were on your own."

He let his gaze skim from my blanched features to Whitmarsh's. The other man wouldn't meet his eyes and I realized that, even though he held the upper hand, Whitmarsh knew only too well what might happen if ever there was a change in the status quo. He was a little afraid of Sean, a little afraid of the monster they'd created and now daren't let go of. No wonder he'd got both his men clamped onto him, leaving Keith standing to one side, submissive and almost forgotten in this exchange.

"So, Charlie," Whitmarsh said with a touch of sneer. "Unless you want to watch your boyfriend's brains getting splattered all over the ceiling for real this time, call the kid in. Don't make me ask a third time."

Come on, Mason. For Christ's sake, man, get on with it!

But even as the thought formed I realized that if Brown's men did ambush us now, Sean was likely to get his head blown off anyway. I told myself that Mason's combat experience, either police or military, was standing him in good stead. He was waiting for his opportunity, biding his time. All I had to do was play along for just a little longer . . .

I lifted the phone again and completed punching in Trey's number. My eyes met Sean's as I hit the send key, looking for reassurance, but I might as well have been hoping for a reaction from a statue. I wondered, if he knew what I was going to do, whether he would have done the same himself.

I tried not to feel pain at the fact that he'd shut down again, shut me out, but it was real and physical. I just had to accept that he was doing what he had to do in order to survive this. Now it was up to me.

Somewhere below me the noise came rushing up again as the mob howled and stamped and cheered for the half-naked girls on the stage. The commentator's voice was a frenetic squawk as he urged them to select a winner like they were choosing a sacrifice.

"It's me," I said when Xander picked up. "Let me speak to Trey."

They were somewhere close. In both ears I could hear the same cheers and catcalls. One reported, one live.

In the pause before Trey came on the line I saw Whitmarsh's fingers flex round the pistol grip of the Beretta, trying to relieve the tension. But his face had already twisted into a triumphant smile. He knew he'd won. Knew he'd beaten me. Beaten the pair of us.

Not quite yet, old son.

"Hi, Trey, I need you to come upstairs, the corner near the stage. Fast as you can," I said, keeping my voice neutral. "Come on your own. Don't bring the others with you."

"All right," he said, nonplussed and cautious. "Is everything OK?"

"Yeah," I said, eyes fixed on Sean's face. "Keith's here. Everything's fine."

I ended the call and threw the phone back to Whitmarsh. He caught it easily, one-handed, and said with some satisfaction, "So now we just wait for him to come to momma."

He never got the chance to be disappointed.

At that moment two of Brown's men came smoothly out of one of the offices behind where Lonnie and Chris were holding Sean, guns out and ready. They must have been using the time they'd been hidden to quietly bypass the connecting doors between the rooms, gaining ground.

Whitmarsh's face sagged in disbelief. Before he had time for response, Mason and the black guy moved out from a doorway to my right and I found out what had been in that gym bag. Both had Mossberg pump-action shotguns pulled up hard into their shoulders like they were doing house clearance, the barrels arcing to cover all the players.

My heart trampolined into my throat as I watched Lonnie's grip tighten on the stock of his own shotgun but he hadn't lived to turn gray in the security field by making rash decisions under fire. After only a fleeting hesitation he delicately removed the Remington from Sean's neck and let it droop.

A spasm of anger passed across Whitmarsh's features, as though recognizing his best hope for negotiation had just slipped away from him. Then he, too, let his gun hand fall to his side.

"I gotta hand it to you, Charlie," he said, his voice bitter. "I didn't think you had the balls for an ambush."

"She didn't," Brown said. He'd followed his men out of the office doorway and was careful now to stand behind them as he spoke. "But I sure did."

Almost to my surprise he had a gun out, too. A little stubby Colt .38 Special revolver that sat firm and steady in his liver-spotted fist. There was more steel to Livingston Brown III than I'd ever suspected.

Lonnie and Chris had sized up the situation enough to step away from Sean, keeping their movements careful and their guns lowered. Sean swayed slightly when they disengaged, the only betrayal of weakness. Then he was steady again. His hands were secured behind his back but I saw him straighten and hunch his constricted shoulders, as though in preparation for release.

Something, I wasn't sure what, stirred in his eyes. Something base and deadly. I could feel it vibrating in the air between us. When he got loose, there was going to be trouble and he could almost taste that freedom.

Whitmarsh just stood and gaped at Brown, gaped all the more as Gerri Raybourn emerged alongside him. His eyes grew wide and not a little wild. "What the—?"

"What, Jim?" Gerri demanded, stalking forward. "You've got a whole heap of explaining to do, feller and, oh boy," she added with low venom, "it better be good. Just what the fuck did you think you were doing here?"

"A little private enterprise, by the looks of it," Brown put in coolly.

Whitmarsh froze, then made a conscious effort to relax, gave a wheezy laugh.

"Just trying to put together the whole package, I guess," he said. His composure seemed to have resurfaced entirely now but it could just have been last-gasp bravado making him sound so cocksure.

Gerri, on the other hand, was shrinking before my eyes. Lines of strain had appeared around her mouth. Her skin had taken on a translucent quality so the matt powder of her subtle makeup now looked false over the top of it.

"You owe your loyalty to the company that employs you," she said, but her voice was hollow.

"Why?" Whitmarsh laughed again. "Over this last year you've weaselled out of paying us overtime, cut our dental and medical, treated us like crap on the sidewalk. Told us the company was going through a rough patch and how we had to suck it in. But you sure didn't have to give up your Mercedes-Benz, now did you? And you expect loyalty for that? Wake up, Gerri! Opportunities like this one don't come along every day."

"So those kids at the motel?" she said quietly. "That really was you?"

Whitmarsh grinned and gave an elaborate nod, almost like he was bowing.

I glanced at her. "Who did you honestly think it was, Gerri?"

She turned her head to stare back at me. "But you'd taken the boy hostage," she said, blankly. Her eyes shifted to skate briefly over Sean and Keith. "We—I—thought you'd taken both of them. I was trying to negotiate with you, going by the book. But Jim insisted he wanted to be the one who went and brought you in. Said he felt responsible that the Pelzners had been taken on his watch . . ."

Her voice trailed off and I thought back to the phone conversation we'd had. Amazing how things altered when you put a different slant on them. The questions she'd asked, the responses she'd made.

It was like adjusting a door that's always been awkward to close and suddenly finding it fits seamlessly. It's not until you look back that you realize how wrong it was before.

"I thought you were trying to set me up," I said.

She heard the doubt in my voice and latched onto it, shaking her head almost violently. "No, no, I wasn't," she said. "You gotta believe me, Charlie. I had no idea what Jim was up to—"

"Well, isn't this nice?" said a new voice at the back of us. "Have I arrived just in time for the group hug?"

I knew the voice before I started to turn but the actual sight of the man behind it still caused my system to spike nastily.

Haines.

A fast little slide show of images projected from the back of my mind. Haines, when all I'd known him by was the make of his Oakley sunglasses; in his police uniform delivering Trey back to the house; at the park going for the gun under his shirt; standing in front of Henry's place calmly explaining how he was going to kill both Trey and me.

What the hell was he doing here? And why weren't Brown's men shooting at him?

Haines came forward, those trademark shades perched on top of his head. I couldn't see his gun but it wouldn't be far away. My eyes flicked just once to the little flowered bag down by the wall but I knew at once he would have drawn on me before I'd ever reached it.

He stopped a few strides away with a smile curling his handsome mouth, as though he recognized my dilemma and could read the utter frustration and confusion going on in my head.

Then he turned to Brown.

"Sorry I'm late, boss," he said easily. "I came soon as I got your call."

Dully, in the background, there came another roar from the crowd in the hall below as the girls who'd made it into the last four came out for their final parade. "There's five hundred bucks to the winner," screamed the commentator, as though to incite competitors and audience alike to an ever more excessive performance.

"Livingston, what the fuck is going on here?" Gerri demanded, raising her voice over the top of it. She stuck her hand into her bag and pulled out a mobile phone. "I'm calling the cops. Right now!"

Brown turned to her, his face still wearing its usual amiable, slightly-bemused-by-life expression. "Gerri," he said with a sigh, "you're a foul-mouthed pain in the ass and you're starting to bore me."

And—just as the bikini winner was announced and the crowd went into deafening overdrive—he shot her.

It was a shockingly careless gesture. Brown didn't even bother to straighten his arm, just swung round slightly and fired from the hip. Gerri was standing less than a couple of meters away from him so he hardly had to aim.

The little Colt bucked and flared in his hand just once and a small scarlet circle appeared on the front of Gerri's suit jacket, just below the curve of her left breast. The bright wet red of it showed up in stark contrast to the delicate lavender shade of the fabric.

She looked down at the dribble of blood that oozed out of the hole with something akin to hurt disbelief on her face.

"But—" she said.

It was as far as she got before her ruined heart simply

stopped beating and she died on her feet. The mobile phone fell to the floor, shattered, then her body dropped and folded, lifeless as a long silk dress sliding off its hanger. She landed in a tumbled pile, arms and legs an inelegant sprawl.

Keith was staring transfixed at the body, murmuring, "For Chrissake. Oh for Chrissake," over and over like a mantra.

I hadn't realized I'd started moving until Brown swung that deadly little gun in my direction.

"She's gone," he said, almost kindly. "Don't waste yourself."

I stopped. Gerri's chest was still. There was very little blood and her eyes were closed as if in sleep. She was way beyond anything I could do for her except make sure I didn't add my own corpse to lie beside her.

"So it was you," I said quietly. "Right from the start it was you."

"Oh yes," Brown said. "And you've led us a merry chase, what with one thing and another. But it's over now. Soon as we get the boy, we're outta here."

"You won't get him."

The certainty in Sean's voice had us all swinging round, startled. Brown recovered faster than the others.

"And what makes you so sure of that?"

"Because I know Charlie and there's no way she would cave just because your man Whitmarsh here was threatening to kill me," Sean said and gave me another perfect smile, one that heartened me far more than it should have done, given the circumstances. It was only then I knew I'd made the right decision.

"No," he went on, shaking his head, "she gave Trey a run signal. I don't know what it was but she's certain to have had one and he'll be long gone by now. You were waiting until she'd called him in but you played your hand too early."

Brown twisted back to me, saw from my face that Sean had got it nailed. Just for a moment his placid facade split and the underlying rage showed through like spite. Then the fissures sealed and it was gone again.

"Well, I guess you'll be needing my services for a little while longer, then?" Haines put in, amusement trailing through his voice as though he was enjoying the whole show.

"I guess so," Brown agreed tightly. "I guess it's damage limitation time." His eyes drifted slowly across the group in front of him. "You can start by helping Mason and the boys dispose of this garbage here."

Jim Whitmarsh can't have been in any doubt at this point what Brown had planned for him. Not after he'd just seen the old guy kill Gerri Raybourn with such casual disregard. Lonnie and Chris had seen it too, and it was Chris whose nerve failed to hold steady.

He sprang into a crouch and brought his gun up, by the looks of it the same 9mm he'd used to help his boss murder the young couple at the motel that first night Trey and I had been on the run. He began to take a bead on Brown himself.

Both Mason and the big black guy with the other Mossberg let fly at the same moment. At that range they couldn't fail to hit their target.

Chris flailed backward, blood spouting from his face and upper body like an industrial sprinkler. His flayed body landed at the base of the nearest wall hard enough to bounce, exposed flesh gleaming. He lay there, convulsing, and made unnerving gurgling sounds from his gaping throat.

Not dead yet, but not going to make it, either.

The noise of the two shotguns discharging inside that confined, reflective corridor was monumental. It sent me staggering, but instinct had me diving for Sean, trying to get him out of the danger zone. Keith had cowered down of his own accord. I didn't particularly care what happened to him anyway.

"Hold your fire, goddammit!" Brown bawled. He glared at Mason, fighting for control. "You trying to have half the cops in the state on our backs with that racket? Goddammit, I didn't mean do it here."

Haines's Smith & Wesson had appeared in his hand the moment Chris had made his play and he held it now to cover Sean and me.

"If you don't mind me making a suggestion," he said to Brown with exaggerated politeness, "we need to get the hell out of here right now." His eyes flicked contemptuously to Mason and the other man. "Security in this place will have dialed nine-one-one soon as they heard those damn cannons go off."

Brown considered for a moment, expressionless, then inclined his head. "OK. Mason, bring the vehicles round to this exit. And let's round up some of those guns, shall we? Before we have any more trouble."

Delegating in turn, Mason jerked his head to the two men behind Whitmarsh and Lonnie. They moved forward quickly, collecting the Beretta and the Remington, retrieving Chris's nine-mil from his unresisting hand with obvious distaste. As Lonnie handed his shotgun over I caught a twinge of regret. Maybe he was wishing he'd pulled the trigger when he'd had the chance, after all.

Mason reclaimed the gym bag from inside the office doorway and the pair of them stashed their armory inside, taking it with them as they went out through the glass doors a little way back along the corridor.

There was a moment's silence after they'd gone. Whitmarsh's tongue wiped nervously over his lower lip.

"So, what are you gonna do with us?" he asked.

"Well, if there's one thing I can't stomach, Jim," Brown said reflectively, "it's people I can't trust."

"We were just trying to get them both for you," Whitmarsh said, hurried now.

"Didn't happen to kinda mention that change of plan to me, now did you?" Haines put in.

"There wasn't time. I—"

"Plenty of time to get Lonnie and his shotgun into position under Henry's place, though, wasn't there?" I asked, using a mild tone to disguise the wedge I was trying to hammer in between them. *Divide and conquer.*

Haines's eyebrows went up then came straight down again as the import of that sank in. "So it was you wasted Chico?" he murmured, glancing at Lonnie. "And there I was thinking the chick had picked up some more armament. I shoulda known it couldn't be her."

He turned to Brown, waving a careless hand toward Whitmarsh and Lonnie. "You want I should get rid of these two when I do the others?"

It was like he was offering to empty a waste paper basket.

Brown shook his head, though frowning like he'd given it serious thought. "We still need to get a hold of the boy and I have plans for Mr. Whitmarsh," he said grimly. "After he's handed over everything useful he got from Keith, he can be the one who gets to dump these three. Take all of them back to the resort and out into the swampland at the back of the place. Wait 'til sundown and in a coupla days there won't be much evidence left."

"Livingston, for Chrissake, please!" Keith looked as if he were about to burst into tears. "You're my friend. Don't do this to me!" *Not "us,"* I noted. *Me.*

Brown regarded him stonily. "You ain't delivered the goods," he said. "You've kinda disappointed me, Keith."

At the far end of the corridor I heard the quiet clank of the push-bar being operated to open another of the doors from the seating area.

I tensed automatically, hearing the guns of Brown's men come up. If it was another security guard, or some stupid lost kids, there was going to be more bloodshed.

A single figure stepped through the opening and froze as he took in the scene of carnage in front of him, his hand still on the latch.

My first reaction was horror but anger wasn't far behind.

"Trey, you dumb little bastard!" I yelled at him, furious. "Get out of here!"

I broke into a run toward him, like I could scare him off. Before I'd taken more than two strides Haines had swung round and caught me a stinger across the base of my skull with the butt of the Smith & Wesson.

The blow was hard enough to put me on the ground. I went sprawling onto my hands and knees, jarring both wrists in the fall. I stayed down, fighting against the pitted blackness that was enveloping my vision, waiting until the floor was steady enough for me to attempt to rise.

At the same moment Sean had ducked his head and charged

the one of Brown's men who was nearest to him, regardless of the weapon. He'd swept the man off his feet before the other reacted. By the time I looked round, Sean was on the ground too, braced against the blows that had put him down and were continuing to keep him there. Well that explained why Brown had contracted in Haines and Whitmarsh to do his dirty work for him. His own guys had come close to being beaten by a man who, quite literally, had both hands tied behind his back.

Haines ignored that scuffle. He leaned over and put the barrel of his gun next to my left eye. The blued steel was cold against my skin.

"Give yourself up or watch her die," he called to Trey.

The kid hesitated, then he edged further into the corridor, skinny shoulders rounded in defeat. He didn't even move when Haines left me and went forward to grab him by the arm, dragging him back to where Brown was waiting.

When the boy tugged against the punishing grip, Haines shook him like a rag, almost throwing him down rather than releasing him. Trey glowered and rubbed his arm where Haines's fingers had left reddened marks.

My head had cleared enough for me to look up at him.

"You stupid little brat," I said bitterly. "Don't you ever listen?"

He scowled some more, defiant. "I couldn't just, like, leave you here."

Haines chuckled. "Well isn't that cute?" he said. "Now you get to all die together."

"No, no, we can work this out, surely?" Keith said. He hurried toward Brown, eager, keeping slightly ducked and submissive. "I didn't know Trey was working on the neural net independent of me. I mean, he's just a kid, y'know? I had no idea he'd made such progress with it." He shoved his glasses back up his nose with a grubby finger and rushed on, his voice almost a gabble. "I need to check out his data, of course, but maybe I can knock it into some kinda shape. Maybe I can still give you what you want. Just give me another chance!"

"*Me?*" Trey said, his voice quietly cutting. "*I?*" He'd gone very still, watching his father with simmering resentment. "What d'you mean, 'maybe *you* can knock it into shape,' huh? It's *my* work, not yours!"

Keith gave a high-pitched nervous laugh, eyes darting from side to side. "Now now, Trey, don't let's argue about this now, son, huh?" he said, in that strained way parents have of speaking out of the side of their mouths when their children are about to monumentally embarrass them in a public place.

"No," Trey said, folding his arms across his chest so his fingers were tucked under his armpits, just leaving the thumbs out, like he was feeling the cold. He shifted his weight down onto one hip, confrontational. "Let's talk about it right now, *Dad.*"

"What's there to talk about, for Chrissake?" Keith snapped, the tension getting the better of him. His hands were a constant jitter. "I evaluate what you've done and, if it holds up, I incorporate it into the program. End of story."

For a moment Trey didn't respond, just stared fixedly at nothing, chewing his lower lip like he was struggling not to cry. "So you, like, actually admit I coulda done something you couldn't, huh?"

Keith frowned. "What do you think?" he said, pained and edgy.

Trey nodded to himself, as though accepting that this was probably the nearest he was going to get to an admission of his own worth in the eyes of his father.

"So what do I get out of this?"

"Oh for crying out loud, Trey!" Now Keith looked as though he was the one about to burst into tears, or wet himself. Or both. "What d'you want, for Chrissake? A raise in your allowance?"

"I just want the truth," he said, stubborn. "The truth about how you murdered my mother."

"*What?*" Keith's voice rose to an outraged squeal. "Of course I didn't murder her. For Chrissake, Trey!" He brought his fists up to the sides of his head like he was about to tear his own hair out. Then he let them fall with a slap against his thighs. "She left us, OK? She walked out."

"She would never have abandoned me like that," Trey said tightly, body rigid to the point of quivering, two splotches of color highlighting his otherwise pale face. "You murdered her. Admit it, or you can go fuck yourself before I'll give you squat!"

"OK, OK!" Keith said, rolling his eyes, desperate now. "I did it, OK? Your mom didn't move to Cleveland with the guy from the Seven-Eleven across the street. I killed her and buried her in the backyard. The front yard. Wherever. Is that what you want to hear?"

"Yeah," Trey said and I saw his shoulders come down a fraction, as though he was relaxing for the first time.

"So, I get your data on the neural net, yeah?" Keith demanded.

But to everyone's surprise, Trey shook his head.

"Oh come on, Trey," Keith managed to force out from between his clenched teeth, "you can't fuck about with these people. If you've got something I can use, then I need it, mister, and I need it right now or—"

Trey shrugged. "That's just it," he said. "I don't, like, have anything. There is no data. There never was any data." His voice broke then, the tears squeezing their way out however much he was willing them back. He scrubbed them away, furious with himself, and lurched on with his fiercely controlled tirade.

"This so-called miracle program you've been, like, telling everyone is almost finished? Well, I got news for you, Dad, *it doesn't work*. It never has worked and it never will. Face it, man, you're a useless piece of shit. The program's fucked."

Keith closed his eyes and let out a long groan, stumbling back.

"Yeah," I heard Whitmarsh murmur heavily behind me, "and so are we."

TWENTY-THREE

FOR SEVERAL SECONDS after Trey had finished speaking there was utter shocked silence. But before the significance of what he'd just announced really had the chance to sink in, the doors at the end of the corridor burst open again.

This time it was the Ocean Center security guards who came charging onto the scene. The first guy through the door took one look at the blood and the guns on show and went into rapid reverse, almost tripping up the man behind him.

Brown's two foot soldiers immediately snapped off half a dozen rounds in their direction, just to encourage the guards to keep up their retreat. The doors slammed hard behind them and even over the ringing in my ears I heard panicked shouting on the other side.

At the same moment the glass doors to the street slammed wide and Mason came through them. He was lucky he didn't get shot by his own team in the process.

"Sir, we need to leave, right now!" he said, terse.

Brown's spine had curved him forward, making him seem older, grayer, more frail. But now he snapped out of the immobility that had gripped him and didn't need telling twice. The old guy scurried down the corridor leaving the rest of us to his men.

The two who'd been grappling with Sean now hauled him roughly to his feet. Mason scooped me up and began herding me toward the exit with the others. Just as we reached the doorway and stepped back out into the fiery sunshine, Mason paused and I realized that Haines had stayed behind.

I looked back, just in time to see Haines swing back to where Chris lay trembling in a spreading pool of his own blood. As I watched, Haines moved in close to the fallen man and stood there for a second, like someone making up their mind about a piece of modern art.

Chris was still alive but only just, if the shallow liquid rasping he was making was anything to go by.

Haines leaned over and calmly put two rounds into the ruin of Chris's face. There wasn't a flicker of pity or remorse on his own features as he did it. The body jerked at the impact, then finally lay still.

Haines carefully picked up both the brass shell casings, then tucked the gun away out of sight in the belt holster under his shirt. As he jogged back to where Brown was waiting for him, all the old man did was raise an eyebrow.

"Never could stand leaving things untidy," Haines said, smiling.

If Brown made any reply to that, I didn't catch it. Mason jerked me forward again and I was too busy trying to keep my feet as he hustled me outside and down the flight of concrete steps to the street. The sunlight was far stronger than the dark tinted glass of the doors had led me to expect and I squinted in the glare.

I could already hear the urgent clamor of the sirens heading toward the scene. Brown's men had heard them too. They started to bundle us into the back of the van that was now waiting by the curb.

"Wait. Put the boy in with us," Brown said. He nodded darkly toward me and Sean. "Just in case they get any fancy ideas."

Panic flared in Trey's face. He tried to dig his heels in, even grabbing hold of the edge of the van door. Haines gave an irritated sigh and took him by the throat almost negligently with one hand, lifting the kid until his toes were barely on the ground.

"Think you're some kinda tough guy, huh?" he growled.

I went for him but never got there. Brown brought the revolver up and the memory of how he'd killed Gerri with so little effort stopped me in my tracks. Mason grabbed my arms,
just in case I thought about risking it anyway.

Trey's face had congested. He let go of the van and
clutched vainly at Haines's hand. I wished fiercely that I'd had
the chance to teach the kid some basic self-defense, how to
break a stranglehold and your attacker's little finger in the
same move. There had never seemed to be the time. Or the
need. He'd always had me to protect him before.

Haines had only been waiting for the boy to let go of the
van door before he slackened his grip. Trey thumped back
onto his heels, thoroughly shaken, and threw me a wounded
glance as though I'd failed him. He allowed them to push him
into the back of the Suburban without further resistance.

The rest of us got the van. Once the doors were slammed
and locked it was stiflingly, suffocatingly hot in there. There
was no handle on the inside of either rear door and no windows we could open—either to escape or to breathe. The air
had a tangible mass, making it almost too heavy to drag into
your lungs. I resisted the urge to pant like a dog.

The back of the van had been lined with cheap plywood,
completely separating the load bay from the front seats and
boxed out over the rear wheels to form a narrow bench. Whitmarsh and Lonnie ended up on one side, with Sean and I facing them and trying not to let our legs tangle in the middle.
The only illumination came from a dim bulb in the center of
the roof.

Keith was forced to sit on the floor, his back to the cab. He
looked insulted at being relegated to the dog shelf but he was
wise enough to realize it wouldn't make any difference if he
voiced his complaint.

Nobody made any attempt to release Sean's hands, which
were still bound behind him with police-issue handcuffs. It
made sitting on the cramped makeshift bench difficult and
probably uncomfortable but with Sean it was difficult to tell.
If he was in pain he didn't show it.

The van pulled out, lurching as it gathered pace. We seemed

to be making a series of sharp turns, weaving through the back streets rather than risking the exposure of the main drag.

I jerked my head to Whitmarsh. "You must have the keys," I said. "Uncuff him."

Whitmarsh just gave Sean a careful glance and shook his head. "I don't think so," he said.

It was pointless to argue with him. I settled for sitting close to Sean, thigh to thigh, needy for any kind of contact. It still didn't quite feel like it was really him. Why, I wondered, had it seemed more real to me to accept that he was gone than it did to find him suddenly resurrected?

I reached up, uncaring of the eyes fixed on us, and touched his face with a gentle hand. The stubble on his cheek prickled against the backs of my fingers. The blood there had dried into black flecks that came away like ash.

"I thought you were dead," I murmured. "I thought they'd killed you." And as I said it I realized with a cold shiver just how close I'd come to executing an innocent woman for that crime. It created a big dark hole somewhere in my mind. I teetered on the edge of falling into it.

"I know. They told me the same about you," he said, adding with a quiet vehemence, "but I knew they were lying."

"How?"

The black, expressionless eyes skimmed across the men opposite, then back to my face. "Because if you had been," he said simply, "they would have had no reason to keep me alive any longer."

I turned my own gaze on Whitmarsh. "So who was the dead guy you dumped with Sean's ID on him?" I asked. "Don't tell me—you keep a stock of corpses in the freezer, just in case?"

"Didn't need to this time," Whitmarsh returned with scorn to match my own. "You helped us out good there, Charlie."

I stilled and he laughed when he saw me do it.

"Remember the two guys who followed you out of the motel before you had that shoot-out with the cop? Well, they were Brown's boys. You plugged the driver in the gut—lucky shot through the door of the car by the look of it. He got away but he bled out before they could treat him. After that, well," he shrugged, "I guess it was just too good an opportunity to waste."

I considered that information for a moment, filing away the fact that I had another death on my hands. I was running out of fingers to count them all on. The mouth of the hole grew larger and more gaping and was lined with jagged teeth like a shark. When I looked down into it I couldn't see the bottom. I closed my mind to the lure of the edge.

"That old Breitling of yours is still ticking, by the way," I said to Sean absently, aware of the inconsequential comment.

"That's good," he said in turn. "It's a nice watch."

Whitmarsh gave one of his gasping laughs. "I hope they bring a good price on the secondhand market," he said, " 'Cos one thing's for sure, neither of you will be the next to wear it."

I tried to keep my face cool and haughty. "Come on, Jim, do you honestly think Brown's going to let you walk after what you've tried to do to him?" I laughed too, but it was a brittle, mirthless sound. "You go through with this and you're going to be looking over your shoulder for the rest of your life."

"Well, whichever way you square it," he said, a touch of bravado creeping in now, "it's gonna be longer than yours."

"Brown will kill you," I said, talking to Lonnie as much as Whitmarsh himself. "He'll kill both of you. There's too much at stake for him not to."

"Brown's an asshole," Whitmarsh dismissed. "He got caught out bad when we had the last big hurricane through here and that fancy time-share he's building is just about to go belly up. Why d'you think he's gotten himself into this?" Another asthmatic laugh. "And for what?" he finished bitterly, with a vicious glance at Keith.

I followed his gaze. Keith was sitting with his thin knees hunched up in front of him, arms wrapped round his shins and his chin tucked down so his straggly little beard nested between his kneecaps.

I had a sudden vision of the way Trey had sat, just like that, in the enameled steel bath at Henry's place. If the boy hadn't lied about his part in the program, I wondered, would Henry have been tortured and murdered? Would Scott have been half-paralyzed?

As if suddenly aware of the hostile scrutiny Keith lifted his head, pushing his glasses back up to the bridge of his nose. "At least we have until sundown," he said, like that made all the difference. "Isn't that what Livingston said?"

Whitmarsh almost snorted. "Yeah," he said, disdainful, "and you know why that is, don't you?"

Keith shook his head.

Whitmarsh waited a beat, like a schoolboy dragging out a gory tale to see if he can make the little girls in his class sick. "That's when the gators come out to feed," he said, baring his teeth in a malicious smile. "That way there ain't no bodies for the cops to find."

For a while after that nobody else had the energy or the inclination to speak. We sat and glared at each other, or avoided eye contact with each other, as the van rocked and bounced and vibrated at speed along the road south.

It seemed to take a hell of a lot longer to get back to Brown's resort than it had done to get from there to the Ocean Center. Maybe they were just taking a more circumspect route.

Eventually, it was the music that gave it away. I heard the same raucous blare of manically cheery pap that had been pouring out of the clubhouse when I'd gone to confront Gerri. Was that really only a few hours ago?

The noise grew louder, then faded as we passed and drew further away from it. Perfect Doppler shift. The comparatively smooth metalled road gave way to what sounded like gravel, then to a rutted track that threw us around like we were the steel ball inside a tin of spray paint. By the time we stopped Keith had started to look slightly green. I don't know if it was travel sickness or just anticipation.

When they opened the van doors Mason and his sidekick had the Mossbergs to hand again. They stood far enough back to make any thought of rushing them a suicidal one.

Whitmarsh and Lonnie got out first, moving smartly aside

so Brown's men had a clear line on the rest of us. I suppose I could understand their caution. If I'd had the opportunity I wouldn't have hesitated to put either one of them between me and a shotgun blast.

As I climbed out I looked around me. We had come far enough on from the time-share so there was no sight or sound of it beyond the impenetrable body of trees that more or less surrounded us. The van and the Suburban had pulled up on a pad of cracked concrete that had been bleached white like old bones by the sun.

There was a single-story building to one side of us, its walls made from silvered timber. Flakes of faded yellow paint still clung to the wood and every metal fastening was pitted with corrosion. A barely readable washed-out sign by the door announced airboat rides twice daily but I doubt it had seen a paying customer in years.

To the other side was the swamp, which was what Brown's development must have looked like before he drained and re-claimed and reshaped the land. The concrete extended down to the edge of the sluggish water where two airboats were tied. Drums of fuel for their massive exposed V8 engines sat on the tiny dock.

Around the boats, spilt fuel created greasy rainbow rings in the water. The whole place had a run-down dirty air to it, but retained a certain picturesque quality, even so. More like a film set than real life.

Next to the building sat the rusting hulk of an old step-side pickup, a relic from the 50s. It was no longer possible to tell what color the body might once have been. Tough grasses and weeds had grown up past the level of the floor and were mak-ing slow but steady progress in retaking the ground they'd lost during the first engagement.

"Where are you planning on putting them?" Haines asked as he approached. He had Trey by the scruff of his neck, casu-ally shoving him along in front of him.

Mason glanced at Brown before replying, as though he didn't like being questioned by the cop. "We've got a couple of storerooms in the back," he said, short, jerking his head toward the timber building. "They can stay there for a couple of hours or so. Until it's time."

Haines shrugged and nodded. "Sounds OK to me," he said and then he turned to Brown. "What do you want to do about the others—the kids she was with in Daytona?"

"Let's make sure this mess is cleared up first, then you can go tie up the loose ends," Brown said.

Trey started to squirm harder, protesting. Haines didn't even bother to look at him, just tightened his grip. I could see his knuckles turning white with the effort he was putting into punishing the boy.

"Let him go," I said with quiet feeling.

Haines looked at me and smiled while Trey thrashed at the end of his arm like a hooked fish.

"Or what?"

"Oh, leave him be," Brown said with mild irritation. "You'll get your chance for that." He checked his watch. "Anyhow, I gotta scoot. It's welcome night and I have to go play genial host up at the clubhouse."

Haines dropped his hold with marked reluctance, even though he was still smiling at me.

Brown ignored him and moved back to the Suburban. He climbed in and cranked up the engine before leaning out of the window. "Let me know when it's done."

He rolled up the tinted window and the Chevy quickly disappeared down the narrow track cut between the Cypress trees. We could see his dust trail long after he had gone.

Mason looked at Whitmarsh and Lonnie. "Well, I guess you got a choice now," he said. "Either you do what the boss man wants with these people, or you join 'em. What'll it be?"

Despite the doubts I'd tried to plant on the ride down there, Whitmarsh barely hesitated. "We'll do it," he said, looking me right in the eye as he spoke. "Don't you worry none about that."

They put Sean and me into one storeroom and Trey and his father into the other. The rooms had bare concrete floors and a row of tiny windows, little more than meshed glass vents up

under the roof line. Apart from that, they were empty of either
creature comforts or possibilities for escape.

Mason's only concession to our well-being was to take the
keys from Whitmarsh and unlock the restraints. I think it was
probably down to Whitmarsh's obvious lack of enthusiasm
for letting Sean loose that made Mason do it, rather than any
particular concern on his part. When Sean shook his hands
free I could see the bloody bracelet marks on both wrists but
he never even winced.

Then they put us inside our prison and locked and pad-
locked the door behind us. We listened in silence as their
booted footsteps receded.

"So this is it." Sean's voice was disembodied in the gloom.

"Maybe," I said. "We still have a chance to get out of this."

I felt him turn. "You reckon?"

"You remember what was said at the Ocean Center?" I
asked. "Well, Trey and I have been helped out over the last
couple of days by a retired FBI man called Walt—lives down
on the beach. He gave me one of those micro-cassette tape
recorders to try and get a confession out of Gerri Raybourn." I
blanked out my own reasons for wanting to confront Gerri and
pushed on. "It was in my bag at the Ocean Center. It should
have got everything that happened there."

For a moment Sean was silent. "*If* it recorded OK from the
inside of a bag," he said at last. "*If* the local cops bother to play
it back. And *if* they recognize its significance and pass it on to
the FBI, we might have a chance. That's a lot of ifs, Charlie."

"I know that," I said, hearing the wobble in my voice. "But
right now it's the only hope we've got of getting out of this, so
please don't take it away from me."

I heard him sigh. "Come here," he said. My eyes were beginning to adjust to the dimness now. I could see his outline
more clearly but I would have known where to find him, in
any case. My system was tuned to his, alert and sensitive.

I walked into his open arms without a stumble and laid my
head against his chest. Under my ear his heartbeat made a
steady hypnotic rhythm. His hands closed gently across my
back, enveloping me.

I wanted to stay like that forever.

"I thought I'd never get to do this again," he said into my hair, so quiet I had to strain to catch the words.

I said nothing. What could I say? That I'd already accepted his death? I kept the cold little secret to myself. It sounded so faithless to admit it out loud.

Sean didn't seem to notice my silence. "They got me getting out of the bloody swimming pool—how stupid is that?" he said, rueful. Those agile fingers had begun to stroke up and down my spine, feeling their way across each vertebra, almost distracted.

"I managed to put Whitmarsh on his arse before Chris waded in, and then Lonnie turned up with that shotgun and made it pretty damned clear I was a disposable item. Chucked some clothes at me, then it was the usual blindfold and cuffs and into the boot of his car." I felt him shrug to try and slacken the tension that was tightening him up as he recounted the story. "I thought that was it. Game over. They'd lined the whole thing with plastic."

"I know," I said, remembering what we'd found in the boot of the Taurus I'd hijacked outside Henry's place.

"The worst thing was knowing what they had planned for you and not being able to do a damned thing about it," he went on. "They were talking about you like you were already dead."

"We probably would have been if I hadn't found the Sig where you left it," I said. And as I said it I remembered that I'd abandoned the gun, too, in the little flowered bag at the Ocean Center. What I would have done to have it back right now.

"I wasn't sure if they'd miss it when they cleaned out my room," Sean said, "but I knew if they did you'd find it. If you made it back to the house."

"Yeah, we made it."

"So I understand. You know where I was when that little bit of news came through?" Sean said and his voice had taken on a flat, dispassionate tone now, like he was debriefing after a disastrous operation, burying the emotion and keeping strictly to the facts.

I gave a slight shake of my head, though I realized his question was largely rhetorical.

"Haines took me out into the Everglades—some godfor-saken track in the middle of nowhere—and they put me on my knees and he put a gun to the back of my head," he said calmly, although under my cheekbone his heart was punching like a fist. "And just before he did it Haines's mobile rang and that's when he found out that they'd missed you at the house, and then again at the motel. And they thought I might still have some value, after all."

"Jesus," I murmured.

He told me the rest then, not that there was much to tell. They'd kept him and Keith in a darkened room not unlike this one and told him nothing. The only time he'd gleaned that something was happening was when Whitmarsh's crew had suddenly tooled up and cleared out in a hurry yesterday. Their mood had been one of jubilation, he said, as though they'd set a trap for me.

Which, of course, they had. With Henry as the bait.

Sean had sat and sweated until their return and then the ill-tempered slamming of doors and kicking of walls and the mo-rose snatches of conversation had made it plain that I'd somehow got Trey away from them again.

"I felt so damned helpless, just waiting for it to happen, and then the relief was just incredible," he confessed. "Not just at your survival but my own too, I suppose. I don't know what you did, Charlie, but it really pissed them off."

So I told him my side of the story. The only part I glossed over was my real intention when I'd gone to face down Gerri. I wasn't quite ready to admit that yet. Even to Sean.

Eventually we sat against the wall opposite the doorway, close together, unashamedly holding hands. The floor was hard and unforgiving, and occasionally things with more legs than I wanted to think about skittered across it but at least they weren't rats. Besides, I was just so glad to be with Sean that I didn't care about the minor problems of insect infestation and my backside going to sleep.

Outside, the sun finally began to lose its harsh edge as another day died in flawless, but largely-ignored tragic beauty. The light filtering through the vents turned mellow, almost misty, as the ferocious heat started to abate a little.

Sean and I sat without speaking as we watched the onset of the end of the day, my head tilted onto his shoulder. There was too much to say to know where to start and so it was better to say none of it than to say it badly.

"If you see a chance, Charlie, take it," Sean said at last. "If I have to go I'd rather go out fighting than being caught with my bloody pants down again."

"You never told me you were skinny-dipping in the pool," I said.

Just for a moment he laughed and squeezed my fingers.

"I'm serious," he said. "If you get an opportunity, don't hesitate. They won't, that's for sure."

He paused and when he spoke again his voice had lost any trace of amusement. "Do you remember you once told me that if I went out of my way to kill a man—even one who blatantly deserved it—you'd feel compelled to try and stop me?"

My mouth had suddenly gone so dry I had to peel my tongue away from the roof of it. "Yes," I said. "I remember."

"You know what you mean to me, don't you, Charlie?"

"Yes."

He nodded. "Good," he said, cool and distant now. "So this time, don't try and stop me."

I should have made some response to that. How could I accept such a sinister statement of intent without argument? If you planned to kill in advance of needing to, it wasn't self-defense any more. It was murder.

But I knew all about planning a murder, didn't I?

And then we heard the footsteps approaching and it was too late for anything else but jumping to our feet, braced and ready.

The light gushed in like floodwater as the door was unlocked and swung wide. Beyond it stood Whitmarsh, now reunited with his Beretta. His jaw was set, determined. He waved us out with a jerk of his head.

"OK, people," he said, tense. "It's time to go for a little ride."

TWENTY-FOUR

I'D NEVER BEEN in an airboat before. Given other circumstances I might even have enjoyed the experience.

Each craft was around eighteen or twenty feet in length, with a flat-bottomed hull that sat less than six inches into the water. Rows of ridged aluminum bench seats for the long-departed day trippers filled the blunt forward part of the boat.

At the rear was the hulking great V8 Chevy motor. It looked like it had been lifted straight out of a Yank truck, leaving the better part of its exhaust silencer system behind in the process.

The motor was connected to a giant carbon fiber prop, mounted inside a mesh guard above the stern. Just in front of that, at the controls, sat Mason. He was wearing a Rolling Rock baseball hat with a pair of camouflage-colored ear defenders jammed over the top and he watched our approach without any expression on his face. One of the Mossberg shotguns was slotted into a rack by his raised seat.

Whitmarsh brought us out first, then unlocked the door to retrieve Trey and his father. Keith came scurrying out, jerking to a stop when the rush of movement brought guns up in his face.

"Look," he said, sly now in his desperation, "we can still work this out! Trey really might have something to offer, y'know? Take him and I'll work on the rest of the program for you. For nothing! I—"

That was as much as I could take of that, but Sean beat me to it. He took one quick step forward and hit Keith in the face with a beautiful right hand, following it up with a left to the solar plexus that dropped the little weasel gasping to his knees. Neither Whitmarsh nor Lonnie made any moves to stop him.

"You have no idea how long I've wanted to see somebody do that to this piece of shit," Whitmarsh said. "You're a jerk, Pelzner. Now stop whining and get up."

Keith regained his feet slowly, holding both hands to his bleeding nose. He glanced at his son for support but Trey wouldn't even look at him.

Whitmarsh kept a hand on the boy's shoulder as we walked single-file down to the waiting boat. It was a canny move on his part. Trey was probably the one person we'd all try to protect—all of us except Keith, that is.

By this time Mason had the motor cranked up and the prop had started to spin. The noise of it set a pair of gangling birds that looked like white herons to flight.

The black guy who'd burst into Brown's office with Mason was waiting for us with the other Mossberg in the bow of the boat. Haines was further back, nonchalantly holding his usual Smith & Wesson pistol. He seemed to have it pointed as much at Whitmarsh as at the rest of us but it was hard to tell because his eyes were hidden behind those Oakleys again.

If Whitmarsh noticed this lack of trust, he gave no sign of it. Despite the fact that the burn had gone out of the day, he was still sweating heavily, his shirt sopping with it now.

What's the matter, Jim? This too cold-blooded for you? Didn't have any trouble at the motel, now did you?

The four of us, the condemned, ended up on one row in the center of the airboat. Trey tucked himself in between me and Sean, leaving Keith to sit, sniffing loudly, on his own at the other side. Shunned even in his final moments.

Lonnie unhooked the bow rope from its post and jumped into the front section with the black guy. Whitmarsh climbed less nimbly into the row immediately behind us, with Haines lurking behind him, still smiling like this was the most fun he'd had with his clothes on.

Mason cranked up the revs and moved away from the dock and I immediately understood why he was wearing those ear defenders. The V8 began to roar as the airboat glided across the small inlet and headed for the open swamp beyond, picking up speed all the while.

The surface of the swamp was coated in a thick layer of water hyacinths but, without any projections from the hull, the airboat scudded over the top of it. It hardly cut a swathe through the vegetation in its wake, leaving very little evidence to mark the trail to our final resting place.

Mason opened the throttle until we were really flying. He handled the airboat with easy confidence, banking into the turns as he skirted round the larger patches of weeds and semi-immersed trees. Insects of all descriptions splatted into us so hard you didn't dare breathe with your mouth open or you would have swallowed enough of them to qualify as a last meal.

And all the time we were moving I was watching the men watching us, looking for a break, a weakness, a moment of inattention that would spell our opportunity.

It never came.

After ten minutes or so Mason eased back and the airboat's speed dropped off until it was dead in the water, letting the motor idle lazily. The sudden reduction in noise was a deafening silence by comparison. Without the cooling breeze whipping past us, the temperature level also rose abruptly, so we almost seemed to be back to the high heat of the day even though the sunset was now in full swing.

We had come far enough to be out of sight of the small dock and the building next to it and had swerved about so much I couldn't even have pointed in the right direction to get back. We were in the middle of nowhere, surrounded by cypress trees that towered out of the turgid water, draped with the Spanish moss that would eventually smother them.

I glanced with growing apprehension at the darkened water alongside the boat. There were snakes in there, I knew, as well as the alligators Livingston Brown was relying upon to dispose of our mortal remains.

A group of bubbles broke the surface close by. I tried to tell myself it was just gas from rotting down plants. I wasn't particularly convincing.

Mason seemed to be looking around, too, with the advantage of his elevated position. After a moment he pointed over to his left and, following his direction, I spotted the long gnarly shape of the submerged gator about a hundred meters away.

If the part of it I could see in the dusky light was anything to go by, it was a big one. I'd never seen anything like it in the wild before and had to admit to a certain stereotyped revulsion at the grotesque appearance, with those twin rows of bony plates along its back and the long flat skull. Maybe knowing we were the feature dish on its dinner menu for this evening had some part to play. As I looked, I caught another stealthy movement, close to the first, then a third.

My God, the place is crawling with them.

I glanced over at Sean. His face was taut, skin stretched tight over his cheekbones, brows pulled down. I could sense his body coiling like a pre-strike snake, alert to the slightest possibility, the faintest quiver in the air.

"This'll do," Mason said, offhand. "Any closer and the sound of the shots will scare 'em off anyhow."

I was at the end of the row and Haines waved me to my feet.

"Ladies first, I do believe," he said.

I stood, trying to keep my knees soft, my arms loose by my sides. Trey looked up at me mutely, shock keeping him passive even though he was clearly on the edge of panic.

"You don't have to do this, Jim," I said to Whitmarsh, achieving an admirably level tone considering my heart rate was redlining, making it hard to draw breath. "You still have a chance to make this right."

Whitmarsh shook his head rather sadly and moved further to the edge of the boat himself, the gun aimed square at the center of my body. "You won't change my mind, Charlie," he said carefully. "It's already made up."

He was looking right into my eyes as he spoke and I could have sworn there was something at the back of his own that hadn't been there before. The barrel of the gun shifted away from me just a fraction.

If you get a chance, take it! Sean's words were roaring in my head. I bunched my muscles, felt rather than saw Sean do the same.

"No, you can't do it!" Suddenly Trey was out of his seat next to me like a rabbit, the fear turning his voice into a shriek. "You can't!" And he dived for Whitmarsh, latching onto his right hand like he was trying to save himself from falling.

Whitmarsh had already started to squeeze the trigger but Trey's reckless act threw his aim off. The gun discharged but the shot went wild and wide.

Which was a damned shame really, because he hadn't been aiming at us.

He'd been aiming at Haines.

At the same moment, by what must have been a prior arrangement, Lonnie swung the Remington up and round toward the black guy standing next to him. Without hesitation, he shot him in the chest.

Lonnie was standing so close to him when he fired that it was almost point-blank. The shot barely had a chance to begin its spread, punching into Brown's security man almost as a solid slug.

Half the back of his shirt exploded outward as his body ripped open, the center of his torso disintegrating in a split second. Debris splashed down beside the boat and then the man toppled backward to join it. The last thing to hit the water, it seemed, was the Mossberg as it dropped from his fingers and sank like a brick.

Lonnie didn't bother to watch him go over. As soon as he'd pulled the trigger he'd racked another fresh cartridge into the chamber and started to twist toward the stern.

Mason saw the move as it happened but he wasn't foolish enough to believe he had the time to reach for his own gun. He just put the rudder hard over and stamped on the throttle, whipping the airboat into a vicious surging turn.

Everyone standing instantly lost their footing, including me. Trey thudded to his knees, almost bringing Whitmarsh down on top of him.

Haines skidded, grabbing at one of the engine supports to keep himself upright. His lips pulled back into a triumphant snarl as he began to bring the Smith & Wesson up to bear on the hampered Whitmarsh.

In the event, though, he never got a shot off.

One moment Sean was sprawled half on the floor beside me, and the next he'd put both hands on the back of the bench seat and vaulted over it, launching himself at Haines. As he leaped he pivoted his legs straight out to the side of him with the easy power of an Olympic gymnast.

One foot landed square in Haines's ribcage, while the other connected with the side of his jaw. The man's head snapped back. He staggered a second time and went down, dropping the semi-automatic into the bottom of the boat.

Like the rest of us, Lonnie had fallen when Mason made his violent maneuver but he'd landed badly. As he started to regain his feet I saw that he'd snapped his right forearm about halfway between wrist and elbow. The break was a nasty one and the lower part of his arm had taken on a rubbery, detached quality.

With a grunt of effort and pain he swapped the Remington into his left hand and pointed it at Mason, sitting exposed at the helm. Mason still hadn't reached for his own gun, but he protected himself the best way he could. He wrenched at the controls again to send the airboat into a series of vicious turns like a gazelle jinking to outwit the pursuing lions.

Lonnie lost his balance again and started to go over backward. He instinctively put his right hand out to catch himself but that action only served to compound the fracture. The arm collapsed under his own weight, sending him tumbling over the side of the boat and into the brackish opaque water of the swamp.

As he went over, Lonnie's finger tightened on the trigger and the Remington let go a second shot. Trey was down below seat level, still grappling with Whitmarsh, and Keith had yet to raise his head. Sean and I dived for cover and by some miracle the stinging spray of pellets missed both of us.

Mason wasn't so lucky. He caught a peppering across the

right-hand side of his body, little more than a glancing blow but bad enough, all the same.

But the bulk of the shot bypassed all the people on board and hit the mesh cage surrounding the propeller. It passed straight through like a magic trick, leaving the guard untouched but the prop inside shattered into fragments, sending shards of carbon fiber zinging across the back end of the airboat like deadly little flechettes.

With the throttle wide open, the prop must have been spinning at close to five thousand revs a minute when it blew. Mason lifted off immediately, but the resulting massive imbalance had already almost shaken the engine to pieces. He grappled with the rudder controls with both hands as it began to veer wildly. His arm and the side of his shirt were already wet with blood.

"Jump!" Sean shouted to me.

I didn't have time to argue with him about the wisdom of that one. Lonnie was already in the water, half-swimming, half-wading for the cover of the nearest clump of cypress trees about sixty meters away to our left. If he could make it with only one arm working . . .

I reached over the back of the seat and grabbed Trey by the collar of his shirt. The adrenaline pumping through my system had the effect of making him weigh almost nothing as I heaved him away from Whitmarsh and all but threw him over the side of the boat. Sean kicked a squealing Keith into the water on the opposite side and jumped in after him.

Hitting flat water, even when you're not traveling that fast is an unpleasant business, not unlike coming off a motorbike and bouncing along the road surface until you've scrubbed off some speed. The only difference was the lack of protective leathers and the fact that you're unlikely to die by drowning at the end of your average bike crash.

Not that drowning was the biggest of my fears right now.

Even so, I was coughing like a consumptive as I surfaced, spitting out gouts of foul-tasting swamp water and scraping at the wet hair that was plastered across my eyes. Then I looked around me, frantic, but in the rapidly encroaching gloom I couldn't spot Trey or Sean anywhere close by.

Just for a second I was assailed by all manner of terrors. Not least of which centered on the presence of the alligators. I splashed in another quick circle but there were no telltale lumps bearing down on me and eyeing me up with a view to dinner. Then I remembered about the poisonous water moccasin snakes.

Oh nice one, Fox.

The airboat thundered on past for a short distance after we'd bailed out of it, describing a big curving turn. Half the rudder system was shot away, too, and Mason wrestled for some semblance of control. The engine sounded raucous in the extreme, barely holding together under the incredible strain of trying to spin the lopsided propeller. It was protesting its mechanical agony loudly in the only way it knew.

I could just about see Whitmarsh up on his feet again now, struggling hand-to-hand with Haines as the airboat bucked and shuddered underneath them.

Whitmarsh had weight on his side but Haines was clearly the stronger party. As I watched he ducked and got a shoulder into Whitmarsh's expansive stomach, ramming him backward and toppling him over the side. He made considerably more of a splash when he hit the water than any of the rest of us had done.

And then, not far behind me I heard a strangled cry that could only be Trey. I spun round toward the sound and saw the kid thrashing in the water. I hoped those long shadows closing on him were just a product of the failing light but I knew I was wrong.

"Trey, for Christ's sake keep still!" I yelled at him. He froze almost instantly, sinking until barely more than his nose and the top of his head were visible out of the water.

Without any clear idea of what the hell I was going to do when I got there, I headed for him in a fast crawl. I arrived at just about the same time as an alligator that must have been twelve feet long, its body a dull grayish black like a slightly scaly nuclear submarine, only not so friendly.

Trey was terrified, incoherent with fright as the reptile approached in its sinuous way through the water. I put myself between it and the boy. My brain inconveniently fed me with an old nature program snippet that an alligator's jaws had the crushing power of 3000 pounds per square inch. I braced myself, still with no idea how to go about winning such an uneven fight.

But then, almost at the last moment, the gator swerved around us, almost graceful in its evasion. I swear the end of its tail brushed past my bare arm in the water but it could have been one of those damned snakes. Another smaller alligator swam by on the other side, moving fast enough to leave a wake.

It was only when I looked at the water that I realized why they hadn't bothered with us.

There was blood in it.

Not from Trey and certainly not from me. It was leaching out of the guy Lonnie had blown away in the front of the boat. His body now floated face down less than twenty feet away, leaving a greasy trail of blood in the water like oil from the wreck of a rusting Panamanian tanker.

The alligators converged on the man's body with a purpose, squabbling over who got first bite of the prize. As I looked one of them seemed to rear up, its massive jaws wide open to show a mouth that was a surprisingly delicate shade of pink inside. A scrap of cloth had snagged on the beast's teeth and flapped when it shook its head. I didn't look too closely at what else might have been in there.

"Come on!" I grabbed Trey's arm, tugged at him. "We've got to get away from here."

Getting him to shift wasn't easy, even though every ounce of logic should have told him that getting away from the vicinity of the corpse—or buffet as the alligators viewed it—was a good idea. Fortunately, Trey was easy to tow through the water, even if the vegetation did seem to constantly tangle round our limbs.

Suddenly, my feet hit the muddy bottom and then I, like Lonnie, was half-swimming, half-staggering with my burden toward the relative safety of the trees.

I still hadn't caught sight of Sean or Keith and that in itself scared me. Not that I cared what happened to Keith, which I recognized wasn't the best attitude for a bodyguard. It was always Trey who'd been my responsibility and I was determined to do my damnedest to save him now.

I glanced behind me. The light levels were dropping fast but I could still make out the collective hump in the water where the alligators were feeding. More of them were gathering all the time until I couldn't count the numbers.

Christ, aren't they supposed to be a threatened species or something?

And, even though I couldn't see it, I could certainly hear the airboat circling back toward us. The trees were almost within reach now. I shoved Trey on faster, slipping in my haste, going down on my knees and taking in another lungful of rancid gloop.

Blinded and gasping, I felt a pair of hands grab hold of the back of my shirt and the seat of my trousers and lift me clear of the water. I began to struggle instinctively until Sean's voice said, "Be still!" in a savage whisper.

He dragged me through a small gap in the trees, and Trey after me. I got to my feet slowly, coughing and retching until there was only air in my lungs again. And not much of that.

On the other side of the trees the area opened out slightly into a pool of fly-blown water with shallow-sloping muddy banks. The trees were close in on all sides, making it darker in there than out on the open swamp.

I squinted suspiciously at a number of dark knobbly stumps protruding out of the pool until I realized they were part of a root system. They stuck up about six inches out of the water and would, at least, be enough to stop the airboat being able to force its way into our sanctuary.

Then, on the other side of the pool, I noticed the elongated shapes of three medium-sized alligators, drawn up on the far bank like beached canoes, watching us unblinkingly.

Keith and Lonnie were standing up to their knees in the water, watching the reptiles and brandishing ripped-out branches just in case any of them decided to make a move. Not that the rotting timber would have lasted long against something with the speed and agility of a hungry gator. For the moment, though, both sides seemed willing to accept the uneasy standoff.

Keith was shaking so hard I'm amazed he could keep hold of his branch, let alone manage to remain at his post. Lonnie looked calmer, cradling his mangled right arm carefully across his body.

"Where's Jim?" Lonnie asked over his shoulder.

I shook my head. "I don't know," I said. "He went into the water but I didn't see what happened after that."

Sean didn't comment, just kept low and peered out through the undergrowth at the airboat. He had mud on his face as makeshift camouflage cream and was blending in to his surroundings perfectly. Something about his movements had changed, gone feral.

"Sean." I put my hand on his arm and he turned his head just enough to look at me. His eyes were as cold and expressionless as those watching us from the far bank. I took my hand back in a reflex, as though he would have bitten me if I hadn't moved. Whatever words I'd been about to say died in my throat.

Sean nodded out into the swamp. "There he is," he said, clipped, and when I looked I saw him too. Whitmarsh must have been disorientated by his submersion and it had taken him a while to get himself together enough to head for cover. He was making slow progress through the congested water in the rough direction of our hide-out.

At that moment, the airboat came into view again. It seemed that Mason had managed to regain some small measure of control by this time. I don't know what happened to Haines's pistol, but he'd taken the Mossberg from its rack and had moved forward to the bow. Even in the low light he spotted Whitmarsh's white shirt against the murky water straight away and signaled Mason to change direction.

"Shit," I whispered. "He's going to lead them right to us."

If he lived that long.

As if doing us a favor, Haines brought the shotgun up to his shoulder and fired. The muzzle flash was a bright spout of flame in the encroaching darkness. Whitmarsh cried out and began to flail in the water. Haines was still too far away for it to have been a killing shot. Maybe that was what he'd intended.

I felt a hand slip into mine and hold on tightly. It was Trey.

"For God's sake, you can't just leave him out there," Lonnie said, his voice hoarse. "He saved your goddamn lives."

Sean shot him a vicious glance but said nothing. There wasn't much he could say, not when Lonnie was right.

Mason began to circle Whitmarsh, passing within a dozen meters of us as he did so. The wash broke over the trees roots and swept into the pool so we had to brace to keep our feet. The Chevy engine sounded almost on its last legs. Mason was having to coax it along and, after Lonnie's wild shot, it was clearly costing him.

"Leave him and let's go back," he called to Haines, his voice scratchy with pain. "We need to go get the other boat. This one's gonna die on us any minute and then we'll be stuck out here. And I need to get fixed up. Jesus, man, this hurts."

"If we don't finish this now, we'll lose 'em," Haines shouted back. "Just keep driving the damned boat."

"Wait until they come round again, then we'll go out behind them," Sean said quietly to me.

I nodded, disengaging my hand from Trey's with some difficulty. Whatever Whitmarsh might have done, we couldn't sit back and let Haines slaughter him.

"Wait a minute, you can't go out there!" Keith protested. "You'll get us all killed."

"Oh for fuck's sake, Dad, shut up," Trey hissed. "They're professionals."

Keith opened his mouth, shut it again, and fell silent.

Haines fired another shot at Whitmarsh. He was close enough for it to have been a final one, close enough to make the water erupt and boil near his head, but Haines was playing with him now, making the older man suffer for his crimes. The airboat came round again and this time Sean and I slipped into the water in its wake.

I struck out for Whitmarsh, reaching him in half a dozen strokes. Haines's first shot had taken him in the side and shoulder and he was losing blood fast enough to be fading. I rolled him over onto his back to stop him drowning, trying not to think about the irresistible taste of meat he was putting into the water.

Haines spotted me and gave a cry of triumph.

"Still trying to play the bodyguard, huh, Charlie?" he jeered, leaning out toward me over the side of the boat. "Well, you can't save everybody. In your case, you can't save anybody." And he started to bring the shotgun up.

But just as he took aim the V8 gave its final rattling splutter and stalled. In the unearthly silence that followed I realized I could hear another engine. It could only be another airboat. Close and closing.

Haines realized it too. He whirled round, eyes scanning the darkness of the swamp.

And, as if waiting just for the split-second of his distraction, a dark shape burst out of the water next to Haines. It knocked him straight off his feet and dragged him over the side of the boat.

TWENTY-FIVE

THE ELEMENT OF surprise Sean achieved was absolute. Haines didn't even have time to gasp as he went under. Mason was the one who got to shout but, wounded and unarmed, there was little more he could do.

A moment later the two of them broke the surface again, fighting over the shotgun which Haines had kept a tight hold of despite the shock of the attack. He was putting up a ferocious struggle but he'd been trained as a policeman, where Sean had been trained as a soldier and there was a big difference.

Besides, Sean had passion driving him on. A cold hard flame of rage that made him far more deadly and more dangerous.

I heaved Whitmarsh closer to the tree-line, then abandoned him to Keith and Trey's care and waded back toward the two men. I was in time to see Sean yank Haines close and headbutt him. Haines's nose broke with an audible crunch and he let go of the Mossberg, falling back into the water.

For a second I expected Sean to turn the gun on him, to force him to surrender, but with a snarl he threw the weapon away behind him and went for Haines with his bare hands.

And that's when I got really scared.

"Sean!" I yelled. "For Christ's sake don't do this."

Sean turned his head and looked straight through me.

It was like staring at a man turned vampire and realizing that although the face was familiar, the soul had been taken.

That what was left was cold and empty and not quite human any more.

The sound of the second airboat was growing louder by the minute. A high-wattage searchlight beam flashed across Mason, making him wince and put up a hand to protect his eyes.

"Don't move!" boomed a megaphone-enhanced voice. "This is the FBI!"

We were shielded from their approach by the hull of Mason's boat so I ignored the instruction, lurching closer to Sean. He was holding Haines under the water now, forearms rigid with the effort of keeping him there as he thrashed and twisted. I couldn't tell from the position of his hands if Sean was strangling the man or simply drowning him.

Either way, it was murder now.

I thought again of Haines calmly pulling the trigger on the woman in the theme park. I remembered the satisfaction in his voice when he'd admitted torturing and killing Henry. I could well imagine him standing behind Sean's kneeling figure with the Smith & Wesson aimed at the back of his skull. And I could just see him smiling while he did it.

But it wasn't Haines I was trying to protect.

"Sean," I said again, more quietly now. "Don't do this to yourself."

For a moment he didn't respond, then he relaxed his shoulders and brought his hands out of the water and I thought I'd got through to him.

But as he did so I realized that Haines had ceased to struggle. He bobbed to the surface and floated lifeless between us, eyes and mouth wide. The swamp water lapped gently into his open throat.

"Sorry, Charlie," Sean said tightly. He sounded weary, but there wasn't a hint of regret in his voice. "You're too late."

And I couldn't find it in myself to be sorry, either.

We both turned, just as the new airboat arrived with a flourish alongside Mason's stricken craft. The wash nearly swept the pair of us off our feet.

Half a dozen black-clad figures with machine pistols jumped from one boat to the other, their boots clattering loudly on the aluminum. They had flashlights attached to their guns and a number pointed them at Mason, but he didn't put up any resistance. In the crossed beams I could now see that one arm of his chair was slick with blood and he could hardly even raise both hands. They had to help him down.

Other hands reached over the side toward us.

"Wait," I said. "We've a man injured here."

Sean cast me a quick glance but I waded back over to Whitmarsh and between us we managed to get him close enough to the airboat for them to grab him and haul him in like a loaded trawler net. He was unconscious and bleeding but they started work on him right away with the urgency to suggest they thought he might survive.

Lonnie and Keith came staggering out of the trees then, still carrying their makeshift clubs. The FBI men were jumpy enough to insist they jettison the branches before they'd take them into the boat.

I waited until they'd got Trey out of the water before I accepted help. It was only then, when everyone else was on board, that Sean pushed Haines's body close enough to be retrieved.

I thought he was being practical, logical, and then it struck me that he'd just been making sure there was no chance of them being able to revive him.

And all the time, around us in the shadows I could hear the rapid movement of the alligators, driven to a frenzy of distraction by the blood in the water. The sudden fear of what might have been bloomed and spread through my imagination faster than I could keep pace with it. And I'd always thought that rats were my biggest phobia.

The reaction started to crowd in then, setting up a trembling in my hands that I had little control over. I sat slumped in the bottom of the airboat, not caring that there were still suspicious guns held over me.

"Well, I guess you're kinda ready to give yourself up now, missy?" said a voice over the top of me.

I raised my head enough to see Special Agent in Charge Till standing above me. His hands were on his hips.

"Not yet," I said, with last-ditch bravado I didn't really feel. "There's still Brown."

He nodded. "We're working on that," he said. His gaze shifted to Sean, eyeing him warily. "So you must be Meyer. Well, I have to say that for a dead guy you're looking pretty healthy."

Sean didn't reply to that. He sat alongside me with his forearms resting on his knees and his hands hanging relaxed. The two of them stared at each other but maybe they were too similar in nature to ever be comfortable in such close proximity.

"Don't tell me—you just happened to be in the neighborhood," I said.

Till tore his gaze away from Sean with difficulty. "We found your tape, missy," he said. "Got the whole thing. Recording's a little fuzzy maybe but the lab boys reckon they can clean it up some and it'll go down a storm at the trial."

"You can thank your Uncle Walt for that," I said.

"Thank him yourself," Till said, jerking his head over his shoulder.

I followed his gaze and saw that it was Walt who was driving the second airboat. The old man gave me a nod and sketched a casual salute.

"You brought your uncle on a trip like this?" I said blankly.

Till shrugged, a little embarrassed. "We found him staking out the front gate when we got here," he admitted, "and we needed someone who could handle an airboat."

I looked at Walt. "I told you I'd find my own way back," I said.

He shrugged. "I had nothing else doing."

Till ran his eye across the other faces his men had pulled out of the swamp and paused when he came to Keith.

"Although I have your confession on record, Mr. Pelzner," he said with a touch of that grim humor, "I'm kinda assuming that you didn't actually murder your wife."

Keith opened his mouth a few times, floundering. "Er, I—"

Till smiled. "Don't sweat it," he said. "I kinda understand that you were under duress at the time."

"So, like, where is she?" Trey demanded. "What happened to her?"

Keith's shoulders bowed even further. "She really did leave, Trey," he said mournfully. I knew he was trying to be gentle about it but it came across as self-pity instead. "She just upped and left the both of us. The divorce papers arrived from Nowheresville, Ohio. She didn't even ask for custody."

Trey looked down at his hands, clasped in front of him, and bit his lip. I scowled at Keith. If he'd had anything about him, he'd have left out that last little piece of information, given the boy something he could still cling to.

Keith twisted and put his hand on Trey's shoulder, gave it a pat. "I'm real sorry, son," he said. "I know how much she meant to you, but it's just you and me now."

Trey looked up at him, tears forming in his eyes, and just for a second I thought he was going to fold.

"You gotta be joking," he snapped, lip curling as he ducked out from under his father's hand. "You were gonna sell me out. I'd rather end up in Juvenile Hall than stay with you, you bastard."

His bottom lip began to quiver. He turned his filling eyes on me. "Why can't I stay with Charlie?"

I put my hands up. "Whoa," I said, more sharply than I'd intended. "That is *not* an option."

"Well I'm not staying with him and you can't make me!" Trey said, a little wildly now, but his face was obstinate. There'd be no shifting him on this one.

Till looked uncomfortable at this display of teenage angst. "Well, I guess we can call in Child Services until we get this one sorted out," he said, his voice dubious.

Trey's lip quivered all the more. I felt like I'd just shot Bambi's mother.

"Don't worry, Trey," Walt said then. "You're welcome to come stay with me and Harriet just as long as you need."

I tried not to make my relief too obvious. The kid had had enough shocks and rejections for one day. Still, what was one more?

Once Till's men had Whitmarsh, Lonnie and Mason

roughly patched up, we all transferred to the undamaged airboat and took the other under tow. I mentioned the black guy Lonnie had dispatched, but it was almost completely dark out on the swamp now and, as none of us could accurately pinpoint his location, Till was reluctant to start a full-scale search.

"First light tomorrow will be soon enough to look for the remains," he said.

I wondered if he'd chosen those particular words deliberately. The way the alligators had been going at the body, there wasn't going to be much left to find.

Conversation became difficult once we were under way but I needed more answers out of Till, even so.

"So when are you planning on picking up Brown?" I shouted over the roar of the engine.

He glanced at me, irritated, but said, "He's making a speech for his fancy clients at the clubhouse right now. My boys have got the place under surveillance. Soon as we get back to the dock we'll go get him."

"I want to be there," I said.

"No way, missy," Till shot back. "I am not taking civilians on an operation like this."

I couldn't help my gaze straying over his shoulder to where Walt was piloting the airboat with the easy skill of long association. I don't know if he could have heard what we were saying, but the old man gave me one of his crinkled-up smiles.

Till caught the gesture. "Oh no, no," he said quickly. "That's way different."

I raised my eyebrows but didn't argue further. Not yet.

Sean was sitting next to me, staring at nothing. As I watched, his hands flexed briefly, just once, as though reliving the moment they'd finished off Haines. He still had the bloody lines around his wrists. A reminder of his captivity, his helplessness.

I wished I knew what thoughts were going round inside his head but he'd got them buttoned down tight. As though aware of my silent scrutiny he turned his head slightly and met my eyes. He didn't need No Entry signs and barbed wire to warn me that I should keep out. I didn't try to go against him.

Maybe we both needed a little time to come to terms with all of this.

More FBI men, with lights and vans and a paramedic ambulance, were waiting for us on the small dockside when Walt brought the two airboats alongside. As soon as the lines were secured and the engine cut, Till jumped out. He immediately started throwing quick and efficient orders to people who appeared by his side then melted away again. It was a pleasure to watch such oiled machinery at work.

They took Whitmarsh away on a stretcher with an oxygen mask strapped to his face. They stabilized Lonnie's smashed arm and bundled him in, too. Somebody appeared with blankets for the rest of us which they draped around our shoulders. How on earth did they know to bring so many blankets, for heaven's sake?

Sean and I stood with Trey and let the mêlée ebb and flow around us. I noticed Walt accost his nephew at one point. I don't know what was said but if the body language was anything to go by, Walt won the argument. Till looked vaguely annoyed as he came back over to us.

"OK," he said. "I'm sticking my neck out here and there'll be hell to pay, but if you want to be in at the finish, let's go."

We were on the move before he'd even finished speaking.

"Not you, Trey," I said as he made to join us.

"Aw, c'mon," Trey complained. "I deserve to be there, too."

"You'll get to hear all about it later," Walt told him. "Let's let these good people go do their job, huh?"

I expected the kid to put up more of a fight than that but he just nodded and hung his head. Walt put an arm around his shoulders and after a moment's hesitation Trey leaned in to him. There was something right about the two of them, standing there like that. If Trey was serious about severing his ties with his father, I reflected, he could do a lot worse than Walt as a surrogate.

Till had already jumped into the passenger side of a dark nondescript saloon and Sean and I jogged across to take the rear seat. The driver gunned the engine and we headed back up the rough track toward Livingston Brown's luxury resort. The lights of at least two other cars followed behind us.

I sat forward in order to talk to Till. "So you found Gerri's body," I said.

He twisted in his seat. "Yeah, and for a little while we thought you were the most likely candidate for the job," he said. "Until we found that recorder in your bag, that is. I gotta hand it to you, Charlie, that tape was pure dynamite."

"Will it be enough to definitely nail Brown for the shooting?"

"Oh yeah, no doubt about that. With that and the other evidence we've uncovered, he won't see daylight again."

"What other evidence?" Sean asked.

"Turns out Brown was investing heavily in the software company Pelzner worked for," Till said. "He didn't just want the program, he wanted the whole nine yards. Hardly surprising considering if that program ever hit the market, they'd all be billionaires. Only problem was, Brown didn't have the money to pay the going price. In fact, he's practically broke."

It was hard to keep focused on him when we were bouncing around over every pothole. I held on to the seat in front of me and tried not to clout my head against the roof of the car. It was like being back on that damned rollercoaster ride with Trey.

"So," Till went on, "it looks like he was trying to destabilize the company, arranging sabotage of property and intimidation of the staff. It all helps rock the boat. I should imagine that's why Ms. Raybourn called in you guys."

Sean nodded.

"The company owner told us that he also secretly leaked some advance news of the program to the financial press, trying to keep the stock price up," Till went on. "Our guess is that's when Brown cooked up the scheme to make it look like Pelzner had run out on the deal."

"But they messed it up," Sean said.

Now it was Till's turn to nod. "Oh yeah, they messed it up all right," he said. He glanced at me, his expression brooding. "I suppose that's all thanks to missy here."

"And then he found out that Keith couldn't make the program work, after all," I put in. "And it was just a case of stopping us falling into the wrong hands and then getting rid of us as fast as possible."

"Well he sure left a trail of destruction trying to do just that," he replied. It's gonna take months just to fill out all the paperwork."

I smiled. "But then Whitmarsh found out from Henry that Trey might just hold the key."

"Which he doesn't."

"I wasn't there for this part," Sean said. "Who's Henry?"

"I'll tell you later," I said. I turned back to the FBI man. "So do I assume from all this that we're more or less off the hook?"

He favored me with a slow appraisal. "Sure looks that way," he said. "Particularly if you was to agree to give evidence in court."

I sat back in my seat. "Well how about that?" I murmured with more than a hint of irony in my tone. "Chief suspect to star witness all in the same day."

The first person I saw when we walked through the main entrance doors to the clubhouse was Randy, the time-share salesman I'd hijacked to get to Brown.

He did a classic double-take. First at the fact that both Sean and I were coated in slime and leaving a wet muddy trail across the tiles behind us. And second when he recognized me underneath it all.

"Oh my God," he yelped, "somebody call the cops!"

"No need, sir, she's with me," Till said, flashing his official ID. "Federal Bureau of Investigation."

"FBI? You're with the FBI?" Randy repeated, looking dazed. He blushed at the memory of what he'd tried to do with me up against a filing cabinet. "Am I under arrest?"

Till sighed. "Just take us to Mr. Brown," he said.

Randy led the way with much more eagerness than he'd shown last time I was there. He eventually stopped just outside a pair of large double doors with a plaque on one that said Party Room. By the sounds of it Brown was just rounding off his big welcome speech on the other side. Nobody listening to the old guy's melodious voice would ever guess he was a vicious murderer.

Till spoke fast and low into his radio, then issued brief instructions to the men he had with him. They all seemed to know the drill without needing long explanations, in any case.

When the moment came they kicked the doors open and went in at a run. There were a few squeals and shrieks from the assembled crowd, but mostly it was all over before anyone had the time to get excited.

It was only then that Sean and I were allowed into the room. Several hundred pairs of shocked and bewildered eyes followed our entrance, but the most stunned belonged to the harmless-looking old guy with the wispy gray hair, currently face down on the floor with two FBI men on top of him, cuffing his hands behind his back.

Brown was loudly announcing his outrage at this manhandling and, I considered, was making a pretty convincing show of wronged innocence along the way.

"You don't begin to have the right to treat me this way," he protested, sounding hurt and a little self-righteous, just as he would if he *was* truly blameless. "You don't have a single shred of evidence against me."

"Oh I'm afraid we do, Mr. Brown," Till said. "Not only do we have a boatload of witnesses, as it were, but thanks to this little lady here, we even have a tape recording of you actually in the act of carrying out a homicide. In fact, we got so much on you it's gonna take from now 'til Thanksgiving just to file the charges."

Brown managed to turn his head enough to look right at

me. The surprise on his face was followed quickly by disgust. Not for me, I realized, but for himself. That he'd been fooled.

"She was just a girl," he muttered as Till's men dragged him to his feet. The disbelief was a faint tinge around the edges of his voice. His eyes slid to Sean and then back again to me. "She was Meyer's goddamn girlfriend. A nobody . . ."

Special Agent in Charge Till put a hold on his satisfaction just sufficiently to give me his own brief, somber appraisal. He took in the sodden filthy shirt and the matted tangle of revolting pink hair. And he saw that above it all I was still standing, still in there. Right to the bitter end.

He nodded to me, just once, and turned back to his prisoner.

"Yeah," he said, and his stern face cracked into the first genuine piece of emotion I'd seen him display. A big grin. His voice had never sounded so laconic, so laid back as it did then.

"I guess if you was a stupid man," he said, "you might just make the mistake of thinking that."

EPILOGUE

"SO, CHARLIE, HOW are you?"

"Fine," I said. "I'm fine." But we both knew I was lying.

"That's good," he said, not fixing me with that piercing stare, careful not to let me know outright that he could tell. That wasn't his way, this quiet man. He made a few notes on the pad in front of him. "And how is Sean?"

"He's fine, too," I said. Another half truth.

The man sighed at that and laid down his pen. It was a nice pen, a shiny chrome Sheaffer and he was careful how he placed it, with precision, between the pristine blotter and the small framed photo of his wife and children. He was a careful man altogether.

We were in his office. A quiet room, but then, I wouldn't have expected anything else. Outside his window was a tranquil view onto public parkland, with trees in the hazy distance.

Nobody disturbed the emptiness of the space except a solitary dog walker. Later, the office workers would be out to sunbathe on the parched grass and return, pink and sleepy, to their afternoon desks. For the moment, though, the dog walker had it all to himself.

"I found a news cutting since your last visit that I thought might be relevant," the man said now. "I saved it for you, if you'd like to see it?"

It was phrased politely but if I refused, it would send up flags. Denial. I shrugged, suddenly reminding myself of Trey.

He reached into the desk and brought it out, a folded magazine rather than a clipping. As he handed it across I looked at the page header out of curiosity and found it was a copy of a US financial journal, dated a week ago.

I opened the magazine out and there right across the top of the left-hand page was a picture of Walt and Harriet. They were standing in front of what could only be described as a mansion in the modern American style. They were arm in arm, and smiling.

I started to read the article, heedless of the fact that the meter was running. The man opposite brought a whole new meaning to the phrase "time is money." My only consolation was that it wasn't me who was footing the bill.

The piece turned out to be an interview, the gist of which was that in the last four months this self-effacing retired law enforcement officer had come from nowhere to become one of the most successful intra-day traders on the US futures market.

I read on, frowning. It wasn't until I turned the page that it all became clear. There were several smaller pictures there, including one, a little group shot tucked away in the bottom right-hand corner, that showed half a dozen kids sitting around a swimming pool and grinning self-consciously. Walt presided over a barbecue nearby. He was wearing a chef's apron and his usual battered Panama hat.

The text told me that Walt and Harriet were using their newfound wealth to continue fostering kids from broken homes. They didn't mention Trey by name, but they didn't need to for me to recognize him.

He was lurking in the background of the photo. The braces had clearly served their purpose and been discarded, and he no longer had his hair short and blond and spiked, but there was something familiar about the eyes, the line of the chin.

And next to him was Scott, looking self-conscious for the photo, standing with his arms folded and his weight on one hip, striking a pose. But he was standing. On his own two feet. That was the main thing.

I put the magazine down slowly onto my lap.

"Son of a bitch," I murmured. "So he really *could* make it work."

"How does that make you feel, Charlie?" He picked up his pen again. Another incomprehensible scribble. Was he condemning or redeeming me?

I stared at him a little blankly. "Feel?" I echoed. "I don't know. Glad, I suppose. Glad that it wasn't all for nothing, just a monumental waste of time and effort and life."

"So you feel regret at the loss of life?"

"Of course I do," I said, but it was the bystanders I was thinking of. The woman at the theme park who'd lost a lung to Haines's wild shot. She would always have that to remind her of the day of fun that turned into a living nightmare.

The young cop, whose only mistake had been eagerness to make his mark but who had never lived long enough to grow out of being known as the rookie. He'd had a wife and a ten-month-old baby son who would never know his father.

And the teenage couple at the motel, away together for the first time, who'd found death instead of love.

Not the men I'd killed, though. Even though I knew their names now, it had failed to make them more real to me. They had been professionals who'd known the risks and gambles when they'd agreed to play the game. And not for Haines, either.

I looked up. "Of course I feel regret," I said again.

But most of all, selfishly, I was regretful for myself and for Sean. For the people we'd been before. The people who had been more or less in control of the demons.

Those people—that control—was gone. The box was open and I was afraid we might never get them back inside.

Which was why I found myself here, in the offices of this eminent psychotherapist. I'd been coming to him once a fortnight since I'd returned from America, but in all honesty I didn't feel we were making any real progress toward fixing what lay inside my head, inside my soul.

I wasn't unrealistic enough to think this man could change that. But if he enabled me to keep a grip on my humanity, to live with myself knowing what I'd done and what I could do,

then it would all have been worthwhile. It would give me
something to take forward. To enable me—and Sean—to
move on.

The worst thing—the thing that frightened me the most
when I woke sweating in the dark hours of the early
morning—was that the greater part of me didn't feel broken.
A part of me felt this was how things ought to be. How they
always had been.

And, just maybe, how they always would be.

"A BODYGUARD?" SIMONE Kerse said blankly to the man sitting next to me. "Rupert, have you gone totally crazy? I absolutely do *not* need a bodyguard." She raked me with a fierce gaze. "Of any description."

My first meeting with Simone, just ten days before I was shot, over a wickedly expensive lunch at a very upmarket restaurant just off Grosvenor Square in the embassy district of London. Not exactly an auspicious start.

Simone had a very slight American accent, more an inflection than anything stronger. She was also young and strikingly good-looking, and nothing at all like my preconception of an engineer.

Just as, it seemed, I was nothing like her preconception of a bodyguard.

Rupert Harrington, on the other hand, could only have been a banker. In his early fifties, tall and thin and bespectacled, he had very little hair and a permanently anxious expression. It crossed my mind after meeting him for the first time that those two facts could easily have been connected.

"I can assure you, my dear," he said to Simone now, with a touch of asperity, "that a number of the bank's clients have had cause to require the services of Mr. Meyer's people and he comes with the highest recommendations. And even you must admit that this has all gone rather beyond a joke, hm?"

He sat back in his chair, careful not to spoil the impeccable line of his conservative dark blue pinstripe suit, and flicked a pained glance in my boss's direction as if to say, *Help me out here, would you?*

"I agree," Sean Meyer said obligingly, his voice bland but with an almost imperceptible underlying thread of amuse-

ment. Not at the situation but at the banker's discomfort because of it. "The threats have been escalating. If you won't go
to the police, you're going to have to take your own measures."

He leaned forwards slightly, resting his forearms on the
starched white tablecloth and looking directly into Simone's
eyes. There was something utterly compelling about Sean
when he pinned you down with that dark gaze, and Simone
was no more immune than anyone else.

"I'm not suggesting we surround you with a bunch of heavies," he went on, "but if you won't accept a full team, then you
should at least consider the kind of discreet, low-profile security we can offer. That's why I brought Charlie along for you
to meet."

He nodded in my direction as he spoke, and both Simone
and Harrington swung skeptical eyes towards me.

In between them, although somewhat closer to tabletop
height, another pair of eyes regarded me unwaveringly. And, I
don't mind admitting, that was the gaze I found the most unnerving.

Simone's young daughter, Ella, sat on a booster cushion
alongside her mother and carefully speared a dessert fork into
the pieces of yellow smoked haddock that had been cut up
into child-friendly pieces on her plate. It wasn't the kind of
food I would have expected a four-year-old to enjoy, but she
was shoveling it in with apparent enthusiasm and chewing
largely with her mouth open. I tried not to watch.

Simone's gaze drifted to her daughter and lingered there
for a moment with no apparent sign of displeasure. I suppose,
if you were maternally minded, Ella was the sort of child who
would induce instant broodiness. She was petite, with a minia-
ture version of her mother's dark ringleted curls framing a
heart-shaped face. Couple that to big violet-colored eyes and
she had "spoiled little brat" written all over her. I wasn't too
disappointed that her mother seemed so set against my being
assigned to protect the pair of them.

Suddenly, Simone let out an annoyed breath through her
nose, as though gathering her internal resources.

"OK, so Matt's having a hard time accepting our breakup—and lately I suppose he has gotten to be something of a pain in the butt," she allowed, her eyes still fixed on Ella. She smiled at the little girl, wiped a rogue piece of fish from her chin and turned away with clear reluctance. Her focus landed squarely on me. "But that doesn't mean I need some kind of nanny."

Much as I didn't particularly want the job, I thought the nanny gibe was a bit below the belt. I'd made an effort to look smart and businesslike for this meeting. Dark brown trouser suit, cream blouse. Under protest, I'd even gunked on some lipstick.

Sean was wearing a charcoal gray made-to-measure that subtly disguised the height and the breadth of him but, to my eyes, did little to hide the deadly grace that was an innate part of his makeup.

I'd caught a glimpse of our reflections in the mirror above the bar when we'd arrived at the restaurant and I reckoned, to the casual observer at least, we probably looked like accountants. That was certainly the effect we'd been aiming for.

Harrington opened his mouth to protest at his client's comments, but before he could speak, Sean cut in again. "As I understand it, you've had constant phone calls and you've been forced to change your mobile number—twice," he said calmly. "Your ex-boyfriend has been hanging around outside both your home and your daughter's nursery school. You've had notes left on your car. Unwanted deliveries. I think you need a little more than some kind of nanny, don't you?"

Simone switched her attention from me back to Sean. In contrast to the rest of us, she was dressed in battleship gray cargo trousers and a dark red chenille sweater with sleeves that came down almost to her fingertips. Her curly dark hair was pulled loosely back into a ponytail. Harrington had told us she was twenty-eight, a year older than I was. She looked about eighteen.

"You make it sound so much worse than it is, Mr. Meyer," she said, folding her arms defensively. "Notes on my car? OK, they're love letters. Unwanted deliveries? Sure, bouquets of flowers. Matt and I were together five years, for heaven's sake! We share a child." She swallowed, lowered her voice. "You're making him out to be some kind of stalker."

"Isn't he?" Sean asked, head tilted slightly on one side. His voice had taken on the same cool note and his face the same impassive watchfulness that had always unnerved me so badly, back when he had been one of my army training instructors, and had always seen entirely too much.

Simone flushed and avoided his gaze. Instead, she spoke to Harrington directly. "I'll talk to Matt again," she said, her tone placatory now. "He'll see sense eventually." She smiled at the banker with a lot more affection than she'd shown to either Sean or me. "I'm sorry you felt you had to take such drastic action on my behalf, Rupert, but there wasn't any need, really."

Harrington looked about to protest further, but he correctly read the stubborn expression on Simone's face and raised both palms in an admission of defeat.

"All right, my dear," he said, rueful. "If you're quite sure."

"Yes," Simone said firmly. "I am."

"Mummy, I need to go wee-wee," Ella piped up in a loud whisper. The smartly dressed elderly couple at the next table clearly subscribed to the unseen-and-unheard school of child raising. They were too British to actually turn around and glare, but I saw their outraged spines stiffen nevertheless.

If Simone noticed their disapproval, she ignored it and smiled at her daughter. "OK, sweetie," she said, sliding her own chair back so she could lift Ella down and take her by the hand as she got to her feet. "If you'll excuse us?"

"Of course," Harrington said, good manners compelling him to stand also.

Sean had already risen, I noted, and for a second I was struck by the air of urbane sophistication he presented. This from a man who had left behind his roots on a run-down housing estate in a small northern city, but who still knew how to slide right back into that rough-diamond skin when the occasion demanded. The banker would not recognize Sean on his home ground.

My eyes followed mother and child as they weaved their

way between the busy tables. Although Simone was not my principal—and at that stage I didn't expect she would become so—watching people was beginning to become a habit, all part of the career I'd chosen. Or maybe the job had ultimately chosen me. I was never too sure about that.

Sean didn't need to learn to watch anyone. For him it was an instinct ingrained deep as an old tattoo, indelible and permanent. He was just too driven, too focused, to ever let himself begin to blur.

"I'm awfully sorry about this," Harrington said as the men sat down again and rearranged their napkins across their knees. "She just won't listen to reason and, quite frankly, her refusal to admit there might be any kind of danger, either to herself or to little Ella, terrifies us, as I'm sure you can appreciate."

"How much did she win?" Sean asked, reaching for his glass of Perrier.

"Thirteen million, four hundred thousand, and change," the banker said with the casual tone of someone used to working with those kinds of figures on a daily basis, but I still heard the trace of a sneer in his voice as he added, "It was, if I understand it correctly, what they term a double rollover."

"Money's still money," Sean said. "Just because her ancestors didn't steal it doesn't make her any less rich."

Harrington had the grace to color. "Oh, quite so, old chap," he murmured. "But Simone is having some difficulty adjusting to the fact that, from the day she bought that winning ticket, her life was never going to be quite the same again. Do you know, she arrived at our office this morning having actually come into town, with the child, on the Tube? Didn't want to have to try to park in the middle of London, she said." He shook his head, as though Simone had suggested walking naked through Trafalgar Square.

"I told her she should have hired a car and driver to take her door-to-door and she looked absolutely baffled," the banker went on. "It simply doesn't cross her mind that she can afford to do these things. Nor does it occur to her that, by *not* doing them, she's putting both herself and her daughter at risk from every crackpot and kidnapper out there—quite apart from the situation with her former, er, boyfriend."

"It does, as you so rightly point out, make them prime targets—Ella especially," Sean agreed. "How serious a threat do *you* consider her ex?"

"Well, if you'd asked me that a few weeks ago, I would have said he was a minor irritation, but now . . ." The banker broke off with an eloquent shrug. "One of the first things Simone did with her money was hire various private investigation agencies to try and trace her estranged father. One of them now believes they have a promising lead, and ever since that report came in, this Matt chap just seems to have become completely unreasonable." Harrington paused, frowning. "Perhaps he believes a reunion between Simone and her father will spoil his own chances of a reconciliation with her," he added with an almost imperceptible curl of his lip. "She'd have to be quite mad to take him back, of course."

"What's the story with Simone's father?" I asked.

Harrington's head came up in surprise. Not at the question, but that I'd been the one who'd put it. Even on such short acquaintance, I'd realized that Harrington didn't speak to anyone he considered at servant level unless he had to, and even then he avoided eye contact. With that in mind I'd let Sean do most of the talking so far. From the expression on the banker's face, he clearly hadn't expected me to wade in at this late stage. His eyes swiveled warily in my direction.

Sean flashed me a lazy smile, one that would have made my knees buckle if I hadn't already been sitting down, and raised an eyebrow to Harrington, as if to repeat the question.

Harrington coughed. "Naturally, one doesn't wish to be indiscreet, but . . . well, as I understand it, Simone's mother was an American, who came over here and married an Englishman, Greg Lucas—an army chap, so I understand. They divorced when Simone was not much more than a baby, and mother and child went back to the States—Chicago, I believe it was—but her father rather dropped off the map, as it were."

He broke off as the wine waiter glided up to the table and

smoothly topped up his glass, finishing the bottle. Harrington ignored him and I wondered briefly what kind of pivotal decisions were made in the afternoons in the world of high finance after boozy lunches just like this one.

"I assume Kerse is Simone's mother's name?" I said when the waiter had departed.

Harrington nodded. "She went back to it after the divorce. Anyway, Simone's mother died a few years ago. There were no siblings, her grandparents on both sides are long gone and Simone herself is currently expending considerable effort— not to mention her now not-insubstantial resources—on attempting to locate this Lucas chap." He stopped to take a sip of his wine.

"Unsuccessfully?"

"Hm." Harrington dabbed fastidiously at his mouth with his napkin. "So far, but then, as I mentioned, a couple of weeks ago one of the firms she's using in Boston thought they'd made some progress and she's been talking about going over there ever since."

"Boston," I repeated blankly, glancing at Sean and finding no reassurance there. "As in Massachusetts, not Lincolnshire?"

Harrington frowned. "Naturally," he said with a flicker of irritation. "The rumor was that Simone's father had followed his ex-wife to the USA, so of course that's where she started looking." He paused, eyes darting from one of us to the other and registering the sudden undercurrents. "Um, one knows America is supposed to be a civilized country and all that, but bearing in mind Simone's somewhat unique circumstances, and given the trouble with her ex, we'd be happier if she had some kind of security consultant along with her when she goes over there." He nodded to Sean but didn't shift his gaze away from me. "Mr. Meyer suggested you'd be just the lady for the job, as it were," he finished with a hearty cheerfulness that didn't quite succeed in masking his natural aversion to female equality in the workplace.

Sean had no such prejudices. During the seven months that had passed since I'd started working full-time for his exclusive close protection agency, he'd sent me on jobs all over Eu-

rope, South Africa, Asia and the Middle East, and I hadn't
turned a hair.

Things didn't always go smoothly, of course, and sometimes that had nothing to do with dangers from outside
sources.

I'd just returned from a month in Prague as part of a four-
man detail. The otherwise all-male team had started out trying
to treat me as a cross between their own personal maid and
private secretary. Three days in, one of them had made what
turned out to be, for him, a very unfortunate remark about the
sexual proclivities of the Women's Royal Army Corps, of
which I'd once been a member, and my temper had finally got
the better of me. Still, they reckoned he should be out of his
cast inside six weeks. His colleagues—and his forewarned
replacement—had treated me with the utmost respect after
that, and the job went off without further unpleasantness.

I'd proved, or so I'd thought, that I was capable of doing
the job. It was just the question of where that job was that was
still causing me some qualms.

America.

There was no logic to it, but when I glanced at Sean I felt a
dull anxiety almost akin to panic. *I'm not ready to go back.*

His face carried no expression beyond a cold determination I barely recognized. *If not now, then when?*

"Um, is there some problem?" Harrington finished, as the
atmosphere finally negotiated its way past the merlot that had
formed a constituent part of his lunch. "If it's a question of
timing, this trip probably wouldn't be for a month or so, if
then. The investigation is still in its early stages at the moment, from what one can gather. There would be no point in
Simone going out there until they've actually found the man,
or at least until they have more information for her, would
there?"

"It's not that." I took a deep breath. "It's just—"

"I think you should check on Simone and Ella, Charlie—
make sure they're OK," Sean said. He spoke quietly, calmly,
but the demand for utter obedience came across loud and clear
in the very softness of his voice, nevertheless. I spiked him

with a short vicious glare, tempted to outright mutiny. I told myself the only reason I didn't was because such behavior would be totally unprofessional in front of a client. Part of me even believed that as a viable excuse.

"Of course," I murmured demurely, pushing my chair back and dumping my napkin onto the tabletop. *Later, Sean . . .* "If you'll excuse me?"

Harrington didn't treat me to the full rise, just lifted himself partly out of his seat. I saw his eyes flicker with curbed curiosity between the two of us, but he didn't ask questions. Or not until I was out of earshot, at least.

I turned my back and stalked through the restaurant away from them, following much the same path between the tables that Simone had taken, trying not to let my anger show as badly on the outside as I felt it raging under the surface.

America.

Sean *knew* how I felt about working there again. We'd practically been living together for six months, so how could he not?

The last time I'd been across the Atlantic was to Florida during the previous March. My first official assignment for Sean, to a holiday destination that had turned out to be anything but.

What should have been a simple babysitting job had escalated into a disaster of major proportions. I'd ended up on the run with my teenage charge and, although I'd got through it, the cost had been a high one on every level. I was still coming to terms with what had happened there. It had taken me several months afterwards to make the decision that close protection was where my future career lay.

Since then, I'd never actually asked Sean *not* to send me to the States and he'd never actually asked me to go back— before today. I tried not to think of the people who'd died in Florida as a result of the unfolding catastrophe I'd found myself caught up in. I'd been personally responsible for three deaths—"personally" being the operative word.

Small wonder, then, that I was in no hurry to return.

*And for an extra added bonus, enjoy this
brand-new, never-before-published
Charlie Fox short story by Zoë Sharp*

POSTCARDS
FROM
ANOTHER COUNTRY

SOMEBODY ONCE SAID that the rich are another country—they do things differently there. It didn't take me very long working in close protection to realize that was true. Hell, some of them were a different planet.

The Dempsey family were old money and that put them at the outer reaches of the solar system as far as real-world living was concerned. Personal danger came a distant second to social disgrace, which was always going to make life tough for those of us tasked to keep them from harm.

The family didn't seem bothered so much by the attempted assassination—and that was how they referred to the botched hit that sparked my involvement—so much as the fact it was carried out with no regard to the correct etiquette.

So, they put up with the movement sensors in the grounds and the increased numbers of staff who regularly patrolled the boundaries, but they balked at having the infrared cameras I'd recommended to blanket the exterior of the house, and absolutely dug their heels in about close-circuit TV coverage inside. It was my job, I was told firmly, to stop anyone from getting that far. *No pressure, then.*

The radio call came in at just after 3:00 AM, when I was in the east wing guest suite I'd commandeered as a temporary central control.

"Hey, Charlie, we just apprehended someone in the summer house," came the crackling voice of one of the new guys. "I think you'd, er, better come and take a look."

"Stay where you are, Pierce," I said, alerted by the hesitation when he'd been well-briefed on how to handle a situation of this type. "I'm on my way."

The summer house was an architectural flight of fancy writ large. Just goes to show what happens when the wealthy get bored and start doodling.

As I made my way across the lawn and skirted the swimming pool, the summer house was lit up like a beacon, lights blazing from every window. I jogged up the steps that led to the ornate entrance and pushed open the door.

As soon as I saw who Pierce had cornered, I understood his reaction. The girl was eighteen but could have passed for twenty-one, and she was utterly beautiful, wearing a mask of blasé bravado and a top that was barely legal. She sat sprawled on one of the cane sofas, one long leg dangling with apparent negligence over the arm. Only the nervous swing of her foot gave lie to her insouciance.

She'd been practicing her best sultry pout on Pierce and did not look pleased when I arrived to spoil her fun. Another few minutes and she'd probably have wheedled her way loose. If the scowl she shot in my direction was anything to go by, she realized it, too.

"OK," I said grimly. "I'll deal with this." As he hurried past me, looking flustered, I added quietly, "Make another sweep of the grounds, Pierce. And wake the boss."

"Oh . . . really?" His eyes flicked longingly over the girl before he caught my eye and mumbled, "Yeah, OK, no problem."

As the door closed behind him, I turned back and found the girl watching his departure with glittering eyes.

"You've obviously made quite a hit there," I said dryly.

"Hm," she agreed, letting a secret little smile briefly curve her lips that died when she switched her gaze back to me. "I get the feeling you're not quite so easily impressed, though."

"No, I'm not," I said, and for nearly half a minute we stared each other out. Then I sighed. "It was foolish to think you could get past us, Amanda," I said, voice mild. "Your father hired us because we know what we're doing."

"Damn watchdogs," Amanda Dempsey said with a sneer. "I've been evading people like you, sneaking out, sneaking in, since I was thirteen years old."

"Well, we caught you this time, didn't we?"

"Yes, you did," she drawled and something flashed through the back of her eyes, quick and bright. Then it was gone. She shrugged. "Well, you can't win them all."

She sat up, suddenly restless, and reached for the inlaid ivory antique cigarette box on the glass table in front of her. "Mind if I smoke?"

"Yes," I said, slamming the lid shut before she had a chance to reach inside, and leaving my hand there. Open-mouthed, she thought about making an issue of it, but took one look at my face and decided not to, shrugging like it was of no importance.

"You know that someone tried to kill your father less than a week ago," I went on, allowing some of the exasperation I was feeling to leak through into my voice. "Is this all just a game to you?"

"What if it is?" she said. "Just because someone's decided to take a potshot at the old man—and the number of likely suspects must be *legion*—and he's chosen to shut himself off like some old hermit, it doesn't mean *I* have to be a virtual prisoner in this moldy old place, too, does it?"

The house had every modern convenience. As well as the outdoor swimming pool and the indoor swimming pool, there were tennis courts, stables, a home gym that made the pro place I used seem positively underequipped, and a dozen full-time staff to pander to the family's every whim. I knew ordinary people who paid a fortune for weekends away at a place like this. I shook my head. What was that about familiarity and contempt?

"You want to go out, you're free to go by the main gate," I said mildly then. "You don't have to scale the back wall."

"Yeah, right." She gave a cynical snort of laughter and threw me a challenging stare. "So I can go out, huh? Alone?"

I smiled and shook my head. "Not a chance."

"OK, so who'll come out with me and spend the night clubbing? You?" She let her eyes flick me up and down, deliberately insulting. "What if I get lucky? Are you going to wait outside the bedroom door like a good little watchdog while I—"

"Only if you let me strip-search the guy at gunpoint first," I said easily. "Mind you, some of the guys you've been hanging around with lately are used to that kind of thing, aren't they?"

"How dare you check up on me," she gritted out, her cheeks flushing, a dull red that did nothing for her porcelain skin.

"We checked up on everyone," I said.

She jumped up. For a moment she just stood there, trembling with anger that had her on the verge of tears.

"I should have known you wouldn't take my side," she said, sounding much younger, almost petulant. "My father says 'jump' and the only thing you spineless wimps give a damn about is how high."

"You have to admit that your old man's money has come in very useful for getting you out of a few scrapes over the years," I said cheerfully. "Drug possession and drunk driving, to name but two."

"How much trouble do you reckon I would have got into," she said bitterly, "if I hadn't spent half my life trying to live up to my father's impossible ideals?"

"You could have got out from under," I pointed out. "He doesn't exactly keep you locked up in the basement."

She laughed as though I'd suggested something ridiculous. "And done what? Gone where?"

I refrained from rolling my eyes. "You're young and moderately bright. You didn't have to be a lapdog all your life," I said, unable to resist getting my own back for her earlier gibe. "You could have gone anywhere and done anything you set your mind to. Most people," I added, "have to work for what they want in life. They don't get it handed to them on a hallmarked silver platter by a flunky wearing white gloves and a tailcoat."

Amanda paced to one of the windows even though the lights made it impossible to see anything outside except her own reflection in the glass. Maybe that was all she was after. Eventually, she turned back.

"You don't come from money, do you, Charlie?"

I thought of my parents' affluent country home in the stockbroker belt of Cheshire and laughed. "My folks aren't quite down to their last farthing, thank you very much."

I shifted slightly so I was between her and the open doorway, just in case, glancing through it as I did so. Lights had come on in the main wing of the house, and I could see figures moving across the lawn. Pierce might be new and green, but it seemed he had remembered what he had to do at least. "I certainly don't go running to *my* father," I went on, "to bail me out every time I hit a problem."

"If that's what I've done," she said, lip twisting, "it's because I'm just doing what Daddy taught me from the cradle."

"Which is?"

"That money is the answer to everything."

Into the silence that followed, my walkie-talkie crackled into life.

"Hey, Charlie," came Pierce's voice, loud and clear, "you were right. We got him. Some punk kid with a sawn-off. Southwest corner. The situation's contained and the police are on their way."

"Good. Thank you." I put the walkie-talkie back in my pocket and glanced across at the girl. "Sorry, Amanda," I said, with no regret in my voice. "Your diversionary tactic didn't work. Who is he, by the way—your latest bit of rough? Did you really think he'd get to your father before we could stop him?"

I put my head on one side and watched her as she turned away from the window and staggered back to the sofa, dropping onto the cushions like her legs would no longer support her. But when she looked up, her eyes were wild, defiant.

"You'll never prove anything," she said. Fine words, spoilt only by the shaky tone.

"She doesn't have to."

Behind me, the door pushed open, and her father stepped into the summer house. He'd put on a silk robe over his pajamas, but he was still a commanding figure.

Amanda stiffened at the sight of him, then dived for the cigarette box on the table in front of her, scrabbling inside it.

"If you're looking for that nice little semiautomatic you hid in there," I said, almost regretful, "I found it this afternoon."

Her color fled. She gave a shriek of rage and flew out of her seat. I was never quite sure if it was me or her father she intended to attack, but I didn't give her the chance. Before she'd taken more than two strides, I'd grabbed her arms, spun her around, and dumped her back onto the sofa. I was tempted to get a punch in, but she *was* my principal's daughter, after all.

I settled for a verbal blow instead. "Not so much watchdog, Amanda," I said. "More guard dog."

She snatched up the cigarette box and hurled it instead. It never came close to target, hitting the wall next to the door and cracking in two, scattering filtertips across the Italian-tiled floor. Then she began to cry.

Her father regarded this display of temper without expression, while I received another message from Pierce to say the police were at the main gate.

"Let them in," I said. I looked across at Dempsey. "Do you want them to take her, too?"

Dempsey pursed his lips briefly before shaking his head. "That won't be necessary." He motioned with a vague hand. "We'll get her . . . help of some kind."

"Your decision, sir, of course."

He hadn't taken his eyes off his daughter. "Why, Amanda?" he asked softly. "What do you possibly gain from my death?"

Her lip curled. "My freedom."

He frowned at that. "But you've had everything you could possibly wish for."

"No. I've had everything money could buy," she said in a brittle voice, throwing her head back. "And if you don't know the difference, there's no earthly point in my trying to explain it."

There was a long pause. Dempsey finally broke his brooding survey and flicked his eyes at me.

"I'm not dealing with this tonight," he said, like it was some minor irritation. "Just get her out of my sight, would you?" And with that he turned on his heel and stumbled from summer house. It doesn't matter how much money you've got if your children hate you enough to try and kill you. Either for or because of it.

I moved over to his daughter. She rose from the sofa. "Not quite such a game now, is it, Amanda?" I said.

"On the contrary," she said, eyes glittering, head high. "Now it gets interesting."

Like I said: The rich are a whole 'nother country—they do things differently there.